THE IMAGE OF THE BEAST

OF THE

BEAST

•

BLOWN

D1826884

THE IMAGE OF THE BEAST • BLOWN
Philip José Farmer
ISBN 1 84068 028 8
Published 2001AD
by Creation Books
www.creationbooks.com
Copyright © Ralph M Vicinanza Ltd 2001
Design:
The Tears Corporation
Cover illustration:
John Coulthart

ONE

THE IMAGE OF THE BEAST

an exorcism: ritual one

Chapter 1

Smoke rose to the light, and smoke and light fused to become green milk. The milk fissioned to become smoke and darkness above. As below.

Smog was outside, and smog was inside.

Green and sour.

The green and sour odour and taste came not only from the smog, which had forced its tendrils into the air-conditioned building, nor from the tobacco plumes in the room. It came from memory of what he had seen that morning and anticipation of what he would see within the next few minutes.

The film room of the Los Angeles Police Department was darker than Herald Childe had ever seen it. The beam of light from the projection booth usually tended to make grey what otherwise would have been black. But the cigar and cigarette smoke, the smog, and the mood of the viewers, blackened everything. Even the silver light from the screen seemed to pull light in instead of casting it back at the viewers.

Where the beam overhead struck the tobacco fumes, green milk formed and curdled and soured. So thought Herald Childe. The image was unforced. The worst smog in history was smothering Los Angeles and Orange counties. Not a mouse of a wind had stirred for a day and a night and a day and a night. On the third day, it seemed that this condition might go on and on.

The smog. He could now forget the smog.

Spread-eagled on the screen was his partner (possibly ex-partner). The wine draperies behind him glowed, and Matthew Colben's face, normally as red as Chianti half-diluted with water, was now the colour of a transparent plastic bag bulging with wine.

The camera swung away to show the rest of his body and some of the room. He was flat on his back and nude. His arms were strapped down beside him and his legs, also strapped down, formed a V. His penis lolled across his left thigh like a fat drunken worm.

The table must have been made for just this purpose of tying down men with their legs separated so others could walk in between the legs.

There was only the Y-shaped wooden table, the thick wine-red carpet, and the wine-red draperies. The camera swept around to show the circle of draperies and then turned back and swooped up to show the full form of Matthew Colben as seen by a fly on the ceiling. Colben's head was on a dark pillow. He looked straight up at the camera and smiled sillily. He did not seem to care that he was bound and helpless.

The previous scenes had shown why he did not care and had demonstrated how Colben had progressed, through conditioning, from impotent fear to rigid anticipation.

Childe, having seen the complete film once, felt his entrails slip about each other and knot each other and, their tails coiled around his backbone, pull until they were choking each other.

Colben grinned, and Childe murmured, "You fool! You poor fucking fool!"

The man in the seat on Childe's right shifted and said, "What'd you say?"

"Nothing, Commissioner."

But his penis felt as if it were being sucked back up into his belly and drawing his testicles after it.

The draperies opened, and the camera moved in to show a huge black-rimmed, long-lashed, dark-blue eye. Then it moved down along a straight narrow nose and broad, full, and bright red lips. A pink-red tongue slipped out between unnaturally white and even teeth, shot back and forth a few times, dropped a bead of saliva on the chin and then disappeared.

The camera moved back, the draperies were thrust open, and a woman entered. Her black glossy hair was combed straight back and fell to her waist. Her face was garish with beauty patches, rouge, powder, green and red and black and azure paint around the eyes and a curl of powder-blue down her cheeks, artificial eyelashes, and a tiny golden nose-ring. A green robe, tied at her neck and waist, was so thin that she might as well have been naked. Despite which she untied the cords about the neck and slid the robe off and showed that she could be even more naked.

The camera moved downward and closer. The hollow at the base of the neck was deep and the bones beneath hinted at exquisiteness. The breasts were full but not large, slightly conical and up-tilted, with narrow and long, almost sharp, nipples. The

Philip José Farmer

breasts were hung upon a large rib cage. The belly sank inwards; she was skinny about the hips, the bones stuck out just a little. The camera went round, or she pivoted – Childe could not tell which because the camera was so close to her and he had no reference point. Her buttocks were like huge unshelled soft-boiled eggs.

The camera travelled around her, showing the narrow waist and ovoid hips and then turned so that it was looking up towards the ceiling – which was covered with a drape-like material the colour of a broken blood vessel in a drunkard's eye. The camera glanced up her white thigh; light was cast into the hollow between the legs – she must have spread her legs then – and there was the little brown eye of the anus and the edge of the mouth of her vagina. The hairs were yellow, which meant that the woman had either dyed her head hairs of her pubic hairs.

The camera, still pointing upwards, passed between her legs – which looked like the colossal limbs of a statue now – and then travelled slowly upward. It straightened out as it rose and was looking directly at her pubes. These were partly covered by a triangular cloth which was taped on. Childe did not know why. Modestly certainly was not the reason.

He had seen this shot before, but he braced himself. The first time, he – in common with the others in the room – had jumped and some had sworn and one had yelled.

The cloth was tight against the genitals, and a shift in angle of lighting suddenly revealed that the cloth was semi-transparent. The hairs formed a dark triangle, and the slit took in the cloth enough to show that the cloth was tight against the slit.

Abruptly, and Childe jumped again even though he knew what was coming, the cloth sank in more deeply, as if something inside the vagina had spread the lips open. Then something bulged against the cloth, something that could only have come from within the woman. It thrust the cloth up; the cloth shook as if a tiny fist or head were beating against it, and then the bulge sank back, and the cloth was quiet again.

The Commissioner, two seats away from Childe, said, "What the hell could that be?" He blew out cigar smoke and then began coughing. Childe coughed too.

"It could be something mechanical up her cunt," Childe said. "Or it could be..." He let the words, and his thoughts, hang. No hermaphrodite, as far as he knew, had a penis within the vaginal canal. Anyway, that wasn't a penis sliding out; that looked like an independent entity – gave the feeling of one, rather – and certainly the thing had beat against the cloth at more than one place.

Now the camera swung around at a level a few inches above Colben and several feet in front of him. It showed the feet, seemingly enormous at this narrow distance, the thickly muscled and hairy calves and thighs spread out on the Y-shaped table, the big testicles, the fat worm of the penis, no longer lolling against the thigh but beginning to get fatter and to lift its swollen red head. Colben could not have seen the woman enter, but he had evidently been conditioned so that he knew she would come in within a certain time after he was strapped to the table. The penis was coming to life as if its ears – buried within the flesh like a snake's – had heard her or as if the slit in its head were a detector of body heat – like an adder's nose pits – and it knew that she was in the room.

The camera moved to one side so that it could start with the profile of Matthew Colben's head. The thick curly grey-and-black hair, the big red ears, the smooth forehead, the big curved nose, the thin lips, massive jawbone, chin thick and heavy as the head of a sledge, big fat chest, the outcurve of a paunch grown with much stuffing of steak and beer, the down-curve to the penis, now fully up and swollen and hard. The camera moved in for a close shot; the veins were ropes run into the lanyard of lust (Childe could not help thinking in such images; he fingered concepts with a Midas touch). The head, fully exposed, glistened with lubricating fluid.

Now the camera moved up and away and took a position where both the man and woman could be seen. She approached slowly, swaying her hips, and came up to Colben and said something. Her lips moved, but there was no sound, and the police lip-reader could not tell what she was saying because her head was bent too far over. Colben said something too, but his words were undecipherable for the same reason.

The woman bent over and let her left breast fall so that Colben could take it in his mouth. He sucked for a while and then the woman removed it. The camera moved in to show the nipple, which was wet and swollen. She kissed him on the mouth; the

Philip José Farmer

camera moved in sidewise to show her as she raised her head a little to permit the camera to record the tongue sliding back and forth into Colben's mouth. Then she began to kiss and to lick his chin, his neck, his chest, his nipples, and she smeared his round belly with saliva. She worked slowly down to his pubic hairs, slobbered on them, gently tapped his penis with her tongue many times, kissed it lightly several times, flicked out her tongue to dab its head with the tip while she held his penis at the root. Then she walked around the leg of the Y and between the legs and began to suck on his penis energetically.

At this point, a tinny piano, like those played in the old-time bars or in the silent movie theatres, began Dvořák's *Humoresque*. The camera shifted to a position above Colben's face; his eyes closed and he was looking ecstatic, that is, stupidly happy.

For the first time, the woman spoke.

"Tell me just before you're ready to come, darling. Maybe thirty or so seconds before, yes? I have a beautiful surprise for you. Something new."

The voice had been printed and run off by the police on an oscilloscope and studied. But distortions had been introduced into it. That was why the voice sounded so hollow and wavery.

"Go slower, baby," Colben said. "Take it easy, put it off like you did last time. That was the greatest orgasm I ever had in my life. You're going a little too fast now. And don't stick your fingers up my ass like you did then. You cut my piles."

The first time the scene had been shown, some of the cops snickered. Nobody snickered now. There was an unheard but easily felt shift in the audience now. The smoke seemed to get hard and brittle; the green milk in the light beam became more sour. The Commissioner sucked in air so hard a rattle sounded in his throat and then he began coughing.

The piano was playing the *William Tell* overture now. The tinny music was so incongruous, and yet it was the incongruity that made it seem so horrible.

The woman raised her head and said, "You are about ready to come, *mon petit?*"

Colben breathed, "Oh, Jesus, just about!"

The woman looked into the camera and smiled. The flesh seemed to fade away, the bones beneath were faintly glowing and cloudy. Then the flesh was cloudy; the skull was hard and bright. And then the skull faded and flesh fell back into place.

She leered into the camera and put her head down again, but this time she went past the corner of the Y and squatted down below the table, where the camera followed her. There was a small shelf fixed to one leg of the table. She picked something off it; the light brightened, the camera moved in nearer.

She held a pair of false teeth. They looked as if they were made of iron; the teeth were sharp as a razor and pointed like a tiger's.

She smiled and put the iron teeth on the shelf and used both hands to remove her own teeth. She looked thirty years older. She placed the white teeth on the shelf and then inserted the iron teeth between her mouth. She held the edge of her forefinger between the two teeth and bit gently down. Then she removed the finger and held it so that the camera could zero in on it. Bright red blood was welling out from the bite.

She stood up and wiped the cut on the fat glass of Colben's penis and she bent over and licked the blood off. Colben groaned and said, "Oh, God. I'm going to come!"

Her mouth went around the head and she sucked in loudly. Colben began to jerk and to groan. The camera showed his face for a second before it moved back to a position alongside the woman's.

She raised her head quickly. The penis was jerking and spurting the thick oily whitish fluid. She opened her mouth widely, bent down swiftly and bit. The muscles along her jaw lumped; her neck muscles became cords.

Colben screamed.

She whipped her head back and forth and bit again and again. Blood ran down from her mouth and reddened the pubic hairs.

The camera moved away from her to show the draperies through which she had entered. There was a flourish of trumpets. A cannon boomed in the distance. The piano played Tchaikovsky's *1812 Overture*.

Trumpets sounded again as the music faded. The draperies shot open, propelled by two stiff arms. A man stepped inside and posed for a moment, his right arm raised so that his black cloak half-hid his face. His hair was black and shiny as patent leather and

Philip José Farmer

was parted down the middle. His forehead and nose were white as the belly of a shark. His eyebrows were thick and black and met over his nose. The eyes were large and black.

He was dressed as if he were going to a movie premiere. He had on a formal suit, a stiff white shirt with a black formal tie and a diagonal red band across his chest and a medal or order on his lapel.

He wore blue sneakers.

Another comic element which only made the situation more horrible.

The man lowered the cloak to show a large hooked nose, a thick black moustache which curved down around the ends of his thick rouged lips, and a prominent cleft chin.

He cackled, and this deliberately corny element was even more horrible than the sneakers. The laugh was a parody of all the gloating laughs cranked forth by all the monsters and Draculas of every horror movie.

Up went the arm, and, his face hidden behind the cloak, the man rushed towards the table. Colben was still screaming. The woman jumped away swiftly and let the man into the Y. The penis was still jerking and emitting blood and spermatic fluid; the head was half bitten off. The camera switched to the woman's face. Blood was running down her chin and over her breasts.

Again, the camera panned back to the Dracula (so Childe thought of him). Dracula crackled again, showing two obviously false canines, long and sharp. Then he bent down and began to chew savagely on the penis but within a short time raised his head. The blood and spermatic fluid was running out of his mouth and making the front of his white shirt crimson. He opened his mouth and spat out the head of the penis on to Colben's belly and laughed, spraying blood over himself and Colben.

The first time, Childe had fainted. This time, he got up and ran towards the door but vomited before he reached it. He was not alone.

Chapter 2

The Dracula and the woman had looked into the camera and laughed wildly as if they had been having a hilarious time. Then, fade-out, and a flash of TO BE CONTINUED? End of film.

Herald Childe did not see the ending the second time. He was too occupied with groaning, with wiping the tears from his eyes and blowing his nose and coughing. The taste and odour of vomit were strong. He felt like apologizing, but he repressed the impulse. He had nothing to apologize for.

The Commissioner, who had not thrown up but who might have looked better if he had, said, "Let's get out of here."

He stepped over the mess on the wooden floor. Childe followed him. The others came out. The Commissioner said, "We're going to have a conference, Childe. You can sit in on it, contribute if you wish."

"I'd like to keep in touch with the police, Commissioner. But I don't have anything to contribute. Not just yet, anyway."

He had told the police, more than once, everything he knew about Matthew Colben, which was much, and everything he knew about his disappearance, which was nothing.

The Commissioner was a tall lean man with a half-bald head and a long thin face and melancholy black moustache. He was always tugging at the right end of his moustache – never the left. Yet he was left-handed. Childe had observed this habit and wondered about its origin. What would the Commissioner say if he were made aware of it?

What could he say? Only he and a psychotherapist would ever be able to find out.

"You realize, Childe, that this comes at a very bad time for us," the Commissioner said. "If it weren't for the... uh, extraordinary aspects of the case... I wouldn't be able to spend more than a few minutes on it. As it is..."

Childe nodded and said, "Yes. I know. The Department will have to get on it later. I'm grateful that you've taken this time."

"Oh, it's not that bad!" the Commissioner said. "Sergeant Bruin will be handling the case. That is, when he has time. You have to realize..."

"I realize," Childe said. "I know Bruin. I'll keep in touch with him. But not so often he'll be bugged."

"Fine, fine!"

The Commissioner stuck out a skinny and cold, but sweating hand, and said, "see you!" and turned and walked off down the hall.

Childe went into the nearest men's room, where several plain clothesmen and two uniformed men were washing the taste of vomit out. Sergeant Bruin was also there, but he had not been sick. He came from the stall zipping up his fly. Bruin was rightly named. He looked like a grizzly, but he was far less easily upset.

As he washed his hands, he said, "I gotta hurry, Childe. The Commissioner wants a quick conference about your partner, and then we all gotta get back on this smog thing."

"You have my phone number, and I got yours," Childe said. He drank another cup of water and crumpled the paper and threw it into the wastepaper basket. "Well, at least I'll be able to move around. I got a permit to use my car."

"That's more'n several million citizens got right now," Bruin said cheerfully. "Be sure you burn the gas in a good cause."

"So far, I haven't got much reason to burn anything," Childe said. "But I'm going to try."

Bruin looked down at him. His big black eyes were as impenetrable as a bear's; they did not look human. He said, "You going to put in time for free on this job?"

"Who's going to pay me?" Childe said. "Colben's divorced. This case is tied up with Budler's, but Budler's wife discharged me yesterday. She says she doesn't give a shit any more."

"He may be dead, just like Colben," Bruin said. "I wouldn't be surprised if we got another package through the mails."

"Me neither," Childe said.

"See you," Bruin said. He put a heavy paw on Childe's shoulder for a second. "Doing it for nothing, eh? He was your partner, right? But you was going to split up, right? Yet you're going to find out who killed him, right?"

"I'll try," Childe said.

"I like that," Bruin said. "There ain't much sense of loyalty kicking around nowadays." He lumbered off; the others trailed out after him. Childe was alone. He looked into the mirror over the washbowl. The pale face resembled Lord Byron's enough to have given him trouble with women – and a number of jealous or desirous men – ever since he was fourteen. Now, it was a little lumpy, and a scar ran down his left cheek. Memento of Korea, when a drunken soldier had objected to being arrested by Childe and had slashed his face with the broken end of a beer bottle. The eyes were dark grey and just now much bloodshot. The neck below the slightly lumpy Byronic head was thick and the shoulders were wide. The face of a poet, he thought as he had thought many times, and the body of a cop, a private investigator. Why did you ever get into this sordid soul-leaching depressing corrupting racket? Why didn't you become a quiet professor of English or psychology in a quiet college town?

Only he and a psychotherapist would ever know, and he evidently did not want to know, since he had never gone to a psychotherapist. He was sure that he enjoyed the sordidness and tears and grief and hatred and the blood, somewhere in him. Something fed on contemptible food. Something enjoyed it, but that something sure as hell wasn't Herald Childe. Not at this moment, anyway.

He left the washroom and went down the hall to an elevator and dropped while he turned his thoughts so inwardly that he did not know whether or not he was alone in the cage. On the way to the exit, he shook his head a little as if to wake himself up. It was dangerous to be so infolded.

Matthew Colben, his partner, had been on his way to being his ex-partner. Colben was a big-mouthed braggart, a Don Juan who let his desire to make a pass interfere with his business. He had not allowed his prick to get in the way of business when he and Childe had become partners six years ago. But Colben was fifty now and perhaps trying to keep the thoughts of a slowing-down body and thickening flesh and a longer time to recover from hangovers away from him. Childe didn't accept this reason; Colben could do whatever he wanted after business hours, but he was cheating his partner when he cheated himself with the booze and the women. After the Budler case, they would be through. So Childe had promised himself.

Now Colben was dead and Budler could be in the hands of the same people who had taken Colben – although there was no evidence to indicate so. But Budler and Colben had disappeared the same night, and Colben had been tailing Budler.

The film had been mailed from a Torrance post office three days ago. Colben and Budler had been missing fourteen days.

Childe stopped at the tobacco stand and bought a morning *Times*. At any other time, the Colben case would have been headline material. Not today. It was, however, a feature on the front page. Childe, hating to go outside, leaned against the wall and read the story. It had been considerably bowdlerized by the reporters who had seen the film. They had not been present at either of the showings he had witnessed, but Bruin had told him they were at a special running. Bruin had laughed like a bear with a sore throat, and described how at least half of them had thrown up or been close to throwing up.

"Some of them been in battles and seen men with their guts blowed inside out!" Bruin had said. "You was in the Korean action and you was an officer, right? Yet you got sick! How come?"

"Didn't you feel your cock drawing up in your belly?" Childe said.

"Naw."

"Maybe you don't have one," Childe had said. Bruin thought that was funny, too.

The whole story was in two columns, and it covered most of what Childe knew except for the details of the film. Colben's car had been found in a parking lot behind a trust and security building on Wilshire Boulevard in Beverly Hills. Colben had been trailing Benjamin Budler, a wealthy Beverly Hills lawyer. Budler had been stepping out on his wife, not to mention his regular mistress. The wife had hired *Childe & Colben, Private Investigators*, to get enough evidence for her to file for divorce.

Colben, using the tape recorder in his car, had described Budler's moves. Budler had picked up a lovely brunette (described in detail but unidentified) on the corner of Olympic and Veteran. The traffic light had been green, but Budler had held up a long line of cars, horns blaring, while he opened the door and let the woman in. She was well-dressed. Colben had surmised that her car was parked somewhere close; she did not look as if she would live in this neighbourhood.

Budler's Rolls-Royce had turned right on Veteran and gone

to Santa Monica, where it had turned left and travelled down Santa Monica Boulevard until it stopped a block from a quiet and expensive restaurant. Here Budler had let the woman off and driven to a parking place on a side street. He had walked to the restaurant where they had dined and wined (presumably) for three hours. Though they went in separately, they came out together. Budler was red-faced, talking loudly and laughing much. The woman laughed much also but she walked steadily. His balance was a little uncertain; he stumbled when he started across the street and almost fell.

They had taken the Rolls-Royce (with Budler driving too swiftly and weaving in and out of traffic) up Santa Monica and turned left at Bedford Drive to go north.

The tape was wiped clean from this point on.

Colben had stated that he had got some long-range pictures of the woman when Budler had picked her up. The camera was in the car but the film had been removed.

The car had been thoroughly cleaned; there was not a single fingerprint. Some dirt particles, presumably from the shoes of whoever had driven the car to the parking lot, were on the mat, but an analysis had shown only that the dirt could have come from anywhere in the area. There were some fibres; these had been rubbed off the rag used to wipe the seats.

Budler's Rolls-Royce was also missing.

The police had not discovered that Budler had dropped out of his normal pattern of life until two days after Colben was reported missing. His wife had known that he was gone, but she had not bothered to report this. Why should she? He often did not come home for two to four days.

As soon as she was informed that her husband might have been kidnapped or murdered, that his disappearance was connected with that of Colben (or seemed likely to be connected), she had told Childe that he was no longer employed by her.

"I hope they find the son of a bitch dead! And soon!" she had screamed over the phone. "I don't want his money tied up forever! I need it now! It's just like him to never be found and tie me up with litigation and red tape and all that shit! Just like him! I hate him!" and so on.

"I'll send you my bill," Childe had replied. "It was nice to be able to work for you," and he had hung up.

His bill would be delivered, but how soon he would be paid was doubtful. Even if a cheque was sent by Mrs Budler by return mail, it might not be cashable for some time. The newspapers reported that the authorities were discussing closing down all banks until the crisis was over. Many people were protesting against this, but it would not make much difference for the protesters if the banks did stay open. What good did that do if most of the customers could not get to their bank unless they were within walking distance or wanted to stand in line for hours to take the infrequent bus?

He looked up from the paper. Two uniformed, gasmasked men were bringing in a tall dark man between them. He held up handcuffed hands as if to demonstrate his martyrdom to the world. One cop carried a third gas mask, and by this Childe knew that the arrested man had probably been using a mask while holding up a store or robbing a loan company or doing something which required concealing his face.

Childe wondered why the cops were bringing him in through this entrance. Perhaps they had caught him just down the street and were taking the short cut.

The situation was advantageous for criminals in one respect. Men wearing gasmasks or water-soaked cloths over their faces were not uncommon. On the other hand, anyone abroad was likely to be stopped and questioned. One thing balances out another.

The cops and the arrestee were coughing. The man behind the tobacco counter was coughing. Childe felt a tickling in his throat. He could not smell the smog, but the thought of smelling it evoked the ghost of a cough.

He checked his ID cards and permit. He did not want to be caught without them, as he had been yesterday. He had lost about an hour because, even after the cops had called in and validated his reasons for being out, he had been required to go home and pick up his papers, and he had been stopped again before he could get home.

He tucked the paper under his arm, walked to the door, looked through the glass, shuddered, wished he had a lightweight scuba diver's equipment, opened the door and plunged in.

Chapter 3

It was like walking at the bottom of a sea of very thin bile.

There were no clouds between the sun and the sea. The sun shone brightly as if it were trying to burn a path through the sea. The August sun burned fiercely and the more it burned, the more it cut with its yellow machetes, the thicker and more poisonous grew the grey-green foliage.

(Childe knew he was mixing metaphors. So what? The Cosmos was a mixed metaphor in the mind of God. The left mind of God did not know what the right mind of God was doing. Or did not care. God was a schizophrenic? Herald Childe, creature of God, image of God, certainly was schizophrenic, Levorotatory image?)

Eyes burned like heretics at the stake. Sinuses were scourged; fire ran along the delicate bones; spermaticky fluid collected to fill the chambers of the sinuses and dripped, waiting for the explosion of air voluntarily or involuntarily set off, to discharge the stuff with the mildest of orgasms.

Not a twitch of wind. The air had been unmoving for a day and a night and half a day, as if the atmosphere had died and was rotting.

The grey-green stuff hung in sheets. Or seemed to. The book of judgement was being read and the pages, the grey-green sheets, were being turned as the eye read and more and more pages were being piled towards the front of the book. How far to read before the end?

Childe could see no farther than one hundred and ten feet, if that. He had walked this path from the door to the parking lot so many times that he could not get lost. But there were those who did not know where they were. A woman, screaming ran by him, and was lost in the greenishness. He stopped. His heart was pounding. Faintly, he could hear a car horn. A siren wailed somewhere. He turned slowly, trying to see or hear the woman or her pursuer, if any, but there was nothing. She ran; no one pursued.

He began to trot. He sweated. His eyes smarted and flowed tears, and little flames seemed to be creeping down his throat towards his lungs. He wanted to get to the car, which held his gas mask. He forced himself to walk. There was panic hanging in the

Philip José Farmer

air, the same panic that came to a man when he felt hands squeezing his neck and thumbs pressing in on his windpipe.

A car emerged from the cloud. It was not his. He passed by it and, ten parking spaces on, found his 1970 Oldsmobile. He put the mask on, started the motor, wincing a little at the thought of the poisons shooting out of the exhaust, turned his lights on and drove out of the lot. The street held more moving bright lights than he had expected. He turned on the radio and found out why. Those who had some place to go outside the area of smog were going whether or not the authorities gave permission, and so the authorities were giving permission. Many who had no place to go, but were going anyway, were also driving out. The flood had started. The streets weren't jammed as yet, but they soon would be.

Childe cursed. He had planned on easy drives to his various destinations that day because, although he could not drive swiftly, he could drive unimpeded by traffic.

The voice of the governor issued from the speaker. The governor pleaded for restraint and calm. Everybody should continue to stay home – if they were able to do so.

However, those who had to get out for health reasons (which would include the entire population now, Childe thought) should drive carefully and should realize that there just were not enough accommodations for them outside the Los Angeles-Orange County area in this state. Nevada and Arizona had been notified of the invasion, and Utah and New Mexico were readying themselves. Troops were being moved into the area but only to act as traffic policemen and to assist the hospitals. There was no martial law; there was no need for it. There was an upswing in crimes of passion, theft, and robbery, but there had been no riots.

No wonder, thought Childe. There was something irritating about smog; it did eat the skin off the nerves, but people did not like to get out in it, and people did not collect in large numbers. To every man, others looked like ghosts coming towards him out of the grey-greenness or like strange fish appearing suddenly from the shadows. Strange fish could be sharks.

He passed a car with three goggled, snouted monstrosities in it. Their heads swivelled, the cyclopean eyes stared blindly, the noses seemed to sniff. He sped away from them until their headlights were muffled and then slowed down. Once, a car suddenly appeared behind him, and a red light flashed. He looked through the rear view mirror before he stopped; there were fake prowl cars stopping motorists and robbing, beating, or even killing them on the streets during daylight, within twenty feet of passers-by. He decided to pull over, eased the car gently towards the dimly visible kerb, and stopped. He kept the motor running and peered at the car and the cop getting out of it on the right side. If he did not like the looks of them he could still get out of the right side of his car and take off into the dimness. But he recognized the cop, although he did not know his name, and stayed behind the wheel. He flipped open his coat and slowly reached within it so that the cop would not get the impression he was reaching for a gun. He had a licence for a gun but it was at home.

The cops had stopped too many to make him get out of the car and assume the stance of the friskee. Besides, there were many legitimate drivers, and within a short time, there would be so many cars on the streets that they might as well give up, except for obvious cases.

Childe established his identity quickly enough. They knew him by hearsay and had also read the papers. One, Chominshi, wanted to discuss the case, but the other was coughing, and Childe started to cough, so they let him go. He continued up Third towards West Los Angeles. His apartment and his office were a few blocks away from Beverly Hills. He planned to go straight home and do some thinking.

If he could think. He was in a mild state of shock. His reflexes seemed to be slow, as if he had been drugged or was recovering from being knocked out. He felt a slight sense of detachment, as if he had been disengaged somewhat from reality, no doubt to soften the effects of the film. The smog did not help him keep an anchor on things; it induced a feeling of slippage of self.

He was not burning with lust for revenge on those who had killed Colben. He had not liked Colben, and he knew that Colben had done some things which were criminal but he had escaped without (as far as Childe knew) even the punishment of conscience. He had knocked up a teenager and kicked her out, and the girl had taken sleeping pills and died. There were others, although none had ended in death for the girls. But some would have been better off

Philip José Farmer

dead. And there was the wife of a client who had been found beaten and would always be an idiot. Childe had had no basis for suspicion of Colben, but he had felt that Colben might have done the beating for the client, especially after he had discovered that Colben was going to bed with the woman. He could prove nothing; he could not even make an accusation which would not sound stupid, because he lacked any evidence. That Colben was neglecting the business, however, was reason enough to get rid of him. Childe did not have enough money to buy Colben out; he had meant to make it so unpleasant for Colben that he would be glad to dissolve the partnership.

Nevertheless, no man deserved to die as Colben had. Or did he? The horror was more in the viewers' minds than in Colben's. He had been hurt very much, but only briefly, and had died quickly.

That did not matter. Childe intended to find out all he could, although he suspected that he would find out very little. And soon enough the need to pay bills would take him off the case; he would only be able to work on it during his leisure moments. Which meant that, in effect, he would be able to accomplish almost nothing.

But he had nothing else to do, and he certainly did not intend to sit still in his apartment and breathe in poison gas. He had to do something to keep going. He could not even read comfortably because of the burning and the tears. He was like a shark that has to keep moving to allow water to flow through the gills. Once he stopped, he would suffocate.

But a shark can breathe and also stand still if the water is moving. Sybil could be his flowingness. Sybil was a name that sounded like running brooks and sunshine in quiet green glades and wisdom like milk from full flowing breasts. Certainly not green milk. White creamy milk of tenderness and good sense.

Childe smiled. The Great Romanticist. He not only looked like Lord Byron, he thought like him. Reincarnation come. George Gordon, Lord Byron, reborn as a private eye and without a club foot. One thing about a club mind, it didn't show. Not at first. But the limp became evident to others who had to walk with him day after day.

The Private Eyes of the novels. They were simply straightforward men with their minds made up – all black and white

– vengeance is mine, saith Lord Hammer – true heroes with whom the big majority of readers had no trouble identifying.

This was strange, because the antiheroes of the existential novels were supposed to be representative of the modern mind, and they certainly were uncertain. The antihero got far more publicity, far more critical trumpeting, than the simple, stable, undoubting private eye, the hero of the masses.

Childe told himself to cut, as if his thoughts were a strip of film. He was exaggerating and also simplifying. Inwardly, he might be an existential antihero, but outwardly he was a man of action, a Shadow, a Doc Savage, a Sam Spade. He smiled again. Truth to tell, he was Herald Sigurd Childe, red-eyed, watery-eyed, drippy-nosed, sickened, wanting to run home to Mother. Or to that image named Sybil.

Mother, unfortunately, became angry if he did not phone her to ask if he could come over. Mother wanted privacy and independence, and if she did not get it, she expressed herself unpleasantly and exiled him for an indeterminate time.

He parked the car outside his apartment, ran up the steps, hearing someone cough behind a door as he passed, and unlocked his door. The apartment was a living room, a kitchenette, and a bedroom. Normally, it was bright with white walls and ceilings and creamy woodwork and lightly coloured, lightly built furniture. Today, it was gloomy; even the unshadowed places had a greenish tinge.

Sybil answered the phone before the second ring had started.

"You must have been expecting me," he said gaily.

"I was expecting," she said. Her voice was not, however, unfriendly.

He did not make the obvious reply. "I'd like to come over," he finally said.

"Why? Because you're hard up?"

"For your company."

"You haven't got anything to do. You have to find some way to spend the time."

"I have a case I'm working on," he said. He hesitated and then, knowing that he was baiting the hook and hating himself for it, said, "It's about Colben. You read the papers?"

Philip José Farmer

"I thought that was what you'd been working on. Isn't it horrible?"

He did not ask her why she was home today. She was the secretary of an advertising agency executive. Neither she nor her boss would have a driving priority.

"I'll be right over," he said. He paused and then said, "Will I be able to stay a while or will I have to get out after a while? Don't get mad! I just want to know; I'd like to be able to relax."

"You can stay for a couple of hours or more, if you like. I'm not going anyplace, and nobody is coming – that I know of."

He took the phone from his ear but her voice was not loud enough for him to hear, and he returned it to his ear. "Herald? I really do want you to come!"

He said, "Good!" and then, "Hell! I've just been thinking of myself! Is there anything I can get you from the store?"

"No, you know there's a supermarket only three blocks from here. I walked."

"OK. I just thought you might not have gone out yet or you forgot something you might want me to pick up for you."

They were both silent for a few seconds. He was thinking about his irritations when they had been married, about how many times he had had to run out to get things that she had forgotten during her shopping. She must be thinking about his recriminations, too; she was always thinking about them when they got together.

"I'll be right over," he said hurriedly. "So long."

He hung up and left the apartment. The man was still coughing behind the door. A stereo suddenly blared Strauss' *Thus Spake Zarathustra* downstairs. Somebody protested feebly; the music continued to play loudly. The protests became louder, and there was a pounding on a wall. The music did not soften.

Herald considered walking the four blocks to Sybil's and then decided against it. He might need to take off suddenly, although there did not seem much chance of it. His answering service was not operating; it had no priority. He did not intend to leave Sybil's number with the police operator or Sergeant Bruin while he was with her. She would get unreasonably angry about this. She did not like to be interrupted by calls while she was with him, at least, not by business calls. That had been one of the things bugging her when they were man and wife. Theoretically, she should not be bothered by such matters now. In practice, which operates more on emotion than logic, she was as enraged as ever. He well knew how enraged. The last time he had been at her apartment, the exchange had interrupted them at a crucial moment, and she had run him out. Since then, he had called several times but had been cooled off. The last time he'd phoned had been two weeks ago.

She was right in one guess. He was hard up. But he did not expect to be any less so after seeing her. He intended to talk, to talk only, to soothe some troublings and to scare away the loneliness that had come more strongly after seeing the film of Colben.

It was strange, or, if not so strange, indicative. He had lived twenty of his thirty-five years in Los Angeles County. Yet he knew only one woman to whom he could really unburden himself and feel relaxed and certain of complete understanding. No. He was wrong. There was not even one woman, because Sybil did not completely understand him, that is, sympathize with him. If she did, she would not now be his ex-wife.

But Sybil had said the same thing about men in general and about him in particular. It was *the human situation* – whatever that phrase meant.

He parked the car in front of her apartment – no trouble finding parking space now – and went into the little lobby. He rang her bell; she buzzed; he went up the steps through the inner door and down the hall to the end. Her door was on the right. He knocked; the door swung open. Sybil was dressed in a floor-length morning robe with large red and black diamond shapes. The black diamonds contained a white ankh, the looped cross of the ancient Egyptians. Her feet were bare.

Sybil was thirty-four and five feet five inches tall. She had long black hair, sharp black eyebrows, large greenish eyes, a slender straight nose perhaps a little bit too long, a full mouth, a pale skin. She was pretty, and the body under the kimono was well built, although she may have been just a little too hippy for some tastes.

Her apartment was light, like his, with much white on the walls and ceilings, and creamy woodwork and light and airy furniture. But a tall gloomy El Greco reproduction hung incongruously on the wall; it hovered over everything said and done

Philip José Farmer

in the one room. Childe always felt as if the elongated man on the cross was delivering judgement upon him as well as upon the city on the plain.

The painting was not as visible as usual. There was almost always a blue haze of tobacco – which accounted for the walls and ceiling not being as white as those of his apartment – and today the blue had become grey-green. Sybil coughed as she lit another cigarette, and then she went into a spasm of coughing and her face became blue. He was not upset by this, no more than usual, anyway. She had incipient emphysema and had been advised by her doctor to chop off the smoking two years ago. Certainly, the smog was accelerating her disease, but he could do nothing about it. Still, it was one more cause for quarrelling.

She finally went into the kitchen for water and came out several minutes later. Her expression was challenging, but he kept his face smooth. He waited until she sat down on the sofa across the room from his easy chair. She ground the freshly lit cigarette out on an ash tray and said, "Oh, God! I can't breathe!"

By which she meant that she could not smoke.

"Tell me about Colben," she said, and then, "first, could I get you...?"

Her voice decayed. She was always forgetting that he had quit drinking four years ago.

"I need to relax," he said. "I'm all out of pot and no chance to get any. You...?"

"I'll get some," she said eagerly. She rose and went into the kitchen. A panel creaked as it slid back; a minute passed; she came back with two cigarettes of white paper twisted at both ends. She handed him one. He said, "Thanks," and sniffed it. The odour always brought visions of flat-topped pyramids, of Aztec priests with sharp obsidian knives, naked brown men and women working in red clay fields under a sun fiercer than an eagle's glare, or Arab feluccas scudding along in the Indian Ocean. Why, he did not know.

He lit up and sucked in the heavy smoke and held it in his lungs as long as he could. He tried at the same time to empty his mind and body of the horror of this morning and the irritations he had felt since calling Sybil. There was no use smoking if he retained the bad feelings. He had to pour them out, and he could do it –

---

sometimes.

The discipline of meditation that a friend had taught him – or tried to teach him – had sometimes been effective. But he was a detective, and the prosecution of human beings, the tracking down, the immersion in hate and misery, negated the ability to meditate. Nevertheless, stubborn, he had persisted in trying, and he could sometimes empty himself. Or seem to. His friend said that he was not truly meditating; he was using a trick, a technique without essence.

Sybil, knowing what he was doing, said nothing. A clock ticked. A horn sounded faintly; a siren wailed. Sirens were always wailing nowadays. Then he breathed out and sucked in again and held his breath, and presently the *crystallization* came. There was a definite shifting of invisible lines, as if the currents of force that thread every centimetre of the universe had rearranged themselves into another *straighter* configuration.

He looked at Sybil and now he loved her very much, as he had loved her when they were first married. The snarls and knots were yanked loose; they were in a beautiful web which vibrated love and harmony through them with every movement they made. Never mind the inevitable spider.

Philip José Farmer

Chapter 4

He had hesitated to stop her when she kissed him all over his belly, although he knew what was coming. He continued to restrain himself when she took his penis and bent down to place her mouth around the head. He felt the tongue flicking it, shuddered, pushed her head away, though gently, and said, "No!"

She looked at him and said, "Why?"

"I never got around to telling you the fine details of the film," he said.

"You're getting soft!"

She sat up in the bed and looked down at him. She was frowning.

"Have you got a disease?"

"For God's sake!" he said, and he sat up, too. "Do you think I'd go to bed with you if I knew I had the syph or the clap? What kind of a question – what kind of a person do you think I am?"

"I'm sorry," she said. "My God! What's wrong? What did I do?"

"Nothing. Nothing under most circumstances. But I felt as if my cock was frozen when you... Never mind. Let me explain why I couldn't let you go down on me."

"I wish you wouldn't use words like that!"

"OK, my thing, then! Let me tell you."

She listened with wide eyes. She was leaning on one arm near him. He could see the swollen nipple, which did not seem to dwindle a bit as she listened. It might have increased. Certainly, her eyes were bright, and, despite her expressed horror, she smiled now and then.

"I really think you'd like to do that to me!" he said.

"You're always saying something stupid like that," she said. "Even now. Do you hate me so much you can't even get a hard-on?"

"You mean erection, don't you?" he said. "If you can't understand why my penis wanted to crawl into my belly for safety, then you can't understand anything about men."

"I won't bite," she said, and she grabbed his penis and lunged for it with her mouth wide open and smiling to show all her teeth.

He jerked himself away, saying, "Don't!"

"Forget about it, I was just kidding you," she said, and she crawled on to him and began kissing him. She thrust her tongue along his tongue and down his throat so far that he choked. "For God's sake!" he said, turning his head away. "What the hell are you trying to do? I can't breathe!"

She sat up and almost hissed at him. "You can't breathe! How do you think I breathe when you're shoving that big thing down my throat? What is the *matter?*"

"I don't know," he said. He sat up. "Let's have a few more drags. Maybe things'll straighten out."

"Do you have to depend upon that to be able to love me?"

He tried to take her hand in his but she snatched it away.

"You didn't see it," he said. "Those iron teeth! The blood! Spitting out that bloody flesh! God!"

"I feel sorry for Colben," she said, "but I don't see what he has to do with us. You never liked him; you were going to get rid of him. And he gave me the creeps. Anyway... oh, I don't know."

She rolled off the bed, went to the closet, and put on the kimono. She lit a cigarette and at once began coughing. It sounded as if her lungs were full of snot.

He felt angry, and opened his mouth to say something – what, he did not know, just so it was something that would hurt. But the taste of cunt made him pause. She had a beautiful cunt, the hair was thick and almost blue-black and so soft it felt almost like a seal pelt. She lubricated freely, perhaps too much, but the oil was sweet and clean. And she could squeeze down on his cock as if she had a hand inside it. And then he remembered the thing bulging out the pad over the woman's cunt in the film, and the blood that had been pouring into his penis became slushy and slowly thawed out and drained back into his body.

Sybil, who had seen the dawning erection, said, "What's wrong *now?*"

"Sybil, there's nothing wrong with *you*. It's me. I'm too upset."

She sucked in some more smoke and managed to check a cough.

"You always did bring your work home. No wonder our life

Philip José Farmer

became such a hell."

He knew that was not true. They had rubbed each other raw for other reasons, the causes of most of which they did not understand. There was, however, no use arguing. He had had enough of that.

He sat up and swung his legs over the bed and stood up and walked to the chair on which he had piled his clothes.

"What are you doing?"

"Some of the smog got in your brain?" he said. "It's obvious I'm going to dress, and it's fairly predictable that I'm getting out of here."

He checked the impulse to say, "Forever!" It sounded so childish. But it could be true.

She said nothing. She swayed back and forth with her eyes closed for a minute, then, after opening them, spun around and walked into the living room. A minute later, he followed her. She was on the divan and glaring at him.

"I haven't had such a ball-ache since I was a teenager and came home from my first necking party," he said. He did not know why he said it; certainly, he did not expect her to feel sorry for him and to do something about it. Or did he?

"Necking party? You're sure dating yourself, old man!" She looked furious. Unfortunately, fury did not make her beautiful.

Yet, he hated to leave; he had a vague feeling that he was somehow at fault.

He took one step towards her and stopped. He was going to kiss her, but it was force of habit that pushed him.

"Good-bye," he said. "I really am sorry, in a way."

"In a way!" she screamed. "Now isn't that just like you! You can't be all sorry or all righteously indignant or all right or all wrong! You have to be half-sorry. You... you... half-assed half-man!"

"And so we leave exotic Sybil-land," he said, as he swung the door open. "It sinks slowly into the smog of fantastic Southern California, and we say aloha, farewell, adieu, and kiss my ass!"

Sybil sprang out of the chair with a scream and came at him with fingers hooked to catch his face with her nails. He caught them and shoved her back so that she staggered against the sofa. She caught herself and then yelled, "You asshole! I hate you! I had a choice to make! I let you come here, instead of Al! I wanted you, not him! He was strictly second-choice, and a bad second at that! I've turned down lots of men because I kept hoping every night you'd call me! I'd eat you up; you'd be days getting out of here. I'd love you, oh, how I'd love you! And now this, you stinking bastard! Well, I'm going to call Al, and he's going to get everything I was going to give you and more! More! More! Do you understand that, you?"

He understood that he could still feel jealous. He felt like punching her and then waiting for Al and kicking him downstairs.

But it would be no good trying to make up with her. Not now. Actually, not ever, but he wasn't quite ready to believe this. Not down there where certainty dwelt.

Trying to grasp what ruined their love was like trying to close your fingers on a handful of smog.

He strode through the door and, knowing that she expected him to slam it behind him, did not.

Perhaps it was this that drove her to the last barbarism.

She stepped into the hall and shouted, "I'll suck his cock! I'll suck his cock, you!"

He turned and shouted, "You're no lady!" and spun around and walked off.

Outside, in the biting veils of grey-green, he laughed until he coughed raspingly, and then he cried. Part of the tears was engendered by the smog, part of his grief and rage. It was sad and heart-rending and disgusting and comical. One-upmanship was all right, but the one-upman actually upped it up his own one.

"When the hell is she going to grow up?" he groaned, and then, "When the hell am *I*? When will the Childe become father to the man?"

Dante was thirty-five, midway in his life's journey, when he went astray from the straight road and woke to find himself alone in a dark wood. But he obtained a professional guide, and he had at least once been on the straight road, the True Way.

Childe did not remember having been on the straight road. And where was his Virgil? The son of a bitch must be striking for higher pay and shorter hours.

Every man his own Virgil, Childe said, and coughing (like Miniver Cheevy), pushed through the smog.

Chapter 5

Somebody had broken the left front window of the Olds while he was with Sybil. A glance at the front seat showed him why. The gas mask was gone. He cursed. The mask had cost him fifty dollars when he purchased it yesterday, and there were no more to be had except in the black market. The masks were selling for two hundred or more dollars, and it took time to locate a seller.

He had the time, but he did not have cash in hand and he doubted that his cheque would be accepted. The banks were closed, and the smog might disappear so suddenly that he would not need the mask and would stop payment of the cheque. There was nothing to do except use a wet handkerchief and a pair of goggles he had worn when he had a motorcycle. That meant he must return to his apartment.

He made up a pile of handkerchiefs and filled a canteen with water as soon as he was home. He dialled the LAPD to report the theft, but, after two minutes, he gave up. The line was likely to be busy all day and all night and indefinitely into the future. He brushed his teeth and washed his face. The wash rag looked yellow. Probably it was his imagination, but the yellow could be the smog coming out. The yellow looked like the stuff that clouded his windshield in the morning after several days of heavy smog. The air of Los Angeles was an ocean in which poisonous plankton drifted.

He ate a sandwich of cold sliced beef with dill pickles and drank a glass of milk, although he did not feel hungry. Visualizations of Sybil with Al troubled him. He didn't know Al, but he could not bar shadowy images whose only bright features – too bright – were a rigid monstrosity and a pair of hairy, never-empty testicles. The pump-pump-pumping sound was also only a shadow, but it would not go away either. Shadows sometimes turned out to be indelible ink blots.

He forced himself to consider Matthew Colben and his murderers. At least, he *thought* they were murderers. There was no proof that Colben had been killed. He might be alive, though not well, somewhere in this area. Or someplace else.

Now that he was recovering from his shock, he could even think that Colben might be untouched and the film faked.

He could think this, but he did not believe it.

The phone rang. Someone was getting through to him, even if he could get through to no one. Suspecting that only the police could ram through a call, he picked up the phone. Sergeant Bruin's voice, husky and growling like a bear just waking up from hibernation, said, "Childe?"

"Yes."

"We got proof that they mean business. That film wasn't faked."

Childe was startled. He said, "I was just thinking about a fraud. How'd you find out?"

"We just opened a package mailed from Pasadena."

Bruin paused. Childe said, "Yeah?"

"Yeah. Colben's prick was in it. The end of it, anyway. Somebody's prick, anyway. It sure as hell had been bitten off."

"No leads yet?" Childe said after three seconds' hesitation.

"The package's being checked, but we don't expect anything, naturally. And I got bad news. I'm being taken off this case, well, almost entirely taken off. We got too many other things just now, you know why. If there's going to be any work done on this, Childe, you'll have to do it. But don't go off half-cocked and don't do nothing if you get a definite lead, which I think you ain't going to get. You know what I mean. You been in the business."

"Yes, I know," Childe said. "I'm going to do what I can, which, as you said, probably won't be much. I have nothing else to do now, anyway."

"You could come down here and swear in," Bruin said. "We need men right now! The traffic all over the city is a mess, like I never saw before. Everybody's trying to get out. This is going to be a ghost town. But it'll be a mess, a bloody mess, today and tomorrow. I'm telling you, I never seen nothing like it before."

Bruin could be stolid about Colben, but the prospect of the greatest traffic jam ever unfroze his bowels. He was really being moved.

"If I need help, or if I stumble – and I mean stumble – across anything significant, should I call you?"

"You can leave a message. I'll call you back when – if – I get in. Good luck, Childe."

"Same to you, Bruin," Childe said and muttered as he hung

Philip José Farmer

up, "*O Ursus Horribilis!* Or whatever the vocative case is."

He became aware that he was sweating, that his eyes felt as if they'd been filed, his sinuses hurt, he had a headache, his throat felt raw, his lungs were wheezing for the first time in five years since he had quit smoking tobacco, and, not too far off, horns were blaring.

He could do something to ease the effects of the poisoned air, but he could do little about the cars out in the street. When he had left his wife's apartment, he had had a surprising amount of trouble getting across Burton Way to San Vicente. There was no stop light at this point on Le Doux. Cars had to buck traffic coming down Burton Way on one side and going up on the other side of the divider. Coming down to the apartment, he had not seen a car or even a pair of headlights in the dimness. But, going back, he had had to be careful in crossing. The lights sprang out of the grey-greenness with startling rapidity as they rounded a nearby curve of Burton Way to the west. He had managed to find a break large enough to justify gunning across. Even so, a pair of lights and a blaring horn and squealing brakes and a shouted curse subject to the Doppler effect – told him that a speeder had come close.

The traffic going west towards Beverly Hills was light, but that coming across Burton Way between the boulevards to cut southeast on San Vicente was heavy. There was panic among the drivers. The cars were two deep, then suddenly three deep, and Childe had barely had room to squeeze through. He was being forced out of his own lane and against the kerb. Several times, he only got by by rubbing his tyres hard against the kerb.

The light at San Vicente and Third was red for him, but the cars coming down San Vicente were going through it. A car going cast on third, horn bellowing, tried to bull its way through. It collided lightly with another. From what Childe could see, the only damage was crumpled fenders. But the two drivers, hopping out and swinging at each other, looked as if they might draw some blood, inept as they were with their fists. He had caught a glimpse of several frightened faces – children – looking through the windows of both damaged cars. Then he was gone.

Now he could hear the steady honking of horns. The great herd was migrating, and God help them.

The deadly stink and blinding smoke had been bad enough

when most cars suddenly ceased operating. But now that two million automobiles were suddenly on the march, the smog was going to be intensified. It was true that, in time, the cars would be gone, and then the atmosphere could be expected to start cleaning itself. If it was going to do it. Childe had the feeling that the smog wasn't going to leave, although he knew that that was irrational.

Meanwhile, he, Childe, was staying. He had work to do. But would he be able to do anything? He had to get around, and it looked as if he might not be able to do that.

He sat down on the sofa, and looked across the room at the dark golden bookcases. *The Annotated Sherlock Holmes*, the two great boxed volumes, was his treasure, the culminating work of his collection unless you counted a copy of *The White Company* personally inscribed by A. Conan Doyle, once the possession of Childe's father. It was his father who had introduced him at an early age to interesting and stimulating books, and his father who had managed to pass on his devotion to the greatest detective to his son. But his father had remained a professor of mathematics; he had felt no burning to emulate The Master.

Nor would any "normal" child. Most kids wanted to be aeroplane pilots or railroad engineers or cowboys or astronauts when they grew up. Many, of course, wanted to be detectives, Sherlock Holmeses, Mark Tidds (what boy nowadays knew of Mark Tidd?), even Nick Carters since he had been revived with modern settings and plots, but few stuck to that wish. Most of the policemen and private investigators whom he knew had not had these professions as boyhood goals. Many had never read Holmes or had done so without enthusiasm; he had never met a Holmes buff among them. But they did read the true detective magazines and devoured the countless paperbacks of murder mysteries and of private eyes. They made fun of the books, but, like cowboys who also deride the genuineness of Westerns, they were addicted.

Childe made no secret of his "vice". He loved them, even the bad ones, and gloried in the "good" ones.

And so why was he trying to justify being a detective? Was it something to be ashamed of?

In one way, it was. There was in every American, even the judge and the policeman, a more-or-less strong contempt for lawmen. This lived side by side with an admiration for the lawman, but for the lawman who is a strong individualist, who fights most of his battles by himself against overwhelming evil, who fights often outside the law in order to bring about justice. In short, the frontier marshal, the Mike Hammerish private eye. This lawman is so close to the criminal that there is a certain sympathy between the lawman and the criminal.

Or so it seemed to Childe, who, as he told himself now, tended to do too much theorizing and also to project his own feelings as those of others.

Matthew Colben. Where was he now? Dead or suffering? Who had forcibly taken him to some dwelling somewhere in this area? Why was the film sent to the LAPD? Why this gesture of mockery and defiance? What could the criminals hope to gain by it, except a perverse pleasure in frustrating the police?

There were no clues, no leads, except the vampire motif, which was nothing but a suggestion of a direction to take. But it was the only handle to grasp, ectoplasmic though it was, and he would try to seize it. At least, it would give him something to do.

He knew something about vampires. He had seen the early Dracula movies and the later movies on TV. Ten years ago, he had read the novel, *Dracula*, and found it surprisingly powerful and vivid and convincing. It was far better than the best Dracula movie, the first; the makers of the movie should have followed the book more closely. He had also read Montague Summers and had been an avid reader of the now-dead *Weird Tales* magazine. But a little knowledge was not dangerous; it was just useless.

There was one man he knew who was deeply interested in the occult and the supernatural. He looked up the number in his record book because it was unlisted and he had not called enough to memorize it. There was no response for about fifty seconds. He waited and then a recording informed him that he would soon be taken care of if he were patient but please not to use the phone unless it was an emergency. He hung up and turned on the radio. There was some news about the international and national situations, but most of the broadcast was about the exodus. A number of stalled cars on the freeways and highways had backed up traffic for a total of several thousand miles. The police were trying to restrict passage on the freeways to a certain number of lanes to permit the police cars, ambulances, and tow trucks to pass through. But all lanes were being used, and the police were having a hell of a time clearing them out. A number of fires had started in homes and buildings, and some of them were burning down with no assistance from the firemen because the trucks could not get through. There were collisions all over the area with no help available, not only because of the traffic but because there just was not enough hospital and police personnel available.

Childe thought, to hell with the case! I'll help!

He called the LAPD and hung on for fifteen minutes, but he got only a busy signal. He then called the Beverly Hills Police Department and got the same result. He had no more luck with the Mount Sinai Hospital on Beverly Boulevard, which was within walking distance. He put drops in his eyes and snuffed up nose drops. He wet a handkerchief to place over his nose and put his goggles on top of his head. He stuck a pencil flashlight in one pocket and switchblade knife in the other. Then he left the apartment building and walked down San Vicente to Beverly Boulevard.

In the half hour that he had been home, the situation had changed. The cars that had been bumper-to-bumper kerb-to-kerb were gone. They were within earshot; he could hear the horns blaring off somewhere around Beverly Boulevard and La Cienega, but there was not a car in sight.

Then he came across one. It was lying on its side. He looked down into the windows, dreading what he might see. It was empty. He could not understand how the vehicle had been overturned, because no one could have gone fast enough in the jam to hit anything and be overturned. Besides, he would have heard the crash. Somebody – somebodies – had rocked it back and forth and then pushed it over. Why? He would probably never know.

The signal lights at the intersection were out. He could see well enough across the street to make out the thin dark shape of the pole. Its lights were not operating. When he got to the foot of the light pole on his corner, he saw why. Broken plastic, which would have been green, red and yellow under more lightened circumstances, lay scattered about.

He stood for a while on the kerb and peered into the sickly grey. If a car were to speed down the street without lights, it could be on him before he could get across the street. Nobody but a

Philip José Farmer

damned fool would go fast or without lights, but there were many damned fools driving the streets of Los Angeles.

The wailing of a siren became stronger, a flashing red light became visible, and an ambulance whizzed by. He looked up and down the street and dashed across, hoping that the light and noise would have made even the damnedest of fools cautious and that anybody following the ambulance would probably be blowing his horn. He got across with only a slight burning of the lungs. The smog was slowly rusting off their lining. His eyes ran as if they were infected.

The sound of bedlam came to him before the hospital building loomed out of the mists. He was stopped by a white-haired man in the uniform of a security guard. Perhaps the old man had worked at an aircraft plant or at a bank as a guard and had been deputized by the police to serve at the hospital. He flashed his light into Childe's face and asked him if he could help him. The smog was not dark enough to make the light brilliant, but it did annoy Childe.

He said, "Take that damned light away! I'm here to offer my services in whatever capacity I'm needed." He opened his wallet and showed his ID.

The guard said, "You better go in the front way. The emergency room entrance is jammed, and they're all too busy to talk to you."

"Who do I see?" Childe said.

The guard hurriedly gave the supervisor's name and directions for getting to his office. Childe entered the lobby and saw at once that his help might be needed, but he was going to have to force it on the hospital. The lobby was jammed and asprawl with people who had been shunted out of the emergency room after more or less complete treatment, relatives of the wounded, people enquiring after lost or injured friends or relatives, and a number who, like Childe, had come to offer their services. The hall outside the supervisor's office was crowded too thickly for him to ram his way through even if he had felt like doing so. He asked a man on the fringes how long he had been trying to get into the office.

"An hour and ten minutes, Mister," the man said disgustedly.

Childe turned to walk away. He would return to his

apartment and do whatever he could to pass the time. Then he would return after a reasonable amount of time (if there were such a thing in this situation), with the hope that some order would have been established. He stopped. There, standing near the front door of the hospital, his head wrapped in a white cloth, was Hamlet Jeremiah.

The cloth could have been a turban, because the last time Childe had seen Jeremiah he was sporting a turban with a spangled hexagram. But the cloth was a bandage with a three-pointed scarlet badge, almost a triskelion. The Mephistophelean moustaches and beard were gone, and he was wearing a grease-smeared T-shirt with the motto: NOLI ME TANGERE SIN AMOR. His pants were white duck, and brown sandals were on his feet.

"Herald Childe!" he called, smiling, and then his face twisted momentarily as if the smile had hurt.
Childe held out his hand.

Jeremiah said, "You touch me with love?"

"I'm very fond of you, Ham," Childe said, "although I can't really say why. Do we have to go through that at this time?"

"Any time and all time," Jeremiah said. "Especially this time."

"OK. It's love then," and Childe shook his head. "What in hell happened? What're you doing down here? Listen, did you know I tried to phone you a little while ago and I was thinking of driving up to see you. Then..."

Jeremiah held up his hand and laughed and said, "One thing at a time! I'm out of my Sunset pad because my wives insisted we get out of town. I told them we ought to wait a day or so until the roads were cleared. By then, the smog'd be gone, anyway, or on its way out. But they wouldn't listen. They cried and carried on something awful, unreeled my entrails and tromped on them. One good thing about tears; they wash out the smog, keep the acids from eating up your corneas. But they're also acid on the nerves, so I said, finally, OK, I love you both, so we'll take off. But if we get screwed up or anything bad happens, don't blame me. Stick it up your own lovely asses. So they smiled and wiped away the tears and packed up and we took off down Doheny. Sheila had a little hand-operated prayer wheel spinning and Lupe was getting three roaches out so we could enjoy what would otherwise be a real

Philip José Farmer

drag, or so we at least could enjoy a facsimile of joy. We came to Melrose, and the light changed to red, so I stopped, being a law-abiding citizen when the law is for the benefit of all and well-founded. Besides, I didn't want to get run into. But the son of Adam behind me got mad; he thought I ought to run the light. His soul was really ruffled, Herald, he was in a coldsweat panic. He honked his horn and when I didn't jump like a dog through a hoop and go through the light, he jumped out of his car and opened my door – dumb bastard, I didn't have it locked – and he jerked me out and whirled me around and shoved my head against the handle. It cut my head open and knocked me half-silly. Naturally, I didn't resist; I really believe this turn-the-other-cheek dictum.

"I was half in the next lane, and the other cars weren't going to stop, so Sheila jumped out and shoved the man in the path of one and pulled me into the car. That Sheila has a temper, you got to forgive her. The man was hit; he bounced off one car and into ours. So Sheila drove the car then, while Lupe was trying to heave the man out. He was lying on the back seat with his legs dragging on the street. I stopped her and told Sheila to take us to the hospital.

"So she did, though reluctantly, I mean reluctantly to take the man, too, and we got here, and my head finally got bandaged, and Sheila and Lupe are helping the nurses up on the second floor. I'll help as soon as I get to feeling better."

"What happened to the man?" Childe said.

"He's on a mattress on the floor of the second level. He's unconscious, breathing a few bubbles of blood, poor unhappy soul, but Sheila's taking care of him, too. She feels bad about shoving him; she's got a hasty temper but underneath it all she truly loves."

"I was going to offer to help," Childe said, "but I can't stay standing around for hours. Besides..."

Jeremiah asked him what the *besides* meant. Childe told him about Colben and the film. Jeremiah was shocked. He said that he had heard a little about it over the radio. He had not received a paper for two days, so he had no chance to read anything about it. Childe wanted somebody with a big library on vampires and on other things that boomp in the unlit halls of the mind?

Well, he knew just the man. And he lived not more than six blocks away, just south of Wilshire. If anybody would have the research material, it would he Woolston Heepish.

"Isn't he likely to be trying to get out of town?"

"Woolie? By Dracula's moustache, no! Nothing, except maybe an atomic attack threat, would get him to desert his collection. Don't worry; he'll be home. There *is* one problem. He doesn't like unexpected visitors, you got to phone him ahead of time and ask if you can come, even his best friends – except may be for D. Nimming Rodder – are no exceptions. Everybody phones and asks permission, and if he isn't expecting you, he usually won't answer the doorbell. But he knows my voice; I'll holler through the door at him."

"*Rodder?* Where have... ? Oh, yes! The book and TV writer! Vampires, werewolves, a lovely young girl trapped in a hideous mansion high on a hill, that sort of thing. He produced and wrote the *Shadow Land* series, right?"

"Please, Herald, don't say anything at all about him if you can't say something good. Woolie worships D. Nimming Rodder. He won't hit you if you say anything disparaging about him, but you sure as Shiva won't get any co-operation and you'll find yourself frozen out."

Childe shifted from one foot to another and coughed. The cough was only partly from the burning air. It indicated that he was having a struggle with his conscience. He wanted to stay here and help – part of him did but the other part, the more powerful, wanted to get out and away on the trail. Actually, he couldn't be much use here, not for some time, anyway. And he had a feeling, only a feeling but one which had ended in something objectively profitable in the past, that something down there in the dark deeps was nibbling at his hook.

He put his hand on Jeremiah's bony shoulder and said, "I'll try to phone him, but if..."

"No use, Herald. He has an answering service, and it's not likely that'll be working now."

"Give me a note of introduction, so I can get my foot in the door."

Jeremiah smiled and said, "I'll do better than that. I'll walk with you to Woolie's. I'm just in the way here, and I'd like to get away from the sight of so much suffering."

"I don't know," Childe said. "You could have a concussion.

Philip José Farmer

Maybe you..."

Jeremiah shrugged and said, "I'm going with you. Just a minute while I find the women and tell them where I'm going."

Childe, waiting for him, and having nothing to do but watch and listen, understood why Jeremiah wanted to get away. The blood and the groans and weeping were bad enough, but the many chopping coughs and loud, long pumping-up-snot-or-blood coughs irritated, perhaps even angered him, although the anger was rammed far down. He did not know why coughs set him on edge so much, but he knew that Sybil's nicotine cough and burbling lungs, occurring at any time of day or night and especially distressing when he was eating or making love, had caused their split as much as anything. Or had made him believe so.

Jeremiah seemed to skate through the crowd. He took Childe's hand and led him out the front door. It was three minutes after 12.00. The sun was a distorted yellow-greenish lobe. A man about a hundred feet east of them was a wavering shadowy figure. There seemed to be thick and thin bands of smog sliding past each other and thus darkening and lightening, squeezing and elongating objects and people. This must have been an illusion or some other phenomenon, because the smog was not moving. There was not a rumour of a breeze. The heat seemed to filter down through the green-greyishness, to slide down the filaments of smog like acrobats with fevers and sprawl outwards and wrap themselves around people.

Childe's armpits and back and face were wet but the perspiration only cooled him a little. His crotch and his feet were also sweating, and he wished that he could wear swimming trunks or a towel. It was better outside than in the hospital, however. The stench of sweaty frightened people had been powerful, but the noise and the sight of the misery and pain had made it less offensive. Now he was aware that Jeremiah, who was, despite being a "hippie", a lover of baths, a true "water brother" as he liked to say, stank. The odour was a peculiar combination of pipe tobacco, marijuana, a pungent heavy unidentifiable something suggestive of spermatic fluid, incense, a soupcon of rosewater on cunt, frightened sweat, extrusion of excited shit, and, perhaps, inhaled smog being sweat out.

Jeremiah looked at Childe, coughed, smiled, and said, "You

smell like something washed up out of the Pacific deeps and two weeks dead yourself, if you'll forgive my saying so."

Childe, although startled, did not comment. Jeremiah had given too many evidences of telepathy or mind-reading. However, there were other explanations which Childe did not really believe. Childe's expression could have told Jeremiah what he was thinking, although Childe would have said that his face was unreadable.

He walked along with Jeremiah. They seemed to be in a tunnel that grew out of the pavement before them and fell flat on to the pavement behind them. Childe felt unaccountably happy for a moment despite the sinus ache, throat and eye burn, insidious crisping of lungs, and stabbing in his testicles. He had not really wanted to be a good servant in the hospital; he had wanted to be sniffing on the track of criminals.

Philip José Farmer

Chapter 6

"You see, Ham," Childe said, "the vampire motif in the film could mean nothing – as a clue – but I feel that it's very important and, in fact, the only thing I can follow up. But the chances..."

His voice died. He and Jeremiah stood on the kerb of the north side of Burton Way and waited. The cars were like elephants in the greyness, grey elephants with trunks to tails, huge eyes glowing in the gloom. The lanes here were one-way for westward traffic, but all traffic was moving eastward.

There was only one thing to do if they wished to cross today. Childe stepped out into the traffic. The cars were going so slowly that it was easy to climb up on the hood of the nearest and jump over on to the next hood and on to a third and then a fourth and on to the grass of the divider.

Startled and outraged drivers and passengers cursed and howled at them, but Jeremiah only laughed and Childe jeered at them. They crossed the divider and jumped from hood to hood again until they got to the other side. They walked down Willaman, and every house was unlit. At Wilshire and Willaman, the street lights were operating, but the cars were paying no attention. All were going eastward on both sides of Wilshire.

The traffic was a little faster here but not too fast.

Childe and Jeremiah got over, although Jeremiah slipped once and fell on top of a hood.

"Middle of this block," Jeremiah said.

The houses and apartments were middle middle-class. The homes were the usual California-Spanish bungalows; the apartment buildings were four or five storey boxes with some attempts at decoration and terracing outside. There were lights in a few windows but the house before which Jeremiah stopped was dark.

"Must not be home," Childe said.

"Doesn't mean a thing. His windows are always dark. Once you get inside, you'll see why. He may not be home just now; he might've gone to the store or the gas station; they're supposed to be open, at least the governor said they would. Let's see."

They crossed the yard. The front window looked boarded

up. At least, something dark and woody-looking covered it on the inside. Closer, he saw that the man-sized figure, which had stood so silently and which he had thought was an iron statue, was a wooden and painted cut-out of Godzilla.

They went around the side of the house to the driveway. There was a large red sign with glaring yellow letters: MISTER HORROR IS ALIVE AND WELL IN HERE.

Beyond was a sort of courtyard with a tree which bent at forty-five degrees and the top of which covered the porch roof and part of the house roof like a great greenish hand. The tree trunk was so grey and twisted and knobbed that Childe thought for a moment that it was artificial. It looked as if it had been designed and built as background to a horror movie.

There were many signs on the door and the walls beside the door, some of them "cute" and others "in" jokes. There were also masks of Frankenstein's Monster, Dracula, and the Wolf-Man nailed against the walls. And several NO SMOKING ABSOLUTELY signs. Another forbade any alcoholic beverages to be brought in.

Jeremiah pressed the button, which was the nose of a gargoyle face painted around it. A loud clanging noise as of large bells came from within and then several bars of organ music: *Gloomy Sunday*.

There was no other response. Jeremiah waited a moment and then rang the bell again. More bells and organ music. But no one at the door.

Jeremiah beat on the door and shouted, "Open up, Woolie! I know you're in there! It's OK! It's me, Hamlet Jeremiah, one of your greatest fans!"

The little peep-window slid back and light rayed out. The light was cut off, came back, was cut off again as the peep-window swung shut. The door opened with a screeching of rusty hinges. A few seconds later, Childe understood that the noise was a recording.

"Welcome," a soft baritone said. Jeremiah tapped Childe's shoulder to indicate he should precede him. They walked in, and the man shut the door, rammed home three large bolts, and hooked two chains.

The room was too confusing for Childe to take it in all at once. He concentrated on the man, whom Jeremiah introduced as Woolston Q. Heepish.

"Woolie" was about six feet in height, portly and soft-looking, moderately paunched, with a bag of skin hanging under his chin, bronze walrus moustache, square rimless spectacles, a handsome profile from the mouth up, a full head of dark-red, straight, slick hair, and pale grey eyes. He hunched forward as if he had spent most of his life over a desk.

The walls and windows of the room were covered with shelves of books and various objects and with paintings, movie stills, posters, masks, plastic busts, framed letters, and blow-ups of movie actors. There was a sofa, several chairs, and a grand piano. The room beyond looked much the same except for its lack of furniture.

If he wanted to learn about vampires, he was at the right place.

The place was jammed with anything and everything concerning Gothic literature, folklore, legendry, the supernatural, lycanthropy, demonology, witchcraft, and the movies made of these subjects.

Woolie shook Childe's hand with a large, wet, plump hand.

"Welcome to the House of Horror," he said.

Jeremiah explained why they were there. Woolie shook his head and said that he had heard about Colben over the radio. The announcer had said that Colben had been "horribly mutilated" but he had not given any details.

Childe told him the details. Heepish shook his head and tsk-tsked while his grey eyes seemed to get brighter and the corners of his lips dimpled.

"How terrible! How awful! Sickening! My God, the savages still in our midst! How can such things be?"

The soft voice murmured and seemed to become lost, as if it were breaking up into a half dozen parts which, like mice, scurried for the dark in the corners. The pale, soft wet hands rubbed together now and then and several times were clasped in a gesture which at first looked prayerful but also gave the impression of being placed around an invisible neck.

"If there is anything I can do to help you track down these monsters: if there is anything in my house to help you, you are welcome," Heepish said. "Though I can't imagine what kind of clue you could find by just browsing through. Still..."

The Image Of The Beast

He spread both hands out and then said, "But let me conduct you through my house. I always have the guided tour first for strangers. Hamlet can come with us or look around on his own, if he wishes. Now, this blow-up here is of Alfred Dummel and Else Bennrich in the German film, *The Blood Drinker*, made in 1928. It had a rather limited distribution in this country, but I was fortunate enough – I have many many friends all over the world and even in Germany – to get a print of the film. It may be the only print now existing; I've made enquiries and never been able to locate another, and I've had many people trying to find another for me..."

Childe restrained the impulse to tell Heepish that he wanted to see the newspaper files at once. He did not wish to waste any time. But Jeremiah had told him how he must behave if he wanted to get maximum co-operation from his host.

The house was crammed with objects of many varieties, all originating in the world of terror and evil shadows but designed and manufactured to make money. The house was bright with illuminations of many shades: bile-yellow, blood-red, decay-purple, rigor mortis-greyblue, repressed-anger orange, but shadows seemed to press in everywhere. Where no shadow could be, there was shadow.

An air-conditioner was moving air slowly and icily, as if the next glacial age were announcing itself. The air was well-filtered, because the burning of eyes and throat and lungs was fading. (Something good to say about ice ages.) Despite this, and the ridges of skin pinched by cold air, Childe felt as if he were suffocating with the closeness and bulk and disorder of the books, the masks, the heads of movie monsters, the distorted wavy menacing paintings, the Frankenstein monsters and Wolf-Men dolls, the little Revolting Robot toys, the Egyptian statues of jackal-headed Anubis, the cat-headed Sekhmet.

The room beyond was smaller but also much more cluttered.

Woolie gestured vaguely at the leaning and sometimes collapsed piles of books and magazines.

"I got a shipment in from a collector in Utica, New York," Heepish said. "He died recently."

His voice deepened and richened almost to oiliness. "Very sad. A fine man. A real fan of the horror. We corresponded for years, more than I care to say, although I never actually got to meet him. But our minds met, we had much in common. His widow sent me this stuff, told me to price it at whatever I thought was fair. There's a complete collection of *Weird Tales* from 1923 through 1954, a first edition of Chambers's *King In Yellow*, a first edition of *Dracula* with a signature from Bram Stoker and Bela Lugosi, and, oh! there is so so much!"

He rubbed his hands and smiled. "So much! But the prize is a letter from Doctor Polidori – he was Byron's personal physician and friend, you know – author of an anonymous book – I have several first editions of the first vampire novel in English – *The Vampyre*. Doctor Polidori! A letter from him to a Lady Milbanks describing how he got the idea for his novel! It's unique! I've been lusting – literally lusting – for it ever since I heard about it in 1941! It'll occupy a prominent place – perhaps the most prominent – on the front room wall as soon as I can get a suitable frame!"

Childe refrained from asking where he would find a bare place on the wall.

Heepish showed him his office, a large room with living dimensions constricted by many rows of ceiling-high bookcases and by a huge old-fashioned rolltop desk engulfed by books, magazines, letters, maps, stills, posters, statuettes, toys, and a headsman's axe that looked genuine, even to the dried blood.

They went back to the room between the office and living room, where Heepish led Childe into the kitchen. This had a stove, a sink, and a refrigerator, but otherwise was full of books, magazines, small filing cases, and some dead insects on the edges of the open cupboards and on the floor.

"I'm having the stove taken out next week," Heepish said. "I don't eat in, and when I give a party, I have everything brought in."

Childe raised his eyebrows but said nothing. Jeremiah had told him that the refrigerator was so full of microfilms that there was little room for food. And at the rate the film was coming in, there would soon not be space enough for a quart of milk.

"I am thinking about building an extension to my house," Heepish said. "As you can see, I'm a teeny-weeny bit crowded now, and heaven knows what it will be like five years from now. Or even one."

Woolston Heepish had been married – for over fifteen years. His wife had wanted children, but he had said no. Children could not be kept away from his books, magazines, paintings and drawings, masks and costumes, toys and statuettes. Little children were very destructive.

After some years, his wife gave up her wish to have babies. Could she have a pet, a cat or a dog? Heepish said that he was indeed very sorry, but cats clawed and dogs chewed and piddled.

The collection increased; the house shrank. Furniture was removed to make room for more objects. The day came when there was no room for Mrs Heepish. *The Bride Of Frankenstein* was elbowing her out. She knew better than to appeal for even a halt to the collecting, and a diminution was unthinkable. She moved out and got a divorce, naming as co-respondent *The Creature From The Black Lagoon*.

It was only fair to Heepish, Jeremiah had said, to let Childe know that Heepish and his wife were the best of friends and went out together as much as when they had lived together. Perhaps, though, this was the ex-Mrs Heepish's way of getting revenge, because she certainly rode herd on him, and he meekly submitted with only a few grumbles now and then.

Now Heepish himself was being forced out. One day, he would come home after a late meeting of *The Count Of Dracula Society* and open the front door, and tons of books, magazines, documents, photographs, and bric-a-brac would cascade out, and the rescuers would tunnel down to find Woolston Heepish pressed flat between the leaves of *The Castle Of Otranto*.

Childe was led into an enclosed back porch, jammed with books like the other rooms. They stepped out the back door into a pale green light and an instant sensation as of diluted sulphuric acid fumes scraping the eyes. Childe blinked, and his eyes began to run. He coughed. Heepish coughed.

Heepish said, "Perhaps we should pass up the grand tour of the garage, but..."

His voice trailed off – Childe had stopped for a moment; Heepish was a figure as dark and bulky and shapeless as a monster in the watery mists of a grade-B movie.

The door squeaked upward. Childe hastened to enter the garage. The door squeaked down and clanged shut. Childe

Philip José Farmer

wondered if this door, too, were connected to a recording taken from the old *Inner Sanctum* radio programme. Heepish turned on the lights. More of the same except that there was dust on the heads, masks, books, and magazines.

"I keep my duplicates, second-rate things, and stuff I just don't have room for in the house here at the moment," Heepish said. Childe felt that he was expected to ejaculate over at least a few items. He wanted to get out of the hot, close and dead air into the house. He hoped that the files he wanted were not stored here.

Childe commented on an entire bookshelf dedicated to the works of D. Nimming Rodder.

Heepish said, "Oh, you noticed that he is the only living author with an individual placard in my collection in the house? Nim is my favourite, of course, I think he's the greatest writer of all time, in the gothic or horror genre, even greater than Monk Lewis or H. P. Lovecraft or Bram Stoker. He is a very good friend of mine.

"I keep many duplicates of his works out here because he needs one now and then to use as tearsheets or reference for a new anthology. He has had many anthologies, you know, just scads of reprints and collections taken from his collections, and collections from these. He's probably the most recollected man on Earth."

Childe did not smile. Heepish shrugged.

There was a large blow-up of Rodder tacked to an upright. In heavy black ink below: TO MY FIRST FAN AND A GREAT FRIEND, MISTER HORROR HIMSELF, WITH INTENSE AFFECTION FROM NIM.

The thin, pale face with the collapsed cheeks, sharp nose, and the huge-rimmed spectacles looked like that of a spooky and spooked primate of the Madagascar jungle, like a lemur's. And lemur, now that Childe considered it, originally meant a ghost. He grinned. He remembered the entry in the big unabridged dictionary he had referred to so often at college.

Lemur – Latin *lemures* nocturnal spirits, ghosts; akin to Greek *lamia,* a devouring monster, *lamas* crop, maw, *lamia,* pl., chasm. Lettish *lamata* mousetrap; basic idea: open jaws.

Chapter 7

Childe, looking at Rodder's photograph, grinned widely.

Heepish said, "What's so funny? I could stand a little laugh in these trying times."

"Nothing, really."

"Don't you like Rodder?"

Heepish's voice was controlled, but it contained a hint of a well-oiled mousetrap aching to snap shut.

Childe said, "I liked his *Shadow Land* series. And I liked his underlying themes, aside from the spooky element. You know, the *little* man fighting bravely against conformity, authoritarianism, vast forces of corruption, and so on, the lone individual, the only honest man in the world – I liked those things. And every time I read an article in the newspapers about Rodder, he's always described as honest, as a man of integrity. Which is really ironic."

Childe stopped and then, not wishing to continue but impelled to, said, "But I know a guy..."

He stopped. Why tell Heepish that the *guy* was Jeremiah?

"This guy was at a party which consisted mainly of science-fiction people. He was standing within earshot of a group of authors. One was the great fantasy writer, Breyleigh Bredburger. You know of him, of course?"

Heepish nodded and said, "After Rodder, Monk Lewis, and Bloch, my favourite."

Childe said, "Another author, I forget his name, was complaining that Rodder had stolen one of his magazine stories for his series. Just lifted it, changed the title and a few things, credited it to somebody with an outlandish Greek name, and had, so far, refused to correspond with the author about the alleged theft. Bredburger said that was nothing. Rodder had stolen three of his stories, giving credit to himself, Rodder, as author. Bredburger cornered Rodder twice and forced him to admit the theft and to pay him. Rodder's excuse was that he'd signed to write two-thirds of the series himself and he wasn't up to it, so, in desperation, he'd lifted Bredburger's stories. He didn't say anything about plagiarizing from other people of course. Bredburger said he'd been promised payment for the third stolen story but so far hadn't got it and wouldn't unless he vigorously pursued Rodder or went through the courts.

"A third author then said that the first would have to stand in line behind about twenty if he wanted to sue or to take it out of Rodder's hide.

"That's your D. Nimming Rodder. Your great champion of the *little* man, of the non-conformist, of the *honest* man."

Childe stopped. He was surprised that he had run on so. He did not want to quarrel. After all, he was to be indebted to this man, if this grand tour ever ended. On the other hand, he was itchy with anger. He had seen too many corrupt men highly honoured by the world, which either did not know the truth or ignored it. Also, the irritation caused by the smog, the repressed panic arising from fear of what the smog might become, Colben's death, the frustrating scene with Sybil, and Heepish's attitude, undefinedly prickly, combined to wear away the skin and fat over his nerves.

Heepish's grey eyes seemed to retreat, as if they were afraid they might combust if they got too close to the light and air. His neck quivered. His moustache grew down; invisible weights had been tied to each end. His nostrils flared like bellows. His pale skin had become red. His hands clenched.

Childe waited while the silence hardened like bird lime. If Heepish got nasty, he would get just as nasty, even though he would lose access to the literature he needed. Childe had been told by Jeremiah that Heepish had got the idea for his collection from observing a man by the name of Forest J. Ackerman, who had probably the greatest private collection of science-fiction and fantasy in the world. In fact, Heepish had been called the poor man's Ackerman, though not to his face. However, he was far from poor, he had much money – from what source nobody knew – and his collection would someday be the world's greatest, private or public.

But at this moment he was very vulnerable, and Childe was willing to thrust through the crack in the armour.

"Well!" Heepish said..

He cocked his head and smiled thinly. The moustache, however, was still swelled like an elephant in mating season, and his fingers were making a steeple, then separating to form the throat-holding attitude.

"Well!" he said again. His voice was as hard, but there was

also a whine in it, like a distant mosquito.

"Well!" Childe said, aware that he would never know what Heepish was going to say and not caring. "I'd like to see the newspaper files, if possible."

"Oh? Oh, yes! They're upstairs. This way, please." They left the garage, but Heepish put the photograph of Rodder under his arm before following him out. Childe had wondered what it was doing out in the garage, anyway, but on re-entering the house, he saw that there were many more photographs – and paintings and pencil sketches and even framed newspaper and magazine clippings containing Rodder's portrait – than he had thought. Heepish had had one too many and stored that one in the garage. But now, as if to show Childe his place, to put him down in some obscure manner, Heepish was also bringing this photograph into the house.

Childe grinned at this as he waited for Heepish to lead him through the kitchen and hall-room and turn right to go up the narrow stairs. The walls were hung with many pictures and paintings of Frankenstein's monster and Dracula and an original by Hannes Bok and another by Virgil Finlay, all leaning at slightly different angles like headstones in an old neglected graveyard.

They went down a short hallway and into a room with the walls covered with paintings and photographs and posters and movie ad stills. There were a number of curious wooden frames, sawhorses with castles on their backs, which held a series of illustrations and photos and newspaper clippings on wooden frames. These could be turned on a central shaft, like pages of a book.

Childe looked through all of them and, at any other time, would have been delighted and would have lingered over various nostalgic items.

Heepish, as if the demands on him were really getting to be too much, sighed when Childe asked to see the scrapbooks. He went into an enormous closet the walls of which were lined with bookshelves stuffed with large scrapbooks, many of them dusty and smelling of decay.

"I really must do something about these before it's too late," Heepish said. "I have some very valuable – some invaluable and irreplaceable – material here."

He was still carrying Rodder's photo under one arm.

It was Childe's turn to sigh as he looked at the growing hill of stuff to peruse. But he sat down in a chair, placed his right ankle over his left thigh, and began to turn the stiff and often yellowed and brittle pages of the scrapbooks. After a while, Heepish said that he would have to excuse himself. If Childe wanted anything, he should just holler. Childe looked up and smiled briefly and said that he did not want to be any more bother than he had to be. Heepish was gone then, but left an almost visible ectoplasm of disdain and hurt feelings behind him.

The scrapbooks were titled with various subjects: MOVIE VAMPIRES, GERMAN AND SCANDINAVIAN, 1919–1939; WEREWOLVES, AMERICAN, 1865–1900; WITCHES, PENNSYLVANIAN, 1880–1965; GOLEM, EXTRAFORTEANA, 1929–1960; SOUTHERN CALIFORNIA VAMPIRE FOLKLORE AND GHOST STORIES, 1910–1967; and so on.

Childe had gone through thirty-two such titles before he came to the last one. They had all been interesting but not very fruitful, and he did not *know* that the one which was in his hands was relevant. But he felt his heart quicken and his back become less stiff. It could not be called a clue, but it at least was something to investigate.

An article from the *Los Angeles Times,* dated 1 May 1958, described a number of reputedly "haunted" houses in the Los Angeles area. Several long paragraphs were devoted to a house in Beverly Hills which not only had a ghost, it had a "vampire".

There was a photograph of the Trolling House taken from the air. According to the article, no one could get close enough to it on the ground to use a camera effectively. The house was set on a low hill in the middle of a large – for Southern California – walled estate. The grounds were well wooded so that the house could not be seen from anywhere outside the walls. The newspaper cameraman had been unable to get photos of it in 1948, when the owner of Trolling House had become temporarily famous, and the newsmen had no better luck in 1958, when this article, recapitulating the events of ten years before, had been published. There was, however, a picture of a pencil sketch made of the "vampire", Baron Igescu, by an artist who had depended upon his memory after seeing the baron at a charity ball. Very few people had seen the baron, although he had made several appearances at charity balls and once at a Beverly Hills taxpayers' protest meeting.

Trolling House was named after the uncle of the present owner. The uncle, also an Igescu, had travelled from Rumania to England in 1887, stayed there one year, and then moved on to America in 1889. Upon becoming a citizen of the United States of America, Igescu had changed his name to Trolling. No one knew why. The mansion was on woodland surrounded on all sides by a high brick wall topped with iron spikes between which barbed wire was strung. Built in very late Victorian style in 1900 in what was then out-of-the-way agricultural land, it was a huge rambling structure. The nucleus was a part of the original house. This was, naturally, a Spanish-style mansion which had been built by the eccentric (some said, mad) Don Pedro del Osorojo in the wilderness of what was to become, a century later, Beverly Hills. Del Osorojo was supposed to have been a relative of the de Villa family, which owned this area, but that was not authenticated. Actually little was known of del Osorojo except that he was a recluse with an unknown source of wealth. His wife came from Spain (this was at a time that California was under Spanish rule) and was supposed to have been of Castilian nobility.

The present owner, Igescu, was involuntarily publicized in 1938 when he was brought dead-on-arrival into the Cedars of Lebanon Hospital after a car collision at Hollywood and La Brea. At twilight of the following day, the county coroner was to perform an inquest. Igescu had no perceptible wounds or injuries.

At the first touch of the knife, Igescu sat up on the dissection slab.

This story was picked up by newspapers throughout the States because a reporter jestingly pointed out that Igescu had (1) never been seen in the daytime, (2) was of Carpathian origin, (3) came from an aristocratic family which had lived for centuries in a castle (now abandoned) on top of a high steep hill in a remote rural area, (4) had shipped his uncle's body back to the old country to be buried in the family tomb, but the coffin had disappeared en route, and (5) was living in a house already well-known because of the ghost of Dolores del Osorojo.

Dolores was supposedly the spirit of Don Pedro's daughter. She had died of grief, or killed herself because of grief. Her lover, or suitor, was a Norwegian sea-captain who had seen Dolores at a governor's ball during one of her rare appearances in town. He

Philip José Farmer

seemed to have lost his sanity over her. He neglected his ship and its business, and his men deserted or were thrown into the local jail for drunkenness and vagrancy.

Lars Ulf Larsson, the captain, barred by the old don from seeing Dolores, managed to sneak into the house and woo her so successfully that she promised to run off with him within a week. But the night of the elopement came, and Larsson did not show up. He was never seen again; a legend had it that Don Pedro had killed him and buried his body on the estate. Another said that the body had been thrown into the sea.

Dolores had gone into mourning and died several weeks later. Her father went hunting into the hills several weeks after she was buried and failed to return. Search parties could not find him; it was said that the Devil had taken him.

Later occupants of the house reported that they sometimes saw Dolores in the house or out on the lawn. She was always dressed in a black formal gown of the 1800s and had black hair, a pale skin, and very red lips. Her appearances were not frequent, but they were nerve-racking enough to cause a long line of tenants and owners to move out. The old mansion had fallen into ruins, except for two rooms, when Uncle Igescu bought the property and built his house around the still-standing part.

Despite the publicity about the present Igescu, not much was really known about him. He had inherited a chain of grocery stores and an export business from his uncle. He, or his managers, had built the stores into a large chain of supermarkets in the Southwest and had expanded the export business.

Childe found the ghost interesting. Whether or not she had been seen recently was not known, because neither Igescu had ever said anything about her. Her last recorded appearance was in 1878, when the Reddes had moved out.

Igescu's sketch in the newspaper showed a long lean face with a high forehead and high cheekbones and large eyes and thick eyebrows. He had a thick down-drooping Slovak coalminer's type of moustache.

Heepish returned, and Childe, holding the sketch so he could see it, said, "This man certainly doesn't look Draculaish does he? More like the grocery store man, which he is, right?"

Heepish poked his head forward and squinted his eyes. He

smiled slightly. "Certainly, he doesn't look like Bela Lugosi. But the Dracula of the book, Bram Stoker's, had just such a moustache. Or one like it, anyway. I tried to get in touch with Igescu several times, you know, but I couldn't get through his secretary. She was nice but very firm. The Baron did not want to be disturbed with any such nonsense."

Heepish's tone and weak hollow chuckle said that, if there were any nonsense, it was on the Baron's part.

"You have his phone number?"

"Yes, but it took me a lot of trouble to get it. It's unlisted."

"You don't owe him anything," Childe said, "I'd like to have it. If I find anything you might be interested in, I'll tell you. How's that? I feel I owe you something for your time and fine co-operation. Perhaps, I might be able to dig up something for your collection."

"Well, you can have the number," Heepish said, warming up. "But it's probably been changed."

He conducted Childe downstairs and, while Childe waited under a shelf which held the heads of Frankenstein's monster, The Naked Brain, and a huge nameless creature from some (deservedly) forgotten movie, Heepish plunged into the rear of the house down a dim corridor with plastic cobwebs between ceiling and wall. He dived out of the shadows and webs with a little black book in his hand. Childe wrote down the number and address in his own little black book and asked permission to try the number. He dialled and got what he expected, a busy signal. The lines were still tied up, unless, that is, he had got through to Igescu's and Igescu's phone was busy. He tried the LAPD number. That was busy. He tried his own phone, and there was a clicking, and then only a hum.

Just for stubbornness, he tried Igescu's number again. And this time, as if the fates had decided that he should be favoured, or by one of those coincidences too implausible to be believed in a novel but sometimes happening in "real" life, the connection went through. A woman's voice said, "Hello? My God, the lines aren't busy any more! What happened?"

"May I speak to Baron Igescu?" Childe said.

"Who?"

"Isn't this Baron Igescu's residence?"

"No! Who is this speaking?"

"Herald Wellston," Childe said, giving the name he had decided to use. "May I ask who is speaking?"

"Go away! Or I'll call the police!" the woman screamed, and she hung up.

"I don't think that was Igescu's secretary," Childe said in answer to Heepish's quizzical expression. "Somebody else has their number now."

Not believing that it would work but willing to try, he dialled information. The call went right through, and he succeeded almost immediately in getting transferred to his contact. She did not have to worry about a supervisor listening in; she was the supervisor.

"What happened, Linda? All of a sudden the lines're wide open."

"I don't know, one of the unexplainable lulls, the eye of the storm, maybe. But it won't last, you can bet your most precious possession on that, Herald. You better hurry."

He told her what he wanted, and she got Igescu's unlisted number for him within a few seconds.

"I'll drop off the usual to you in the mail before evening. Thanks, Linda, you beautiful beautiful."

"I may not be here to get it if this smog keeps up," she said. "Or the mailman may have skipped town with everyone and his brother."

He hung up the telephone. Heepish, who had stepped out of the room but not out of hearing range, raised his eyebrows. Childe did not feel that he had to justify himself, but, since he was using Heepish's phone, he did owe him some explanation.

"The forces of good must use corruption to fight corruption," he said. "I occasionally have to find a number, and I send a ten to my informant, or used to; now it's a twenty, what with inflation. In this case, I suspect I've wasted my money."

Heepish harrumphed. Childe got out quickly; he felt as if he could no longer stand this shadowy, musky place with its monsters frozen in various attitudes of attack and their horrified paralysed victims. Nor could he endure the custodian of the museum any longer.

Yet, when he stood at the door to say good-bye and to thank his host, he felt ashamed. Certainly, the man's hobby –

passion, rather – was harmless enough and even entertaining – even emotionally purgative – for millions of children and adults who had never quite ceased being children. Though dedicated to archetypal horror and its Hollywood sophisticated developments, the house had defeated itself, hence, had a therapeutic value. Where there is a surfeit of horrors, horror becomes hokum.

And this man had helped him to the best of his ability.

He thanked Heepish and shook his hand, and perhaps Heepish felt the change in his guest, because he smiled broadly and radiated warmth and asked Childe to come back – any time.

The door swung shut with the Inner-Sanctum creakings, but it did not propel Childe and Jeremiah into the acid-droplet mist. A breeze ruffled them, and sunshine was bright, and the sky was blue.

Childe had not known until then how depressed and miserable he had been. Now, he blinked his eyes that did not burn or weep and sucked in the precious clean air. He chortled and did a little jig arm in arm with Jeremiah. The walk back to his apartment was the most delightful walk in his life. Its delight exceeded even that of his first walk with Sybil when he was courting her. The yards and sidewalks held a surprising number of people, all enjoying the air and the sun. Apparently, fewer than he – and the radio and TV experts – had thought had fled the area.

There were, however, few cars on the streets. Wilshire Boulevard held only one auto between La Cienega and Robertson, and when they crossed Burton Way on Willaman, they could see no cars.

However, there were great green-grey clouds piled against the mountains. Pasadena and Glendale and other inland cities were still in the fist of the smog.

By the time he had said good-bye to Jeremiah, who turned off towards Mt Sinai Hospital, the wind had slid to a halt, and the air was as still as a dead jellyfish again. There was a peculiar glow on the western horizon; a hush descended as if a finger had been placed against the lips of the world.

He still felt happy as he went into the apartment building. The phone lines were busy again, but he stuck it out, and, within three hundred seconds by his wristwatch, the phone rang. The voice that answered was female, low, and lovely.

Magda Holyani was Mr Igescu's secretary; she stressed the

"Mister".

No, Mr Igescu could not talk to him. Mr Igescu never talked to anybody without an appointment. No, he would not grant an interview to Mr Herald Wellston, no matter how far Mr Wellston had travelled for it nor how important the magazine Mr Wellston represented. Mr Igescu never gave interviews, and if Mr Wellston was thinking of that silly vampire and ghost story in the *Times*, he had better forget it – as far as talking to Mr Igescu about it. Or about anything.

And how had Mr Wellston got this unlisted number?

Childe did not answer the last. He asked that his request be forwarded to her employer. She said that he would be informed of it as soon as possible. Childe gave her his number – he said he was staying with a friend and told her that if Igescu should change his mind, he should call him at that number. He thanked her and hung up. Throughout the conversation, neither had said a word about the smog. Childe decided to do some thinking, and, while he was doing that, he had better attend to some immediate matters – such as his survival. He drove to the supermarket and found that it had just been reopened. Apparently, the manager was staying on the premises, and several of the checkout women and the liquor store clerk lived nearby. Cars were beginning to fill the parking lot, and people on foot were numerous. Childe was glad that he had thought of this, because the shelves were beginning to look bare. He stocked up on canned goods and powdered milk and purchased a five-gallon bottle of distilled water.

On the way back, he heard six sirens and saw two ambulances. The hospital was not about to complain of lack of business.

By the time he had put away the groceries, he had made up his mind. He would drive out and scout around the Igescu estate. He had no rational cause to do so. There was not the thinnest of threads to connect Igescu with Colben. Nevertheless, he meant to investigate. He had nowhere else to go and nothing to do. He could spend the rest of the day with this doubtless unrewarding lead, and tomorrow, if the city began to return to normal, he would start on a definite and profitable case, if one showed up. And one should. There were bound to be many missing persons, gone somewhere with the smog.

Chapter 8

The drive out was pleasant. He saw only ten cars on the streets; two were police. The black-and-whites, red lights flashing but sirens quiet, raced past him.

Childe went west on Santa Monica Boulevard, turned right at Rexford Drive, and began the safari through the ever wealthier and more exclusive houses and mansions (northward was the hierarchical goal). He went up Coldwater Canyon and into the hills, which are labelled on the map as the Santa Monica Mountains. He swung left on to Mariconado Lane, drove for a mile and a half on the narrow, winding, macadam road, almost solidly walled with great oaks, firs, and high thick bushes and hedges, turned right on Daimon Drive, drove for a mile past several high-walled estates, and came finally to Igescu's (if Heepish had given him correct directions).

At the end of the high brick mortared-with-white wall, three hundred yards past the gateway, the road ended. There were no walls to keep anybody from walking past the end of the drive. Whoever owned the land next to the Baron's felt no need for enforcing privacy. Childe drove to the end of the pavement, and after some manoeuvring, turned the car around. He left it with its rear against a bush and facing the road. If he had to leave suddenly, he would not be delayed by having to go back and forwards several times. After locking the doors, he put an extra key in the earth under a bush (always prepare for emergencies) and then walked to the gateway.

The wall was ten feet high and topped by iron spikes between which were from four to six strands of barbed wire. The gateway was a single heavy iron grille-work which swung out when electrically actuated. He could see no keyholes. A tongue of metal must insert into a slot in a metal fitting on the side of the gateway. The grille-work was painted a dull black and separated into eight squares by thick iron bars. Each square held a sheet of iron formed into a profile of a griffin with the wings of a bat. This was a grade-B movie touch, but, of course, only coincidence. The bat wings probably had some heraldic significance.

A metal box six feet up on the right post could be a voice

Philip José Farmer

transceiver. Beyond the gate was a narrow tar-topped road which curved and disappeared into thick woods. The only sign of life was a listless black squirrel. (The radio had reported that all wild land birds had fled the area.)

Childe walked into the woods at the end of the road. He ignored the TRESPASSERS WILL BE VIGOROUSLY PROSECUTED sign – he liked the VIGOROUSLY – to walk along the wall. The going was not easy. The bushes and thorns seemed determined to hold him back. He shoved against them and wriggled a few times and then the wall curved to the right and went up a steep hill. Panting, he scrambled up on all fours to the top. He wondered if he were that much out of shape or if the smog had cut down his ability to take in enough oxygen.

The wall still barred his way. After resting, he climbed a big oak. Near the top, he looked around, but he could see only more trees beyond the wall. No branches offered passage over the walls.

He climbed down slowly and carefully. When he was a child, he had at times thought that he might prefer to be Lord Greystoke instead of Sherlock Holmes. He had grown up to be neither, but he was much closer to Holmes than Greystoke. He wouldn't even make a good Jane.

Sweat ran down his face and soaked his undershirt below the armpits. His pants were torn in two places, a small scratch on the back of his left hand was bleeding, his hands were sore on the palms and dirty all over, and his shoes were badly scuffed. The sun, in sympathetic altitude with his spirits, was low. It was just about to touch the ridge of the western hills he could see through a break. He would have to go back now and conduct a tour of the wall some other time – if ever. To ram and bumble through the woods in the dark would be more than exasperating.

He hastened back to the car, tearing a button off his shirt this time, and got to it just at dusk. The silence was like that in a deep cave. No birds twittered or chirped. Even the buzz and hum of insects were absent. Perhaps the smog had killed them off. Or, at least, thinned their ranks or discouraged them. There were no sounds of aeroplanes or cars, sounds which it had been difficult to escape anywhere in Los Angeles County night or day. The atmosphere seemed heavy with a spirit of – what? – of waiting. Whether it was waiting for him or something else, and what it was waiting for, was dubious. And, after he considered the feeling, he found it ridiculous.

He got into the car behind the wheel, remembered that he had left a key in the dirt under a bush, started to get out to retrieve it, then thought better of it, and closed the door again. He drummed his fingers, wished he had not quit smoking, and chewed some gum. He almost turned the radio on but decided that, in this stillness, its sound would go too far.

The suncast fell away from the sky at last. The darkness around him became thicker, as if it were the sediment of night. The glow thrown by the million lights of the city and reflected back on to the earth was missing tonight. There were no clouds to act as mirrors, and the surrounding hills and trees barred the horizon-shine. Stars began to thrust through the black. After a while, the almost full moon, edged in black, like a card announcing a death, rose above the trees.

Childe waited. He got out after a while and went to the gate and looked through, but he could not even see a faint nimbus which might have revealed that, somewhere in that dense blackness, was a large house with many lights and at least two people. He returned to the car, sat for perhaps fifteen minutes longer, and then reached for the ignition key. His hand stopped an inch from the key.

He heard a sound which turned his scalp cold.

He had hunted enough in Montana and the Yukon to recognize the sound. It was the howling of wolves. It rose from somewhere in the trees behind the walls of Igescu's estate.

Philip José Farmer

Chapter 9

He was tired when he returned to his apartment. It was only ten P.M. but he had been through much. Besides, the poisoned air had burned away his vitality. The respite of the breeze had not helped much. The air was still dead, and it seemed to him that it was getting grey again. That must be one of the tricks his imagination was playing him, because there were not enough cars on the streets to account for another build-up of smog.

He called the LAPD and asked for Sergeant Bruin. He did not expect Bruin to be there, but he was lucky. Bruin had much to say about his troubles with traffic that day. Not to mention that his wife had suddenly decided to get out of town. For Christ's sake! The smog was gone! For a while, anyway. No telling what would happen if this crazy weather continued. He had to get to bed now, because tomorrow looked even worse. Not the traffic. Most of the refugees should be past the state line by now. But they'd be back. That wasn't what was worrying him. The crazy weather and the smog, the sudden departure of the smog, rather, had resulted in a soaring upward of murders and suicides. He'd talk to Childe tomorrow, if he had time.

"You sound as if you're out on your feet, Bruin," Childe said. "Don't you want to hear about what I've been doing on the Colben case?"

"You found out anything definite?" Bruin said.

"I'm on to something, I got a hunch..."

"A hunch! A hunch! For God's sake, Childe, I'm tired! See you!"

The phone clicked.

Childe cursed, but after a while he had to admit that Bruin's reaction was justified. He decided to go to bed. He checked his automatic-answer device. There was one call. At 9.45, just before he had got home. Magda Holyani had phoned to inform him that Mr Igescu had changed his mind and would grant him an interview. He could call back if he got in before ten. If he didn't, he was not to phone until after three the following afternoon.

Childe could not go to sleep for a long time because of wondering what could have made the Baron change his mind.

Could he have seen Childe outside the walls and decided to invite him within for some sinister reason?

He awoke suddenly, sitting up, his heart racing. The phone was ringing on the stand beside him. He knocked it over and had to climb down out of bed to get it off the floor. Sergeant Bruin's voice answered him.

The crooked hands of the clock on the stand touched the Gothic style twelve and eight.

"Childe? Childe. OK! I'd feel bad about getting you up, but I been up since six myself. Listen, Budler's car was found this morning! In the same lot Colben's car was found in, how you like that? The lab boys, what're available, are going over it now."

"What time in the morning?" Childe said.

"About six, why, what difference does that make? You got something?"

"No. Listen, if you got time," and Childe outlined what he had done. "I just wanted you to know that I was going there tonight in case I didn't..."

He stopped. He suddenly felt foolish, and Bruin's chuckle deepened the feeling.

"In case you don't report back? Haw! Haw!" Bruin's laughter was loud. Finally, he said, "OK, Childe. I'll watch out you check in. But this deal about this vampire – a baron, no shit? A real live Transylvanian vampire-type Rumanian baron, what runs a line of supermarkets, right? Haw! Haw! Childe, you sure the smog ain't been eating away your brain cells?"

"Have your fun," Childe said dignifiedly. "Have you got any leads, by the way?"

"How the hell could we? You know we've had no time!"

"What about the wolves, then?" Childe said. "Isn't there some sort of law about having wild animals, dangerous animals, on the premises. These sounded as if they were running loose."

"How do you know they were wolves? Did you actually see them?"

Childe admitted that he hadn't. Bruin said that even if there were laws against keeping wolves in that area, it would be the business of the Beverly Hills Police or perhaps the county police. He wasn't sure, because that area was doubtful; it was on the very edge of Beverly Hills, if he remembered right. He'd have to look it up.

Childe did not insist on finding out. He knew that Bruin was too busy to be interested and even if he wasn't busy he probably thought Childe was on a false trail. Childe admitted to himself that this was most likely. But he had nothing else to do.

The rest of the day he spent cleaning up his apartment, doing his washing in the apartment's basement machines, planning what he would do that evening, speculating, and collecting some material, which he put into his trunk.

He also watched the TV news. The air was as motionless and as grey as lead. Despite this, most of the citizens seemed to think that conditions were returning to normal. Businesses were open again, and cars were filling the streets. The authorities, however, had warned those who had left the area not to return if they had some place to stay. The "unnatural" weather might continue indefinitely. There was no explanation for it which could be proved or even convincingly presented. But if normal atmospheric conditions did return, it would be best for those whose health was endangered by smog to stay away, or to plan on returning only long enough to settle their affairs before getting out.

Childe went to the supermarket, which was operating almost one hundred percent normalcy, to stock up. The sky was greying swiftly, and the peculiar ghastly light had now spread over the sky from the horizon. It subdued the human beings under its dome; they spoke less frequently and more quietly and even the blaring of horns was reduced.

The birds had not returned.

Childe called Igescu twice. The first time, a recording said that all calls would be answered only after six. Childe wondered why the recorded call of the evening before had said he could phone in after three. Childe called again a few minutes after six. Magda Holyani's low voice answered.

Yes, Mr Igescu would see him at eight that evening. Sharp. And the interview would be over at nine. Mr Wellston would have to sign a paper which would require that any material to be published could be blue-lined by Mr Igescu. He could not bring a camera. The chauffeur, Eric Glam, would meet Mr Wellston at the gate and would drive him up. Mr Wellston's car would have to be parked outside the wall.

Childe had hung up and taken three steps from the phone when it rang. Bruin was calling. "Childe, the report from the lab had been in for some time but I didn't have a chance to see it until a coupla minutes ago." He paused. Childe said, "Well?"

"It was clean, just like Colben's car. Except for one thing."

Bruin paused again. Childe felt a chill run over his back and then up his neck and over his scalp. When he heard Bruin, he had the feeling of *déjà vu*, of having heard the words before under exactly identical circumstances. But it was not so much *déjà vu* as expectation.

"There were hairs on the front seat. Wolf hairs."

"You've changed your mind about the possible worthwhileness of investigating Igescu?"

Bruin grunted and said, "We can't. Not just now. But, yeah, I think you ought to. The wolf hairs were put on the seat on purpose, obviously, since everything else was so clean. Why? Who knows? I was looking for another film, this time about Budler, but we didn't get any in. So far."

"It could be just a coincidence," Childe said. "But in case I don't report in to you by ten tonight, if it's OK for me to call your house, then you better call on the baron."

"Hell, I probably won't be off duty by ten and no telling where I'll be. I could have your call relayed, but the lieutenant wouldn't like that, we're pretty tied up with official calls and this wouldn't rate as that. No, call Sergeant Mustanoja, he'll be on duty, and he'll take a message for me. I'll contact him when I get time."

"Then let's make it eleven," Childe said. "Maybe I'll get hung up out there."

"Not by the balls, I hope," Bruin said, and laughing, clicked the phone.

Childe felt his testicles withdraw a little. He did not care much for Bruin's humour. Not while the film about Colben was still bright in his mind.

He took three paces, and the phone rang again. Magda Holyani said that she was sorry, but it was necessary that the interview be put off until nine.

Childe said that it would make little difference to him. Holyani said that that was nice and please make it nine *sharp*.

Childe called Bruin back to report the change in plans.

Bruin was gone, so he left a note with Sergeant Mustanoja.

At 8.30 he drove out. From Beverly Boulevard, the hills appeared like ghosts too timorous or too weak as yet to clothe themselves with dense ectoplasm.

By the time he had pulled up before the gateway to the Igescu estate, night had settled. A big car inside the gate was pouring out light from its beams up the private road away from the gate.

A large form leaned against the gate. It turned, and the extraordinarily broad-shouldered and lean-waisted figure of a giant was silhouetted against the lights. It wore a chauffeur's cap.

"I'm Mr Wellston. I have an appointment at nine."

"Yes, sir. May I see your ID, sir?"

Childe produced several cards, a driver's licence, and a letter, all counterfeit. The chauffeur looked them over with the aid of a pencil-thin flashlight, handed them back through the opening in the gate, and walked off to one side. He disappeared behind the wall. The gate noiselessly swung inward. Childe walked in, and the gate swung back. Glam strode up, opened the rear door for him, and then shut it after Childe was in the back seat. He got into the driver's seat, and Childe could see that his ears were huge and at right angles to his head, seemingly as big as bats' wings. This was an exaggeration, of course, but they were enormous.

The drive was made in silence; the big Rolls-Royce swung back and forth effortlessly and without any noticeable motor noise. Its beams sprayed trees, firs, maples, oaks, and many thick bushes trimmed into various shapes. The light seemed to bring the vegetation into existence. After going perhaps half a mile as the crow flies, but two miles back and forth, the car stopped before another wall.

This was of red brick, about nine feet high, and also had iron spikes with barbed wire between the spikes. Glam pressed something on the dashboard, and the gate's grille ironwork swung inward.

Childe looked through the windows but could see only more road and woods. Then, as the car came around the first bend, he saw the beams reflected against four gleaming eyes. The beams turned away, the eyes disappeared, but not before he had seen two wolfish shapes slinking off into the brush.

The car started up a steep hill and as it got near the top, its beams struck a Victorian cupola. The drive curved in front of the house and, as the beams swept across the building, Childe saw that it was, as the newspaper article had described it, rambling. The central part was obviously older and of adobe. The wings were of wood, painted grey, except for the red-trimmed windows, and they extended part way down the side of the hill, so that the house seemed to be like a huge octopus squatting on a rock.

This flashed across his mind, like a frame irrelevantly inserted in a reel, and then it became just a monstrous and incongruous building.

The original building had a broad porch and the added-on buildings had also been equipped with porches. Most of the porch was in shadows, but the central portion was faintly illuminated with light leaking through thin blinds. A shadow passed across a blind and then was gone.

The car stopped. Glam lunged out and opened the door for Childe. Childe stood for a minute, listening. The wolves had not howled once. He wondered what was to keep them from attacking the people in the house. Glam did not seem worried about them.

"This way, sir," Glam said and led him up the porch and to the front door. He pressed a button, and a light over the door came on. The door was of massive highly polished hardwood – mahogany? – carved to represent a scene from (it seemed likely) Hieronymus Bosch. But a closer look convinced him that the artist had been Spanish. There was something indefinably Iberian about the beings (demons, monsters, humans) undergoing various tortures or fornicating in some rather peculiar fashions with some rather peculiar organs.

Glam had left his chauffeur's cap on the front seat of the Rolls. He was dressed in a black flannel suit, and his trousers were stuffed into his boot-tops. He unlocked the door with a large key he produced from a pocket, swung the door open (it was well-oiled, no Inner-Sanctum squeaks), and bowed Childe on through. The room inside was a large (it could even be called great) hall. Two halls, rather, because one ran along the front of the house and halfway down it was a broad entrance to another hall which seemed to run the depth of the house. The carpets were thick and wine-coloured with a very faint pattern in green. A few pieces of heavy, solid Spanish-looking furniture sat against the walls.

Glam asked Childe to wait while he announced him. Childe watched the giant stoop to go through the doorway to the centre hall. Then he jerked his head to the right because he had caught a glimpse of somebody down at the far end just going around the corner. He was startled, because he had seen no one at that end when he came in. Now he saw the back of a tall woman, the floor-length full black skirt, white flesh of the back revealed in the V of the cut, high-piled black hair, a tall black comb.

He felt cold and, for a second, disoriented.

He had no more time to think about the woman then, because his host came to greet him. Igescu was a tall slim man with thick, wavy, brown-blond hair, large, bright green eyes, pointed features, a large curving nose, and a dimple in his right cheek. The moustache was gone. He seemed to be about sixty-five years old, a vigorous athletic sixty-five. He wore a dark-blue business suit. His tie was black with a faint bluish symbol in its centre. Childe could not make it out; the outlines seemed to be fluid, to change as Igescu changed position.

His voice was deep and pleasant, and he spoke with only a tinge of foreign pronunciation. He shook hands with Childe. His hands were large and strong-looking and his grip was powerful. His hand was cold but not abnormally so. He was a very amiable and easy-going host but made it clear that he intended to allow his guest to remain only an hour. He asked Childe a few questions about his work and the magazine he represented. Childe gave him glib answers; he was prepared for more interrogation than he got.

Glam had disappeared somewhere. Igescu immediately took Childe on a guided tour. This lasted about five minutes and was confined to a few rooms on the first floor. Childe could not get much idea of the layout of the house. They returned to a large room off the centre hall where Igescu asked Childe to sit down. This was also fitted with Spanish-type furniture and a grand piano. There was a fireplace, above the mantel of which was a large oil painting. Childe, sipping on an excellent brandy, listened to his host but studied the portrait. The subject was a beautiful young woman dressed in Spanish costume and holding a large ivory-yellowish fan. She had unusually heavy eyebrows and extremely dark eyes, as if the painter had invented a paint able to concentrate blackness.

There was a faint smile about the lips – not Mona Lisaish, however – the smile seemed to indicate a determination to – what? Studying the lips, Childe thought that there was something nasty about the smile, as if there were a deep hatred there and a desire to get revenge. Perhaps the brandy and his surroundings made him think that or perhaps the artist was the nasty and hateful one and he had projected on to the innocent blankness of the subject his own feelings. Whatever the truth, the artist had talent. He had given the painting the authenticity of more than life.

He interrupted Igescu to ask him about the painting. Igescu did not seem annoyed.

"The artist's name was Krebens," he said. "If you get close to the painting, you'll see it in minuscule letters at the left-hand corner. I have a fairly good knowledge of art history and local history, but I have never seen another painting by him. The painting came with the house, it is said to be of Dolores del Osorojo. I am convinced that it is, since I have seen the subject."

He smiled. Childe felt cold again. He said, "Just after I came in, I saw a woman going around the corner down the hall. She was dressed in old-fashioned Spanish clothes. Could that be... ?"

Igescu said, "There are only three women in this house. My secretary, my great-grandmother, and a house guest. None of them wear the clothes you describe."

"The ghost seems to have been seen by quite a few people," Childe said. "You don't seem to be upset, however."

Igescu shrugged and said, "Three of us, Holyani, Glam, and I, have seen Dolores many times, although always at a distance and fleetingly. She is no illusion or delusion. But she seems harmless, and I find it easier to put up with her than with many flesh and blood people."

"I wish you had permitted me to bring a camera. This house is very colourful, and if I could have caught her on film... or have you tried that and found out she doesn't photograph?"

"She didn't when I first moved in," Igescu said. "But I caught her a year ago and the developed film showed her quite clearly. The furniture behind her showed dimly, but she's much more opaque than she used to be. Given time, and enough people to feed off..."

He waved his hand as if that would complete the sentence.

Childe wondered if Igescu were putting him on. He said, "Could I see that photo?"

Certainly," Igescu said. "But it won't prove anything, of course. There is very little that can't be faked."

He spoke into an intercom disguised as a cigar humidor in a language Childe did not recognize. It certainly did not sound Latin, although, unacquainted with Rumanian, he had no way of identifying it. He doubted that Rumanian would have such back-of-the-throat sounds.

He heard the click of billiard balls, and turned to look down into the next room. Two people were playing. They were both blond, of medium height, well built, and clothed in tight-fitting white sweaters, tight-fitting white jeans, and black sandals. They looked as if they could be brother and sister. Their eyebrows were high and arched and the eye sockets were deep. Their lips were peculiar. The upper lip was so thin it looked like the edge of a bloody knife; the lower lip was so swollen that it looked as if it had been cut and infected by the upper.

Igescu called to them. They raised their heads with such a lupine air that Childe could not help thinking of the wolves he had glimpsed on the way up. They nodded at Childe when Igescu introduced them as Vasili Chornkin and Mrs Krautschner but they did not smile or say anything. They seemed eager to get back to their game. Igescu did not explain what their status was but Childe thought that the girl must be the house guest he had mentioned.

Glam appeared suddenly and noiselessly, as if he slid spaces around him instead of moving himself. He gave a manila envelope to Igescu. Childe glanced at Igescu as he removed the photo from the envelope, then he looked up. Glam had gone as swiftly and silently as he had entered.

The photo was taken from about forty feet during the daytime. Light flooding in from the large window showed everything in detail. There was Dolores del Osorojo just about to leave the hall through a doorway. The edge of the doorway and part of a chair nearby could be faintly made out through her. She was looking back at the camera with the same faint smile as in her painting.

"I'll have to have it back," Igescu said.

Chapter 10

"As you say, a photo proves nothing," Childe said. He looked at his wristwatch. A half hour left. He opened his mouth to ask about the car accident and the morgue incident but Magda Holyani entered.

She was a tall, slim, small-breasted woman of about thirty with beautiful although disproportioned features and thick pale-yellow hair. She walked as if her bones were flexible or as if her flesh encased ten thousand delicate intricately articulated bones. The bones of her head seemed to be thin; her cheekbones were high, and her eyes were tilted. The mouth was too thin. There was something indefinably reptilian about her, or, to be more exact, snakish. This was not repulsive. After all, many snakes are beautiful.

Her eyes were so light he thought at first they were colourless, but, closer, they became a very light grey. Her skin was very white, as if she shunned not only the sun but the day. It was, however, flawless. She had no make-up whatever. The lips would have looked pale if she had been standing next to a woman with rouged lips, but set against her own white skin they seemed dark and bright.

She wore a tight-fitting black dress with a deep squarecut bodice and almost no back. Her stockings were black nylon, and the high-heeled shoes were black. She sat down after being introduced, revealing beautiful, but seemingly boneless, legs from the mid-thigh down. She took over the conversation from Igescu, who lit up an expensive cigar and seemed to become lost in gazing into the smoke.

Childe tried to keep the conversation to a question-and-answer interview, but she replied briefly and unsatisfactorily and followed with a question each time about himself or his work. He felt that he was being interviewed.

He was becoming desperate. This would be his only chance to find out anything, and he was not even getting a "feel" of rightness or wrongness about this place and its tenants. They were a little odd, but this meant nothing, especially in Southern California.

He noticed that Glam was busying himself nearby with emptying the Baron's and Magda's ash trays, refilling the glasses,

Philip José Farmer

and at the same time managing to keep his eyes on the woman. Once, he touched her, and she snapped her head back and glared at him. Igescu was aware that Childe was taking this in, but he only smiled.

Finally, Childe ignored her to ask Igescu directly if he would care to comment on the much-publicized "vampire" incident. After all, it was this that had brought him out here. And so far he had not learned much. The article would be spare, if indeed he had enough data to make an article.

"Frankly, Mr Wellston," Igescu said, "I permitted this interview because I wanted to kill people's curiosity about this once and for all. Essentially, I am a man who likes privacy; I am wealthy but I leave the conduct of my business to others and enjoy myself. You have seen my library. It is very extensive and expensive and contains many first editions. It covers a wide variety of subjects. I can say without bragging that I am an extremely well-read man in many languages. Ten shelves are filled with books on my hobby: precious stones. But you may also have observed several shelves filled with books on such subjects as witchcraft, vampirism, lycanthropy, and so on. I am somewhat interested in these, but not, Mr Wellston, because I take a professional interest."

He smiled over his cigar and said, "No, it is not because I am a vampire, Mr Wellston, that I have read in these subjects. I took no interest in them until after the incident that caused you to come here. I thought that if I were to be accused of being a vampire, I had better find out just what a vampire was. I knew something about them, of course, because, after all, I do come from the Carpathians and from an area in which the peasants believe more in vampires and the devil than they do in God. But my tutors never went much into folk-lore, and my contacts with the local non-nobility were not intimate.

"I decided to give you this interview so that, once and for all, this nonsense about my vampirism could be quelled. And also, to divert attention from me towards the only truly supernatural feature of this house: Dolores del Osorojo. I have changed my mind about photographs for your article. I will have Magda send you a number. These will show some of the rooms in the house and various photos of the ghost. I will do this on the condition that you make it clear in your article that I am a man who likes privacy and a quiet life and that the vampire talk is nonsense. After getting that out of the way, you may stress the ghost as much as you like. But you must also make it clear that there will be no other interviews with anybody and that I do not like to be disturbed by curiosity-seekers, eccentric spiritualists or journalists. Agreed?"

"Certainly, Mr Igescu. You have my word. And of course, as agreed, you will edit the article before it's published."

Childe felt a little dizzy. He wished that he had not accepted the brandy. It had been four years since he had drunk anything, and he would not have broken his rule now, except that Igescu had praised the brandy as being so rare that he had been tempted to try it. And he had also not wanted to offend his host in any way if he could help it. He had, however, not had more than one tumbler. The stuff was either very potent or he was vulnerable after the long dry period.

Igescu turned his head to look at the tall dark grandfather clock. "Your time is about up, Mr Wellston."

Childe wondered why the baron was so concerned with time, when, by his own admission, he seldom went any place or did anything particularly pressing. But he did not ask. The baron would have regarded such a question as too impertinent to answer with anything but cold silence.

Igescu stood up. Childe rose also. Magda Holyani finished her drink and got up from the chair. Glam appeared in the doorway, but Igescu said, "Miss Holyani will drive Mr Wellston to the gate, Glam. I need you for another duty."

Glam opened his mouth as if he meant to object but shut it immediately. He said, "Very well, sir," and wheeled around and walked away.

Igescu said, "If you'd like some more material for your article, Mr Wellston, you might look up Michel Le Garrault in the UCLA library. I have copies of two of his works, first editions, by the way. The old Belgian had some very interesting and original theories about vampires, werewolves, and other so-called supernatural phenomena. His theory of *psychic imprinting* is fascinating. Have you read him? Can you read French?"

"Never heard of him," Childe said, wondering if he would have fallen into a trap if he had professed familiarity. "I do read French."

Philip José Farmer

"There are many so-called authorities on the occult and supernatural who have not heard of Le Garrault or had no chance to read him. I recommend that you go to the rare book section of the UCLA library and ask for *Les Murs S'écroulés*. Translations of the original Latin were made in French, and curiously, in Bohemian, and these are very rare indeed. There are, as far as I know, only ten Latin copies in the world. The Vatican has one; a Swedish monastery has two; I have one; the Kaiser of Germany had one but it was lost or, probably, stolen after he died at Doorn; and the other five are in state libraries at Moscow, Paris, Washington, London, and Edinburgh."

"I'll look him up," Childe said. "Thanks very much for the information."

He turned to follow Igescu out and saw the woman in Spanish dress, high comb stuck in her black hair, just stepping into a doorway at the end of the ball. She turned her head and smiled and then was gone.

Igescu said, calmly, "Did you see her, too?"

"Yes, I did. But I couldn't see through her," Childe said.

"I did," Magda Holyani said. Her voice shook a little. Childe looked at her. She seemed to be angry, not frightened.

"As I said, she has been getting more and more opaque," Igescu said. "The solidifying is so subtle, that it's only noticeable if you compare what she was six months ago with what she now is. The process has been very slow but steady. When I first moved in here, she was almost invisible."

Childe shook his head. Was he really discussing a ghost as if it existed? And why was Magda so upset? She had stopped and was staring at the doorway as if she were resisting the impulse to chase off after the thing.

"Many people, more people than care to admit, have seen ghostly phenomena – something weird and unexplainable, anyway – but either the phenomenon doesn't repeat itself or else the people 'visited' ignore it and it goes away. But Dolores, ah, there is another story! Dolores is ignored by me, except for an occasional picture-taking. Magda used to ignore her but now she seems to be getting on her nerves. Dolores is gaining substance from somewhere, perhaps from someone in this house."

Certainly, the story of Dolores was gaining substance. If a

photo of her was no evidence that she existed, neither was the fact that he had seen her. For some reason, Igescu might have planned this whole thing, and if he, Childe, were to run after Dolores and try to seize her, what would his hands close on? He had a feeling that he would grip solid flesh and that the young woman would turn out to have come into existence about twenty years ago, not one hundred and fifty.

At the door, he shook hands with Igescu, thanked him, and promised to send him a carbon of the article for editing. He followed Magda to the car and turned once before getting in to look back. Igescu was gone, but a blind had been half-raised and Glam's bulldog face and batwing ears were plainly visible.

He got into the front seat with Magda, at her invitation. She said, "My job pays very well, you know. It has to. It's the only thing that would make it endurable. I almost never get a chance to go to town and the only ones I can talk to, ever, are my boss and a few servants and occasionally a guest."

"Is it hard work?" Childe asked, wondering why she was telling him this. Perhaps she had to unburden herself to someone.

"No. I take care of his few social obligations, make appointments, act as middle man between him and his business managers, do some typing on the book he's writing on jewels, and spend more time than I care to staying away from that monster, Glam."

"He did nothing definite, but I got the idea that he's quite attached to you," Childe said.

The beams swept across the trees as the car went around a corner. The moon was up now, and he could see more distinctly. He could be wrong, but it seemed to him that they were not on the same road he had travelled on the way up.

"I'm taking the longer, no less scenic, route," she said, as if she had read his mind. "I hope you don't mind. I feel that I just have to talk to somebody. You don't have to listen to me, of course, there's no reason why you should."

"Pour it on me," he said. "I like to hear your voice."

They passed through the gateway of the inner wall. She drove slowly, in first gear, as she talked, and once she put her hand on his leg. He did not move. She took her hand off after a minute when she had to stop the car. They had driven off the road on to a narrow stone-covered path which led through a break in the trees to a clearing. A small summerhouse, a rough wooden structure on a high round cement base, stood there. Its open sides were partially covered with vines, so that its interior was dark. A flight of cement steps led up to the wide entrance.

"I get very lonely," she said, "although the baron is charming and does talk a lot. But he's not interested in me in the way some employers are in their female employees."

He did not have to ask her what she meant by that. She had put her hand on his leg again, seemingly as accidentally or unselfconsciously as before. He said, "Are there wolves out here, too? Or are they all inside the inner wall?"

She was leaning closer now, and her perfume was so strong that it seemed to soak into his pores. He felt his penis swelling and he took her hand and moved it so that it was on his penis. She did not try to take her hand away.

He reached over and ran a finger down along the curve of the left breast and down the cleavage into the breast.

His hand went on down and slid between the cloth and breast and rubbed over the nipple. The nipple swelled, and she shuddered. He kissed her with many slidings of his tongue along hers and over her teeth. She fumbled along his zipper, found it, pulled it slowly down, and then probed through the openings of his jockey shorts. He unbuttoned the front of her dress and quickly verified what he had suspected. She wore nothing beneath the dress except for a narrow suspender belt. The breasts were small but shapely and were swelling with blood. He bent over and took a nipple in his mouth and began sucking. She was breathing as hard as he.

"Let's go in the summerhouse," she said softly. "There's a couch in there."

"All right," he said. "But before we go any further, you should know I'm unprepared. I don't have any rubbers." He would not have been surprised if she'd said that she had some in her handbag. It wouldn't have been the first time that this had happened to him.

But she said, "Never mind. I won't get pregnant." Shakily, he followed her out of the car, sliding past the wheel. She turned and slid the dress off her shoulders. The moonlight gleamed on the whitest flesh possible, on dark wet nipples, and a dark triangle of pubic hairs below the suspender belt. She kicked her shoes off and, clad only in belt and stockings, swayed towards the summerhouse.

He followed her, but he was not so excited that he did not wonder about cameras and sound devices in the summerhouse. He knew that he was good-looking, but he was not, after all, a god who swept all women before him on a tide of desire. If Magda Holyani seduced him on such short acquaintance, she either was very hard-up or had a motive that he might not like if he knew. Or possibly, both. She did not seem to be faking her passion.

If, for some reason, she thought she could lead him so far, turn him on and then turn him off, she was going to be surprised. He had suffered a good part of yesterday with a painful ball-ache because of his unfinished love-making with Sybil, and he did not intend to suffer again.

Inside the house, he looked around. There could be no cameras hidden here. If there were any, they'd have to be attached to the trees on the edge of the clearing, and he could not see how they would be able to film much, even if they were equipped with black-light devices. The vines and their supports would bar anything except patches of skin and an occasional glimpse of a head or limb. Besides, what did he have to lose? Blackmail could not be the object of such a game.

Magda yanked off the blanket acting as a dust cover for the sofa. She turned then, the moonlight falling through the vines dappling her pale skin. Childe took her in his arms and kissed her again, ran his hands down her back, feeling the hard muscles – she had the muscle tone of a young puma – the inward fall of the waist and the outward fall of the hips. The suspender belt annoyed him, so he sank to his knees and unfastened the stockings and pulled them down and then pulled down on the belt. She kicked them to one side and put her hands on the back of his head and pulled him towards her cunt. He allowed her to press his face against the hairs, and ran his tongue out and inserted it just below the opening of the lips and tickled her clitoris with its tip. She moaned and clutched him tighter.

But he stood up, sliding his tongue up from her cunt again and along her belly and up to her nipple, which he began to suck again. He stepped her backwards until she fell on the sofa, her legs

Philip José Farmer

sticking out, her heels resting on the floor. Then he got down on his knees again and licked her clitoris once more and then slid down and thrust his tongue again and again into her vagina. She began to twist her hips a little, but he reached up and pressed down on her belly to indicate that she should hold still.

Her cunt tasted as sweet as Sybil's, and the hairs seemed to be softer. He put one finger inside her cunt and another finger of the same hand up her anus and then, working the hand slowly in and out, rubbed his tongue back and forth over her clitoris and then later tongue-fucked her while his fingers increased the speed of their in-and-out into her cunt and anus.

She came with a scream and a sudden tightening of thighs about his head. The grip was so strong that he could not move his fingers.

He could stand it no longer. He had had no emissions for two weeks because of his involvement in a case which he had wound up just before Colben disappeared. He had been busy night and day and when he managed to snatch some sleep even his unconscious had been too tired to whip up a sexual dream. Then the frustrations with Sybil had made him hypersensitive. In a minute, he was going to come, whether he was in Magda or the air. "I can't wait," he said. "It's been too long."

He started to get down beside her and to help her scoot up on the sofa so she could lie full length. But she said, "You're ready to come?"

"It's been too long. I'm full to bursting," he groaned.

She pushed him down and ran her tongue along his belly and wet his pubic hairs with her saliva and tongue and then closed her lips upon the head of his cock. She slid it back and forth in her lips twice, and with a scream that matched hers of a moment ago, he burst in her mouth.

He lay there, feeling as if a tide inside him were withdrawing to some far-off horizon. He did not say anything; he'd expected her to get up and spit out the stuff, as Sybil always did. Sybil also always immediately brushed her teeth and gargled with Listerine. Not that he blamed her, certainly. He could understand that, once the excitement was gone, the thick ropy stuff could become disgusting. He knew how it tasted. When he had been fourteen, he and his fifteen-year-old brother had gone through a period of about six months when they had sucked each other off. And then, by mutual and silent consent, they had quit and that had been the last of his homosexual experiences and, as far as he knew, of his brother's. Certainly, his brother, who was such a cocksman that he must be a compulsive, hated fairies, and once, many years later, when Childe had referred to their experimentations, his brother had not known what he was talking about. He was either too ashamed of it now to admit it or else had actually buried it so deep that he did not remember.

But Magda did not leave him. She audibly swallowed several times and then renewed her sucking. He sat up and bent over so he could cup her breasts in his hands while she was mouthing his glans. And then, just as his penis was at almost full erection, he thought of Colben and the iron teeth. This woman could be the actress in that movie.

She looked up at him suddenly and said, "What's wrong?"

"Listen," he said, "and don't get mad. Or laugh. But do you have false teeth?"

She sat up and said, "What?" Her voice was thick with fluid.

"Do you have false teeth?"

"Why do you want to know?" Then she laughed and said, "You want me to take them out?"

"If you have false teeth."

"Do I look that old?"

"I've known several nineteen-year-olds who had choppers," he said.

"Kiss me and I'll tell you," she said.

"Certainly."

He held her tightly while he probed her mouth with his tongue. He sniffed the wild-beast odour of his own semen and tasted the thick-oil gluey-seeming product of his own body. Far from being unpleasant, it excited him. She had her hand on his cock, and, feeling it swell, immediately withdrew from his arms and went down on him again. Evidently, she did not intend for him to find out if she did have false teeth, or perhaps she thought that his tongue would have determined that.

Whatever her reasons, she would not tell him, unless he were to use force, he was sure of that. He leaned back and let her work on him. And after a while he rolled her over and she opened her legs and took his penis gently in her fingers and guided him in. He had no sooner sunk in to the hairs than she squeezed down on his cock with her muscles and continued to squeeze as if she had a hand inside her cunt. And then, once again, thinking of the film, he became soft. He remembered that bulge behind the G-string of the woman in the film.

"For God's sake," she said. "What's the matter now?"

"I thought I saw somebody in the shadows," he said, the only excuse he could grasp at the moment. "Glam?"

"It had better not be," she said. "I'll kill him if it is. So will the baron."

She stood up on the sofa and called, "Glam? Glam? If you're there, you asshole, you better start running and fast. Otherwise, it's the other end of the wolf for you."

There was no answer. Childe said, "The other end of the wolf? What do you mean?"

"I'll tell you later," she said. "He's not out there; if he is, he isn't going to bother us. Come on, please. I'm ready to explode."

Instead of reaching for him, she got down off the sofa and crossed the summerhouse to a small cabinet on a stand in the shadows. She came back with a bottle with a squat body and a long narrow neck with a wide mouth. It was half-full. She drank some, swished some in her mouth, and still holding it, pressed her lips against his and squirted the liquid into his mouth. It was hot and thick and slightly tart. He swallowed some and immediately felt his anxieties draining off.

"What the hell is that?"

"It's a liqueur made in Igescu's native province," she said. It's supposed to have an aphrodisiac effect. I understand that there isn't any true aphrodisiac, but this stuff does one thing. It burns away the inhibitions. Not that I thought I'd ever have to use it on you."

"I won't need any more of it," he said. His penis was rising as if it were a balloon being filled for a transatlantic voyage. A beam of moonlight fell on it, and Magda, seeing it, squealed with delight.

"Oh, you beauty! You great big beauty!"

She lay down and raised her legs and he entered again and then, for a long time, said nothing. It was a peculiarity of his that if he were blown at the beginning, he took a long time coming the second time. Magda seemed to have an almost unbroken series of orgasms during this time and when he finally came she clawed his back until the blood ran off. He did not mind at the time, but later he cursed her. It was a theory of his that women who clawed your back when they came were actually attempting to prove how passionate they were, but he was willing to admit that he could be wrong.

They lay there for some time by each other, not saying a word. They were sheathed in sweat and would have been grateful for a breeze. But the air was as still as before.

Finally, he said, "There's no use your playing with it. Not for some time. I'm shot out. I could stay and be all right within an hour, but I have to go pretty soon."

He was thinking that he was supposed to have called Mustanoja by now.

"I'm not unsatisfied, baby," she said, "but I could be whipped up into enthusiasm again, and I'd like to be. You don't know how long it's been for me!"

She reached for the bottle, which was on the floor by the sofa.

"Let's have another drink and see what happens."

He watched her to make sure that she drank again out of the bottle before he drank. He took a small swallow and then said, "What's this about Glam and the other end of the wolf?"

She laughed and said, "That big ugly dumbshit! He wants me, but I can't stand him, and he'd probably try to rape me, he's such a moron, but he knows that if I didn't kill him, Igescu would! You must know about the wolves, since you mentioned them. I was walking in the woods one evening when I heard one of the wolves howling and snarling. It sounded as if it were in pain, or at least, in trouble of some kind. I went up a hill and looked down in a hollow, and there was the female wolf, her head in four nooses, and the ends of the nooses tied to trees. She couldn't go back or forward, and there was Glam, all his clothes off except for his socks and shoes, holding the wolf by the tail and fucking her. I think he must have been hurting her, I don't know how big a female wolf's cunt is, but I don't think they're built to take an enormous cock like Glam's. I really think she was hurt. But Glam, that animal Glam, was

Philip José Farmer

fucking her."

Childe was silent for a moment and then he said, "What about the male wolf? Wasn't Glam afraid of the male wolf?"

She laughed and said, "Oh, that's another story," and she laughed for a long time.

When she stopped, she raised the bottle and poured liquid on her nipples and then on her pubic hairs.

"Lick it off, baby, and then we'll make love again."

"It won't do any good," Childe said. But he rolled over and sucked on her nipples for a while and fingerfucked her until she came again and again and then he kissed her belly, travelling downward until his mouth was against the tight hairs of her cunt. He tongued off the liqueur and then jabbed his tongue as far as he could until his jaws and tongue hurt. When he stopped, he was rolled over by her strong hands and she gently nibbled at his penis until it rose like a trout to a fly. This time, he mounted her from behind, and she told him to be quiet, he did not have to wear himself out. She contracted the muscles of her vagina as if it were a hand and this time he kept his erection. He seemed to be getting a little dizzy and a little fuzzy. He knew that he had made a mistake drinking that liquid. But he wondered if it had a property of becoming narcotic if it were on epidermis. Could its interaction with the skin of her nipples and cunt have produced something dangerous only to him? Then the thought and the alarm were gone.

He remembered vaguely an orgasm that seemed to go on forever, like the thousand-year orgasm promised the faithful of Islam in heaven when they are enfolded by an houri. There were blanks thereafter. He could remember, as if he were seeing himself in a fog, getting his car and driving off while the road wiggled like a snake and the trees bent over and made passes at him with their branches. Some of the trees seemed to have big knotty eyes and mouths like barky cunts. The eyes became nipples; sap oozed out of them. A tree gave him the finger with the end of a branch.

"Up yours, too," he remembered yelling, and then he was on a broad road with many lights around him and horns blaring and then there was the same tree again and could this time it beckoned at him and as he got closer he could see that its mouth *was* a barky cunt and that promising him something he had never had before.

And so it was. Death.

Chapter 11

He awoke in the emergency room of the Doctors Hospital in Beverly Hills. His only complaint was sluggishness. He was unconscious when he had been pulled out of the car by a good Samaritan. The Beverly Hills officer told him that his car had run into a tree off the side of the road but the collision was so light that the only damage was a slightly bent-in bumper and a broken headlamp.

The officer evidently suspected first, drunkenness, and second, drugs. Childe told him that he had been forced off the road and had been knocked out when the car hit the tree. That he had no visible injury on his head meant nothing.

Fortunately, there were no witnesses to the crash. The man who had pulled him from the car had come around the curve just in time to see the impact. Another car was going in the opposite direction; it was not driving erratically, as Childe had reported, but this meant nothing because the car could have straightened out. Childe gave Bruin and several others as references. Fifteen minutes later, he was discharged, although the doctors warned him that he should take it easy even if there was no evidence of concussion.

His car was still on the roadside. The police had not had it towed in because the trucks were too busy, but the officer had removed the key from the ignition. Unfortunately, the officer had also forgotten to give it back to Childe, and Childe then had to walk to the Beverly Hills Police Department to retrieve it. The officer was on duty. A radio call resulted in the information that he was tied up and would not be able to drop by the department for at least an hour. Childe made sure that the key would be given to the officer in charge of the desk, and he walked home through the night. He cursed himself for having buried the extra key under the bush outside Igescu's and then forgetting to dig it up again.

He had tried to get a taxi to take him home, but these were too busy. It seemed that everybody thought that the smog was over for good and was celebrating. Or perhaps everybody wanted to have some fun before the air became too poisoned again.

There were three parties going on in his building. He put ear plugs in as soon as he had showered, and went to bed. The

Philip José Farmer

plugs kept most of the noise out but did not help bar his thoughts.

He had been drugged and sent out with the hope that he would kill himself in a car-accident. Why the drug had affected him and not Magda was an interesting question but one that did not have to be considered at this time. She could have taken an antidote or relied on someone else to take care of her after Childe was gone. Or it was possible – he remembered what he had thought during the time – that the liquid contained something which did not become a drug unless it contacted human exterior epidermis?

He sat up in bed then. Sergeant Mustanoja! He should have been worrying about Childe's failure to call in. What had he done – if anything?

He phoned the LAPD and got Mustanoja. Yeah, he had the note but Bruin didn't seem to think it was important and, anyway, what with being so busy – what a night! – he had forgotten it. That is, until this Beverly Hills officer called in about him and then Mustanoja had found out what happened and knew he was not at Igescu's so what was there to worry about, huh? How was Childe?

Childe said he was home and OK. He hung up with some anger at Bruin for making light of his concern. However, he had to admit that there was no reason for Bruin to do otherwise. He would change his opinion after he found out what had happened last night. Perhaps, Bruin could arrange with the Beverly Hills Police Department... No, that wasn't going to work. The BHPD had far more immediate duties than investigating what was, objectively speaking, a very hazy lead. And there were certain things, important things, about the events that Childe was not going to tell them. He could skip the summerhouse activities and just say that he had been drugged with the brandy in the drawing room, but the officers were shrewd, they had known so many false tales and part-true tales, so many omissions and hesitations, that they picked up untruths and distortions as easily as radar distinguished an eagle from an airliner.

Besides, he had the feeling that Magda would not hesitate to claim that Childe had raped her and forced perversions upon her.

He had got into bed again but now he climbed out swiftly once more. He felt ashamed and sick. That drug had overcome his normal fastidiousness and caution. He would never have gone down on a woman he just met. He always reserved this act – even if he were strongly tempted to do it – for women whom he knew well, liked or loved, and was reasonably sure were free from syphilis or gonorrhoea.

Although he had brushed his teeth, he went into the bathroom and brushed them again and gargled deeply ten times with a burning mouthwash. From the kitchen cabinet he took a bottle of bourbon, which he kept for guests, and drank it straight. It was a dumb act, because he doubted that the alcohol would kill any germs he had swallowed so many hours ago, but it, like many purely ritual acts, made him feel better and cleaner.

He started for bed again and then stopped. He had been so upset that he had forgotten to check in with the exchange or turn on the recorder. He tried the exchange and hung up after the phone rang thirty times. Apparently, the exchange was not yet operating again or had lost its third-shift operator. The recorder yielded one call. It was from Sybil, at nine o'clock. She asked him to please call her as soon as he came in, no matter what time it was.

It was now three-ten in the morning.

Her phone rang uninterruptedly. The ring seemed to him like the tolling of a faraway bell. He envisioned her lying on the bed, one hand drooping over the edge of the bed, her mouth open, the eyes open and glazed. On the little table by the bed was an empty bottle of phenobarbital.

If she had tried to kill herself again, she would be dead by now. That is, if she had taken the same amount as the last time.

He had sworn that if she tried again, she would have to go through with it, at least as far as he was concerned.

Nevertheless, he dressed and was out on the street and walking within a minute. He arrived at her apartment panting, his eyes burning, his lungs doubly burned from exertion and smog. The poison was accumulating swiftly, so swiftly that by tomorrow evening it would be as thick as before – unless the winds came.

Her apartment was silent. His heart was beating and his stomach clenching as he entered her bedroom and switched on the light. Her bed was not only empty, it had not been slept in. And her suitcases were gone.

He went over the apartment carefully but could find nothing to indicate "foul play". Either she had gone on a trip or someone had taken the suitcases so that that impression would be given.

Philip José Farmer

If she had wanted him to know that she was leaving, why hadn't she left a message?

Perhaps her call and her sudden departure were unrelated.

There was the possibility that they were directly related but that she had told him only enough to get him over here so that he would worry about her. She could be angry enough to want to punish him. She had been mean enough to do similar things. But she had always quickly relented and tearfully and shamefully called him.

He sat down in an easy chair, then got up again and went into the kitchen and opened the *secret* compartment in the wall of the cabinet rear, second shelf up. The little round candy cup and its contents of white-paper-wrapped marijuana sticks – fifteen in all – were still there.

if she had left willingly, she would have disposed of this first.

Unless she were very upset.

He had not found her address book in any of the drawers when he had searched, but he looked again to make sure. The book was not there, and he doubted that any of the friends she had when they were married would know her whereabouts. She had been dropped by them or she had dropped them after the divorce. There was one, a life-long friend, whom she still wrote to now and then, but she had moved from California over a year ago.

Perhaps her mother was ill, and Sybil had left in a hurry. But she wouldn't be in such a hurry that she wouldn't have left the message with the recorder.

He did not remember her mother's number but he knew her address. He got the information from the operator and put a call through to the San Francisco address. The phone rang for a long time. Finally, he hung up and then thought of what he should have immediately checked. He was deeply upset to have overlooked that.

He went into the basement garage. Her car was still there.

By then he was considering the fantastic – or was it fantastic – possibility that Igescu had taken her.

First, why would Igescu do this?

If Igescu had been responsible for Colben's death and Budler's disappearance, then he might have designs on the detective investigating the case. Childe had pretended to be Wellston, the magazine reporter, but he had been forced to give his own phone number. And Igescu might have checked out the so-called Wellston. Certainly, Igescu had the money to do this.

What if Igescu had found out that Wellston was really Childe? And, having found out that Childe had not got into the serious car accident he had hoped for, he had taken Sybil away. Perhaps Igescu planned to let Childe know that he had better drop the investigation... no, it would be more probable that Igescu wanted to force him to break into the estate, to trespass. For reasons of his own, of course.

Childe shook his head. If Igescu were guilty, if he, say, had been guilty of other crimes, why was he suddenly letting the police know that these crimes had been committed?

This question was not one to be answered immediately. The only thing as of this moment was whether or not Sybil had gone voluntarily and, if she had not, with whom had she gone?

He had not checked the airports. He sat down and began dialling. The phones of every airline were busy, but he hung on until he got through to each and then went through more exasperating waits while passenger lists were checked. At the end of two hours, he knew that she had not taken a plane out. She might have intended to, but the airlines had been over-burdened ever since the smog had become serious. The waiting lists were staggeringly long, and the facilities at the ports, the restaurants and toilets, had long queues. Parking facilities no longer existed for newcomers. Too many people had simply left their cars and taken off with no intention of returning immediately. The authorities had imposed an emergency time limitation, but the process of towing away cars to make room for others was tedious, involved, and slow. The traffic jam-up around International Airport demanded more police officers than were available.

He ate some cereal and milk and then, though it hurt him to think of all the money wasted, he flushed the marijuana down the toilet. If she continued to be missing and he had to notify the police, her apartment would be searched. On the other hand, if she were to return soon and find her supply gone, she would be in a rage. But surely she would understand why he had had to get rid of that stuff.

Dawn had arrived by then. The sun was a twisted pale-yellow thing in the sky. Visibility was limited to a hundred feet. The eye-burning and the nostril-scorching and the lung-searing were back.

He decided to call Bruin and to tell him about Sybil. Bruin would, of course, think that he was being unduly concerned and would think, even if he didn't say so, that she had simply left for an extended shacking-up with some man. Or, possibly, Bruin being the cynic he was, she was shacking up with some woman.

He did not have to phone Bruin. Bruin called him as he stood before the phone.

"We got a package in the late mail yesterday afternoon but it wasn't opened until a little while ago. You better get down here, Childe. Can you make it in half an hour?"

"What's it about? Budler?" And then, "Never mind. But how did you know I was here?"

"I tried your place and you didn't answer, so I thought I'd try your ex-wife's. I knew you was still friendly with her."

"Yeah," Childe said, realizing that it was too early to report her missing. "I'll be down in time. See you. Unhunh! Maybe I can't! I have to get my car first and that may take some time."

He told Bruin what had happened but censored the summerhouse activities. Bruin was silent for a long time and then said, "You realize, Childe, that we're all doing a juggling act now, keeping three balls or more in the air at the same time? I'd investigate Igescu even if you don't have anything tangible or provable, because they sure sound like a fishy lot, but I doubt we could get into that place without a court order and we don't have any evidence to get an order. You know that. So it's up to you. Those wolf hairs in Budler's car and now this film – well, I ain't going to tell you about it, you got to see it to believe it – but if you can't get down here on time... listen, I could have a squad car pick you up. I would if this was ordinary times, but there's none available. Tell you what, if I'm out, you can get the film run off again, I'll leave word it's OK. Anyway, it might be shown again for the Commissioner. He's up to his ass in work, but he's taking a special interest in this case, and no wonder."

Childe drank some orange juice, shaved (Sybil kept a man's razor and shaving cream for him and – he suspected – for other men) and then walked to the Beverly Hills Police Department. He got his key from the desk sergeant and asked if it were possible to get a ride with a squad car out to his car. He was told it was not possible. He tried to get a taxi, could not, and decided to hitchhike out. After fifteen minutes, he gave up. There were not many autos on Santa Monica Boulevard and Rexford, and the few that did go by ignored him. He did not blame them.

Picking up hitchhikers at any time was potentially dangerous, but in this eerie white-lighted smog anybody would have looked sinister. Moreover, the radio, TV, and newspapers were advising caution because of the number of crimes in the streets.

His eyes teary and the interior of his nostrils and throat feeling as if he were sniffing in fumes from boiling metal, he stood upon the corner. He could see the house across the street and make out the city hall and the public library across the street from it as dim bulks, motionless icebergs in a fog. Far down, or seemingly far down, Rexford Avenue, a pair of headlights appeared and then swung out of sight.

Presently a black-and-white squad car passed him. When it was almost out of sight up Rexford, it stopped and then backed up until it was by him. The officer on the right, without getting out of the car, asked him what he was doing there. Childe told him. Fortunately, the officer had heard about him. He invited Childe to get in and ride with them. They had no definite goal at that moment; they were cruising around the area (the wealthy residential district, of course) but there was nothing to stop them from going that far out. Childe had to understand that if they got a call, they might have to dump him out on the spot and he would be stranded again. Childe said that he would take a chance.

It took fifteen minutes to get to his car. Only an emergency would have forced them to speed through this thick milky stuff. He thanked them and then started the car without any trouble, backed up, and swung towards town. Forty minutes later, he was parked in the LAPD visitors' lot.

Philip José Farmer

Chapter 12

Budler was in the same room in which Colben had been killed. The first scenes had shown Budler being conditioned, going through fear and impotence at first and then confidence and active, eager participation. In the beginning, he had been strapped to the same table but later the table was gone and a bed took its place.

Budler was a little man with narrow shoulders and skinny hips and legs, but he had a tremendous penis. He was pale-skinned and had light blue eyes and straw-coloured hair on his head. His pubic hairs were a light brown. His penis, however, was dark, as if blood always filled it. He had an unusual capacity for sustaining erections after orgasms and an unusual supply of seminal fluid.

(Both victims had been men with hypersex drives, or, at least, men whose lives seemed to be dominated by sex. Both were promiscuous, both had made a number of girls pregnant, been arrested or suspected of statutory rape, and were known as loudmouths about their conquests. Both were what his wife described as 'creeps'. There was something nasty about them. Childe thought that the victims had possibly been selected with poetic justice in mind.)

The woman with the garish make-up, and the creature? – machine? organ? – concealed behind her G-string, was an actor; she specialized in sucking cock and she took out her teeth several times but she did not use the iron teeth. Every time he saw her remove her false teeth, Childe tensed and felt sick but he was spared the mutilation.

There were other actors, also. One was an enormously fat woman with beautiful white skin. Her face never appeared. There was another woman, whose figure was superb, whose face was always hidden, usually by a mask. Both of these used their mouths and cunts, and once Budler buggered the fat woman.

There were also two men, their faces masked. Childe studied their bodies carefully, but he could not say that either was Igescu or Glam or the youth who had been playing billiards. One of the men had a build similar to Igescu's and another was a very big and muscular man. But he could not identify them as anyone he had seen at Igescu's.

Budler must have had a latent homosexual tendency which was developed, possibly under the influence of drugs, during the conditioning. One of the men blew him several times, and twice Budler buggered the big man. The third man appeared in one scene only, and this time it was in what Childe thought would be the grand finale. He braced himself for something terrible to happen to Budler, but aside from being exhausted, Budler seemed to suffer no ill effects. Budler and the three men and three women formed many configurations with, usually, Budler as the focus of the group.

The Commissioner, sitting by Childe, said at this point, "This is quite an organization. Besides the six there, there must be two, at least, handling the cameras."

The last scene (Childe knew it was the last because the Commissioner told him just as it flashed on) showed Budler screwing one of the well-built women dog-fashion. The cameras came in at every angle except that which would show the woman's face. There were a number of shots which must have been taken through a long flexible optical fibre device, because there were close-ups of a seemingly gargantuan penis driving in under a cavernous anus into an elephantine slit. The lubricating fluid flowed like spillage over a too-full dam.

And then the camera seemed to inch forward along the penis, now quiescent, and into the slit. Light blazed up, and the viewers seemed to be surrounded by thousands of tons of flesh. They were looking down at the penis, a whale that had crashed into an underseas cave. Then they were looking up at the ceiling of wet pale red flesh.

Suddenly, the light went out and they were back again, looking at Budler and the woman from the side. The two were on the bed, she face-down and her arms to one side and her buttocks raised by a pillow under her stomach. He was straddling her, one knee between the legs, and rocking back and forth.

Suddenly, so suddenly that Childe gasped and thought his heart would stop, the woman became a female wolf. Budler was still astride her and pumping slowly away when the transformation took place. (A trick of photography, of course. A trick involving drugs, surely, because Budler acted as if the woman had metamorphosed.) He stopped, raised his hands, and then sat up, his penis withdrawing and beginning to droop. He looked shocked.

Philip José Farmer

Snarling, the wolf turned and slashed at his penis.

It happened so quickly that Childe did not understand immediately that the powerful jaws had taken the penis off close to the root.

Blood spurted out of the stump and over the wolf and the bed.

Screaming, Budler fell backward. The wolf bolted the penis down and then began biting at the man's testicles. Budler quit screaming. His skin turned blue-grey, and the camera left the wounds where the genitals had been and travelled up to show his dying face.

There was the tinny piano music again, Dvorak's *Humoresque*. The Dracula burst through the curtains with the same dramatic gesture of the cape thrown aside to reveal his face. The camera travelled down then and verified what Childe thought he had seen when the man entered but had not been certain about. The Dracula's penis, a very long and thin organ, was sticking out of the fly. The Dracula cackled and bounded forward and leaped upon the bed and grabbed the wolf by the hairs of its flanks and sank its penis into it from behind.

The wolf yowled, its mouth open, a piece of testicle falling out. Then, as the Dracula rammed it, driving her forward and inching along on his knees, the wolf began tearing at the flesh between the legs of Budler.

Fadeout. TO BE CONTINUED: in blazing white letters across the screen. End of film.

Childe became sick again. Afterward, he talked with the Commissioner, who was also pale and shaking. But he was not shaky in his refusal to take any action about Igescu. He explained (which Childe knew) that the evidence was too slight, in fact, it was nonexistent. The "vampire" angle, the wolves on the estate, the (supposed) drugging of him by Igescu's secretary, the wolf hairs found in Budler's car, the wolf in the film, all these certainly would make investigation of Igescu legitimate. But Igescu was a very rich and powerful man with no known criminal records or any suspicions by the authorities of criminal connections. If the police were to do anything, and he did not see how they could, the Beverly Hills Police would have to handle the investigation.

The essence of his remarks was what Childe had expected.

He would have to get more conclusive evidence, and he would have to do it without any help from the police.

Childe drove back through a darkening air. The weird white light was slowly turning grey-green. He stopped at a service station to fill his tank and also to replace the broken headlamp. The attendant, after stamping the form for his credit card, said, "You may be my last customer. I'm taking off just as soon as I get the paperwork out of the way. Getting out of town, friend. This place has had it!"

"I may follow you," Childe said. "But I got some unfinished business to attend to first."

"Yeah? This town's gonna be a ghost town; it's already on the way."

Childe drove into Beverly Hills to shop. He had a difficult time finding a parking space. If it was going to be a ghost town, it did not seem that it would be so soon. Perhaps most of the people were getting supplies for the second exodus or were stocking up before the stores were again closed. Whatever the reason, it was two and a half hours before he got all he wanted, and it took a half-hour to drive the mile and a half to his apartment. The streets were again jammed with cars. Which, of course, only speeded up the poisoning of air.

Childe had intended to drive out to Igescu's at once, but he knew that he might as well wait until the traffic thinned out. He spent an hour reviewing what he meant to do and then tried to call Sybil, but the lines were busy again. He walked to her apartment. He was goggled and snouted with a gas mask he had purchased at a store which had just got a shipment in. So many others were similarly masked, the street looked like a scene on Mars.

Sybil was not home. Her car was still in the garage. The note he had left in her apartment was in the exact position in which he had placed it. He tried to get a long-distance call to her mother put through but had enough trouble getting the operator, who told him he would have to wait for a long time. She had been ordered to put through only emergency calls. He told her it *was* an emergency, his wife had disappeared and he wanted to find out if she had gone to San Francisco. The operator said that he would still have to wait, no telling how long. Should she call him back at that number when his turn came?

He said no and thank you and hung up. He walked back to his apartment and re-checked the automatic recorder with the same negative results. For a while he watched the news, most of which was a repetition or very slight updating of accounts of the smog and the emigration. It was too depressing, and he could not get interested in the only non-news programme, Shirley Temple in *Little Miss Marker*. He tried to read, but his mind kept jumping back and forth from Budler to his wife.

It was maddening not to be able to act. He almost decided to buck the traffic, because he might as well be doing something and, moreover, once off the main roads, he might be able to travel speedily. He looked out at the street, packed with cars going one way, horns blaring, drivers cursing out' their windows or sitting stoic, tight-lipped, hands gripping the wheels. He would not be able to get his car out of the driveway.

At seven, the traffic suddenly became normal, as if a plug had been pulled some place and the extra vehicles gulped down it. He went into the basement, drove the car out, and got into the street without any trouble. A few cars drove down the wrong side, but these quickly pulled over into the right lane. He got to Igescu's before dusk; he had had to stop to change a flat tyre. The roads were littered with many objects, and one of these, a nail, had driven into his left rear tyre. Also, he was stopped by the police. They were looking for a service station robber driving a car of his make and colour. He satisfied them that he was not a criminal, not the one they were looking for, anyway, and continued on. The fact that they could concern themselves with a mere hold-up at this time showed that the traffic had eased up considerably, in this area, at least.

At the end of the road outside Igescu's, he turned the car around and backed it into the bushes. He got out and, after removing the gas mask, raised the boot and took out the bundle he had prepared. It took him some time to carry the cumbersome load through the thick woods and up the hill to the wall. Here he unfolded the aluminium ladder, locked the joints, and, with the pack on his back, climbed up until his head was above the wire. He did not intend to find out if the wire was electrified. To do so might set off an alarm. He pulled up the long rubberized flexible tunnel, a child's plaything, by the rope tied around its end.

He hoisted it until half its length was over the wire and then began the unavoidably clumsy and slow manoeuvre of crawling, not into it but over it. His weight pressed it down so that he had a double thickness between him and the sharp points of the wire. He was able to turn, straddling the wire, and pull the ladder slowly up after him with the rope, which he had taken from the tunnel and tied to the ladder. He was very careful not to touch the wire with the ladder.

He lifted it up and turned it and deposited its end upon the ground on the inside of the wall. Once his feet were on the rungs, he lifted up the tunnel and dropped it on the ground and then climbed down. He repeated this procedure at the inner wall up to the point where he reached the top of the wall. Instead of climbing on over, he took two large steaks from his backpack and threw them as far as he could. Both landed upon leaves near the foot of a large oak. Then he pulled the tunnel back and retreated down the ladder. He sat with his back against the wall and waited. If he did not succeed with this step within two hours, he would go on in, anyway.

The darkness settled, but it did not seem to get any cooler. There was no air moving, no sound of bird or insect. The moon rose. A few minutes later, a howling jerked him to his feet. His scalp moved as if rubbed by a cold hand. The howling, distant at first, came closer. Soon there was a snuffling and then a growling and gobbling. Childe waited and checked his Smith & Wesson Terrier .32 revolver again. After five minutes by his wristwatch, he climbed over the wall, pulling the tunnel and ladder after him as he had done at the first wall. He laid them on the ground behind a tree in case anybody should be patrolling the wall. Gun in hand, he set out to look for the wolves. The bones of the steaks had been cracked and partially swallowed; the rest was gone.

He did not find the wolves. Or he was not sure that what he did find were the wolves.

He stepped into a clearing and then sucked in his breath. Two bodies lay in the moonlight. They were unconscious, which state he had expected from the eating of drugged meat. But these were not the hairy, four-legged, long-muzzled bodies he had thought to see. These were the nude bodies of the young couple who had played billiards in the Igescu house. Vasili Chornkin and

Philip José Farmer

Mrs Krautschner slept on the grass under the moon. The boy was on his face, his legs under him and his hands by his face. The girl was on her side, her legs drawn up and her arms folded beside her head. She had a beautiful body. It reminded him of one of the girls he had seen in the films and especially of the girl Budler had been fucking dog style.

He had to sit down for a while. He felt shaky. He did not think that this was possible or impossible. It just *was,* and the *was* threatened him. It threatened his belief in the order of the universe, which meant that it threatened him.

After a while he was able to act. He used tape from his backpack to secure their hands behind them and their ankles together. Then he taped their mouths tightly and placed them on their sides, facing each other and as close together as possible and taped them together around the necks and ankles. He was sweating by the time he had finished. He left them in the glade and hoped that they would be very happy together. (That he could think this showed him that he was recovering swiftly.) They should be happy if they knew that he had planned to cut the throats of the wolves.

He headed towards where the house should be and within five minutes saw its bulk on top of the hill and some rectangles of light. Approaching it on the left, he stopped suddenly and almost fired his revolver, he was so upset by the abrupt appearance of the figure. It flitted from shadow into moonlight and back into shadow and was gone. It looked as if it were a woman wearing an ankle-length dress with a bare back.

For the third time that night, he felt a chill. It must have been Dolores. Or a woman playing the ghost. And why should a fraud be out here when there was no need to play the ghost? They did not know that he was here. At least, he hoped not.

It was possible that the baron wanted to shock another guest tonight and so was using this woman.

The driveway had five cars besides the Rolls-Royce Silver Cloud. There were two Cadillacs, a Lincoln, a Cord, and a 1929 Duesenberg. Neither wing showed a light, but the central part was well-lit.

Childe looked for Glam, did not see him, and went around the side. There was a vine-covered trellis which afforded easy access to the second storey balcony. The window was closed but not locked. The room was dark and hot and musty. He groped along the wall until he found a door and slowly swung it out. It opened on a closet in which hung dark musty clothes. He closed the door and felt along it until he discovered another door. This led to a hallway which was dimly lit by moonlight through a window. He used his pencil-thin flashlight now and then to guide himself. He passed by a stairway leading to the storey below and the storey above and pushed open a door to another hallway. This had no illumination at all; he fingered his way to the other end with his flashlight.

Sometimes he stopped to put his ear against a doorway. He had thought he had heard the murmurs of voices behind them. Intent listening convinced him that nobody was there, that his imagination was tricking him.

At the end of this hallway, twice as long as the first, he found a locked door. A series of keys left the lock unturned. He used his pick and, after several minutes' work, during which the sweat ran down his eyes and his ribs and he had to stop several times because he thought he heard footsteps and, once, a breathing, he solved the puzzle of the tumblers.

The door opened to a shaft of light and a puff of cold air.

As he stepped through into the hallway, he caught a flash of something on his left at the far end. It had moved too swiftly for him to identify it, but he thought that it was the tail end of Dolores' skirt. He ran down the hallway as quietly as he could with his sneakers on the marble tile floor (this was done in much-marbled and ornate-woodworked Victorian style, even if it was in the Spanish part). At the corner, he halted and stuck his head around.

The woman at the extreme end was facing him. By the light of a floor lamp near her, he could see that she was tall and black-haired and beautiful – the woman in the portrait above the mantel in the drawing room.

She beckoned to him and turned and disappeared around the corner.

He felt a little disoriented, not so much as if he were being disconnected from a part of himself inside himself but as if the walls around him were being subtly warped.

Just as he rounded the corner, he saw her skirt going into a doorway. This led to a room halfway down the hall. The only light was that from the lamp on a stand in the hallway. He groped around until he felt the light switch. The response was the illumination of a small lamp at the other end on a stand by a huge bed with a canopy. He did not know much about furniture, but it looked like a bed from one of the Louis series, Louis Quatorze, perhaps. The rest of the expensive-looking furniture seemed to go with the bed. A large crystal chandelier hung from the centre of the ceiling.

The wall was white panelling, and one of the panels was just swinging shut.

Childe thought it was swinging shut. He had blinked, and then the wall seemed solid.

There was no other way for the woman to have gone.

Do ghosts have to open doors, or panels, to go from one room to another?

Perhaps they did, if they existed. However, he had seen nothing to indicate that Dolores – or whoever the woman was – must be a ghost.

If she were a hoax set up by Baron Igescu for the benefit of others, and particularly for Childe, she was leading him on for a reason that he could only believe was sinister. The panel led to a passage between the walls, and Igescu must want him to go through the panel.

The newspaper article had said that the original house had contained between-walls passages and underground passages and several secret tunnels which led to exits in the woods. Don del Osorojo had built these because he feared attacks from bandits, wild Indians, revolting peasants, and, possibly, government troops. The Don, it seemed, was having trouble with tax-collectors; the government claimed that he was hiding gold and silver.

When the first Baron Igescu, the present owner's uncle, had added the wings he had also built secret passageways which connected to those in the central house. Not so secret, actually, since the workers had talked about them, but no drawings or blueprints of the house's construction existed, as far as anybody knew. And most of the workers would now be dead or so old that they could not remember the layout, even if any of them could be found.

The panel had been opened long enough for him to know

that it was an entrance. Perhaps the baron wanted him to know it; perhaps Dolores, the ghost. In any event, he meant to go through it.

Finding the actuator of the entrance was another matter. He pressed the wood around the panel, tried to move strips around it, knocked at various places on the panel (it sounded hollow), and examined the wood closely for holes. He found nothing out-of-the-way.

Straightening up, he half-turned in an angry movement and then turned back again, as if he would catch something – or somebody – doing something behind his back. There was nothing behind him that had not been there before. But he did glimpse himself in the huge floor-to-ceiling mirror that constituted half of the wall across the room.

Chapter 13

The mirror certainly was not reflecting as a mirror should. Nor was it reflecting grossly or exaggeratedly, like a funny-house mirror. The distortions – if they could be called distortions – were subtle. And as evasive as drops of mercury.

There were slight shiftings of everything reflected, of the wall behind him, the painting on the wall to one side of him, the canopied bed, and himself. It was as if he were looking at an underwater room through a window, with himself deep in the water and the mirror a window, or porthole, to a room in a subaquatic palace. The objects in the room, and he seemed to be as much an object as the bed or a chair, swayed a little. As if currents of cold water succeeded by warmer water compressed or expanded the water and so changed the intensity and the refraction of lighting.

There was more to the shifting than that, however. At one place, the room and everything in it, including himself, seemed almost – not quite – normal. As they should be or as it seemed that they should be. Seemed, he thought, because it struck him that things as they are were not necessarily things as they should be, that custom had made strangeness, or outrageousness (a peculiar word, what made him think of that?), comfortable.

Then the "normality" disappeared as the objects twisted or swayed, he was not sure which they did, and the room, and he, became "evil".

He did not look "weak" nor "petty" nor "sneaky" nor "selfish" nor "indifferent", all of which he felt himself to be at various times. He looked "evil". Malignant, destroying, utterly loveless.

He walked slowly towards the mirror. His image, wavering, advanced. It smiled, and he suddenly realized that he was smiling. That smile was not utterly loveless; it was a smile of pure love. Love of hatred of and the corruption of all living things.
He could almost smell the stink of hate and of death.

Then he thought that the smile was not of love but of greed, unless greed was a form of love. It could be.

The meanings of words were as shifting and elusive as the images in the mirror.

He became sick; something was gnawing at his nerves in the pit of his stomach.

It was a form of sea-sickness, he thought. See-sickness, rather.

He turned away from the mirror, feeling as he did so a chill pass over his scalp and a vulnerability – a hollowness – between his shoulders, as if the man in the mirror would stick him in the back with a knife if he exposed his back to him.

He hated the mirror and the room it mirrored. He had to get out of it. If he could not get the panel open in a few seconds, he would have to leave by the door.

There was no use in repeating his first efforts. The key to the panel was not in its immediate neighbourhood, so he would have to look elsewhere. Perhaps its actuator, a button, a stud, something, could be behind the large oil painting. This was of a man who looked much like the baron and was probably his uncle. Childe lifted it up and off its hooks and placed it upright on the floor, leaning against the wall. The space behind where it had been was smooth. No actuator mechanism here.

He replaced the painting. It seemed twice as heavy when he lifted it up as it had when he had taken it down. This room was draining him of his strength.

He turned away from the painting and stopped. The panel had swung inward into the darkness behind the wall.

Childe, keeping an eye on the panel, placed a hand on the lower corner of the portrait-frame and moved it slightly. The panel, however, had already started to close. Evidently the actuating mechanism opened it briefly and then closed it automatically.

He waited until the panel shut and again moved the frame sideways. Nothing happened. But when he lifted the painting slightly, the panel again swung open.

Childe did not hesitate. He ran to the panel, stepped through cautiously, making sure that there was firm footing in the darkness, and then got to one side to permit the panel to swing shut. He was in unrelieved black; the air was dead and odorous of decaying wood, plaster falling apart, and a trace of long-dead mice. There was also a teaser (was it there or not?) of perfume.

The flashlight showed a dusty corridor about four feet wide and seven high. It did not end against the wall of the hallway, as he

Philip José Farmer

had expected. A well of blackness turned out to be a stairway under the hall. At its bottom was a small platform and another stairway leading up, he presumed, to another passageway on the other side of the hall.

In the opposite direction, the passageway ran straight for about fifty feet and then disappeared around a corner. He walked slowly in that direction and examined the walls, ceiling, and floor carefully. When he had gone far enough to be past the baron's bedroom, he found a panel on hinges. It was too small and too far up the wall for passage. He unlocked its latch, turned his flashlight off, and swung it slowly out to avoid squeaking of hinges.

They gave no sound. The panel hid a one-way mirror. He was looking into a bedroom. A titian-haired woman came through the door from the hall about seven seconds later. She walked past him, only five feet away, and disappeared into another doorway. She was wearing a print dress with large red flowers; her legs were bare and her feet were sandalled.

The woman was so beautiful that he had felt sick in his solar plexus for a moment, a feeling he had experienced three times, when seeing for the first time women so beautiful that he was agonized because he would never have them.

Childe thought that it would be better to continue his exploring, but he could not resist the feeling that he might see something significant if he stayed there. The woman had looked so determined, as if she had something important to do. He placed his ear against the glass and could hear, faintly, Richard Strauss' *Thus Spake Zarathustra*. It must be coming from the room into which she had gone.

The bedroom was in rather sombre taste for a beautiful young woman; the baron's room, if it had been the baron's room, would have been more appropriate for her. It was far cheerier, if you excepted the wall-mirror. The walls were of dark dull wooden panelling about six feet up from the floor; above them was a dull dark wallpaper with faint images: queer birds, twisted dragons, and the recurring figures of what could be a nude Adam and Eve and an apple tree. There were no snakes.

The carpet was thick and also dull and dark with images too faded to be identified. The bed was, like the baron's, canopied, but it was of a period he did not recognize, although this did not mean much, because he knew very little about furniture or furnishings. Its legs were wrought-iron in the form of dragons' claws, the bedspread and the canopy were a dark red. There was a mirror on the wall opposite. It was three-sided, like the mirrors used in the clothing departments of stores. It seemed to be nothing extraordinary; it reflected the window through which Childe was looking as another mirror above a large dull red-brown dresser.

There was a chandelier of cut quartz with dull yellow sockets for candles. The light in the room, however, came from a number of table and floor lamps. The corners of the room were in shadow.

Childe waited for a while and sweated. It was hot in the corridor, and the various odours, of wood, plaster, and long-dead mice, became stronger instead of dying on a dulling nose. The teaser of perfume was entirely gone. Finally, just as he decided that he should be moving on and why was he standing here in the first place – the woman came through the door. She was naked; her titian-red hair hung loosely around her shoulders and down her back. She held a long-necked bottle to her lips as she walked towards the dresser. She paused before it and continued to drink until only about two inches of the liquid was left. Then she put the bottle on the dresser and leaned forward to look into the mirror.

She had taken her make-up off. She peered into the mirror as if she were searching for defects. Childe stepped back, because it seemed impossible that she would not see him. Then he stepped forward again. If she knew that this was a one-way mirror, she did not care if another was on the other side. Or supposed that no hostile person would be there. Perhaps only the baron knew of this passageway.

She seemed to find her inspection of her face satisfactory, and she might have found it very pleasing, to judge from her smile. She straightened up and looked at her body and also seemed pleased at this. Childe felt uncomfortable, as if he were doing something perverted by spying on her, but he also began to get excited.

She wriggled a little, swayed her hips from side to side, and ran her hands up and down her ribs and hips and then cupped them over her breasts and rubbed the nipples with the ends of her thumbs. The nipples swelled. Childe's penis swelled, also.

Philip José Farmer

Keeping her left hand busy with her breast, she put her right hand on her pubes, and opened the top of the slit with one finger and began to rub her clitoris. She worked swiftly at it, rubbing vigorously, and suddenly she threw her head back, her mouth open, ecstasy on her face.

Childe felt both excited and repulsed. Part of the repulsion was because he was no voyeur; he felt that it was indecent to watch anyone under these circumstances. It was true that he did not have to stay, but he was here to investigate kidnapping and murder, and this certainly looked worth investigating.

She continued to rub her clitoris and the hairy lips. And then – here Childe was startled and shaken but also knew that he had somehow expected it – a tiny thing, like a slender white tongue, spurted from the slit.

It was not a tongue. It was more like a snake or an eel.

It was as small in diameter as a garter snake but much longer. How long it was he could not determine yet, because its body kept sliding out and out. It kept coming, and its skin was smooth and hairless, as smooth as the woman's belly and as white, and the skin glistened with the fluid from her cunt.

It shot out in a downward arc, like a half-erect penis, and then it turned and flopped over against her belly and began to zigzag upwards. It continued to slide out from the slit as if yards of it were still coiled inside her womb, and it continued to ooze up until its snaky length was coiled once around her left breast.

Childe could see the details of the thing's head, which was the size of a golf ball. It turned twice to look directly at him. Into the mirror, rather.

Its head was bald except for a fringe of oil-plastered black hair around the tiny ears. It had two thin but wet black eyebrows and a wet black Mephistophelean moustache and beard. The nose was relatively large and meat cleaver shaped. The eyes were dark, but they were so small and set so far back that they would have seemed dark to Childe even if they had been palest blue. The mouth was as much a slit as the vagina from which the creature had issued, but it briefly opened its mouth, and Childe could see two rows of little yellow teeth and a pink-red tongue.

The face was tiny, but there was nothing feeble about its malignancy.

The woman's lips moved. Childe could not hear her, but he thought she was crooning.

The snake body resumed its climbing while more of its body slid out of the pink fissure and the dark-red bush. It rounded her breast and went up her shoulder and around her neck and came around the right side and extended a loop outwards and then in so that the Lilliputian head faced her. The woman turned a little then, thus permitting Childe a quarter-view of her profile.

Her hands moved along the ophidian shaft as if she were feeling an unnaturally long penis – hers. Her slim fingers – beautiful fingers – traced the length and then, while one hand curled gently around the back of the head to support the body, the other slid back and forth from a few inches behind the head on down to the slit, as if she were masturbating the snake-penis.

The thing quivered. Then the head moved forward, and its minute lips touched her lower lip. It bit down, or seemed to, because she jerked her head back a little as if stung. Her head moved forward again, however, and her mouth was wide open. The head was engulfed in her mouth; she began to suck.

Childe had been too shocked to do anything but react emotionally. Now he began to think. He wondered how the thing could breathe with its head in her mouth. Then it occurred to him that it would be even more difficult for it to breathe when it was coiled in her womb or whatever recess of her body it lived in. So, though it had a nose, it perhaps did not need it. Its oxygen could be supplied by the woman's circulatory system, which surely must be connected through some umbilical device to the other end of the thing.

That head. It had belonged at one time to a full-grown man. Childe, with no rational reason, knew this. The head had belonged to the body of an adult male. Now, through some unbelievable science, the head had been reduced to the size of a golf ball, and it had been attached to this uterine snake, or the original human body had been altered, or...

He shook his head. How could this be? Had he been drugged? That mirror and now this.

The body bent, and the head withdrew from the woman's mouth. It swayed back and forth like a cobra to a flute, while the woman put her hands to her mouth and then removed a set of false

　　　　　　　　　　　　　　　Philip José Farmer

teeth. Her lips fell in; she was an old woman – from the neck up. But the thing thrust forward before she had put the teeth on the dresser, and the tiny head and part of the body disappeared into the toothless cavity. The body bent and unbent, slid back and forth between her lips.

At first, the movements were slow. Then her body trembled, and her skin became paler, except around the mouth and the pubes, where the intense darkening spoke of the concentration of blood. She shook; her great eyes fluttered open; she stared as if she were half-stunned. The thrustings of the body became swifter, and more of the body appeared and disappeared. She staggered backwards until she fell back upon the bed with her legs hanging over the edge and one foot resting on the floor, the other lifted up.

For perhaps ninety seconds, she jerked. Then, she was quiet. The snaky body lifted; the head came out of the lips and turned with the turning of the upper quarter of body. A thick whitish fluid was dribbling out of the open mouth.

The shaft rose up and up until all but the last six inches were lifted from the woman's body. It teetered like a sunflower in a flood and then collapsed. The tiny mouth chewed on a nipple for a while. The woman's hands moved like sleeping birds half-roused by a noise, then they became quiet again.

The mouth quit chewing. The body began a slow zigzag retreat into the dark-red bush and the fissure, trailing the head behind it. Presently, the body was gone and the head was swallowed up, bulging open the labia as it sank out of sight.

Childe thought, Werewolf? Vampire? Lamia? Vodyanoi? What?

He had never read of anything like this woman and the thing in her womb. Where did they fit in with the theories of Le Garrault as expounded by Igescu?

The woman rose from the bed and walked to the dresser. Looking into the mirror, she fitted the false teeth into her mouth and once more was the most beautiful woman in the world.

But she was also the most horrifying woman he had ever seen. He was shaking as much as she had been in her orgasm, and he was sick.

At that moment, the door that opened on to the hallway moved inward.

Childe felt as cold as if he had been dipped into an opening in polar ice.

The pale-skinned, scarlet-lipped, black-haired head of Dolores del Osorojo had appeared around the doorway.

The woman, who must have seen Dolores in the mirror, greyed. Her mouth dropped open; saliva and the spermy fluid dribbled out. Her eyes became huge. Her hands flew up – like birds again – to cover her breasts. Then she screamed so loudly that Childe could hear her, and she whirled and ran towards the door. She had snatched up the bottle by the neck so swiftly that Childe was not aware of it until she was halfway across the room. She was terrified. No doubt about that. But she was also courageous. She was attacking the cause of her terror.

Dolores smiled, and a white arm came around the door and pointed at the woman.

The woman stopped, the bottle raised above her head, and she quivered.

Then Childe saw that Dolores was not pointing at the woman. She was pointing past her. At him.

At the mirror behind which he stood rather. The woman whirled and looked at it and then, bewildered, looked around. Again, she whirled, and this time she shouted something in an unidentifiable language at the woman. The woman smiled once more, withdrew her arm, and then her head. The door closed.

Shaking, the woman walked slowly to the door, slowly opened it, and slowly looked through the doorway into the hall. If she saw anything, she did not care to pursue it, because she closed the door. She emptied the bottle then and returned to the dresser, where she pulled up a chair and sat down on it and then put her head on her arms on the table. After a while, the pinkish glow returned to her skin. She sat up again. Her eyes were bright with tears and her face seemed to have got about ten years older. She leaned close to the mirror to look at it, grimaced, got up, and went through the other door, which Childe presumed led to a bathroom or to a room which led to a bathroom.

Her reaction to Dolores certainly was not the baron's, who had seemed blasé, or even her reaction when she had seen Dolores in the living room. But here, where she was alone, the sight of the supposed ghost had terrified her.

Philip José Farmer

If Dolores were a hoax, one of which the woman would surely be aware, why should she react so?

Childe had a more-than-uneasy feeling that Dolores del Osorojo was not a woman hired to play ghost.

It was, however, possible that the woman was terrified for other reasons.

He had no time to find out what. He used the flashlight in quick stabs to determine if there was an entrance to her room, but he could find none. He went on then and came across another panel which opened to another one-way mirror. This showed him a small living room done in Spanish colonial style. Except for the telephone on a table, it could have been a room in the house shortly after it was built. There was nobody in it.

The corridor turned past the room. Along the wall here was a hinged panel large enough to give entrance to the other side. There was also a peephole behind a small sliding panel. He put his eye to it and could see only a darkened room. At the periphery of his vision was a lightening of the darkness, as if light were leaking through a barely opened door or a keyhole. A voice was coming from somewhere far off. It was in a strange language, and it seemed to be carrying on a monologue or a telephone conversation.

Beyond this room the corridor became two, the legs of a Y. He went down each for a short distance and found that two entrance panels existed on opposite walls of one leg and an entrance panel and peephole on opposite walls of the other. If, at another time, he could locate a triangular-shaped room, he would know where these passageways were.

He looked through the peephole but could see nothing. He went back up the passageway and up the other leg to the panel and opened this. His hand, thrust through the opening, felt a heavy cloth. He slid through carefully so that he would not push the cloth. It could be a drapery heavy enough to keep light on the other side from shining through. If anybody were in that room, he must not see the drapery move.

Squatting, his shoulder to the wall and squeezing his shoulders so that he would not disturb the cloth, he duckwalked until he had come to the juncture of two walls. Here the edges of the draperies met. He turned and pulled the edges apart and looked through with one eye.

The room was dark. He rose and stepped through and turned his flashlight on. The beam swept across a movie camera on a dolly and then stopped on a Y-shaped table.

He was in the room, or one like it, in which Colben and Budler had spent their – presumably – last few hours.

There was a bed in one corner, a number of movie cameras, some devices the use of which he did not know, and a large ashtray of some dark-green material. In the centre of its roughly circular dish stood a long thin statue. It looked like a nude man in the process of turning into a wolf, or vice versa. The body up to the chest was human; from there on it was hairy and the arms had become legs and the face had wolf-like ears and was caught in metamorphosis. There were about thirty cigarette stubs in the dish. Some had lipstick marks. One had a streak of dried blood, or it looked like dried blood, around the filter.

Childe turned on the lights and with the tiny Japanese camera took twenty shots. He had what he needed now, and he should get out. But he did not know whether or not Sybil was in this house.

And there might be other, even more impressive, evidence to get the police here.

He turned off the lights and crawled out of the panel into the passageway. He had a choice of routes then and decided to take the right leg of the Y. This led to another hall – the horizontal bar of a T. He turned right again and came to a stairway. The treads were of a glassy substance; it would have been easy to slip on them if he had not been wearing sneakers. He walked down six steps, and then his feet slid out from under him and he fell heavily on his back.

He struck a smooth slab and shot downward as if on a chutey-chute, which, in a sense, he was on. He put out his hands against the walls to brake himself but the walls, which had not seemed vitreous, were. The flashlight showed him a trapdoor opening at the bottom of the steps – these had straightened out to fall against each other and form a smooth surface – and then he slid through the dark opening. He struck heavily but was unhurt. The trapdoor closed above him. The flashlight showed him the padded ceiling, walls, and floor of a room seven feet high, six broad, ten deep. There were no apparent doors or windows.

Philip José Farmer

He smelled nothing nor heard anything but gas must have been let into the room. He fell asleep before he knew what was happening.

Chapter 14

He did not know how long he had been there. When he awoke, his flashlight, his wristwatch, his revolver, and his camera were missing. His head ached, and his mouth was as dry as if he were waking up after a three-day drunk. The gas must have had a very relaxing effect, because he had wet his shorts and pants. Or else he had wet them when the steps had dropped out from under him and he had begun to slide. He had needed to piss just before the trap caught him.

Five lights came on. Four were from floor-lamps set in the corners, and one was from an iron wall-lamp shaped like a torch and set at forty-five degrees to the wall.

He was not in the padded chamber. He was lying on a huge four-poster bed with scarlet sheets and bedspread and a scarlet black-edged canopy. The room was not one he had seen before. It was large; its black walls were hung with scarlet yellow-trimmed drapes and two sets of crossed rapiers. The floor was dark-glossy brown hardwood with a few crimson starfish-shaped thick-fibred rugs. There were some slender wrought-iron chairs with high skeletal backs and crimson cushions on the seats and a tall dresser of dense-grained brown wood.

It was while looking around that he thought of the dread of iron and the cross that vampires were supposed to have. There were iron objects all over the house, and, while he had seen no crucifixes, he had seen plenty of objects, such as these crossed rapiers, which made cruciforms. If Igescu was a vampire (Childe felt ridiculous even thinking this), he certainly did not object to contact with iron or sight of the cross.

Perhaps (just perhaps), these creatures had acquired an immunity from these once-abhorred things during thousands of years. If they *had* ever dreaded iron and the cross, that is. What about the years before iron was used by man? Or the cross was used by man? What guards and wards did man have then against these creatures?

Shakily, Childe got out of the bed and stood up. He had no time to search for a secret wall-exit, which he thought could exist here and which he might find before his captors returned. But the

Philip José Farmer

door at the far end swung open, and Glam entered, and the big room seemed much smaller. He stopped very close to Childe and looked down at him. For the first time, Childe saw that his eyes were light russet. The face was heavy and massive as a boulder, but those eyes seemed to glow as if they were rocks which had been subjected to radioactivity. Hairs hung from the cavernous nostrils like stalactites. His breath stank as if he had been eating rotten octopus.

"The baron says you should come to dinner," he rumbled.

"In these clothes?"

Glam looked down at the wet patch on the front of Childe's pants. When he looked up, he smiled briefly, like a jack-o'lantern just before the candle died.

"The baron says you can dress if you want to. There's clothes your size or near enough in the closet."

The closet was almost big enough to be a small room. His eyebrows rose when he saw the variety of male and female clothing. Who were the owners and where were they? Were they dead? Did some of the clothes bear labels with the names of Colben and Budler, or had they borne the labels, since the baron would not be stupid enough, surely, to leave such identification on.

Perhaps he *was* stupid. Otherwise, why the sending of the films to the Los Angeles Police Department?

But he did not really believe this about the baron.

Childe, after washing his hands and face and genitals and thighs in the most luxurious bathroom he had ever been in, and after dressing in a tuxedo, followed Glam down several hallways and then downstairs. He did not recognize any of the corridors nor the dining room. He had expected to be in the dining room he had seen yesterday, but this was another. The house was truly enormous.

The motif of this room was, in some respects, Early Grandiose Victorian-Italian, or so it seemed to him. The walls were grey black-streaked marble. A huge red marble fireplace and mantel were at one end, and above the mantel was a painting of a fierce old white-haired man with long moustachioes. He wore a wine-red coat with wide lapels and a white shirt with thick ruffles around the neck.

The floor was of black marble with small mosaics at each

---

of the eight corners. The furniture was massive and of a black dense-grained wood. A white damascene cloth covered the main table; it was set with massive silver dishes and goblets and tableware and tall thick silver candle-holders which supported thick red candles. There were at least fifty candles, all lit. A large cut-quartz chandelier held a number of red candles, also, but these were unlit.

Glam stopped to indicate a chair. Childe advanced slowly to it. The baron, at the head of the table, rose to greet him. His smile was broad but fleeting. He said, "Welcome, Mr Childe, despite the circumstances. Please sit down there. Next to Mrs Grasatchow."

There were four men and six women at the table.

The baron.

Magda Holyani.

Mrs Grasatchow, who was almost the fattest woman he had ever seen.

The baron's great-grandmother, who had to be at least a hundred.

Vivienne Mabcrough, the titian-haired woman with the man-headed snake-thing in her womb.

O'Riley O'Faithair, a handsome black-haired man of about thirty-five who spoke a charming Irish brogue. And now and then a few sentences in an unknown language to the baron and the Mabcrough woman.

Mr Bending Grass, who had a very broad and high-cheekboned face with a huge aquiline nose and huge, slightly slanted, very dark eyes. He could have been Sitting Bull's twin, but something he said to Mrs Grasatchow indicated that he was Crow. He spoke of the mountain man, John Johnston, "Liver Eating Johnston", as if he had been a contemporary.

Fred Pao, a tall slender Chinese with features that could have been carved out of teak and a Fu Manchu moustache and goatee.

Panchita Pocyotl, a short petite and beautiful Mexican Indian.

Rebecca Ngima, a handsome lithe black African dressed in a long white native costume.

They were all expensively and tastefully dressed and, though their speech was not free of foreign pronunciation, their

English was fluent, "correct", and rich with literary, philosophical, historical, and musical allusions. There were also references to events and persons and places that puzzled Childe, who was well-read. They seemed to have been everywhere and, here he felt cold threading the needle of his nerves, to have lived in times long dead.

Was this for his benefit? An addition to the hoax?

What hoax?

It was then that he got another shock, because the baron addressed him again as Mr Childe. With a start, he remembered the first time. He had been too dull to have realized then what that meant.

"How did you learn my name?" he said. "I carried no identification with me."

The baron smiled and said, "You don't really expect me to tell you?"

Childe shrugged and began eating. There were many different dishes on the sideboard; he had been given a wide choice but had decided on New York-cut steak and baked potato. Mrs Grasatchow, who sat on his left, had a platter with an entire bonita fish and a huge bowl of salad. She drank before, during, and after the meal from a gallon decanter of bourbon. The decanter was full when she sat down and empty when the dishes were cleared off the table.

Glam and two short, dark, and shapely women in maids' uniforms served. The women did not act like servants, however, they frequently talked with the guests and the host and several times made remarks in the foreign tongue that caused the others to laugh. Glam spoke only when his duties required. He glanced at Magda far more than his duties required.

The baroness, seated at the opposite end from her great-grandson, bent like a living question mark, or vulture, over her soup. This was the only food she was served, and she allowed it to get cold before she finally finished it. She said very little and only looked up twice, once to stare a long time at Childe. She looked as if she had only recently been brought out of an Egyptian pyramid and as if she would just as soon go back into the crypt. Her dinner gown, high-necked, ruffle-bosomed, diamond-sequined, red velvet, looked as if she had purchased it in 1890.

Mrs Grasatchow, although as fat as two sows put together,

had a remarkably white, flawless, and creamy skin and enormous purplish eyes. When she had been younger and thinner, she must have been a beautiful woman. She talked now as if she thought she was still beautiful, perhaps the most beautiful and desirable woman in the world. She talked loudly and uninhibitedly about the men who had died – some of them literally – for her love. Halfway through the dinner, and two-thirds through the gallon of whisky, her speech began to get slurred. Childe was awed. She had drunk enough to kill him, or most men, and she only had a little trouble with her speech.

She had drunk far more than the Chinese, Pao, who had downed much wine during the evening, but not much relative to her. Yet nobody reprimanded her, but Igescu seemed concerned about Pao. He was speaking to him in a corner, and though Childe could not hear them, he saw Igescu's hand come down on Pao's wrist, and Igescu shook his head and then jerked the thumb of his other hand at Childe.

Suddenly, Pao began to shake, and he ran out of the room. He was in a hurry to get out, but Childe did not think that he was about to vomit. He did not have the pale skin and desperate expression of one whose guts are ready to launch their contents.

The dishes were cleared and cigars and brandy and wine were served. (My God! was Mrs Grasatchow really going to smoke that ten-dollar cigar and pour down a huge snifter of brandy on top of the whisky?)

The baron spoke to Childe:

"You realize, of course, that I could easily have had you killed for trespassing, for entering, for voyeurism, et cetera, but mostly for entering? Now, perhaps, you would like to tell me what you are up to?"

Childe hesitated. The baron knew his name and must, therefore, know that he was a private investigator. And that he had been a partner of Colben. He must realize that, somehow, Childe had tracked him down, and he must be curious about what had led Childe here. He might be wondering if Childe had told anybody that he was coming here.

Childe decided to be frank. He also decided that he would tell the baron that the LAPD knew he was here and that if they did not hear from him at a certain time, they would come out here to find out why.

Igescu listened with a smile that seemed amused. He said, "Of course! And what would they find if they did come out here, which they are not likely to do?"

Perhaps they would find something Igescu did not suspect. They might find two naked people tied to each other. Igescu might have a difficult time explaining them, but they would not be a dangerous liability. Just puzzling to the police and inconvenient to Igescu.

At that moment Vasili Chornkin and Mrs Krautschner, fully clothed, entered. They stopped for a moment, stared at Childe, and then walked on in. The blonde stopped by Igescu to whisper in his ear; the man sat down and ordered something to eat. Igescu looked at Childe, frowned, and then smiled. He said something to Mrs Krautschner. She laughed and sat down by Chornkin.

Childe felt even more trapped. He could do nothing except, perhaps, make a break for it, but he doubted that he would get far. There was nothing for him to do except drift with the current of Igescu's wishes and hope that he would get a chance to escape.

The baron, looking over the brandy snifter just below his nose, said, "Did you get a chance to read Le Garrault, Mr Childe?"

"No, I didn't. But I understand the UCLA library is closed because of the smog."

The baron stood up. "Let's go into the library and talk where it's quieter."

Mrs Grasatchow heaved up from the chair, blowing like an alcoholic whale. She put an arm around Childe's shoulder; the flesh drooped like tangles of jungle vines. "I'll go with you, baby, you don't want to go without me."

"You can stay here for the time being," Igescu said.

Mrs Grasatchow glared at the baron, but she dropped her arm from Childe and sat down.

The library was a large dark room with dark leather-covered walls and massive dark-wood built-in shelves and at least five thousand books, some of them looking centuries old. The baron sat down in an over-stuffed leather-covered chair with a wooden back carved in the form of a bat-winged Satan. Childe sat down in a similar chair, the back of which was carved as a troll.

"Le Garrault..." the baron said.

"What's going on here?" Childe said. "Why the party?"

"You aren't interested in Le Garrault?"

"Sure, I'm interested. But I think there are things of much more interest just now. For instance, my survival."

"That is up to you, of course. One's survival is always up to one's self. Other people only play the part that you permit. But then, that's another theory. For the present, let's pretend that you are my guest and may leave at any time you wish – which can be the true situation. For all you know. Believe me, I am not telling you about Le Garrault just to pass the time. Am I?"

The baron continued to smile. Childe thought about Sybil and got angry. But he knew that it would do no good to ask the baron about her. If the baron had her, he would admit it only if it served some purpose of his.

"The old Belgian scholar knew more about the occult and the supernatural and the so-called *weird* than any other man who ever lived. I don't mean that he knew more than *anybody* else. I mean that he knew more than any other *man*."

The baron paused to draw in cigar smoke. Childe felt himself getting tense, although he was making an effort to relax.

"Old Le Garrault found records which other scholars did not find or else saw in these records what other scholars missed. Or possibly he may have talked to some of the – what should I call them? Unmen? – some of the unmen, the pseudo-men, and got his facts, which we shall call theory, directly from them.

"In any event, Le Garrault speculated that the so-called vampires, werewolves, poltergeists, ghosts, and so on, might be living creatures from a parallel universe. You know what a parallel universe is?"

"It's a concept originated by some science-fiction author, I believe," Childe said. "I think that the theory is that a number, perhaps an infinite number, of universes may occupy the same space. They can do this because they are all *polarized* or *at right angles* to each other. Those terms are actually meaningless, but they do signify that some physical mechanism enables more than one cosmos to fill the same quote *space* unquote. The concept of parallel universes was used and is being used by science-fiction writers to depict worlds just like ours, or only slightly differing, or wildly different. Like a universe where the South won the Civil War.

Philip José Farmer

That idea has been used at least three times, that I know of."

"Very good," the baron said. "Except that your examples are not quite correct. None of the three stories you are thinking about postulated a parallel universe. Churchill's and Kantor's were *what if* stories, and Moore's was a time travel story. But you have the right idea. However, Le Garrault was the first to publish the theory of parallel universes, although the publication was so restricted and so obscure that very few people knew about it. And Le Garrault did not postulate a series of universes which diverged only slightly at one end of the series, that is, the end nearest to Earth's cosmos, and diverged more the further away you got from the Earth's.

"No, he speculated that these other universes were nothing at all like Earth's, that they had different physical 'laws', that many of them would be completely incomprehensible to Earthmen who might broach the 'walls' between the universes."

"Then he said that there might be 'gates' or 'breaks' in the 'walls' and that occasionally a dweller of one universe might go into another?"

"He said more than that. He called his speculation a theory, but he believed that the theory was a fact. He believed that there were temporary breaks in the walls, accidental cracks, or openings which sometimes existed because of weaknesses or flaws.

"He said that creatures – sentient and non-sentient – sometimes entered our universe through these breaks. But they have forms so alien that the human brain has no forms to *explain* them. He said that it was not just a matter of humans *seeing* the aliens as such and such. It is a matter of the aliens actually being moulded into these forms because they cannot survive long in this universe unless they have forms that conform to the physical 'laws' of this universe. The forms may not conform one hundred percent, but they are close enough. And, in fact, an alien may have more than one form, because that is the way the human sees him. Hence, the werewolf, who has a human form and wolf form, and the vampire, who has a human form and a bat form."

This man is really putting me on, Childe thought. Or else he is so insane that he actually believes this. But what is he leading up to, that he is one of the aliens?

The baron said, "Some of the extra-universals came here accidentally, were caught in the flaws, and were unable to get back.

Others were exiles or criminals, sent by the people of their world to this Botany Bay – this Earth."

"Fascinating speculation," Childe said. "But why do these take certain forms and not others?"

"Because, in their case, the myth, the legend, the superstition, call it what you will, gave birth to the reality. First, there were the beliefs and tales about the werebeast and the vampire and the ghost and the et cetera. These beliefs and tales existed long ago, long before history, long before civilization. In one form or another, these beliefs existed in the Old Stone Age."

Childe shifted to relieve his discomfort. He felt cold again. He felt as if a shadow had slid over him. That shadow was of a great hulking half-brute figure, bulge-browed, ape-jawed. And behind it were other shadows of figures with long fangs and great claws and strange shapes.

The baron continued, "There is, according to Le Garrault, a *psychic imprinting*. He did not use the word *imprinting*, but his description meant that. He said that the aliens are able to survive for a short while in their own form when they come to this universe. They are in a state of fluidity, of dying fluidity."

"Fluidity?"

"Their forms are trying to change to conform to the physical laws of this universe. A universe which is as incomprehensible to them as theirs would be to an Earthman. The effort sets up stresses and strains which would inevitably tear them apart, kill them. Unless they encounter a human being. And, if they are lucky enough to be from a universe which enables them to receive – telepathically, I suppose, although that term is too restricted – enables them to receive the impressions of the human mind, then the alien is able to make the adaptation. He is enabled because he comprehends the form in which he can survive in this world. Do you follow me?"

"In a way. But not too well."

"It's almost as difficult to explain this as it is for a mystic to explain his visions. You realize that my explanations no more fit the facts, the true processes, than the description of the atom as a sort of miniature solar system fitted the true processes."

"I understand that, at least. You're using analogies."

"Strained analogies. But the theory says that the alien, if he is lucky, encounters human beings who perceive him as something

Philip José Farmer

unnatural, which he is, in a sense, since he is not natural to the human universe. The humans do not absolutely reject him; it is the nature of humans to try to explain every phenomenon or, should I say, describe it, classify it, fit it into the order of natural things.

"And so the alien is given his form, and a certain part of his nature, by the humans. There is a process of *psychic imprinting*, you understand. And so, willynilly, the alien becomes what the human believes him to be. But the alien still retains some of his otherworld characteristics, or I should say powers or abilities, and these he can use under certain circumstances. He can use them because they are part of the structure of this universe, even though most humans, that is, the educated, that is, the reconditioned, deny that such powers, or even such beings, can exist in this universe."

"You were enjoying your filet mignon and your salad," Childe said. "I thought vampires lived only on blood?"

"Who said I was a vampire?" the baron replied, smiling. "Or who said that vampires live on blood only? Or, who, saying that, knew what he was talking about?"

"Ghosts," Childe said. "How does this theory explain ghosts?"

"Le Garrault said that ghosts are the results of imperfect *psychic imprinting.* In their case, they assume, partially assume, the form of the human being first encountered or, sometimes, they result from the belief of a human being that they are the ghost of a departed. Thus, a man who believes in ghosts sees something he thinks is the ghost of his dead wife, and the alien becomes that ghost. But ghosts have a precarious off-and-on existence. They are never quite of this world. Le Garrault even said that it was possible that some aliens kept shuttling back and forth between this world and the native world and were actually ghosts in both worlds."

"Do you really expect me to believe that?" Childe said.

The baron puffed again and looked at the smoke as if it were a suddenly realized phantom. He said, "No. Because I don't believe the ghost theory myself. Not as Le Garrault expounded it."

"What do you believe then?"

"I really don't know," the baron said, shrugging. "Ghosts don't come from any universe I am familiar with. Their origin, their *modus operandi,* are mysterious. They exist. They can be dangerous."

Childe laughed and said, "You mean that vampires and werewolves, or whatever the hell they are, fear spooks?"

The baron shrugged again and said, "Some fear them."

Childe wanted to ask more questions but decided not to do so. He did not want the baron to know that he had found the room with the cameras and the Y-shaped table. It was possible that the baron intended to let him go, because he could dispose of the incriminating evidence before Childe could get the police here. For this reason, Childe did not ask him why Colben and Budler had happened to be his victims. Besides, it seemed obvious that Budler had been picked up by one of this group as a victim of their "fun". Magda or Vivienne or Mrs Krautschner, probably, had been the woman Colben had seen with Budler. And Colben, following Budler and the woman, had been detected and taken prisoner.

The baron rose and said, "We might as well rejoin the others. From the sounds, I'd say the party is far from dead."

Childe stood up and glanced at the open doorway, through which laughter and shrieks and hand-clapping spurted.

He jumped, and his heart lurched. Dolores del Osorojo was walking by the doorway. She turned her head and smiled at him and then was gone.

Philip José Farmer

Chapter 15

If the baron had seen her, he gave no sign. He bowed slightly and gestured Childe to precede him. They went down the hall – no Dolores anywhere – and were back in the dining room. O'Faithair was playing wildly on the grand piano. Childe did not recognize the music. The others were sitting at the table or on sofas or standing by the piano. Glam and the two women had cleared off the table and were carrying off the dishes from the sideboards. Mrs Grasatchow was now drinking from a bottle of champagne. Magda Holyani was sitting on an iron skeletal chair, her formal floor-length skirt pulled up around her waist to expose her perfect legs to the suspender belt. Dark-red hair stuck out from below the suspender belt. A half-smoked marijuana cigarette was on the table by her side.

She was looking through an old-time stereoscope at a photograph. Childe pulled her skirt down because the sight of her pubic hairs bothered him and disgusted him, and he said, "That's a curious amusement for you. Or is the picture...?"

She looked up smiling, and said, "Here. Take a look yourself."

He placed the stereopticon against his eyes and adjusted the slide holding the picture until the details became clear and in three dimensions. The photograph was innocent enough. It showed three men on a sail boat with a large mountain in the distant background. The photograph had been taken close enough so that the features of the men could be distinguished.

"One of them looks like me," he said.

"That's why I got this album out," she said. She paused, drew in deeply on the marijuana, held the smoke in her lungs for a long time and then puffed out. "That's Byron. The others are Shelley and Leigh Hunt."

"Oh, really," Childe said, still looking at the picture. "But I thought... I know it... the camera wasn't invented yet."

"That's true," Magda said. "That's not a photograph."

He did not get a chance to ask her to explain because two enormous white arms went around him from behind and lifted him to a sofa and dropped him on it. He started to get up. He was angry

---

enough to hit her, and had his fist cocked, when she shoved him back again. She was not only very heavy; she had powerful muscles under the fat.

"Stay there, I want to talk to you and other things!" she said.

He shrugged. She sat down by him, and the sofa sank under her. She held his hand and leaned against him and continued the near-monologue she had been maintaining at the table. She told him of the men who had lusted after her and what she'd done to them. Childe was beginning to feel a little peculiar then. Things were not quite focused. He realized that he must be drugged.

A moment later, he was sure of it. He had seen the baron walk to the doorway and looked away for a second. When he looked back, he saw that the baron was gone. A bat was flying off down the hallway.

The change had taken place so quickly that it was as if several frames of film had been spliced in.

Or was it a change? There was nothing to have kept the baron from slipping off around the corner and releasing the bat. Or it was possible that there was, objectively, no bat, that he was seeing it because he had been drugged and because of the suggestions that Igescu was a vampire?

Childe decided to say nothing about it. Nobody seemed to have noticed it. They were not in shape to have noticed anything except what they were concentrating upon. O'Faithair was still playing madly. Bending Grass and Mrs Pocyotl were facing each other, writhing and shuffling in a parody of the latest dance. The redhead beauty, Vivienne Mabcrough, was sitting on another sofa with Rebecca Ngima, the beautiful Negress. Vivienne was drinking from a goblet in one hand while the other was slipped into the front of Ngima's dress. Ngima had her hand under Vivienne's dress. Pao, the Chinese, was on his back, his legs bent to support Magda, who was standing on his feet and getting ready to do a backward flip. She had taken off her shoes and dress and was clad only in her suspender belt, stockings, and net bra. She steadied herself and then, as Pao shoved upwards, soared up and over and landed on her feet. Childe thought that her unshod feet would have broken with the impact, but she did not seem to be bothered. She laughed and ran forward and did a forward flip over Pao and landed in front of a sofa on which Igescu's great-grandmother sat. The old woman

Philip José Farmer

reached out a claw and ripped off Magda's bra. Magda laughed and pirouetted away across the floor.

The baron had sauntered over to behind the baroness and had leaned over to whisper something to her. She smiled and cackled shrilly.

And then Magda ended her crazy whirl on Childe's lap. His head was pressed forward against her breasts. They smelled of a heady perfume and sweat and something indefinable.

Mrs Grasatchow shoved Magda so vigorously that she fell off Childe's lap and on to the floor. She looked up dizzily for a moment, her legs widespread to reveal the red-haired slit.

"He's mine!" Mrs Grasatchow shrilled. "Mine! You snake-bitch!"

Magda got to her feet unsteadily. Her eyes uncrossed. She opened her mouth and her tongue flickered in and out and she hissed.

"Stay away!" Mrs Grasatchow said in a deeper voice. Had she really grunted?

Glam entered the room. He scowled at Magda. Evidently he did not like to see her in the almost-nude and making a play for Childe. But the baron froze him with a glare and motioned him to leave the room.

"Stay away, huh?" Magda said. "You have no authority over me, pig-woman, nor am I afraid of you."

"Pigs eat snakes," Mrs Grasatchow replied. She grunted – yes, she grunted this time – and put one flesh-festooned arm over his shoulders and began to unzip his fly with the other hand.

"You've eaten everything and everybody else, but you haven't, and you aren't going to, eat this snake," Magda said, spraying saliva.

Childe looked around and said, "Where are the cameras?"

"Everything's impromptu tonight," Mrs Grasatchow said. "Oh, you look so much like George."

Childe presumed that she meant George Gordon, Lord Byron, but he could not be sure and he did not care to play her game, anyway.

He pushed her hand away just as she closed two fingers on his penis, which, to his chagrin, was swelling. He felt nothing but repulsion for the fat woman, yet a part of him was responding. Or was it seeing Magda and also sharing in the general atmosphere of excitement? The drug, which he was sure he had been given, was basically responsible, of course.

Magda sat down on his lap again and put her arms around his neck. Mrs Grasatchow, snarling, raised her hand as if to strike Magda, but she let it drop when the baron called shrilly across the room. At that moment, a pair of large doors swung open. Childe, catching the movement at the corner of his eyes, turned his head. The baron was standing in the doorway. Behind him was *the* billiard room or *a* billiard room. It looked much like the first one he had seen. The two blonds, Chornkin and Krautschner, were playing.

The baron advanced across the room and, when a few paces behind Childe, said, "The police don't know he's here."

Childe erupted. He came off the sofa, tossing Magda away and then leaping over her and running towards the nearest door. He got to the hallway and was jerked violently off his feet, swung around, and pressed close to Glam. The great arms made him powerless to do anything except kick. And Glam must have been wearing heavy boots under his pants legs. Certainly he acted as if he did not feel the kicks. Perhaps he didn't. Childe may have had little strength.

As if he were a small child, he was led into the room. Glam holding his hand. The baron said, "Good. Good for him and good for you. You restrained your impulse to kill him. Very commendable, Glam."

"My reward?" Glam said.

"You'll get it. A share. As for Magda, if she doesn't want you, and she says she doesn't, she can continue to tell you to go to hell. My authority has its limits. Besides, you aren't really one of us."

"You're lucky I haven't killed you, Glam!" Magda said.

"You have depraved tastes, Glam," Mrs Grasatchow said. "You'd fuck a snake if someone held its head, wouldn't you? I've offered you help..."

"That's enough of that," Igescu said. "You two can play dice or a game of billiards for him. But the winner saves a piece for me, understood?"

"Dice won't take so long," Magda said.

The baron nodded at Glam, who clamped a hand on Childe's shoulder from behind and steered him out of the room.

Philip José Farmer

Magda called, "See you soon, lover!"

Mrs Grasatchow said, "In a pig's ass, you will!" Magda laughed and said, "He'll be in a pig's ass if you win!"

"Don't push me too far!" the fat woman shrilled.

Then Childe was being steered down the hall to its end and around the corner and down two flights of stairs. The hall here was of large grey blocks of stone. The door before which they halted was of thick black wood with iron bosses forming the outline of an archaic and grinning face. Glam shifted his grip from the shoulder to the neck and squeezed. Childe thought the blood would be pushed out of the top of his head. He went to his knees and leaned his head against the wall while his senses, and the pain in his neck, returned. Glam unlocked the door, dragged Childe into the room by one hand and dropped the hand when he came to the far wall. He completely undressed the feebly resisting Childe, lifted him up and snapped a metal collar shut around his neck. Glam picked up the clothes and went out, locking the door behind him.

There was a single unshaded light in the centre of the ceiling. The floor was covered with straw and a few blankets. The walls and ceiling were painted a light red.

When his strength came back, Childe found that the metal collar was attached by a four-foot long lightweight chain to an eyebolt sunk into the stone of the wall. He looked around but could see nothing to indicate that cameras or eyes were on him. The walls and ceiling seemed to be unbroken. However, it was possible that one or more of the stones was actually a one-way window.

There was a rattle at the door. A key clicked in the lock. The door swung open. Magda entered. She wore nothing unless you could count the key in her hand. She stood there smiling at him. Suddenly, she whirled. She said, "Who is that?" and he got a glimpse of her back, of the egg-shaped hips, as she went swiftly into the hall.

There was a thump and a gasp. Then, silence.

Childe had no idea of what was happening, but he supposed that Glam or Grasatchow had attacked Magda. He had not thought that they would dare, since the baron had made it plain exactly how far they might go.

He waited. A sound as of a bare body being dragged along the stone floor came to him. Then, more silence. Then, a whispering. This sound was not that of a human voice but the friction of silk against silk.

He jerked with fright.

Dolores del Osorojo entered the doorway. With a swirl of skirts, she turned and closed the door. She faced him then and advanced slowly towards him, her white arms held out to him. She was not transparent or semi-opaque. She was as solid as young flesh could be. Her black hair and white face and red lips and white swelling bust were solid. And sweet.

Childe was too scared to respond to the arms around him and the breasts and lips pressed close to him. He was cold, although her breath was hot and the tongue she slid back and forth over his tongue was hot. Warm saliva leaked from her mouth over his chin and down his chest.

She was panting.

Childe tried to back away. The wall stopped him. She pressed against him, and he lacked the will, or the strength, to try to push her away. He was still trembling.

The woman muttered something in Spanish. He did not understand the words, but her tone was intended to be soothing. She backed away and began to undress swiftly. The dress slid off, and the three petticoats, and then the knee-length underwear and the long black stockings and corset. Dolores, in the nude, was a magnificent woman. The breasts were full and the nipples, almost as large as the ends of his thumbs, pointed upwards slightly. The pubic hair was thick and black and a line extended from it upward, like the smoke from a distant fire, to her navel. The fluid beginning to soak her hair and run down her leg showed how deeply impatient she was.

Childe, seeing these, felt less afraid. She looked too much of the protoplasm, too little of the ectoplasm, for him to believe to the core of his mind that she was truly a ghost.

He was far from being at ease, however. And when he tried his little Spanish to ask her if she could release him, he realized that she had no intention of letting him loose. Or else she was not able to do so.

He repeated his request that she got the key from Magda. She shook her head, indicating that she would not do so or she did not understand him. Perhaps – he hoped – she meant to release him

Philip José Farmer

but only after she got what she wanted. What she wanted, for some reason or other, was Childe.

Not that it was any mystery about what she wanted. The reason why he was her choice was the mystery. At present, he could do nothing to find out.

She kissed him again and again and finally she began to play with his penis while she kissed him. He could not get an erection; the touch of her fingers turned his flesh cold as a dying man's and he shrank from her. He was, literally, spooked.

Finally, she quit kissing him. She backed away again and inspected him with stabs of her black eyes and then frowned. But she approached him again, speaking in soothing but incomprehensible Spanish, and got down on her knees in the straw. She took his limp penis into her warm mouth. She began to suck slowly, while the tips of her fingers touched the insides of his thighs where the thigh and belly met. His flesh began to warm, and the penis, as if the blood, once frozen, had suddenly become fluid, began to fill out. The old familiar but never boring sensations began to come back. He put his hands on her hair and pulled the high comb out and let it flood loose around her shoulders. He moved his hips back and forth.

Suddenly, she had unmouthed his penis and was kissing him again, running her tongue around his mouth. Then she took his penis and, rising to her toes, let herself down upon it. It slid up into her cunt; she moved back and forth a few times, and he came. There are orgasms and there are orgasms.

This was so exquisite that he passed out, very briefly, during the ejaculations.

It was as if she had sparked within the chamber of her cunt, as if a century and a half of chastity were loosed along the shaft of his cock. Or as if she had generated a current that shot lightning down his nerves. So intense was the sensation, he was not sure that he was not burned out – literally. Perhaps something electrical *had been* discharged.

Childe was restricted to an upright position because of the chain. He told the woman, the ghost, or whatever she was, to get the key from Magda, but she paid him no attention except to look at him when he was talking. He could not understand why she did not get the key, since it was to her advantage to do so. And then it occurred to him that she was probably afraid that he would take off and leave her. And she did not want that, because she had too much to unloose. Or so it seemed to him.

He was limited in his area of activity and angle of position, but Dolores was ingenious. After she had stacked his penis into a full rigidity again, drawing in on it with just the reverse action of blowing up a balloon but with the direct effect of blowing and had licked off and swallowed the spermatic fluid and cleaned off his penis in the process, she released it. She got down on her hands and knees and turned away from him and then stood up on her hands, her legs spread wide. She let herself fall frontward, towards him, and her feet struck the wall on each side of him. After working her way forward on her hands a little, she was in a position she wanted. He thought at first of refusing her, but after considering that she might leave him locked up if he did, he grabbed her hips. His penis went past and under the anus and into the slit and she rocked back and forth.

Like Magda, she could squeeze and relax upon his penis with the muscles of the vaginal sheath. He moved only a little, pulling her hips in to him with short savage jerks. Within a few seconds, she was shuddering and sobbing, apparently having one orgasm on the heels of the next. Her cries were in Spanish. He knew little of that, but he could catch, "Oh, holy fucking virgin mother Maria! Oh, father of the big cock! Fuck! Fuck! Shit! Shit! Oh, Christ, blessed Jesus, oh, sweet Jesus, he's fucking me! Fuck me, blessed flesh! Sweet flesh, fuck me!"

At that time he did not think about her words; he was just reacting. But he would remember and wonder. If she were the daughter of old Don del Osorojo, the sheltered daughter of the weird old grandee, she had a surprising vocabulary. But then, during a century and a half of hanging around live people, she could be expected to pick up words she might not have heard before death. But why hadn't she learned English in that time?

Now, he did not think of what she was saying. He was taking a long time coming, so long that he was able to turn her over, or around. Her arms were then braced below her, her feet against the wall, her cunt rammed against him, and she pushed back and forth while he reached down and rubbed her breasts and nipples with his hands. She had strong muscles; she could remain in that human-arch position, her head hanging down, and rock back and forth and occasionally stab her ass forward with no support of his hands under her hips.

After what seemed a long time, he jetted. Dolores screamed with the crescendo of climaxes. Then she let her feet slide down the wall while he helped ease her weight with his hands on her buttocks and then clamped her legs between his arms and let her slide on down. On the floor, she lay on her back, panting and looking up while spermatic fluid fell drop by drop into her open mouth. Then she scooted a little to one side to let the drops fall on her breasts and rubbed the sticky stuff over them. The chlorox odour of the fluid and the odour of sweat were strong in the chamber.

Then her breathing became normal. Dolores rose and gave him a long tonguey spermaticky kiss. Her hand fondled his testicles.

He turned his head away and said, "No more, Dolores. Or whoever or whatever you are."

His legs trembled. Fucking in bed was demanding enough, but fucking standing up took twice as much out of him. And it seemed to him that Dolores had means for draining him of more than the normal quota of energy. For a few seconds, she had given him energy – he would swear that she had discharged a current down his penis – but then the orgasms had been so exquisite that they had opened the gates to drain the reservoir.

He had no objective reason for thinking so, but he *felt* that she had robbed him of a certain amount of vital energy and strengthened and solidified herself. Certainly, she had seemed flesh enough when he had felt her. But now, she seemed to have somehow become even more solid.

Dolores, seeing him shake so, said something, smiled, and held her finger up as if to tell him to wait there. (What the hell else could he do?) And she left the room. In a few seconds, she was back with a bottle of red wine and a big chunk of filet mignon. (Did she have quick and secret access to the kitchen?) He said no to the wine but eagerly ate the meat. Although he had finished supper only a half hour ago, or so it seemed, he was very hungry.

Dolores tilted the bottle to her lips and drank. Almost, he expected to see a dark column going down the throat and into the stomach, as if she were a transparent figure in a stomach-acid commercial. But he could see only the Adam's apple moving.

If he was hungry, she was thirsty. She kept the bottle to her lips until it was half empty. She may have intended to fully empty it, but a noise came through the door, which she had left ajar. Dolores jerked and dropped the bottle. It fell on its side and spurted red wine on the straw.

She bent down and scooped up all her clothes, rolled them into a bundle, which she placed under her right arm, and then kissed him swiftly, breathing wine and sperm. She ran to the wall on his right; her left hand pushed along the juncture of two grey blocks. With a groan and a squeak, a section of wall, consisting of blocks six high and four wide, swung inward on the left side. The interior was dark. Dolores turned and smiled and threw something that glittered. He lunged for it, but the chain jerked him back, cutting off his breath, and the object bounced off his fingertips and fell on the straw.

It was the key to the lock on the metal collar.

The darkness swallowed Dolores. The section, squeaking and groaning again, swung shut.

A huge head with huge jowls, large purplish eyes, and a high-piled blue-black hairdo, came around the corner of the doorway. Mrs Grasatchow.

From behind her came excited voices. The fat woman's eyes widened. She pushed the door open and waddled across the straw to Childe. He slowly drew back the foot he had extended to try to move the key towards him.

Mrs Grasatchow sniffed loudly and then screamed. "Jism!" She grunted like a sow about to give birth. "Who's been here? Who? Tell me! Who?"

"Didn't you see her?" Childe said. "She went down the hall!"

"Who?"

"Dolores del Osorojo!"

Mrs Grasatchow's skin was naturally pale and made even whiter by her powder. But she managed to turn more white.

The baron, a long cigar in one hand, entered the room. He said, "I thought it would be Dolores. Only she..." The fat woman whirled swiftly, as graceful as a rhinoceros, which is huge but can be very graceful in certain movements.

"You said... you pooh-poohed Dolores! You said she

couldn't be any danger to us!"

The baron looked shrewdly at Childe before answering. He puffed on his cigar, and said, "It didn't seem likely that she would ever get enough plasm long enough to harden it. But I was wrong."

"What did she do to Magda?" Mrs Grasatchow said.

The baron shrugged. "We'll have to ask Magda that when she comes to. If she does."

The doorway was filled with the body of Glam. He carried Magda, still naked, in his arms. Her head lolled, her long blonde hair hung down, her arms and legs were limp.

Glam said, "What do I do with her?"

"Take her upstairs to her room. Put her to bed. Tell Vivienne to look at her."

Glam's expression flickered from stone-mask to something unreadable, and back to stone-mask. The baron said, "She's defenceless now, true. But if I were you, I wouldn't try anything."

Glam said nothing. He turned and carried the woman off. The two blonds, Chornkin and Krautschner, looked in, each from a side of the doorway.

"Did you see Dolores?" the baron said.

They shook their heads. The baron glanced at the section of wall which had opened for Dolores. He opened his mouth as if he were going to tell the two where she had gone and to send them after her. But he closed his lips.

Childe thought that perhaps the baron preferred to keep certain secrets. Didn't he trust the two? Or did he think it would be futile to chase after her? In any event, he must think that Childe had seen the exit.

"She has to be flesh enough to fuck," Mrs Grasatchow said. "Look at the redness of his cock and the jism."

"I can see," the baron said dryly. "Magda's key was gone. Childe, do you have it?"

Childe shook his head. Igescu went to the two young people and they whispered for a moment. Then they turned their backs to each other and went off down the hall, bent over, searching. The baron came back in and said, "Take your eyes off his cock, and help me look for that key."

"Here it is!" Mrs Grasatchow said.

She stooped, picked it up, and straightened, groaning. The

baron took it and put it in his jacket pocket.

Childe tightened his lips. He had no chance now, unless Dolores came back to help him. He doubted that she would. Although she had thrown the key to him, she had not made sure he had had it, and she had had time to do so. The gesture had seemed to say that he could escape if he were agile enough and clever enough. Perhaps she was resentful of her long, long frustrating imprisonment in incorporeality. She might have wanted him to suffer, too. After all, she had taken him, not because of affection or love but because she needed an object to relieve herself on.

But she was partly on his side. That was his only hope, at present.

The baron left the room, and, in a few seconds, the young people entered. The boy had the key. He unlocked the collar, and he and the girl, each holding Childe by an arm, hustled him out of the room. They passed two doors and entered the third, which was already open. This was a room the size of the one he had just left, but the walls were oak-panelled, the ceiling was painted light blue, and the floor was covered with a thick Persian rug with swastikas inside circles. There were a number of collars hanging from chains attached to bolts sunk into the wall, however. Childe was again held by a metal collar.

This room must have no secret entrances.

The baron looked at his wristwatch and said, "We have to do something about her. She wasn't dangerous until she got enfleshed. But everything has its disadvantage. Now she's dangerous, she's also vulnerable. We can do something about her, and we will. I'm going to call a conference."

Mrs Grasatchow pouted. She said, "Now Magda's out of the way, I'd thought..."

"Half an hour. No more," Igescu said. "I'll send somebody down to escort you. You wouldn't want to be alone on the way up."

The fat woman started. It was as if a tidal wave were racing through her flesh.

"You mean *I*... *I*... have to worry? That *I'm* in danger?"

She bellowed with laughter.

"We all are," the baron said. "All of a sudden, our security is gone. This," he stabbed a thumb at Childe, "has something to do with it but I don't know what. He's a focus of some sort. Maybe Dolores has been waiting for someone like him all these years.

"Half an hour," he said. "I mean it. And don't use him up. I still want a piece of him."

The baron left, closing the door behind him. Mrs Grasatchow started to take her clothes off. Childe's legs began to shake again.

Chapter 16

He told her that she was wasting her time. He did not tell her that, even if he had not been drained and weakened, he would have been unable to respond positively to her. The enormous hanging breasts, the tremendous belly, which curved out and overhung the genitals so far that they could not be seen in the shadows of the folds, the hips, sackish with fat, the tree-trunk legs, repulsed him. He doubted that he could have got a hard-on even if he were in full strength and had not had an emission for a month.

Mrs Grasatchow said, "That spook-bitch sucked you dry, heh?" And then she laughed. She was close to him; the blast of alcohol made him feel like vomiting. There must be two gallons in that pony-sized gut.

She had brought into the room a large bearskin-purse and a bottle of wine and a bottle of Scotch. She poured the wine over his belly and genitals and then got on her knees and licked them off. He did not respond.

She came up off her knees like a boulder tossed up by a volcanic explosion. Her hand struck him on the side his jaw. He saw comets and fell back, half-conscious, against the wall.

"You little asshole!" she screamed. "You may look like George, but you sure aren't the man he was!"

She waddled to her purse and took out a silvery cone about two inches long. "This will put some life into you! Once it's in you!"

Grinning, she approached him. He shrank back against the wall and then leaped out at her, striking at her. Laughing, she caught his wrist and turned it until he cried out in agony and sank to his knees as far as the chain would allow. Choking, he tried to stand up again, but she forced him down until he was almost unconscious again.

He regained his senses to find himself turned around, his face to the wall. Something – he knew it was the cone – was being shoved up his anus.

"You've never had anything like this, little man!" she crooned. "Never! You'll not forget this night, as long as you live. Oh, little man, I wish I were you just now, so I could fuck me!"

The cone burned at first and made him feel as if he had to

shit. After about half a minute, it seemed to turn icy and to become heavy, as if it were a lead sinker just removed from a freezer. The coldness and heaviness spread out, up his intestines, coil after coil, like a snake racing ahead of the Ice Age but too slow, into his testicles, which became bells ringing with chilliness, into his solar plexus, and, at the other terminus, into his penis. Liquid nitrogen pumping into every tube of his body.

He squirmed as the stuff fell down the shafts of his legs and flapped slowly spiralling up the shaft of his trunk. The powerful hands of the fat woman tightened, and she said, "Quiet, little lover. This won't hurt you, and you'll be a man such as you never were!"

The icy weight lapped at the base of his brain. His neckbones and hindbrain felt crystallized. He could distinguish each vertebra and each cell of the cerebellum as a frozen entity. He could also feel the individual vessels of his penis slowly filling with half-frozen blood. By then, Mrs Grasatchow had turned him around again and was down on her elephantine knees and sucking on his penis. She grunted as if she were a sow tearing into a corncob, but, as far as he could detect, he was being treated gently enough. Her jaws did not move, only her lips, shaped around the glans, moved. He could feel nothing. He might as well have had a hundred local shots of morphine over his body and one massive shot in his penis. But if his brain was receiving no tactile message, part of his body was. The penis, like an independent creature, a leech stuck in her mouth and drawing blood from her tongue, was gradually filling up.

When she felt that it was as swollen and rigid as it could be, she stood up. She said, "You're not going any place, not now!" She unlocked the collar and put the key in her purse. He tried to run from her to the door, but his legs would not move.

She lay down on the floor and spread her thighs open – it was like the Red Sea splitting to make passage for the horde of Moses – and she said, "Eat me!"

Obediently, although his frozen brain tried to push out a message of resistance to his nerves, he got down and spread the slit open and prepared to tongue the clitoris first, as was his habit.

She said, "No, idiot! The other way! Sixty-nine!"

He crawled up on to her and swivelled around. She took in his penis until his hairs pressed against her lips. He could not feel this, but he looked through the space that existed briefly between their bodies and saw the hairs and the narrow band of the root. He flicked the tip of his tongue over the "little penis". A "little penis" this clitoris was. He had never seen such an enormous one. He did have some difficulty getting to it, however, because her belly was so huge. It was like having to curve over a hill, hanging upside down, to lick at a spring in a crevasse at the bottom of the hill.

The worst of it was, he felt no sexual stimulation only disgust. But he had to do exactly as she said, and his organs, outside of the brain, must be responding to some sensory input.

At another order, he withdrew his penis from her mouth and turned around and inserted his penis into her vagina. He began pumping slowly but soon speeded up in response to her command. She began groaning and moaning, turning her head from side to side, crying out in a foreign language, rolling the great hips sideways and then thrusting and now and then lifting herself up from the waist and grabbing his buttocks and pulling and pushing him.

He did not know how long they were in this position nor whether or not he had an orgasm. But the time came when she rolled him off her, the uncoupling wetly announced itself, and she got above him and eased herself down upon his penis and moved the great body as lightly and swiftly as a toy balloon on the end of a string. After what seemed to be a hundred orgasms, judging by her number of frenzies, she got off him and went to the corner after her bottle of whisky. He seemed able to move a little on his own volition, so he turned to watch her. She sat on the rug, leaning against the wall, looking like an over-yeasted mass of dough.

Childe became aware that he was gasping. He could hear his breath rattling in and out, but he could not feel the thudding of his heart nor the moving of his ribs.

Mrs Grasatchow downed at least a fourth of the quart and then looked at her wristwatch.

"Forty-five minutes," she said. "Igescu will be furious."

She heaved herself up and said, "Hmm! What's wrong? He said he'd send somebody after me."

She opened the door and looked down the hallway. Childe tried to run towards her then, hoping to knock her down with his momentum and get away down the hall. He only managed, after a seemingly long time, to get to his feet. If he had exerted himself prodigiously, he did not know it. Reception from his muscles was still cut off.

On seeing him move, the woman's eyebrows went up, and she said, "Do you feel that suppository burning now?"

"No," he said. "It's still cold and heavy."

"You'll feel it in a moment. You'll think a hot-air balloon is going up your ass!"

A laughquake shook her. Afterward, she said, "That stuff has a very peculiar effect. You didn't feel anything while you were fucking me, but wait. I wish I could take advantage of you then, but you'll have to enjoy yourself with yourself."

She looked at her wristwatch again. "Maybe I won't go. I think Igescu has forgotten me. Or he knows I'll be very angry indeed if I don't get all of you. Now, you just stand right there, little Georgey Porgey Pudding and Pie. I'll fix you up again, and double the effect. I don't want you acting up on me."

As if a bore tide had reversed and was running back to sea, the coldness and heaviness became warmth and lightness. The second effect started where the first had ended, in the brain and the tip of his glans. The warmth and lightness raced inward from all borders and met in the region of the cone, in his anus, where, for a second, it burned as if a meteorite had just ended its fiery curve there.

He cried out with the pain.

The fat woman said, "Oh, oh! It's happened!" and she charged, one hand open to grab him and another cone in the other hand. She seemed to grow as large as the wall. Her flesh shook like a loose robe in a stiff wind. Childe launched himself at her, his hands out to grab her ears, because he meant to tear them off. He would have had to fight savagely to get past her to the door. Even when he had his full strength, he would have been out-muscled by her, not to mention outweighed.

His hands caught her ears, and his face thrust into one breast as violently as if he had been dropped from the ceiling on to her. She screamed, because he had bitten down on the excrescence suddenly appearing between his teeth. It was her nipple, as he found out when he got up from the floor where she had thrown him. He spat out the piece of flesh – the nipple and some white skin around it – and rose shakily. She was still screaming and rolling back and forth and clutching her mutilated breast.

Childe did not wait to completely recover from the impact of the floor. Fighting dizziness and a pain in his shoulder, he kicked her between her legs as she started to roll towards him. His big toe disappeared momentarily in her slit. She screamed again. A flailing arm knocked his leg out from under him. He fell crosswise on top of her belly. She clamped her arms down on his buttocks and then one hand slid down to grab his testicles. With a desperate jerk, he turned over to face her, still crosswise, seized a breast, and twisted.

Her arms came up; she screamed again. Childe rolled away across her belly and down her legs. It was like rolling down a small hill. He got out of the way of her kicking legs and leaped up and came down with both bare feet on her face. Her head was driven back against the floor; her nose smashed; blood burst; her eyes crossed.

Again, he leaped and came down with both feet on her belly. He sank deep. Her wind whooshed out, as if somebody had opened a big door to a distillery with a strong cross-draught. He almost gagged. But he jumped a third time, once more on her face. Her nose became even flatter. Her eyes rolled up until only the whites showed. Her mouth was wide open, braced like a sail against the wind of her agony to get her breath back.

And, at that moment, the cone reversed its effect. It was as if the entire coition with her had been recorded with a glass window between himself and his nerve endings. He could see but could not hear. Now, the glass was gone, and he could hear the rerun. With this difference. He was no longer frozen. He now felt everything exquisitely; he could feel his cock in her mouth and between her breasts and in her cunt, even though they were no longer there.

During the fight, though he had not been aware of it, he had had an erection. Now, he jetted, and the delayed reaction orgasm stormed his body. He fell to the floor and writhed helplessly, if ecstatically in its lightnings. There was nothing else, for the moment, he could do.

Philip José Farmer

Chapter 17

When he could regain control, he got up and staggered towards the door. Although his penis no longer spouted, it remained as hard as before and did not have the delicious emptied-to-good-purpose feeling of an after-orgasm. It did feel pleasurable, increasingly pleasurable, as if he were again working up to coition. He could, however, ignore it for the present.

Mrs Grasatchow still lay on her back, arms and legs outflung, her mouth open, and her eyes open and showing white, as if hardboiled eggs had been stuffed into the sockets.

He noticed a large turd spread out on the rug between him and Mrs Grasatchow. So, he had been "scared shitless" sometime during the fight. He had not known when he spurted out the excrement; it did not matter. He was sure he had expelled the turd and not she, although it was possible that she had when he had jumped on her face. It was, however, so far from her that he doubted it.

Gingerly stepping by the turd, he walked to her purse, which was near the door. In it he found the key to the door. She had locked the door after looking down the hallway the last time. He unlocked it and, carrying her purse, went down the hall towards the room in which he had been originally imprisoned.

First, though he hated the idea of any delay, he had to investigate the other rooms along the hall. There was always the chance of other prisoners there. Perhaps Sybil was in one. Six doors were closed. Three were unlocked and contained not much of interest. Three opened to the key from the fat woman's purse.

The first two were small rooms with padded walls and floor. The third contained some furniture, modern Danish, with a colour TV set, a well-stocked bar, a pool table, and cartons of cigarettes and cigars and boxes of marijuana sticks and bottles of pills of various sizes, shapes, and colours. It looked as if it might be a rest room or recreation room. The occupants could relax here between their working bouts in the other room. There was also a large bureau with a mirror, which he did not think was one-way. The top of it was crowded with cosmetics and held some wigs.

He opened the drawers, hoping to find some clothes he

could wear. Before he could examine one, he was overcome with another semi-epileptic orgasm and jetted over the clothes in the top drawer. There was a wash room which he used to clean his genitals, face and hands, and his mouth. He drank several glasses of water and returned to the bureau.

There were some T-shirts and gym shorts. He found some that were near enough to his size and put them on. Then it occurred to him that he was going to have another ejaculation soon and would be very uncomfortable. It was either that or stick his cock out. He decided on the latter, although he felt ridiculous. And he looked ridiculous in the mirror. A knight with a stubby delicate lance. Some knight! Some detective! A private dick become public.

There were some socks but no shoes. He put the socks on and continued his search. If only a weapon were here. No luck. Too much to hope for, of course. The two lower drawers were crammed with flat transparent plastic envelopes containing something unidentifiable. He opened one and shook out the contents. It fluttered out like a transparent flag to a length of about six feet. It had four extensions, a thick mass of hair on one end, and a circular mass of hair in the middle. Just beside the thick mass of hair was a small red valve like that on a child's plastic inflatable swimming pool. He blew it up and felt weakened by the exertion before he had completed the job.

After seeing what he had, he was horrified, although he had suspected what the result would be.

Somehow, Colben's skin had been stripped from his body and made into a balloon. The apertures: earholes, mouth, anus, and the mutilated penis, had been sewn over with the flaps of skin. His eyes had been painted blue, and the mouth was painted with a facsimile of labial red. The pubic hairs were still attached, and these, together with the sewed fold between his legs, gave him a womanish appearance.

Childe did not have time to deflate him. He pushed him sailing away, and frantically removed the contents of the other envelopes. One was the head of Budler. He presumed that the wolf in the film had eaten the rest of Budler or so mangled it that it could not be used for a balloon. His head went spinning over and over towards the corner, where Colben, turned upside down by the weight of his hair and the valve on the back of his neck, stood on

Philip José Farmer

his head.

There were a number of women, only four of whom had the right length or colour of hair for Sybil. Despite this, he inflated all of them. When he had blown up the last one, he was panting as if he had run a half-mile through the smog. The effort was only partly responsible. He had been so certain that the last one would have Sybil's features.

He sat down and sipped on another glass of water. There were thirty-eight skins at one end of the room. Most of them were upside down, but a few had fallen against the others and leaned one way or another. The light from a lamp in the corner shone through many of them so that they seemed a mob of drunken ghosts. The draught from the air-conditioning moved them back and forth a little so that they also seemed like phantoms of the drowned.

Thirty-eight. Twenty-five males. Thirteen females. Of the males, fifteen were Caucasians, seven were Negroes, three were Mongolians or Indians. Of the females, nine were Caucasians and four were Negresses.

All were adults. If any had been children, he would not have been able to endure it. He would have run screaming down the hall. He thought he was tough, but he would not have been able to stand the sight of the inflated skins of children.

As it was, he was angry and sick. More angry than sick at the moment. What were they planning on doing with these... these corpse-balloons? Fill them with hydrogen and send them flying over Los Angeles?

That was probably exactly what they did plan on doing. It would be on a par with, no, would surpass, the effrontery of the films.

He rose and took a bottle of vodka by the neck and went back to the doorway of the room in which he had left Mrs Grasatchow. She was sitting up and vomiting. Blood was still trickling from her nostrils. On seeing Childe, she snarled and managed to lift herself to her feet. Blood and vomit smeared her immense belly.

"You'll beg me to kill you!" she screamed.

"Why will I?" he said. He stepped inside the room. "Before I kill you, I want you to tell me why you did that to all those people? And why did you strip off their skins?"

"I'll rip your balls off!" she shouted. She charged him then; he braced himself, the bottle lifted high. But she stepped on the turd and her feet shot up and ahead of her and she fell heavily on her back. She lay there, groaning but seemingly knocked out. He hit her, once, on the side of her head with the bottle she had dropped and then locked the door to the room. The bottle in one hand and her purse on the other arm, and his penis sticking out what a hero I make! he thought – he entered the room in which he had first been chained.

But he came out of it at once and went into the recreation room. He needed evidence. The police wouldn't believe much of his story after he told it, but they would have to believe that a part of it was true when he showed them Colben and Budler. And another picked at random who might turn out to have been reported missing.

The deflation was as ghastly as he had expected. The air hissed out, and Budler and the woman shrank like the witch on whom Dorothy had thrown water. But Colben – he always was slippery – got away and shot around the room, butting into several of the phantoms and knocking them head over heels. He came to rest draped over the bar. Childe pulled him off the bar then as he had pulled him away several times when he was living. He rolled him up and stuffed him into the purse on top of Budler's head and the red-headed woman.

The section of wall opened for him after a number of experiments of running his hand along the juncture of the blocks which Dolores had pressed. He stepped inside with a pencil-flashlight taken from the purse. The section swung shut behind him, and he began walking slowly. The passageway was warm and dusty and narrow. It led past several rooms, each of which had a one-way mirror but no entrance that he could detect. They were similar to those lining the other hallway. A stairway confronted him. He walked up this uneasily, although he did not think that it could be a trap, since he was deep in the earth. But he could not be sure. At the top, he was in a passageway which offered him two routes. There were prints in the dust, a long pointed shoeprint which he presumed was the baron's and those of a dog or a wolf. The latest led to the right, so he decided to follow them. One way was as good as another, and something had to decide him.

Philip José Farmer

His flashlight showed him several squares in the walls. When he opened these, he saw through one-way mirrors into a number of rooms, one of which he thought he remembered. It was a Louis Quatorze bedroom, but it did not seem quite like the one he remembered. It did have an entrance through the panelling. He took it and after stepping softly around it and looking into the bathroom, knew this was not the same room. The queer disturbing mirror was missing. He started to open the door to look out into the next room or the hallway but thought better of it. He placed his ear against the wood and was glad that he had done so. The murmur of voices came through the wood.

The keyhole let him hear more clearly but not clearly enough. After turning off all the lights in the room, he turned the knob carefully and eased the door open. The voices came from the end of the hall. He could see partway down it but not far enough to see the speakers. The voices were identifiable, except for two. These could be Chornkin's and Krautschner's since they had not spoken when introduced or at the dinner table. They could also be those of newcomers.

"...much energy from Magda, as I said before," Igescu was saying loudly. He seemed exasperated and, perhaps, a little frightened. "I think Dolores had gathered enough around her to take a tangible and enduring shape, enough to render Magda powerless for a moment and suck her almost dry. She didn't kill Magda but she came damn close. And then Glam, that damn fool! He deserved what he got! But then what can you expect from his kind? Glam fucked her, although I'd warned him often enough, what might happen. I think he thought he was safe. But the very act of fucking gave her energy enough; she came to and found Glam in her, how she hated him! And you saw Glam!"

The strange male voice interrupted softly. Childe could not understand what he was saying. Igescu's reply was loud enough.

"Yes, Magda got the energy but not enough! She's stuck in stasis, and she won't get out unless she kills another! Which will mean someone here, in this house!"

The strange female voice spoke then; it was even softer than the male's. Igescu said, "Childe would do it! I had other plans for him, but I can give them up! We have to find Magda first and get her to Childe! Otherwise...!"

"Dolores?" Mrs Pocyotl said.

Childe could almost see the baron's shrug. The baron said, "Who knows? She's X! A dangerous X! If she can do that to Magda, she can do that to any of us. But I doubt that she could attack more than one of us at a time and I think she'd have to surprise us, just as she must have surprised Magda! So, we'd better hang together, as..."

A shout interrupted him. Footsteps sounded. The group was going around the corner and down the stairs to the cause of commotion. More shouts. He swung the door wider and peeped down the hall. The only one there was Bending Grass, who leaned his stocky form against the wall and cocked his head to look down the stairway. Then somebody called his name and he disappeared.

Childe ran down the hallway to the only door opened. This was by the head of the steps, and the group had been assembled outside it. He stuck his head in. The room was strange, looked more like a movie director's idea of a Turkish harem than anything else. There were rugs and drapes and cushions and ottomans and even a hookah and a dresser so low that Magda must have had to sit cross-legged while she looked in the mirror. There was a marble-lined bath sunk level with the floor. It was almost large enough to qualify as a small swimming pool. Beyond it was a low marble enclosure which presumably had served Magda as a bed, since it was piled with cushions and pillows and canopied with many silk veils.

Glam's black soft-leather boots stuck out over the enclosure. Childe walked swiftly in, past the bath, which was full of cold water, and looked over the marble railing. Glam had died with his boots on. Also, his pants. He had stripped off his shirt and undershirt and pulled his pants down around his knees, but he had been too eager to bother taking all his clothes off.

There was blood on his pants and much blood on his body. Blood had spurted out from his ears, nostrils, eyes, mouth, anus, and penis. Something had violently squeezed him. The ribs were caved in; the arms were flattened; the hip bones had been pushed inward towards each other. Not only blood had been expelled from every aperture. The contents of the bowels and about six feet of the bowels themselves had been pressed out of his anus.

Near the bed, a section of wall stood open. Whether Magda

Philip José Farmer

had taken this or Igescu had opened it to see if she had taken it, Childe could not know. But he could not linger long here; his route of escape was suddenly no longer a matter of choice. Voices announced the return of the others. He might have had time to slip back through the door and up the hallway, but he did not dare chance it. He went through the opening in the wall.

Before he had taken a dozen steps, he was seized. He groaned with a despairing ecstasy and braced himself with both hands against the walls while he spouted and shook. Afterwards, he cursed, but he could do nothing about his condition. He walked on. His penis still stuck straight out and slightly at an upward angle, like the bowsprit of a ship. The cone was working within him. God knew how long its effect lasted, how long it would take to melt entirely away.

Almost, he decided to hide in the passageway near the still open panel and eavesdrop. But every second he was in the house meant recapture or death, and he was frightened because of what had happened to Glam and of what the others had said about Magda. Frightened was not strong enough. He was close to panic. And this was strange, because the terror should have taken from him any sexual stimulation whatsoever. Under these circumstances, he should have been unable to retain an erection. But there it was, independent of his other feelings, as if a switch had been thrown to place his genitals on a separate circuit. The cone, whatever it was, must not only be the prime mover of his state, it must also be the prime feeder. It had to be furnishing the energy to keep manufacturing all this spermatic fluid at such an extraordinary – for him – rate of speed. Generally, when unusually stimulated, when first in love, or sometimes when the marijuana hit him just right, he could have three or four orgasms within several hours. But, usually, one or two in an hour, and he was done for four or five hours. He had sometimes twitted himself with being the most undersexed private eye in history, without, of course, really believing his self-deprecation. But now, he seemed to be a fountain with a never-ending reservoir. And, of course, he *would* be so in a situation where it was the last thing he wanted.

Thus, when he thought he was far enough away from the panelling, he turned on the flashlight. And he saw the white figure of Dolores coming towards him. Her arms were open and she was smiling. Her eyes were half-lidded but bright, and two patches of wetness shone on her thighs. It seemed to be his misfortune to encounter over-lubricating women. However, after a century and a half of enforced abstinence, she could not be blamed.

She barred his way. She was solid flesh enough, no man knew that better than he, yet he hesitated to attack her. The fate of Magda was warning enough. Moreover, there was the chance that if he did what she wanted, he might work off the effect of the cone. It was just possible. And he thought that he probably had no choice, anyway. So he put down his purse, turned off the flashlight, and dropped his pants. She pulled him down on her and he put his penis in swiftly and began to thrust without preliminaries of any kind. He had hoped that he would come at once, but even though he now had her soft wet flesh around his penis, and though the pleasure was somewhat heightened, he was unable to disengage himself from the automatic effects of the cone.

At length he came and then, when he tried to pull himself away, he found himself unable to. Her arms looked feminine and soft enough and felt so, but she had the strength of a python in each.

Thinking of pythons made him think of Magda, and he became even more alarmed. If she came upon them now, she would have him helpless... those coils... Glam... He shuddered even as he began to pump again. His skin had turned cold and his hairs felt as if they were bristling in the static of terror. His anus was a dot of ice, a bull's eye for Magda if she crawled up behind him and raised her head to unloose a hammer stroke.

He groaned and muttered, "I must be out of my mind, I'm really believing that crap!" and then he groaned this time because he was coming once more.

It was no use. Lying with Dolores was not cancelling or even diminishing the effects of the cone. And he was certainly not stupid enough to bang away at her for the sheer pleasure of it while his life was in danger. Especially since he had had enough of this "pleasure" to last him for a long time.

He tried to break loose. Her arms did not tighten, but they also did not relax. He was not going to get out until he had satisfied her or was unable to keep an erection, and she was not going to be satisfied for a long time and he did not know how long he would

Philip José Farmer

last, but he suspected that he would last for hours and hours.

Remembering what he had done to Mrs Grasatchow during the fight, he bit down upon Dolores' nipple. His bite did not take the nipple off, but it was painful enough to cause her to open her arms and to scream. He was out of her embrace and had jumped away to where she could not reach him, pulling up his pants, stooped to pick up the flashlight and purse, and was running down the passageway, before she had stopped screaming.

The noise, of course, would be heard in Magda's room if the panelling were still open, and they would be investigating. His flashlight beam bounded up and down and then went off into darkness at a corner. He stopped and probed around. Apparently, he was at a dead end, but he did not believe it. Shouts behind him sent him into a frenzy of tapping and poking against the wall to activate whatever mechanism moved this section. He felt somebody brush his shoulder, somebody spoke in Spanish, and a white arm reached past him and touched a cornice. Another arm pushed in on another cornice. The blank wall became a blank darkness in which the thin beam was lost. A hand pushed him on through – he seemed to be paralysed for a few seconds – and then he turned just in time to see the section swing back into place. Beyond, the beam from a large flashlight flicked into existence.

A hand, still greasy from playing with his penis, slipped in his and the white figure led him down a passageway and up a flight of steps. The dust was thick here; he sneezed resoundingly several times, Igescu would have no trouble following them because of their newly made footprints. They had to get out of the secret ways, for a while, anyway.

Dolores, whose footprints were as clear as his, seemed to realize that they betrayed them. She stopped before a wall, unfastened several latches and slid back the section. They stepped into a room with grey-and-white marble walls, red marble ceiling, black-and-red marble floor, and furniture of white or black marble. The chandelier was a mobile composed of thin curved pieces of coloured marble with sockets for candles.

Dolores led him across the room. She dropped his hand and her right hand was pressed against her breast, which must hurt very much. Her face was expressionless, but the hot black eyes seemed to promise him revenge. If she had wanted it, she could have abandoned him in the passageway, he thought. Perhaps she wanted to take revenge personally.

He caught a glimpse of them as they passed a tall mirror. They looked like two lovers who had been interrupted in bed and who were fleeing a jealous husband. She was naked, and his penis, still wet and tipped with a globule of spermatic fluid, was projecting from his fly. They looked comical enough; the purse added an incongruous, doubtful touch.

There was nothing comical about the pack behind them. He crowded on Dolores' heels and urged her to go faster. She said something and half-ran through the door and down and down a luxurious hall with thick carpeting. Near the end of the hall, by a curving stairway with marble steps and a carved mahogany handrail, she pushed open another door. There was a suite of four rooms done in opulent Edwardian style. The bedroom contained the entrance to the intramural passageway; a bookcase slid aside to reveal an iron gate of two sections locked by a combination lock. Dolores turned the knob swiftly as if she had much practice with it. The two sections of gate could then be pushed aside. When they were on the other side, she pushed them together and spun the combination dial on this side. Apparently, this action activated a mechanism, because the bookcase slid back into place. The light through the opening had shown him that they were not in a passageway but in a small room. Cool air moved past him. Dolores turned on a lamp. He saw several chairs, a bed, a TV set, a bar, a dresser with mirror, books, and cabinets. The cabinets held cans of food and delicacies; one cabinet was the door to a well-stocked refrigerator. A door off the room led to a bathroom and a closet full of clothes. Igescu could hide here for a long time if he wished.

Dolores spoke in Spanish, slowly. He understood the simple sentence. "Here we are safe for a while."

"About my biting you, Dolores," he said. "I had to. I must get out of here."

She paid him no attention. She looked at her breast in the mirror and murmured something. Teethmarks and a red aureole ringed the nipple. She turned and shook her finger at him and then smiled, and he understood that she was gently reprimanding him for being over-passionate. He must not bite her again. After which warning, she took his hand and pulled him towards the bed.

He lunged away, tearing loose from her grip, and said, "Nothing doing! Show me the way out of here! *Vámanos! Pronto!*"

He began to inspect the walls. She spoke slowly behind him. Her words were clear and simple enough. If he would stay for a little, he would be shown the way out. But no more biting.

"No more nothing," he said. He found the control, a piece of corner carving which could be moved on a pivot. The dresser moved out on one side. He went through while Dolores yelled at him from the room. She sounded so much like Sybil giving him hell, although he understood not a word, that he was able to ignore her. He carried a sharp-edged rapier, one of a set on the wall, in one hand and the flashlight in the other. The handle of the purse was over his left shoulder. The blade gave him confidence. He did not feel so helpless now. In fact, if he got a chance, he would leave the passageway and walk out the front door and if they got in his way, they would get the blade where it would do them the least good and him the most.

The way out did not come easily, however. The passageway ran into a stairway which led steeply upward into the shadows. He backtracked to look for one-way windows or entrances to rooms but could find no unlocking controls. So he returned to the stairway, which he walked up with as little weight on his feet as possible. He stuck the sword through his belt and held the flashlight in his teeth while he braced his arms against the walls. If the stairway straightened out, it would not drop him down a chutey-chute.

The stairs held, and he was on a narrow landing. The door was easily opened by a conventional knob. He stepped cautiously out into a curving-walled room with a great window lit by the moon, a dim pale eye in the haze. Looking through the window, he saw the yard and trees and driveway at the front of the central portion. He was in the cupola on the left wing, just beside the original Spanish building. It contained three rooms, two of which were empty. The door to the third was part way open, and light streamed through it. He crouched by it and slowly extended his head, then had to withdraw it while he shook and spurted and clenched his teeth and clamped his lips to keep from groaning.

Chapter 18

Afterwards, he looked through the doorway again. The baron's great-grandmother was sitting on a high stool before a high table with a sloping top, such as old-time bookkeepers (Bob Cratchit) used when they wrote accounts (for Ebenezer Scrooge). He could not see what was on the table except that it was a large paper of some sort. Her jaws were moving, and now and then he could hear something but could not tell if the words were English or not. The only light was from a single lamp suspended from the ceiling directly overhead. It dimly showed walls with large, thick, black painted symbols, none of which he recognized; a long table with racks of bottles containing fluids; a globe of Earth with all sorts of curlicues painted in thin lines over it, sitting at the end of the table; a large birdcage on a stand in one corner with a raven, its head stuck under a wing; and a robe hanging on a hook on the wall.

After a few minutes of muttering, the baroness got down off the stool. Her bones snapped and creaked, and he did not think she would make it to the robe, she shuffled so slowly and shakily. But she got the robe down and put it on with some difficulty and then proceeded with one foot dragging after the other towards the long table. She stooped, groaning, and straightened up with more creakings and with an enormous book in her arms which she had taken off a shelf beneath the table.

It did not seem likely that she would get far with this additional burden, but she made it, huffing and creaking and even lifted the book above her head to slide it over the front of the tilted-top table. The book slid down until stopped by a strip of wood fixed horizontally halfway up the top. Another strip at the lower edge of the top kept the paper from falling off. He could see that it was a map of the Los Angeles area, just like the maps service stations give to their customers.

His view of it was blocked by the baroness, who climbed back upon the stool, swaying so that he once started to go after her to catch her. She did not fall, and he settled back, asking himself what he cared if she fell. But conditioning took over at the oddest moments, and he had been taught to be kind and respectful to old ladies.

Philip José Farmer

The back of the robe was white with a number of large symbols, some of which duplicated those on the wall. The old woman lifted her arms to flap the wide sleeves as if she were an ancient bird about to make a final flight. She began chanting loudly in a foreign tongue which sounded like that used at times by others in the household. Her arms waved; a large gold ring on a finger glinted dully at times, seeming like an eye winking at him.

After a while she stopped chanting and clambered down off the stool again. She tottered to the table and mixed up several of the fluids in the bottles in a glass and drank the contents. She belched loudly; he jumped at its loudness and unexpectedness. She got back on the stool and began to turn the pages of the huge book and, apparently, read a few phrases from each page.

Childe guessed that he was looking upon a genuine magical ritual, genuine in that the witch believed in her magic. What its object was, he did not know. But he felt chilled when he suddenly thought that perhaps she was trying to locate him or influence him by means of this ritual. Not that he believed she could. It was just that he did not like the idea. At another time and under different circumstances, he would have laughed. Too much had happened tonight, however, for him to make light of anything in this house.

Nor did he have any reason to crouch here in the doorway as if waiting to be born. He had to get out, and the only way was past the baroness. There was a door beyond the table; that door, as far as he knew, was the sole exit from the cupola, except for the way by which he had come. That door probably led to a hallway which would lead to a stairway to the lower floors or to a window to the top of a porch.

He doubted that he could get by her without being seen. He would have to knock her out or, if necessary, kill her. There was no reason why he should be gentle. She had to know what was going on here and probably had participated in her younger days or, for all he knew, still did.

Sword in hand, he stood up and walked slowly towards her. Then he stopped. Above her, a very thin haze, greenish-grey, shapeless with some short curling tentacles, had appeared. It could be accounted for if she were smoking. She was not. And the haze grew thicker and spread out sideways and down but not upward.

Childe tried to blink it away. The smoke flowed over her

grey Psyche knot of hair and down her neck and over the shoulders of the robe. She was chanting even more loudly and turning the pages of the book more swiftly. She could not be looking up to read the book; her head was bent so far forward that she had to be staring at the map.

Childe felt a little disorientated again. It was as if something were wrong with the world, however, not with him. Then he shook his head and decided to tiptoe by her if he could. She seemed so intent, she might not see him. If the smoke grew thicker, that is, if there indeed *was* smoke and he was not suffering another hallucination, he would be hidden from her.

The smoke did expand and become denser. She was sitting in a ragged column of it. And she was suddenly coughing. Smoke blew out of the way of her breath and then coiled back in to fill the gap. He caught a whiff of a tendril and stepped back. It was acrid, burning, filled with the essence of a million automobile exhausts and smokestack products of chemical factories and refineries.

By now, he was opposite her and could see that the cloud had spread downward and was beginning to cover the map.

She looked up, as if she had suddenly detected his presence. She squalled and fell backward off the stool but whirled and landed on all fours and then was up and running towards the doorway through which he had just come. He was startled for a second at her swiftness and agility but recovered and went after her. She had slammed the door before he could stop her, and when he turned the knob and pulled on it, he found that the door was locked. To break it down was useless, since she would be long gone down the stairway and the passageway.

No, there was Dolores. She might stop the old woman. Then, again, she might not. Her position in this situation was ambiguous. He suspected that her attitude would be what was best for Dolores and that might not coincide with what would be good for him. It would be good sense to quit chasing after the baroness and try to get out before she could warn the others.

The smog over the table was disappearing swiftly and was gone by the time he left the room. The door led directly into an elevator cage which must have been made about 1890. He hated the idea of being trapped in it but he had no other way out. He pressed the DOWN button. Nothing happened except that a small light glowed above the button and a lever near it. He pushed down the lever, and the elevator began to sink. When he pushed the lever upward past the neutral position, the elevator stopped. He pressed the UP button and then pushed the lever upward, and the elevator began to ascend. Satisfied that he could operate it, he started it downward and stopped at the second storey. If the alarm had been given, they would be waiting for him on the ground floor. They might also be waiting on every floor, but he had to take some chances.

The door was just like the other doors, which was why he may not have known about the elevator. He turned the knob and pushed it and found himself near the door to Magda's bedroom. At the same time, increasingly loud voices and rapid footsteps came up the stairway. He didn't have time to run down the hall and try other doors. He slipped into the room again. Glam's body was still in the marble enclosure, the boots sticking over it. The wall-section was open. He considered for a moment hiding under the many pillows and cushions inside the enclosure but decided that he would be found if they moved Glam's body. There was nothing to do except enter again the passage behind the wall.

He hid behind the inner wall and waited. The first one to step through was going to get a sword in his neck or his guts. The sword trembled in his grip, partly from weariness and partly from nervousness. He had had no experience in swordplay, no fencing lessons, no instructions or conditioned reflexes built up, and so he suddenly realized that he was not as dangerous as he would have liked to be. To handle a sword expertly, a man had to know where to thrust and where not to thrust. An ill-placed stab could hit a bone and glance off and leave the intended victim only lightly wounded and able to run off or attack, if he were tough and experienced. Even a hard musculature could turn an inept thrust.

He swore. He had been so intent on what he was going to do with the sword that he had not noticed that his penis was working up to another orgasm. Stormed, he dropped the sword with a clatter but did not care about the noise for a few seconds. He jetted, the chlorox odour rising strong in the dusty hot passageway. Then he picked up the sword and waited, but he was even more uneasy. Those people out there might have nostrils more sensitive than human beings – he admitted by now that they were not human, as he knew human – and they might easily detect the jism. Should he move on? If so, where? To the same circuit?

He had been running long enough. It was time to fight fire with fire.

Fire.

He looked through the opening. The door of the room was still shut. Loud voices came through it. A savage squeal which chased cold over him. It sounded like an enraged hog. More shouts. Another squeal. The voices seemed to drift away, down the hall. He crept out and inspected the room and found what he wanted. There were books in the shelves, the pages of which he tore out. He crumpled up a *Los Angeles Times* and piled crumpled book-pages over them and ripped open several pillows and sprinkled their contents on the pile. The cigarette lighter in the purse touched off the papers, which soon blazed up and began feeding on the wall-drapes under which the fire had been built.

He opened the door to the hall to open the way for a draught – if it should exist. Taking the classified ad sections of the *Times* and a number of books, he went into the passageway. Having found a one-way mirror, he broke it with the hilt of his sword to make another draught or a reinforcement of the first. He started a fire in the passageway, which was made of old and dry wood and should soon be blazing like the underbrush in the hills at the end of a long dry season. He then entered the room with the broken mirror and built a fire under a huge canopied bed.

Why hadn't he done this before? Because he had been too harried to have time to think, that was why. No more. He was fighting back.

If he could find a room with windows to the outside, he would go through it, even if it meant a drop from the second storey. He'd let them worry about the fire while he got over the walls to his car and back to the police.

He heard voices outside the door to the room and went back into the passageway. He ran down it, using his flashlight, although the fire was providing an adequate twilight for him. A corner took him away from it, however. He stopped and sent the beam down one corridor to check ahead of him. Nothing there. He started to turn to probe the corridor on the other side of the intersection, and he froze. Something had growled at the far end.

Faint clicks sounded. Claws or nails on the naked boards of the floor?

A howl made him jump.

It was a wolf.

Suddenly, the clicking, which had been leisurely, became rapid. The wolf howled again. He turned his flashlight on the corner of the passageway at the far end just in time to see a big grey shape come around it, eyes glowing in the beam. Then, the shape, snarling, was bounding towards him.

And behind it came another.

Childe thrust almost blindly at the hurtling shape. His sword travelled in the general direction of the beast as it sprang, but its speed and ferocious voice disconcerted him. Despite this, the blade struck it squarely somewhere. A shock ran along his arm, and, although he had leaned forward in what he hoped was a reasonable imitation of a fencer's lunge, he was thrown backward. He landed on his rump but scrambled to his feet, yelling as he did so. The flashlight, which had fallen, was pointing down along the floor at the second wolf. This was several yards away and crouching as it advanced slowly towards Childe.

It was smaller, the bitch of the pair, and presumably had slowed down to find out what was going on before it attacked.

Childe did not want to expose his side to the bitch, but he did not want to meet her charge without a weapon. He grabbed the hilt of the rapier, put his foot on the body, and pulled savagely. The carcass was palely illuminated in the side-wash of the flashlight. The sword shone dully, and darkness stained the fur around the beast's neck. The rapier had gone in three-quarters of its length, through the neck and out past the bottom rear of the skull.

The rapier pulled out reluctantly but swiftly. The she-wolf snarled and bounded forward, her nails clicking briefly. Childe had a few inches of blade to withdraw yet and would have been taken on the side. Her jaws would probably have clamped on his shoulder or head, and that would have been the end of him. A wolf's jaws were strong enough to sever a man's wrist with one snap.

The bitch, however, slipped on something and skidded on one shoulder into the rump of the dead wolf. Childe leaped backward, taking the sword with him and then as quickly lunged and ran her through the shoulder as she bounded to her feet. She snarled again and her jaws clashed at him, but he pushed with all his weight against the hilt and drove her back so that she fell over the dead wolf. He continued to push, digging his heels into the wood. The blade sank deeper and presently the tip ground against the floor. Before that, the bitch was silent and still.

Shaking, breathing as if his lungs needed oil, he pulled the rapier out and wiped it on the she-wolf's fur. He picked up the flashlight and ran its beam over the wolves to make sure they were dead. Their outlines were becoming indistinct. He felt dizzy and had to shut his eyes and lean against the wall. But he had seen what the bitch had slipped on. A smear of his semen.

Voices drifted around the corner from which the wolves had come. He ran down the passageway, hoping that they would become too occupied with fighting the fires to chase him. The corridor ran into another at right angles to it, and he took the left turn. His beam, dancing ahead of him, picked out a section of wall, and a locking mechanism. He went through it, his sword ready, but he was unable to restrain his wheezing. Any occupant of the room, unless he were deaf, would be warned.

The room was broad and high-ceilinged, so high that it must have displaced two rooms above it and may have gone almost to the roof. The walls were panelled in dark oak, and huge rough-hewn oak beams ran just below the heavily shadowed ceiling. The floor was dark polished oak. Here and there was a wolf or bear skin. The bed was a framework with eight thick rough-hewn oaken logs, low footboard and headboard, and planks laid across the framework.

Lying on the planks was a huge oak log squared off at the corners. It had been gouged out on its top with axe and chisel. The gouge was wide and deep enough to hold a tall man. It did hold a man. The baron, covered with a bearskin to his neck, lay on his back in the hollow. There was dirt beneath him and dirt humped under his head for a pillow.

His face was turned straight upward. His nose looked huge and long. His lower lip had slipped a little to reveal the long white teeth. His face was as greenish-grey as if he had just died. This may have been because of the peculiar greenish light flickering from four fat green candles, two at each corner of the log-coffin.

Childe pulled the bearskin back. The baron was naked. He

Philip José Farmer

put his hand on the baron's chest and then on his wrist pulse. There was no detectable heartbeat, and the chest did not move. An eyelid, peeled back, showed only white.

Childe left the baron and pulled two drapes back. Two enormous french windows were greyly bared. It was daytime, but the light was very dark, as if night had left an indelible stain. The sky was dark grey with streamers of green-grey dangling here and there.

Childe looked in the darkness under the planks supporting the log-coffin. He found a roughly-worked oaken lid. He felt cold. The silence, the sputtering green candles, the heavy dark wood everywhere, the ponderous beams, which seemed to drip shadows, the roughness, indeed, the archaicness, of the room, and the corpselike sleeper, who was so expected and yet so unexpected – these fell like heavy shrouds, one over the other, upon him. His breath sawed in his throat.

Was this room supposed to be a reproduction of a room in the ancestral castle in the Carpathians? Why the ubiquitous primitively worked oak? And why this coffin when Igescu could afford the best?

Some things here accorded with the superstitions (which, as far as he was concerned, were not superstitions). Other things he could not account for.

He had a hunch that this room was built to conform to specifications far more ancient than medieval ones, that the oak and the log and the candles had been in use long before the Carpathian mountains were so named, long before Rumania existed as a colony of the Romans, long before the mother city, Rome, existed, and probably long before the primitive Indo-European speakers began to spread out of the homeland of what would someday be called Austria and Hungary. A type of this room, and a type of this man who slept in the log, in one form or another, had existed in central Europe, and elsewhere, when men spoke languages now perished without a record and when they still used flint tools.

Whatever the origin of his kind, however closely or distantly he resembled the creature of folklore, legend, and superstition, Igescu was forced to be as good as dead when daylight arrived. The rays of the sun contained some force responsible for diurnal suspended animation. Perhaps some other phenomenon connected with the impact of the sun caused this strange sleep. Or, perhaps, it was the other way around, with the absence of the moon? No, that wasn't logical because the moon was often present in the daytime. But then, maybe the moon's effect was greatly reduced by the other luminary.

If Igeseu had not been forced to do so, he would never have quit the search for Dolores and Childe. Why, then, had he not made sure that he would not be so vulnerable? He knew that both Dolores and Childe were in the intramural passageways.

Childe felt colder than before except for a hot spot between his shoulder blades, the focus of something hidden somewhere and staring at his back.

He looked swiftly around the room, at the ceiling, where the shadows clung above the beams, under the oaken frame of the bed, although he had looked there once, and behind the few chairs. There was nothing.

The bathroom was empty. So was the room beyond the thick rough oaken door on the west wall. Nothing living was there but a massive mahogany coffin with gold trimming and gold-plated handles stood in one corner.

Childe raised the lid, fully expecting to find a body. It was empty. Either it had housed a daylight sleeper at one time or it was to be used in some emergency by the baron. Childe pulled up the satin lining and found earth beneath it.

He went back to the oaken room. Nothing had visibly changed. Yet the silence seemed to creak. It was as if the intrusion of another had hauled in the slack of the atmosphere, had hauled it in too tightly. The shadows abruptly seemed darker; the green light of the candies was heavier and, in some way, even more sinister.

He stood in the doorway, sword ready, motionless, repressing his breathing so he could listen better.

Something had come into this room, either from the passageway entrance or through the door at the west wall. He doubted that it had used the passageway entrance, because any guard stationed there would have challenged him before he could get into the room.

It had to have been in the other room, and it must have been watching him through some aperture, which Childe could not discern. It had not moved against him immediately because he had not tried to harm the baron.

Perhaps the feeling was only too-strained nerves. He could see nothing, nothing at all to alarm him.

But the baron would not have left himself unguarded.

Chapter 19

Childe took one step forward. There was still no sound except that which his mental ear heard. It was a crackling, as if the intrusion of a new mass had bent a magnetic field. The lines of force had been pushed out.

The rapier held point up, he advanced towards the enormous log on the bed. The noiseless crackling became louder. He stooped and looked under the frame. There was nothing there.

Something heavy struck him on his back and drove him face down. He screamed and rolled over. Fire tore at his back and his hips and the back of his thighs, but he was up and away, while something snarled and spat behind him. He rounded the bed and whirled, the sword still in his hand although he had no memory of consciously clinging to it or of even thinking of it. But if his spirit had unclenched for a moment, his fist had not.

The thing was a beauty and terror of white and black rosetted fur, and taut yellow-green eyes which seemed to reflect the ghastly light of the candles, and thin black lips, and sharp yellow teeth. It was small for a leopard but large enough to scare him even after most of the fright of the unexpected and unknown had left him. It had hidden in the cavity of the log, crouching flattened on top of Igescu until Childe had come close enough for it.

Now it crouched again and snarled, eyes spurting ferocity, claws unsheathed.

Now it launched itself over the bed and the coffin, Childe, leaning over the baron's body, thrust outward. The cat was spitted on the blade, which drove through the neck. A paw flashed before his eyes, but the tips of the claws were not quite close enough. Childe went over backward, and the rapier was torn from his hand. When he got up, he saw that the leopard, a female, was kicking its last. It lay on its right side, mouth open, the life in its eyes flying away bit by bit, like a flock of bright birds leaving a branch one by one as they started south to avoid the coming of winter.

Childe was panting and shaking, and his heart was threatening to butt through his ribs. He pulled the sword out, shoving with his foot against the body, and then climbed upon the oaken frame. He raised the sword before him by the hilt with both hands. Its point was downward, parallel with his body. He held it as if he were a monk holding a cross up to ward off evil which, in a way, he was. He brought the blade down savagely with all his weight and drove it through the skin and heart and, judging from the resistance and muted cracking sound, some bones.

The body moved with the impact, and the head turned a little to one side. That was all. There was no sighing or rattling of breath. No blood spurted from around the wound or even seeped out.

The instrument of execution was steel, not wood, but the hilt formed a cross. He hoped that the symbol was more important than the material. Perhaps neither meant anything. It might be mistaken lore which said that a vampire, to be truly killed, must be pierced through the heart with a stake or that the undead feared the cross with an unholy dread and were deprived of force in its presence.

Also, he remembered from his reading of *Dracula*, many years ago, something about the head having to be removed.

He felt that probably there were many things said about this creature that were not true and also there were many things unknown. Whether the lore was superstition or not, he had done his best, was going to do his best, to ensure that it died a permanent death.

As for the leopard, it might be just that – a leopard. He suspected that it was Ngima or Mrs Pocyotl because it was so small. It did not seem likely that Pocyotl, who was Mexican, some of whose ancestors undoubtedly spoke one form or another of Nahuatl, would be a wereleopard. A werejaguar, yes. No, it must be, if not a genuine leopard, Ngima or the Chinaman Pao.

Whatever it was, it showed no sign of changing after death. Perhaps it really was not a metamorph, but a pet trained to guard Igescu.

What am I thinking of? he thought. Of course, it is. There are no such creatures as werewolves and wereleopards and vampires. Maybe there are vampires, psychological vampires, psychotics who think they are vampires. But the actual metamorphosis! What kind of mechanism would be involved, what mechanism could affect a change like that? Bones become fluid, change shape even in the cellular structure, and harden again? Well, maybe the bones are not *our* kind of bones. But what about the energy involved? And even if the body could shift shape, the brain surely couldn't! The brain would have to retain its human size and shape.

He looked at the leopard and he remembered the wolves. Their heads were wolf-sized, their brains were small.

He should forget this nonsense. He had been drugged; the rest was suggestion.

Not until then did he become aware that the leopard, when it had been fastened to him for such a short time, had done more than he had thought. It had torn off his shirt and pants and belt, and his hand, feeling his back and hips and legs, was wet with blood. He hurt, and he was alarmed, but a closer examination convinced him that the leopard had done more harm to his clothes than to him. The wounds were superficial or seemed so.

He went into the next room, which was a small study and picked up an armful of newspapers and magazines. Returning to the huge room, he wadded up the papers and ripped out pages and stacked a pile on each side of the baron's neck. After dripping some lighter fluid on the two piles and over the baron's hair and chest, he touched off the fluid.

Childe then opened the large windows and built another fire below the central plank. A third pile below the left side of the framework blazed up. In a few minutes, he added a wooden chair to that fire. After a while, the oak of the frame and the plank were blazing, and the log was blackening and smoking. The stench of burned hair and flesh rose from the baron.

More paper and lighter fluid got the drapes over the windows to burning. Then he struggled with the body of the leopard until he had dropped it on the fire. Its head burned fiercely with lighter fluid; its black nose lost its wet shininess and wrinkled with heat.

Opening the entrance to the passageway made a stronger draught. The smoke in the room streamed out through the hole to meet the smoke in the passageway.

The entrance did not seem big enough to handle all the smoke, which soon filled the room. He began to cough and, suddenly, as if the coughs had triggered him, he had a long shuddering orgasm the roots of which seemed to be wrapped around his spine and to be pulling his spine down his back and out through his penis.

Just as the last spurt came, a shriek tore from the smoke in the centre of the room. He spun around and could see nothing. One of the two had not been dead and still was not dead because the shrieks were continuing with full strength.

And then, before he could turn again to face the new sound, a grunting and squealing shot from the wall-entrance. There was a rapid clicking, much louder than the wolves' claws, a tremble of the boards under his feet and he was knocked upward to one side. Half-stunned, his left leg hurting, he sat up. He began coughing. The squealing became louder and the boards shook under him. He rolled away under cover of the smoke, while the thing that had hit him charged around, hunting for him.

Crawling on his hands and knees along the wall, his head bent near the floor to keep from breathing the smoke, he headed for the french windows. The swine noises had now given way to a deep coughing. After a dozen racks that seemed strong enough to suck in all the smoke in the room during the in-breaths, the hooves clattered again. Childe rounded the corner and slid along the wall until he came to the next corner. His hand, groping upward into the smoke, felt the lower edges of the french windows. The open ones were about ten feet away, as he remembered them.

The hooves abruptly stopped. The squealing was even more ferocious, less questing and more challenging. Hooves hit the floorboards again. Punctuating the two sounds was a loud hissing.

A battle was taking place somewhere in the smoke. Several times, the walls shook as heavy bodies hit them, and the floor seldom ceased to tremble. Blows – a great hand hammering into a thick solid body – added codas to the crackling of the fires.

Childe could not have waited to see what was going on even if he had wished. The smoke would kill him sooner, the fire would kill him later, but not so much later, if he did not get out. There was no time to crawl on around until he got to the west door. The windows were the only way out. He climbed out after unfastening and pushing out the lower edge of the screen, let himself down until he clung by his hands, and then dropped. He struck a bush, broke it, felt as if he had broken himself too, rolled off it and then stood up. His left leg hurt even more, but he could see no blood.

And then he jetted again – at least, his penis had not been hurt in the fall – and was helpless while two bodies hurtled through the window he had just left. The screen, torn off, struck near him. Magda Holyani and Mrs Grasatchow crushed more bushes and rolled off them on to the ground near the driveway.

Immediately after, several people ran out of the house on to the porch.

Both the women were bleeding from many wounds and blackened with smoke. Magda had ended her roll at his feet in time to receive a few drops on her forehead. This, he could not help thinking even in his pain, was an appropriate extreme unction for her. The fat woman had struck as heavily as a sack of wet flour and now lay unconscious, a grey bone sticking out of the flesh of one leg and blood running from her ears and nostrils.

Bending Grass, Mrs Pocyotl, and O'Faithair were on the porch. That left Chornkin, Krautschner, Ngima, Pao, Vivienne, the two maids, the baroness, and Dolores unaccounted for. He thought he knew what had happened to the first three. Two were dead of rapier thrusts in the passageway and one was burning with Igescu.

The clothes of the three on the porch were ripped, their hair was disarrayed, and they were bleeding from wounds. They must have tangled with Magda or Mrs Grasatchow or Dolores or any combination thereof. But they were not disabled, and they were now looking for him, their mouths moving, their hands moving to indicate him now and then.

Childe limped, but swiftly, to the Rolls-Royce parked twenty feet away on the driveway. Behind came a shout and shoes slapping against the porchsteps. The Rolls was unlocked, and the key was in the ignition lock. He drove away while Bending Grass and O'Faithair beat on the windows with their fists and howled like wolves at him. Then they had dropped off and were racing towards another car, a red Jaguar.

Childe stopped the Rolls, reversed, and pressed the accelerator to the floor. Going backward, the Rolls bounced O'Faithair off the right rear fender and then crashed to a halt. Bending Grass had whirled just before it pinned him against the Jaguar. His dark broad face stared into the rear window for a few seconds. Then it was gone.

Childe drove forward until he could see the Indian's body, red and mashed from the thighs down, face downward on the pavement. The outlines of his body looked fuzzy; he seemed to be swelling.

Childe had no time to keep looking. He stopped the Rolls again, backed it up over O'Faithair, who was just beginning to sit up, went forward over him again, turned around, and drove the wheels back and forth three times each over the bodies of Holyani, Grasatchow, Bending Grass, and O'Faithair. Mrs Pocyotl, who had been screaming at him and shaking her fist, ran back into the house when he drove towards the porch.

Flames and smoke were pouring out of a dozen windows on all three storeys of the left wing and out of one window of the central house. Unchecked, the first would destroy the entire building in an hour or two. And there was nobody to check it.

He drove away. Coming around the curve just before entering the road through the woods, he saw part of the yard to one side of the house. The red-headed Vivienne, her naked body white in the ghastly half-dark daylight, Mrs Pocyotl with her shoes off, and the two maids were running for the woods. Behind them came the nude Dolores, her long dark hair flying. She looked grim and determined. The others looked determined also, but their determination was inspired by fright.

Childe did not know what she would do if she caught them, but he was sure that they knew and were not standing to fight for good reasons. He also suspected that Pao and the baroness had not come out of the house because of what Dolores had done to them, although it was possible that Magda or Mrs Grasatchow had killed them. He could not be sure, of course, but he suspected that the two had been in metamorphosis as pig and snake and that they had been unmanageable.

The three women disappeared in the trees.

He struck himself on the forehead. Was he really believing all this metamorphosis nonsense?

He looked back. From this slight rise, he could see Bending Grass and Mrs Grasatchow. The clothes seemed to have split off the Indian, and he looked black and bulky, like a bear. The fat woman was also dark and there was something non-human about the corpse.

At that moment, from behind the house, the biggest black fox he had ever seen raced out and tore off towards the woods into which the three women had disappeared. It barked three times and then turned its head and seemed to grin at him.

The chill that had transfixed him when he first saw Dolores went through him again. He remembered something now, something he had read long ago. The shapeshifting fox-people of China. They lost control of their ability to change form if they drank too much wine. And, that first evening, the baron had been trying to restrain Pao's wine consumption. Why? Because he had not wanted Childe to witness the metamorphosis? Or for some other reason? For some other reason, probably, since the baron could not have been worried about Childe escaping to tell what he had seen.

He shrugged and drove on. He had had too much of this and wanted only to get away. He was beginning to believe that a 150 pound man could become fluid, twist bone and flesh into a non-human mould, and, somewhere along the transformation, shed 125 pounds, just tuck them away some place to be withdrawn later when needed. Or, if not cached, the discarded mass trailed along, like an invisible jet exhaust, an attached plume of energy ready for reconversion.

The gate of the inner wall was before him. He opened this and drove through, and soon was stopped by the outer wall. Here he left the Rolls on the driveway, after wiping off his prints with a rag from the glove compartment, and walked through the big gate to his own car, parked under the trees at the end of the road.

He found the key he had hidden – how long ago? it seemed days – and drove away. He was naked, bloody, bruised, and hurting, and he still had an erection that was automatically working up to yet another – oh, God! – orgasm, but he did not care. He would get into his apartment, and the rest of the world, smog, monsters, and all, could go to hell, which they were doing, anyway.

A half-mile down the road, a big black Lincoln shot by him towards the Igescu estate. It held three men and three women, all of whom were handsome or beautiful and well dressed. Their faces were, however, grim, and he knew that their destination was Igescu's and that they were speeding because they were late for whatever sinister conference they had been scheduled to attend. Or because someone in the house had called them for help. The car had California licence plates. Perhaps they were from San Francisco.

He smiled feebly. They would be unpleasantly surprised. Meanwhile, he had better get out of here, because he did not know whether or not they had noted his licence plate.

Before he had gone a mile, the sky had become darker, growled, thundered, lightninged. A strong wind tore the smog apart, and then the rains washed the air and the earth without let-up for an hour and a half.

He parked the car in the underground garage and took the elevator up to his floor. No one saw him, although he expected to be observed. He had no excuse for being naked and with a hard-on and it would be just like life, the great ironist, to have him arrested for indecent exposure and God knows what else after all he had been through, he, the abused innocent. But no one saw him, and, after locking the door and chaining it, he showered, dried himself, put on pyjamas, ate a ham and cheese sandwich and drank half a quart of milk, and crawled into bed.

Just before he fell asleep, a few seconds later, he put out his hand to feel for something. What did he want? Then he realized that it was Mrs Grasatchow's purse, which contained the skins. Somewhere between the baron's bedroom and this bedroom, he had lost the purse.

Chapter 20

Childe slept, though often restlessly, for a day, a night, and most of the next day. He got up to empty bladder and bowels, to eat cereal or a sandwich and sometimes woke up at the end of a wet dream.

His dreams were often terrors, but were sometimes quite pleasant copulations. Sometimes Mrs Grasatchow or Vivienne or Dolores rode him, and he woke up jetting and groaning. Other times, he was riding Sybil or some woman he had known or some faceless woman. And there were at least two dreams in which he was mounting a female animal from the rear, once with a beautiful leopardess and once with a bitch wolf.

When he was awake, he wondered about the dreams, because he knew that the Freudians insisted that all dreams, no matter how terrifying or horrible, were wishes.

By the time he was slept out, pyjamas and sheets were a mess, but the effects of the cone were gone. He was very happy to have a flaccid penis. He showered and breakfasted, and then read the latest *Los Angeles Times*. Life was almost normal now; the papers were being delivered on schedule. Industries were running full-time. The migration back was still going on but was only a trickle now. The mortuaries were overloaded, and funerals were taking place far into the night. The police were swamped with missing persons reports. Otherwise, the city was functioning as usual. The smog was beginning to build up but would not become alarming while the present breeze continued.

Childe read the front page and some articles. Then he used the phone to check on Sybil. She had not come home. A call to San Francisco was answered by Sybil's sister, Cherril. She said that the mother had died, and Sybil was supposed to have come for the funeral. She presumably left as soon as she had packed. She had been unable to get a plane out, and her car wouldn't start, so she had phoned back that she was coming up with a friend who also wanted to get out of town.

Who was the friend? Cherril did not know. But she was frantic, and she had tried to get hold of Childe. When he had not answered after five tries, she had given up on him. The state police had reported that Sybil was not involved in any of the many

Philip José Farmer

accidents between Los Angeles and San Francisco during that time.

Childe told Cherril not to worry, that many people were still missing. Sybil would show up safe and sound. He would not rest until he found her. And so on.

When he hung up the phone, he felt empty. The next day, he was as hollow, and he had to admit that he knew no more than what Cherril had told him. The "friend" he suspected Sybil to have driven off with, Al Porthouse, denied having seen her for two weeks.

Childe gave up, temporarily, and turned his attention elsewhere. The baron's house had been burned out, although the rains had kept it from being completely destroyed. There were no bodies in the ruins, in the yard, or in the woods. Mrs Grasatchow's purse was not found.

Childe remembered the automobile that had raced by him after he had driven away from the baron's. Whoever the six had been, they had cleaned up thoroughly.

But what had happened to Dolores?

He drove out to the estate and went over the wall again, the police having locked the main gate. His poking around uncovered nothing. The police did not know his story, of course. He knew better than to tell them anything except that he had visited the baron just once and that briefly. They had questioned him and then had said that they were puzzled by the disappearance of the baron, secretary, servants, and chauffeur, but so far no information had come in. For all they knew, the household had left for parts unknown, the house had burned by accident, and any day now they might hear from the baron.

Late that afternoon, he returned to his apartment. He was shrouded in his thoughts, which were concerned with moving elsewhere, to some place where smog would not be a problem for years to come. It was some time before he realized that the phone must have rung at least a dozen times. It had started while he was unlocking the door.

The voice was a pleasant baritone.

"Mr Childe? You don't know me. We haven't met, fortunately for you, although I think we passed each other on the road outside the Baron Igescu's estate several days ago."

Childe did not reply for a moment, then he said, "What do

you want?"

His voice was steady. He had thought it would crack, as if it were crystallized with the ice encasing him.

"You have been very discreet, Mr Childe, in not telling the police. Or as far as we know, anybody. But we want to ensure your silence, Mr Childe. We could easily do that by methods you well know by now. But it pleases us to have you know about us and yet be able to do nothing."

Childe shouted, "What did you do with Sybil?"

There was a silence. And then the voice, "Sybil? Who's she?"

"My wife! My ex-wife, I mean! You know, damn you! What have you done with her, you filthy monster, unnatural...!"

"Nothing, I assure you, Mr Childe."

The voice was cool and mocking.

"We rather admire you, Mr Childe, because of what you accomplished. Congratulations. You managed to kill, permanently, a number of our friends who have survived for a very long time indeed, Mr Childe. You could not have done it without the help of del Osorojo, of course, but that was something we did not foresee. The baron did not anticipate it, and for his carelessness, or ignorance, he paid, and those with him. Some of them, anyway."

This was his last chance to find out anything about them.

He said, "Why the films? Why were they sent in to the police?"

"The films are made for our private use, for our entertainment, Mister Childe. We send them to each other all over the world. Via private couriers, of course. The baron decided to break a precedent and to let the *others* in on some of them. Because we would enjoy the furore and the shaking up of the police. The shaking up of all humans, in fact. The baron and his group were going to move out soon, anyway, so there was no chance of our being connected with the films.

"The baron planned on mailing the films of earlier subjects, working backward chronologically, to the police. Most of the subjects had been listed as missing persons, you know, and the earliest had been dropped by the police because the cases were so old. You found their skins. And lost them.

"You were lucky or smart. You used an unorthodox method of investigation and stumbled across the truth. The baron couldn't

Philip José Farmer

let you go then because you knew too much, so he decided you would become the latest subject. Now, the baron won't have to leave this area to get away from the smog..."

"I saw the old woman, the baroness, trying to conjure up smog!" Childe said. "What..."

"She was trying to get rid of it, you fool! This used to be a nice place to live in, but you humans... !"

Childe could feel the fury making the man inarticulate. However, when the voice returned, it was again cool and mocking.

"I suggest you look in your bedroom. And remember to keep silent, Mister Childe. Otherwise..."

The phone must have been travelling down to the rest. But, before the click, he heard bells tolling, and an organ playing the first bar of *Gloomy Sunday*. He could imagine the rest of the music and the Inner-Sanctum rusty-hinge screeching.

He stood for a while with the phone in his hand. Woolston Heepish? That call came from the house of Woolston Heepish?

Nonsense! There must be another explanation. He did not even want to think about the implications, if... no, forget this.

He put the phone down, and then remembered with a start what the man had advised. He slowly walked into the bedroom. The bedside lamp had been turned on during his absence.

She was in bed, staring straight up. A sheet was draped over her to just below the naked breasts. Her black hair was spread out on the pillow.

He came closer and murmured, "I didn't think they could harm you, Dolores."

He pulled the sheet back, expecting to find the evidences of some horror committed upon her. She was unmarked.

But her body tilted upward, the feet rising first, the stiff legs following, and then, as the body began to point straight upward, it rose towards the ceiling. The heavy hair, and the little red valve on the back of the neck, stopped it from floating up all the way.

The make-up was very good. It had given her skin a solid fleshy appearance and kept him from seeing through it.

Childe had to leave the room for a while and sit down.

When he came back, he stuck a pin in her. She exploded with a bang as loud as a pistol's. He cut her up into strips with scissors and flushed her down the toilet, except for the head of hair, which he put into the garbage.

A century and a half of haunting, a brief fleshing, a few short and wild copulations, a few killings of ancient enemies, and here she was. Rather, there she went. One dark eye, long lashes, a thick eyebrow whirled around then were sucked down.

At least, he had not found Sybil's skin in his bed.

Where was she? He might never find out. He did not think those "people" knew. The "man" had sounded genuinely puzzled.

It was not necessary to postulate those "people" to account for her disappearance. Human beings had enough monsters of their own.

TWO

BLOWN

*sketches among
the ruins of my mind;
an exorcism: ritual two*

Chapter 1

It seemed that the rain would never stop.

On the evening of the sixth day, in a city like the planet of Venus in a 1932 science-fiction story, Herald Childe followed Vivienne Mabcrough.

A few minutes before, he had stopped behind a big black Rolls-Royce, waiting for a light change at the intersection of Santa Monica Boulevard and Canon Drive in Beverly Hills. The Rolls was equipped with rear window wipers, and these enabled Childe to see Vivienne Mabcrough.

She was in the back seat with a man and turned her head just as the light changed to green. Childe would never forget that profile. It was not only the most beautiful he had ever seen, but the last time he had seen it, he had been in a situation he would like to forget but could not.

For several seconds, while horns blared behind him, he had an impulse to let her go. If he trailed her, he might find himself the object of attention from her and her kind. And that was something no sane man and very few insane would wish.

Despite this, he moved the 1972 Pontiac across the street after the Rolls, cutting off a Jaguar which had swung illegally to his left to pass him. The Jaguar's horn blared, and the driver mouthed curses behind his glass and plastic enclosure. A spray of water covered Childe's car, and then the wipers removed it. He could see the Rolls turn west on Little Santa Monica, going through a yellow light. He stopped for the red and, seeing no police car in any direction – though he could not see far because of the grey curtains of water – he went left on the red light. He saw the tail lights of the Rolls turn right and followed. The Rolls was stopped before the Moonlark Restaurant, and Vivienne and her escort were getting out. They only had to take one step to be under the canopy and a doorman assisted them. The Rolls drove off then, and Childe decided to follow it. The driver was a uniformed chauffeur, and possibly he would take the car back to Vivienne's residence. Of course, the car could be her partner's, but that did not matter. Childe wanted to know where he lived, too.

Although he was no longer a private detective, Childe had

---

kept his recording equipment in the car. He described the car and the license plate number into the microphone while he tracked it back across Santa Monica and then north of Sunset Boulevard. The car swung on to Lexington, and in two blocks drove on to the circular driveway before a huge Georgian mansion. The chauffeur got out and went down the walk along the side of the house to the rear. Childe drove half a block and then got out and walked back. The rain and the dusky light made it impossible for him to see any house addresses from the street. He had to go up the driveway, hoping that no one would look out. The house was lit within, but he could see no sign of life.

He returned to the car, which he entered on the right side because he did not wish to wet his shoes and legs. The dirty grey-brown water had filled the street from curb to curb and was running over on to the strips of grass between street and sidewalk.

In the car, he recorded the address. But instead of driving off, he sat for a long time and considered what he should do next.

They had not bothered him since that night in Baron Igescu's house, so why should he bother them?

They were murderers, torturers, abductors. He knew this with the certainty of personal experience. Yet he could not prove what he knew. And if he told exactly what had happened, he would be committed to a mental institution. Moreover, he could not blame the authorities for putting him away.

There were times when he could not believe his own vivid memories. Even the most piercing, that of the time when he had flushed the complete skin of Dolores del Osorojo, eyes and all, down the toilet, was beginning to seem unbelievable.

The mind accepted certain forms and categories, and his experiences with Igescu, Vivienne Mabcrough, Standing Grass, Fred Pao, and others in that enormous old house in northern Beverly Hills were outside the accepted. And so it had been natural that his mind should be busy trying to bury these forms and categories. Shove them down, choke them off in the dusty dusky cellar of the unconscious.

He could just go home to his place in Topanga Canyon and forget all about this, or try to.

He groaned. He was hooked and couldn't fight loose. He had always wondered about the true identity of Igeseu and his

Philip José Farmer

people. Were they really vampires, werewolves, werebears, werefoxes, and other creatures which mankind generally considered only to be superstitions? Even Igescu's seemingly "scientific" account of their origins and nature, which were detailed by the old French scholar Le Garrault, now sounded outrageous. But Igescu's explanation was better than just superstition.

He groaned again and then swore. He was going to pursue this. If he had not seen Vivienne, he might have continued to ignore his desires to take up the trail once more. But the sight of her had gotten him as eager as an old bloodhound that smells a whiff of fox on the wind from the hills.

He drove away and did not stop until he pulled into a Santa Monica service station. There was a public phone booth here, which he used to call the Los Angeles Police Department. His friend, Sergeant Furr, finally answered. Childe asked him to check out the license number of the Rolls. Furr said he would call him back within a few minutes. Three minutes later, the phone in the booth rang.

"Hal? I got it for you. The Rolls belongs to a Mrs Vivienne – V-I-V-I-E-N-N-E – Mabcrough. I don't know how you pronounce that last name. M-A-B-C-R-O-U-G-H. Mabcrow? Mabcruff? I dunno. Anyway..."

The address was that of the house where the Rolls was parked.

Childe thanked Furr and hung up. Vivienne was confident that he would not bother her anymore. Even after she had been in conspiracy to kill him, and after he knew that she had killed his partner by biting his penis off, she had not changed her name. Evidently she believed that he had had such a scare thrown into him, he would under no circumstances come near her or her kind – whatever that was.

He trudged through the rain and got into the car and drove slowly and carefully back to the house in which Vivienne Mabcrough lived. It was nightfall now, and the streets of Beverly Hills in the downtown district were little rivers, curb to curb and overflowing. Although this was a Thursday night, there were very few pedestrians out. The usual bumper to bumper traffic was missing. Not half a dozen cars were in sight within the distance of three blocks in any direction. Santa Monica Boulevard traffic was heavier, because it served as a main avenue for those on their way to Westwood or West Los Angeles or Santa Monica on one side of the street, and on their way to Los Angeles, or parts of Beverly Hills, on the other.

The headlights looked like the eyes of diluvian monsters burning with a fever to get on the Ark. A car had stalled as it was halfway through making a left turn from Santa Monica on to Beverly Drive, and the monsters were blaring or hooting at it. Childe nudged his car through the intersection, taking two changes of light to do so because cars in the lanes at right angles insisted on coming through instead of waiting so that the intersection could be cleared.

When he got through, he proceeded up Beverly Drive at about twenty miles an hour but slowed down to fifteen after several blocks. The water was so high that he was afraid of drowning out his motor, and his brakes were getting wet. He kept applying a little pressure intermittently to the pedal in order to keep the brakes dry, but he did not think he was having much success. Four cars went by him, passing from behind or going the other way, and these travelled so fast they threw water all over his car. He wanted to stick his head out of the window and curse at them for their stupidity and general swinishness, but he did not care to be drenched by the next car.

He parked half a block down from the Mabcrough residence. Hours passed. He was impatient at first, and then the habits of years of sitting and waiting while he was a private eye locked into his nervous system. He pissed a couple of times into a device much like airplane pilots use. He munched on some crackers and a stick of beef jerky and drank some coffee from a canteen. Midnight came, and his patience was beginning to thin out against the grindstone of time. His nerves were jumping, and he was about to surrender to them.

Then the chauffeur came out from behind the house, got into the Rolls, and drove off. Childe could see the dark figure, outlined by the lights from within the house. He wore a slicker and a shiny transparent covering over his cap. As the car went by, Childe hunkered down behind the wheel. He waited until it was a block away and then swung out to follow it without turning his lights on immediately. The rain had not ceased, and the streets were even deeper in water.

The Rolls picked up Vivienne and her escort at the club and

then went back towards the mansion. Childe had hoped it would; he did not feel like trailing her from one spot to another. The Rolls stopped before the big porch to let its passengers off, and they went into the house. The chauffeur drove the car away, presumably to the side entrance and into the garage behind the house. Childe had gotten out of the car by then and walked down along the side of the house. He saw the lights in the storey above the garage come on. The chauffeur, he hoped, lived there.

He went to the side door, which was surrounded by dense shrubbery and a wall behind him. The people next door could not see him, and anybody passing by on the street would not be likely to see him.

The door opened after a few minutes of trying a number of keys. He shot his flashlight around, looking for evidences of a burglar alarm, and could not find any. He went on slowly into the house, ready to run if a dog gave warning. There was no sound except the chiming of a big grandfather clock on the second floor.

A moment later, he was crouched outside the partly opened door of Vivienne's bedroom.

Chapter Two

The room was very large. There was a single light on, coming from the lamp which rested on the floor. Its base was at least four feet high and was some red-shot quartz-like stone sculptured into two naked nymphs – or female satyrs – back to back. The shade looked like thin parchment. Childe, seeing this, was chilled through as if a huge icicle had been shoved up his anus all the way to his hindbrain. He remembered the many skins of human beings he had found inside the drawer in a room in Igescu's house. These had been stripped from the corpses – or perhaps the living owners – and resewn so that they could be blown up like balloons.

There were paintings in red, blue, and purple on the lampshade, outlines of semi-human figures writhing in flames.

The walls were covered with what looked like heavy quiltwork. This had three figures, repeated over and over. There was a satyr standing on a low stone on one hoof, the other slightly raised. His back was arched and his arms and head were raised while he blew a syrinx. A nymph was crouched before him sucking on an enormous purple penis. Behind her was a half-human, half-snake creature. Its lower part was that of a gargantuan python with white and purple markings, and the upper part was a woman's from the belly button up. She had full and well-shaped breasts with spearpoint scarlet nipples, a lovely three-cornered face and long silver hair. Her slender fingers were spreading the egg-shaped buttocks of the nymph, who was bent over, and a long forked tongue was issuing from the snake-woman's mouth and just about to enter the anus or the vagina of the nymph.

Beyond the lamp was a tremendous twelve-postered bed with a crimson many-tasseled canopy. On it were Vivienne and the man, both naked.

She was on her back and he was on top with her legs over his shoulders. He was just about to insert his cock.

Childe watched. He expected either something strange coming from the man or something strange, but not unfamiliar, from the woman. When he had been prowling the secret tunnels between the walls of the Igescu mansion, he had seen her in her bedroom. She had thought she was alone, and she had made love to herself in the most outré fashion. He would never forget that.

"Put it in for me, baby," the man said. He was about thirty-five, dark and hairy and beginning to flesh out.

And then the man screamed and soared backwards off the bed, propelled by his sudden movement and his push upwards with one arm and by a snapping movement of his body that could only have been induced by utmost terror.

He went back and up, trying to stand up at the same time that he moved away from Vivienne. Her legs flew apart as if they were two white birds that had startled each other.

The man fell off the bed and crashed on to the floor. By then, he had quit screaming, but he shook and moaned.

Vivienne got on to her knees and crawled over to look over the edge of the bed at him. Something long and dark-headed between her legs slid back into the slit and disappeared.

"What's the matter, Bill?" she said, looking down at him. "Did the cat get your cock?"

He was sitting up by then, intently handling and eyeing his penis. He looked up at her with surprise.

"My God! What happened? You ask what happened? I thought... I really did think... you got teeth in your cunt?"

He stood up. The grey of his skin was beginning to redden out. He waved his prick at her.

"Look at that! There are teeth marks there!"

She took the limp organ, which looked like a giant but sick worm, and bent over to examine it.

"How can you say those are teeth marks?" she said. "There are some tiny little indentations there, but nothing serious. There! Does that make Mommy's boy feel better?"

She had kissed the big purple-red glans then run her tongue along the shaft.

He backed away, saying, "Keep your distance, woman!"

"Are you out of your mind?" she said. She was sitting up on the edge of the bed with the magnificently full and conical breasts pointed at him. Her pubis was a large triangle of thick dark-red hair, almost the same shade as the long thick rich auburn hair on her head. The legs were extraordinarily long and very white.

Bill continued to keep his distance. He said, "I tell you; something bit me. You got teeth in your cunt!"

She lay back down on the bed with her legs stretched out so that the tips of her toes touched the floor. She said, "Put your finger in, darling, and find out what a fool you are."

He eyed the reddish fleece and the slit, somewhat opened by the posture.

He said, "I like my finger, too!"

Vivienne sat up suddenly, her beautiful face twisted. "You asshole! I thought you were a normal healthy man! I didn't know you were psychotic! Teeth in my cunt, indeed! Get to hell out of here before I call the men from the psycho ward!"

Bill looked as if he felt foolish. He said, "Honest to God, I don't know how to explain it! Maybe I am going nuts! Or maybe I just had a sudden strain, maybe that was the burning sensation I felt! No, by God, it felt like tiny teeth! Or a bunch of needles!"

Vivienne got down off the bed and reached out a hand to Bill.

"Come here, baby. Sit down on the bed. Here!" She patted the edge of the bed.

Bill must have decided that he was making a fool of himself. Moreover, the sight of the superbly shaped Vivienne, with her outrageously beautiful face, overcame his fears. His penis began to swell, but it did not rise. He seated himself on the bed, and Vivienne walked around the side and got a pillow. Returning, she threw it on the floor and got down on her knees on it.

"I've got teeth in my mouth, baby, but I know how to use them," she said. She picked up the semi-flaccid organ and ran her tongue out to flick the slit on the end of the glans. He jumped a little but settled back to look down at her while she took half of the cock into her mouth. She began to work her head back and forth, slowly, and the organ disappeared entirely, then emerged slick and shining red as far as the head.

Bill shook and moaned and kept his gaze fixed upon the penis diving in and out of those full red lips. He was evidently getting a heightened ecstasy out of watching his cock pistoning into her mouth.

Herald Childe did not know whether he should stay there or not. He wanted to explore the house for anything he might be able to use for evidence against Vivienne and her partners. If he could find the names and addresses, documents, recordings, films,

Philip José Farmer

anything that would tend to prove their criminal activities, he should do it now. Vivienne was occupied, and she was unlikely to notice any noise outside this bedroom.

However, he was worried about the man. His behaviour made it evident that he was not aware of Vivienne's peculiarities of physiology or her fatal actions. At least, Childe supposed that they were fatal for others. He had never seen her kill anyone or even harm anyone, but he was certain that she was no different than her monstrous associates.

Bill was an innocent in the sense that he was a victim. He had probably never done anything to offend or hurt Vivienne and her group. He was probably just a pick-up, as Childe's partner had been a pick-up.

Childe shuddered at the memory of that film that had been shipped to the LAPD by the killers. It had shown his partner being sucked off, as Bill now was. The woman had removed her false teeth and inserted razor-edged iron teeth, and bitten off the end of his partner's cock.

The blood was a crimson fountain that burst out frequently in his visions and his dreams.

Childe decided that he would have to interfere. This meant that he could not prowl around the house now. He would have to make sure the man was safe. And he should do so now. But he could not. He wanted to find out what would happen. He would wait a while and then stop it.

Vivienne abruptly stood up, revealing Bill's red and pulsing beak sticking out at a 45-degree angle.

She said, "Slide back on to the bed, baby, and lie down."

Whatever reservations he had about her had diminished with the increase in blood pressure. He moved back and lay down with his head on the pillow while she climbed on to the bed. She mouthed the head of his penis for a minute and then said, "Bill?"

He was flat on his back, his hands spread out, his face turned upwards. His eyes were open. He did not answer.

"Bill?" she said again, a little louder.

When he did not respond, she crawled down to him and looked into his face. She pinched his cheek and then raked it with her fingernails. Blood flowed from four rows on his flesh, but he did not move. His penis, however, reared up, thick, squat, red-purplish, glistening.

Vivienne turned then, and Childe saw the smirk. Whatever she was planning, it was proceeding smoothly.

It was then that he should walk into the room, but he was too fascinated to make his move as yet. Bill seemed to be paralysed, though how it had happened, Childe could not guess. Not at first. Then he realized that that thing had bitten Bill's peter with poisonous teeth. The venom had frozen him, with the exception of his prick. The blood was still pumping into it.

The woman straddled him with the intention of easing down on his cock and letting it slide up into the slit of her vagina. But she only allowed the head to enter and then she stopped descending. She crouched there for about thirty seconds, during which she shook as if she were having an orgasm.

Immediately after, she withdrew, exposing the penis, which was still upright. But there were tiny rills of blood running down its side from several places between the head and the shaft.

Vivienne turned around to straddle him facing away from him. She put her hand below her buttocks to grab the penis and to slide it in again. This time, however, she let her weight slowly down to guide the cock into her anus. And when its head was engulfed, she stopped.

Childe anticipated what would happen next. He felt sick, and he knew he should halt the monstrous rape, but he was also gripped with the desire to witness what, as far as he knew, no man alive had seen. Emphasis on the alive.

Vivienne waited, and then the lips of her slit bulged open. The thick mat of rich red hair was pushed aside, and a tiny head emerged. It was soaked with the lubricating fluids within her cunt, and it had the features of a man. Its hair was black; it had a tiny moustache and goatee; its eyes were two garnets under eyebrows no thicker than the leg of a black widow spider. The lips were so thin as to be invisible; the nose was long and curved.

The head moved forward as the body continued to slide out from the vagina. It raised up on the shaft of the body like a snake, and Childe heard it hiss but knew that that had to be his imagination. It glided on over the wrinkled sac of the testicles and underneath, apparently headed for the anus. Then, it disappeared while the uncoiling body kept issuing from the slit. By then, its head

Philip José Farmer

must have gone deep into the man's bowels.

Childe unfroze abruptly. He shook his head as if trying to clear away sleep. He was not sure that he had not fallen into a semi-hypnotic state while watching the bizarre scene.

He stepped through the door just as Vivienne eased herself down on the penis, driving it all the way up her own anus. Her eyes were closed, and her face was ecstatic. He managed to get close to her while she was moving up and down on the shaft and moaning phrases in a foreign language. The only sounds were her voice, the striking of rain against the windows, and the squeak of the bed springs as she slid up and down on the cock like a monkey on a stick.

Now that he was closer, he could see that the pale and slimy body of the thing was in the man's anus. It apparently had gone in as deeply as it could, or as it cared to, because the motion was stopped. Childe felt sick because he could imagine that golf-sized head with its vicious eyes blind in the night of the bowels and its mouth chewing on whatever it was that it found delectable in there.

Chapter 3

He reached out and touched the pink-red and swollen nipple on that superb breast.

She reacted violently. Her eyes flew open, exposing the beautiful violet, and she rose up off the bed, leaving the throbbing penis sticking up and dragging the body of the thing out of the man's body. Both came loose with a slurping sound, and the tiny mouth of the thing chattered a high-pitched and angry stream of expletives. At least, they sounded like cursing to Childe, although he did not know the language. The words seemed to be Latin in origin; they were vaguely French or perhaps Catalan or something in between.

On seeing Childe, the thing reared up on its body, which coiled behind the head as if it were a rattlesnake. Vivienne continued to move away from Childe, however, retreating to the opposite end of the bed. There she crouched, while the thing swung between her legs and then started to slide back into the vagina. The head was fixed on Childe while this withdrawal occurred. Its red-gleaming eyes were so hateful and deadly that Childe felt as if he had been bitten. Then the head was gone into the slit; the labia closed; it was as if the thing had never existed. Certainly, the thing should *not* exist.

Childe moved up along the bed and reached out and slapped the man in the face. The hand left a red imprint, but that was the only reaction from him. He continued to stare upwards, and his chest rose and fell slowly. His dong was beginning to dwindle and sag.

"That will do no good unless I give him the antidote," Vivienne said. Her colour was beginning to return, and she was even smiling at him.

"Then give it to him!" Childe said.

"Or you'll do what?"

The tone was not hostile, just questioning.

"I'll call the cops."

"If you do," she said evenly, "you'll be the one hauled away. I'll charge you with breaking and entering, threatened rape, and assault and battery on my friend here and maybe even

Philip José Farmer

attempted murder."

Childe wondered why she would not charge him with actual rape, then it occurred to him that she would not want a physical examination.

He said, "I'm not in too good a position, it's true. But I don't think you could stand much publicity."

She climbed down off the bed, brushing against him with one soft hip, and walked to her dresser. She picked up a cigarette, lit it, and then offered him one. He shook his head.

"Then it's a Mexican stand-off?" she said.

"Not unless you give this man the antidote," he said. "I don't care what it costs me, I'll raise a howl that'll bring this place down around your ears."

"Very well," she said.

She opened a drawer while he stood behind her to make sure that there was no weapon in it. She picked up a large sewing needle from a little depression in the top of a block of dark-red wood and walked with it to the man. She inserted its tip into the jugular vein and then walked back to the dresser. By the time she had replaced the needle, Bill was beginning to move his legs and his head. A few minutes later, he groaned and then sat up, his feet on the floor. He looked at the naked Vivienne and at Childe as if he was not sure what was happening.

Childe said, "Were you conscious?"

Bill nodded. He was concentrating on Vivienne with a peculiar expression.

"I can't believe it!" he said. "What the hell were you doing with me? You pervert!"

Childe did not understand for a moment. The accusation seemed so mild compared with what had happened. Then he saw that Bill had not witnessed the thing issuing from her vagina. He must have believed that she had stuck some object up his anus.

"Your clothes are over there," she said, pointing at a chair on the other side of the bed. "Get dressed and get out."

Bill stood up unsteadily and walked around the bed. While he dressed clumsily, he said, "I'll have the cops down here so fast your head'll swim. *Drugging* me! Drugging *me!* What the hell for? What did you intend to do?"

"I wouldn't call the cops," Childe said. "You heard what she said she'd do. You'd end up with all sorts of charges flung at you, and, believe me, this woman has some powerful connections. Moreover, she is quite capable of murder."

Bill, looking scared, dressed more swiftly.

Vivienne looked at her wristwatch and said, "Herald and I have some things we're eager to discuss. Please hurry."

"Yeah, I'll bet you two perverts do!" Bill said, glaring at both.

"For Christ's sake!" Childe said. "I saved your life!"

Childe watched Vivienne. She was leaning against the dresser with her weight on one leg, throwing a hip into relief. He hated her. She was so agonizingly beautiful, so desirable. And so coldly fatal, so monstrous, in all senses of that overused and misused word.

Bill finally had his clothes on, except for his raincoat and rubbers. These, Childe supposed, would be in the closet in the vestibule downstairs just off the entrance.

"So long, you queers!" Bill mumbled as he stumbled through the door. "I'll see you in jail, you can bet on that!"

Vivienne laughed. Childe wondered if he should go with him. Now that he had followed her and was in this den of whatever it was that she and her colleagues were, he wondered if he had made a very wrong decision. It was true he had rescued a victim, but the victim was so stupid he did not realize what he had escaped. Certainly, he did not seem worth the trouble or the risk.

Vivienne waited until the front door loudly slammed. Then she moved slowly towards him, rolling her hips.

He backed away, saying, "Keep your distance, Vivienne. I have no desire for you; you couldn't possibly seduce me, if that's what you have in mind."

She laughed again and sat down on the edge of the bed. "No, of course not! But why are you here? We left you alone, though we could have killed you easily enough at any time. And perhaps we should have, after what you did to us."

"If you were human, you'd understand why."

"Oh, you mean the monkey sense of curiosity? Let me remind you of how Malayans catch monkeys. They put food in a jar with a mouth large enough for the monkey to get his paw into but too small for him to withdraw the hand unless he lets loose of the

Philip José Farmer

food. Of course, he doesn't let loose, and so the trapper takes him easily."

"Yes, I know that," he said. "Your analogy may be a fairly exact one. I'm here because I still think that your bunch had something to do with my wife's disappearance. I know you denied that, but I can't get it out of my mind that you did away with Sybil. You're certainly capable of doing that. You're capable of anything that's cruel and inhuman."

"Inhuman?" she said, smiling.

"All right. Point well taken," he said. "However, here we are, alone together in this house with no one except Bill knowing that I am here. And he not only does not know who I am, he isn't going to say anything about me. Not after he considers the possible repercussions, especially the fact that he might be suspected."

"Suspected of what?" she said, her eyes widening. Before he could reply, she said, "I doubt that he'll say anything to anybody."

"What do you mean?" he said, although he thought he knew what she was going to say.

She looked at her watch and said, "He ought to be dying of a heart attack about now."

She looked up at him and smiled again. "So pale! So shocked! What did you expect, you babe in the woods? Did you think I'd let him go so he could talk to the police? I could make him regret it, of course, with charges that would put him in jail, but I don't want any publicity whatsoever. Now, really, Herald Childe, how could you be so naive?"

Childe broke loose from the casing of ice that had seemed to be around him. He leaped at her, his hands outstretched, and she tried to roll away from him on the bed to the other side, but he seized her ankle. He dragged her to him, although she slammed one heel into his shoulder. He leaned down between her legs and thrust three fingers into the wet vagina and probed. Something fiery touched one of his fingers, and he knew he had been bitten, but he plunged his hand in as far as he could.

Vivienne screamed with the pain then, but he kept his hand in and, despite the agony of more bites on his other fingers, managed to seize that tiny head. It was slippery, and it resisted, but it came out of her cunt, its mouth working, the minute teeth glittering in the light, its eyes looking like red jewels stuck into its

---

bearded doll face.

He pressed his left shoulder against her right leg to keep it from kicking him and braced his right shoulder against her other leg. She reached down and grabbed his hair and pulled, and the pain was so intense he almost let loose of the thing. But he clung to it and then threw himself backward as hard as he could. The snakelike body shot out from the slit while the tiny mouth screamed like a rabbit dying.

As he fell on his back on the floor, he saw the tail slide out of the slit. It came loose much easier than he thought it would. Perhaps he had been wrong in thinking that it was anchored to her in a plexus of flesh.

But there *were* red and bloody roots hanging from the end of the tail, and Vivienne was down on the floor by him writhing and screaming.

He jumped and threw the thing away. Its slimy muscle-packed body and the grease-soaked head and unadulterated viciousness of the face and eyes were so loathsome he was afraid he was going to vomit.

The body soared across the bed, hit the other edge, flopped, and then slithered off the edge to fall out of sight.

Vivienne quit screaming, though her skin was grey and her eyes were great areas of white with violet islets. She said, "Now you've done it! I hope I can get back together again!"

He said, "What?"

He was having difficulty standing. The pain in his fingers was lessening, but that was because a numbness was shooting up his arm and down his side. The room was beginning to be blurred, and Vivienne's white body with the auburn triangle between the legs and torn fleshy roots hanging out of the slit was starting to spin and, at the same time, to recede.

"You wouldn't understand, you stupid human!"

He sank to his knees and then sat down, lowering himself with one arm that threatened to turn into rubber under him. Vivienne's pubis was directly under his eyes, so he saw what was happening despite the increasing fuzziness of vision.

The skin was splitting along the hairline of the pubis. The split became a definite and deep cleavage as if invisible knives were cutting into her and the operators of the knives intended to scoop out the vagina and the womb in one section.

Cracks were appearing across her waist, across her thighs, her knees, her calves, and her feet.

He bent over to see more clearly. There were cracks on her wrists, her elbows, around her breasts, her neck. She looked like a china doll that had fallen on to a cement sidewalk.

When he looked back at her cunt, it had walked out of the space it had occupied between her legs. It was staggering on its own legs, a score or more of needle-thin many-jointed members with a red-flesh colour. Its back was the pubis, the rich auburn hair, the slit, and the mound of Venus. Its underside was the protective coating of the vaginal canal. The uterus came next on its many tiny legs, following the vagina as if it hoped to reconnect.

Out from the cavity left by the exodus came other organs, some of which he recognized. That knot and fold of flesh certainly must be the fallopian tube and ovary, and that, what the hell was that?

By then the cleavages around the base of the breasts had met, and the breasts reeled off the steep slope of the ribs and fell down, turning over. One landed on its legs and scuttled off, but the other breast lay on its back – its front, actually – and kicked its many spider legs until it succeeded in getting on its feet – so-called.

The belly had split across and down, as had the upper part of the trunk. The anus and the two cheeks of the buttocks crawled off. The legs of this creature were thicker but the weight of the flesh seemed to be almost too much. It moved slowly, whereas the hands, using the fingers as legs, ran across the room quickly and disappeared under the bed.

The head was also walking towards the underside of the bed. It was lifted off the floor by legs about three inches high and perhaps a sixteenth of an inch thick. Four longer legs that had sprouted from behind her ears supported the head and kept it from falling to one side or another. Vivienne's eyes were wide open and blinking, so that she seemed to be as aware in this state as she was in the other. She did not, however, look at Childe.

He felt sick, but he did not think he was going to vomit. If he was, he could not feel anything churning up. His insides were too numb for anything except a vague feeling of queasiness.

He fell over on his side and could not get up again no

matter how hard he struggled. Or tried to struggle, rather, because his efforts were all mental. His muscles, as far as he could tell, failed to respond with even a tremor.

Chapter 4

When he saw the golfball-sized head of the thing poke out from beyond the end of the bed, Childe realized what he had done. By yanking so savagely on that thing, he had jerked it loose from some base in her body, probably in her uterus. This was what he had intended. But he could never have visualized that pulling the thing was like pulling the cord on one of those burro dolls – what were they called? – that were hung up in Mexican homes on Christmas. Pull the string and they ripped open, and all the goodies spilled out.

The thing had been her string, and when it was torn out, she fell apart, and all her goodies, separate entities, spilled out. And began a walk that only a Bosch could paint.

Now the thing was gliding snakelike towards him, its forepart raised off the ground and the slimy, goateed, shark-toothed, scimitar-nosed, garnet-eyed head was pointed at him. Its mouth was writhing, and a piping was issuing from the invisible lips.

Childe could do nothing but lie on his side, his eyes fixed on the approaching thing. He wondered what it had in mind for him. Its bite was poisonous, and while its poison had paralysed Bill but left his sexual organs active, it might be fatal it he were bitten again. Moreover, Vivienne said an antidote had to be given, and she, as far as he knew, was the only one who could do that. But not while she was in this condition.

A glob of coiled intestines crossed before him, cutting off his view of the snake-thing. Behind it came the spinal area, a flesh centipede. This reeled blindly into a foot, which was travelling upside down, its sole pointed towards the ceiling, while twenty legs bore it to wherever it was going. The spine and the foot fell over on their side and kicked their legs for a while before managing to get back up.

The snake-thing crawled nearer. Childe watched it and speculated on whether or not its underside was equipped with many moving plates to enable it to progress so serpentinely. Did it have an ophidian skeleton?

He was so numb that it did not occur to him to wonder how this whole process could come about. He just accepted it.

Presently, the many-legged cunt, still followed by the many-legged uterus, walked towards him. The hairy-back animal bumped into his stomach, staggered back, half-turned, and bumped along his body. It stopped when it came into contact with his chin, slid along it and around to his mouth, where it stopped. He could not see it, but he had the feeling that it was leaning against his lips. Its hairs brushed his nose and made him sneeze. The odour from it was clean and faintly musky, and under other circumstances he would have enjoyed it very much.

The cunt remained by him, pressing on his mouth, as if it recognized something familiar in its blind and deaf world. The uterus was nestled against his neck, its wet skin on his skin.

The snake-thing kept on coming towards him and then it disappeared around his head. He tried to throw his head back and to turn it, but he could not. Within a few seconds, he felt it crawling up over the back of his head. He wanted to scream, to make a superhuman effort that would enable him to burst out of his own skin and run out of the room. Then the thing was coiled up on his cheek, and the wet beard was tickling the lobe of his ear.

The voice was tiny and tinny.

The words were unintelligible. They were in that same language he had heard before, in between French and Spanish. Like an unnasalized, untruncated French. An archaic French, perhaps.

The tiny tinny voice raged on. Its forked tongue flicked against the inner part of his ear.

Suddenly, there was a silence. The body was still there, but it was motionless. The vagina-thing abruptly scuttled away with the uterus-thing nosing after it. Vivienne's head appeared from under the bed and stalked slowly towards him. Her tongue was sticking out from her lax lips, and her bright eyes stared at him.

Her head stopped a few feet from his eyes. Her eyes looked up, evidently at the thing on his cheek. Her lips moved, but no voice issued. This was to be expected, since she had no lungs. The lungs were twin creatures lurching like sick dinosaurs along a drying swamp towards the far wall.

Maybe, Childe thought, maybe the thing can lip-read. Maybe she's giving him instructions for starting the reassembly process.

But what if there is no reassembly? What if this is final? What do I know about her or others of her kind? All were strange,

Philip José Farmer

but some were stranger than others. Vivienne was the strongest. She did not fit into any categories of vampire or werewolf or lamia or ghost. Maybe, when the cord is yanked, the lanyard pulled, she has had it. Surely, she – her parts that is – can't survive long in this condition. They have to eat and to excrete, they are as subject to natural laws as any other creatures, even if they seem to be unnatural.

There is nothing unnatural in this universe. Anything that seems so just isn't explained yet. All things can be explained by natural laws. If you don't know certain laws, then you think a thing is unnatural.

The snake-thing slid down over his eyes on to the floor. It crawled to Vivienne's head and coiled there while the upper part rose to a point a few inches before her eyes. It swayed back and forth like a cobra, and sometimes its head turned. Its mouth was working, and its face was twisted with rage. Only when its head was turned towards him could Childe hear the faint piping voice. It was still using the unknown tongue.

Presently it communicated something or it tired of trying to communicate. It turned and crawled to a point just past his chin. He could not see what it was doing until a moment later. It crawled out past him, towing the uterus behind it. Its tail had been inserted into the interior and probably was being implanted again.

When it was a little distance past his head, it stopped and turned again. It crawled back towards him, stopping with the uterus leaning up against his forehead. The vagina moved away, and he was able to see that the snake-thing was butting it with its head. Herding it.

When it had the vagina manoeuvred into the proper position, it slipped through from the rear of the vagina and emerged through the slit. The vagina moved backwards as if impelled by telepathy until it was reunited with the uterus-thing.

Now what? Childe thought, and then he was able to worry about himself for the first time. Maybe the poison did wear off; maybe Vivienne had been lying about the necessity of the antidote. She must have wanted to give Bill an antidote to get him going more quickly. And at the same time she had administered the poison that would stop his heart. If she had not lied about that, of course.

He tried to move but was as unable as before. However, his thinking and his vision were not as unfocused.

Now he began to be impressed with the utter alienness of the life before him. That a living body could fall apart into discrete creatures which were mobile was unthinkable. But there they were. And how did they survive so long? The blood system, for instance, had been cut off, sealed into each creature, but the circulation, of course, had stopped. There was the heart, its veins and arteries closed up, moving away from him towards the underside of the bed on thirty frail legs. Something about it reminded him of a headless chicken.

But how did these things live without the bringing in of oxygen and the carrying away of waste? They had to have some auxiliary source of energy and excretion. Had to have!

And how did Vivienne manage to hide all these fissures and cleavages, all these legs and God knew what other biological mechanisms, in her body? She should have looked fat and lumpy, but she had not. She had a superb body and that face, that painfully beautiful face, now walking around on a score of skinny legs and four support legs from behind her ears!

The snake-thing dragged itself in front of him, trailing the uterus, in chase of the anus and buttocks. Obviously it intended to unite with them. But what then? It was becoming unwieldy and could not corner too many other pieces and unite before it became too heavy and too awkward.

The head had been busy while he watched the snake-thing. It had kicked and pushed the two shoulders until they were huddled together in a corner of the room. Then the head went off in pursuit of various entrail things while the snake-thing backed into the buttocks and anus and hooked up as a railroad engine would hook up several cars with another.

At that moment, he felt the floor vibrate slightly under him. A second later, two large shoes were by his head. Then the shoes moved on out past him, and he saw the chauffeur. He was a big man with a skin as dark as a sunburned Sicilian's, but his features were Baltic. He had a broad face with high cheekbones and a high forehead and straight dark hair. The scene before him did not seem to bother him in the least.

With swift but efficient movements, he began to reassemble

Philip José Farmer

Vivienne Mabcrough. The parts were placed together or one inserted into another, and presently she was stretched out on the floor in a unit. The fissures closed; the cracks disappeared; the cleavages filled out. When her skin was again unbroken, he hit her over the heart with his fist. She gasped for air, breathed for a while, and then sat up. She was a little unsteady but waved the hand of the chauffeur away.

The head of the snake-thing came out of her slit and stared angrily at him.

"Barton," she said, "put him on the bed and undress him."

Wordlessly, Barton picked Childe up in his arms and laid him out on the bed. He proceeded to take off all of Childe's clothes and to hang them up neatly in the closet. The shoes and socks went under a chair. Childe could see this because he was able by then to turn his head. He could not, however, talk.

"You can go now, Barton," Vivienne said.

The big dark man looked emotionlessly at Childe. Then he said, "Very well, madame," and left.

Childe wondered what his place was in Vivienne's group. He remembered Glam, the giant servant of Baron Igescu. That man had been a strange one, but he was entirely human, or of human origin anyway. He had made the mistake of falling in love with Magda Holyani, who seemed to be a werepython. She had rejected him, and Glam had tried to rape her. The result: most of his bones broken and his blood and guts squeezed out.

If Barton was wholly of human origin, then he was one of the vilest collaborators in history. Or in unhistory, since history, or any human science or scientific discipline, refused to acknowledge the existence, or the possibility of existence, of these beings.

Vivienne stood over him and bent down so that one breast hung above his mouth a few inches.

She said, "You frustrated me, my beautiful Herald Childe, and I don't like to be frustrated. You took away my Bill, a stupid ass of a man but a great cock. So you will substitute for him, even though you are now forbidden."

He wanted to ask what she meant by "forbidden" but could not even open his mouth.

Vivienne kissed him and thrust her tongue into his mouth and felt his tongue and teeth and gums while she played with his cock with one hand. Despite himself, he responded. His cock felt slightly titillated; it warmed up and swelled a little, if his sense of feel was any indication.

Vivienne moved herself up then and put her nipple in his mouth, but he was unable to suck on it. If he had been able, he would have refused. She was the most beautiful woman he had ever seen, but she was by now far from the most desirable. He did not care for murderesses at all, and he loathed her for that thing coiled in her womb. He hoped it was still coiled there, but he doubted it. His anus was beginning to contract in dread of its coming.

Even though he did not suck or tongue it, her nipple grew large and hard in his mouth. She withdrew it and put the other one between his lips, and it grew large. Then she began to kiss his nipples and to stroke his cheeks with her fingers. She slowly traced her tongue down his belly, working back and forth and across, drawing geometric designs with its tip.

When she came to his pubic hairs, she ran her tongue along the edge of the hairline and then worked her tongue over the hairs until they were wet. His penis swelled some more. He did not want it to be affected in the least by her, but something, perhaps the paralysing effect of the bite, made him unable to resist. He loathed her and he wanted to scream at the thought of the snake-thing. But the loathing and the horror were numbed, far away. The pleasure of her tongue and lips was the immediate entity.

When he felt her mouth closing around his testicles, he began to be flooded with a hot sensation. It arose from under his navel and spread outwards but chiefly towards the base of his penis. When it oozed into his penis, it filled it out so that it rose up straight and hard.

After a while, she pushed the testicles out with her tongue and lowered her head over his cock. Her lips went softly and wetly around the head, and her tongue pressed against the slit in its end. He groaned deep within himself and could not repress a desire to move his hips upward to drive his prick deeper into her mouth. The desire was all that resulted; his hips remained motionless.

Vivienne continued to suck on the glans and occasionally to move her head down so that the shaft went in all the way. The warmth at the base of his penis became a rod of fire which stretched from the tip of his spine to the tip of his cock. The heavy

Philip José Farmer

grey fluid was moving slowly, rubbing against excited nerves, towards the entrance to his shaft.

Suddenly, Vivienne got up and turned around, presenting that lovely back and the egg-shaped buttocks. She squatted over him and reached down and tenderly took the head between her fingers. This she guided into her anus as she lowered herself down on it. The head stuck in the tight mouth for a minute and then abruptly slid in. It moved against a warm slick surface until the flesh of her ass was against his pubic hairs.

She lowered and raised herself slowly several times, causing him to feel ecstatic. It would not take much of this to make him come. And he did not like buggering. Though he had done it several times, in response to women who liked it, he had a distaste for it. Now his repulsion was on the edge of his mind. It bulked large enough for him to be aware of it, but it did not bother him.

She stopped on an upward movement, leaving his cock half in.

Knowing what was about to happen, he mentally gritted his teeth. The horror did not draw any blood from his engorged penis, however.

Suddenly, something slipped down over his testicles. It slid over the sac and under, and something – the thing's bearded little head, of course – touched his anus. Then it entered and was pushing into his anus and then up his rectum. It felt hard and solid and unpleasant, as when a doctor stuck a finger up him for a prostate examination. But this disagreeable sensation did not last long. Something, perhaps its bite or the substance released by its bite, turned unpleasantness into a warm and relaxing feeling.

A few seconds later, Vivienne began to move up and down on his cock, and he could feel the body of the snake-thing sliding back and forth in him. Its motion seemed to be independent of hers; it was moving much faster than her motions could account for.

The warmth and relaxation within his rectum and his bowels gave way to an almost hot feeling and a tension. The tension was, however, near-ecstatic. His insides felt as ready for orgasm as his penis. Both exquisitenesses acted as sine waves out of phase with each other. But as Vivienne increased her slidings up and down his pole, and as the snake-thing continued at the same rapid pace, the waves slowly came into phase.

There was a moment of glory: a flashing red light across his eyes, a spurt of metal rubbing against his pleasure nerves, a breaking through of a red-hot drill in the centre of his brain, and he exploded. It was as if he had been turned inside out as he passed through some fifth-dimensional continuum. He was a glove of flesh removed from a hand, inverted, and exposed to radiations.

Vivienne sat on him for a while but rotated on his cock so that she could face him. The action pulled the snake-thing along, but it, apparently, was through. It slid into her slit and out of his anus and then was facing him. Its shaft and head were smeared and it was still expelling a musky grey fluid from its mouth. When the flow had ceased, its forked tongue flickered out and began to clean its face. Within a few minutes, its face and beard looked as if it had showered.

Though it did not look as vicious as before, it still looked dangerous.

Childe was glad to see it withdraw, although he wished that it had not first moved up her body and kissed her on the lower lip with its thin mouth.

Vivienne scooted up when the thing disappeared into her cunt, and his penis slipped out of her anus. She kissed him and said, "I love you."

He could not reply, but he thought, "Love?" He wished he could vomit.

At that moment, three men entered the room. One of them had a cane, from which he pulled a thin-bladed sword. He stuck the point of it against Vivienne's neck.

She turned pale and said, "Why are you breaking the truce?"

Chapter 5

Forrest J Ackerman, hiding in the bushes, was getting wetter. He was also becoming madder.

Three days ago he had received through the mail a large flat box. This had come from England, and it contained an original painting by Bram Stoker. The painting depicted Count Dracula in the act of sucking blood from the throat of a young blonde. Many illustrations have done this; a number of reprints of *Dracula*, written by Bram Stoker, have shown Dracula going down on a sleeping young beauty, and innumerable advertisements and stills for various Dracula movies have shown this.

But this was the only painting of Dracula done by the author himself. Until a few months ago, its existence had been unknown. Then a dozen oil paintings and a score of ink drawings had been found in a house in Dublin, once owned by a friend of Stoker's. The present owner had discovered the works in a boarded-up closet in the attic. He had not known what the paintings and drawings represented in money. He had sold them to an art dealer for several pounds and thought himself well ahead.

But the dealer had brought in handwriting experts who verified that the signature on the illustrations was indeed Bram Stoker's. Forry Ackerman, reading of this, had sent a wire to the Dublin art dealer and offered to top any price submitted. The result was that he got his painting but had to go to the bank to get a loan. Since then, he had been waiting anxiously and could talk of little but the expected arrival.

When he unwrapped it, he was not disappointed. Admittedly, Stoker was no St John, Bok, Finlay, or even a Paul. But his work had a certain crude force that a number of people commented upon. It was a primitive, no doubt of that, but a powerful primitive. Forry was glad that it had some artistic merit, although he had no knowledge of what constituted "good art" and no desire to learn. He knew what he liked, and he liked this.

Besides, even if it had been less powerful, even crude, he would not have cared. He had the *only original painting* of Dracula by the author of *Dracula*. No one else in the world could claim that.

This was no longer true.

That night he had come home to his house in the 800 block of Sherbourne Drive. It was raining then as now, and the water was pouring down his driveway into the street. The street was flooded but the water had not yet risen to cover the sidewalk. It was after one o'clock, and he had just left a party at Wendy's to come here because he had to get out one of his comic magazines. As editor of *Vampirella* and some horror magazines, he had hard schedules to meet. He had to edit *Vampirella* tonight and get it out in the morning, air mail, special delivery, to his publisher in New York.

He had unlocked the door and entered the front room. This was a rather large room decorated with large and small original paintings of science-fiction and fantasy magazine covers, paintings done on commission, stills from various horror and so-called science-fiction movies, photographs of Lon Chaney, Jr as the Wolf Man, Boris Karloff as Boris Karloff, and Bela Lugosi as Dracula. Each bore a signature and a dedication of best wishes and fondest regards to "Forry". There were also heads and masks of Frankenstein's monster, the Creature from the Black Lagoon, King Kong, and a number of other fictional monsters. The bookshelves reached from floor to ceiling at several places, and these were jammed with the works of science-fiction authors, Gothic novel writers, and some volumes on exotic sexual practices.

Forry's house had to be seen to be visualized. It had once been his residence, but he had filled it with works evaluated at over a million dollars. He had moved into Wendy's apartment and now used the house as his business office and as his private museum. The day would come – perish the day! – when he would no longer be around to enjoy, to vibrate with joy, in the midst of his dream come true. Then it would become a public museum with the great Ray Bradbury as trustee, and people would come from all over the world to view his collection or to do research in the rare books and with the paintings and manuscripts and letters. He was thinking about having his ashes placed in a bronze bust of Karloff as Frankenstein's monster and the bust put on a pedestal in the middle of this room. Thus he would be here in physical fact, though not in spirit, since he refused to believe in any survival after death.

California law, however, forbade any such deposit of one's ashes. The morticians' and cemetery owners' lobby had ensured that the legislature passed laws beneficial to their interests. Even a man's ashes had to be buried in a cemetery, no matter what his wishes. There was a provision that ashes could be scattered out over the sea, but only from an airplane at a suitable distance and height. And the ashes of only one person at a time could be done so. The lobby ensured that the ashes of a number of deceased were not stored until a mass, thus economical, flight could be made. The lobby ensured that the bereaved made tribute to the jackals of the dead, to the worshippers of Anubis.

Forry, thinking about this, suppressed his anger at the money-hungry and essentially soulless robbers of the bereaved. He wondered if he could not make some arrangements for an illegal placing of his ashes in the bust. Why not? He could get some friends to do it. They were a wild bunch – some of them were – and they would not be stopped by a little illegality.

While he was standing there, taking off his raincoat, he looked around. There was the J. Allen St John painting of Circe and the swine, Ulysses' buddies. And there, pride of his prides, and there... and there...

The Stoker was gone.

It had been hung on a place opposite the door so that anybody entering could not miss seeing it. It had displaced two paintings. Forry had had a hard time finding space in this house where every inch of the wall was accounted for.

Now, a blank spot showed where it had been.

·Forry crossed the room and sat down. His heart beat only a little faster. He had a faulty pacemaker; it controlled the heart within a narrow range, and that explained why he had to take stairs slowly and could not run. Nor did excitement step up the heart. The emotions were there, however, and they made him quiver when he should have beat.

He thought of calling the police, as he had done several times in the past. His collection had been the object of attentions of many a burglar, usually a science-fiction or horror addict who brushed aside any honesty he might have possessed in his lust to get his hands on books, paintings, stills, manuscripts, masks, photographs of the famous and so forth. He had lost thousands of dollars from this thievery which was bad enough. But the realization that some of the works were irreplaceable hurt him far worse. And the thought that anybody could do these evil things to him, who loved the world as he did not love God, hurt. Who loved people, rather, since he was no Nature lover.

Putting aside his first inclination to call the police, he decided to check with the Dummocks. These were a young couple who had moved in shortly after the previous caretakers, the Wards, had moved out. Lorenzo and Hulia Dummock were broke and houseless, as usual, so he had offered them his hospitality. All they had to do was keep the house clean and fairly well ordered and act as helpers sometimes when he gave a party. Also, they would be his burglar insurance, since he no longer lived in the house.

He went upstairs after calling a number of times and getting no answer. The bedroom was the only room in the house which had space for residents. There was a bed and a dresser and a closet, all of which the Dummocks used. Their clothes were thrown on the bed, the floor, the dresser top, and on a pile of books in one corner. The bed had been unmade for days.

The Dummocks were not there, and he doubted they could be anyplace else in the house. They had gone out for the night, as they quite often did. He did not know where they got their money to spend, since Hulia was the only one working and she did that only between sieges of asthma. Lorenzo wrote stories but had so far been able to sell only his hard-core pornography and not much of that. Forry thought they must be visiting somebody off whom they were undoubtedly sponging. This increased his anger, since he asked very little of them in return for room and board. Being here nights to watch for burglars had been their main job. And if he reproached them for falling down on this, they would sneer at him and accuse him of exploiting them.

He searched through the house and then put on his raincoat and went out to the garage. The Stoker painting was not there.

Five minutes later, he got a phone call. The voice was muffled and unrecognizable, although the caller had identified himself as Rupert Vlad, a friend and a committeeman in the Count Dracula Society. Since Forry took all his calls through the answering service, he could listen in and determine if he wished to answer any. This voice was unfamiliar, but the name got the caller through.

"Forry, this isn't Vlad. Guess you know that?"

Philip José Farmer

"I know," said Forry softly. "Who is it?"

"A friend, Forry. You know me, but I'd just as soon not tell you who I really am. I belong to the Lord Ruthven League and the Count Dracula Society, too. I don't want to get anybody mad at me. But I'll tell you something. I heard about you getting that painting of Dracula by Stoker. I was going to come over and see it. But I attended a meeting of the Lord Ruthven League... and I saw it there."

"You what?" Forry said shrilly. For once he had lost his self-control.

"Yeah. I saw it on the wall of, uh, well..."

There was a pause.

Forry said, "For the sake of Hugo, man, don't keep me hanging in air! I have a right to know!"

"Yeah, but I feel such a shit finking on this guy. He..."

"He's a thief!" Forry said. "A terrible thief! You wouldn't be a fink. You'd – be doing a public service! Not to mention servicing me!"

Even in his excitement and indignation, he could not keep from punning.

"Yeah, uh, well, I guess you're right. I'll tell you. You go right over to Woolston Heepish's house. You'll see what I'm talking about."

"Woolston Heepish!" Forry said. He groaned and then added, "Oh, no!"

"Uh, yeah! I guess he's been bugging you for years, right? I kinda feel sorry for you, Forry, having to put up with him, though I must say he does have a magnificent collection. I guess he should, since he got some of it from you."

"I never gave him anything!"

"No, but he took. So long, Forry."

Chapter 6

Fifteen minutes later, Forry was outside the Heepish residence. This was two blocks over from Forry's own house, almost even with it. In the dark and the driving rain, it looked an exact duplicate of the Ackermansion. It was a California pseudo-Spanish bungalow with a green-painted stucco exterior. The driveway was on the left as you approached the house, and when you stepped past the extension of the house, a wall, you saw the big tree that grew in the patio. It leaned at a forty-five-degree angle across the house, and its branches lay like a great hand over part of the tiled roof. At the end of the driveway was the garage, and in front of the garage was a huge wooden cutout of a movie monster.

You turned to the right and on to a small porch to face a wooden door plastered with various signs: NO SMOKING PERMITTED. WIPE YOUR FEET AND YOUR MIND BEFORE ENTERING. THE EYES OF HEEPISH ARE ON YOU (hinting at the closed-circuit TV with which Heepish scanned his visitors before admitting them). ESPERANTO AND VOLAPUK SPOKEN HERE. (This bugged Forry, who was a long-time and ardent Esperantist. Heepish not only imitated Ackerman with the Esperanto, but, in his efforts to go him one better, had learned Esperanto's closest rival, Volapuk.)

Forry stood for some time before the door, his finger held out to press on the doorbell. The skies were still emptying their bins; the splash of water was all around. Water roared out of the gutter drains and covered the patio. The light above the door gave a ghostly green illumination. All that the scene needed was thunder and lightning, the door swinging open slowly and creakingly, and a tall pale-faced, red-lipped man with sharp features and black hair plastered close to his head, and a deep voice with a Hungarian accent saying, "Good evening!"

There was no light from the interior of the house. Every window was curtained off or boarded up or barred by bookcases. Forry had not seen the interior of the house, but it had been described to him. His own house was so furnished.

Finally, he dropped his hand from the doorbell. He would scout around a little. After all, he would look like an ass if he barged in demanding to have his painting back, only to find that his informant had lied. It would not be the first time that he had been

Philip José Farmer

maliciously misinformed so he would get into an embarrassing situation.

He walked around the side of the house and then to the back. There should be a room here which had once been an anteroom or pantry for the kitchen. In his own house, it was now piled with books and magazines; in fact, he kept his collection of *Doc Savage* magazines just off the kitchen door.

The curtains over the windows were shut tight. He placed his ear against the window in the door but could hear nothing. After a while, he returned to the front. That there were two cars in the driveway and a number parked in the street might indicate that Heepish had guests. Perhaps he should return to his house and phone Heepish.

Then he decided that he would confront Heepish directly. He would not give him a chance to deny he had the painting or to hide it.

Having made up his mind, he still could not bring himself to ring the doorbell. He went to the front of the house and stood in the bushes for a while while the rain pelted him and water dripped off the branches. The confrontation was going to be dreadful. Highly embarrassing. For both of them. Well, maybe not for Heepish. That man had more nerve than a barrel of brass monkeys.

A car passing by threw its water-soaked beams on him for a minute. He blinked against the diffused illumination and then walked from under the shelter of the bush. Why wait any longer? Heepish was not going to come out and invite him in.

He pressed the button, which was the nose of a gargoyle face painted on the door. A loud clanging as of bells came from within followed by several bars of organ music: *Gloomy Sunday*.

There was a peephole in the large door, but Heepish no longer used this, according to Forry's informants. The pressing of the doorbell now activated a TV camera located behind a one-way window on the left of the porch.

A voice from the Frankenstein mask nailed on the door said, "As I live and don't breathe! Forrest J (no period) Ackerman! Thrice welcome!"

A moment later, the door swung open with a loud squeaking as of rusty hinges. This, of course, was a recording synchronized to the door.

Woolston Heepish himself greeted Forry. He was six feet tall, portly, soft-looking, somewhat paunched, and had a prominent dewlap. His walrus moustache was bronzish, and his hair was dark red, straight, and slick. He wore square rimless spectacles behind which grey eyes blinked. He hunched forward as if he had spent most of his life reading books or working at a desk. Or standing under a rainy bush, Forry thought.

"Come in!" he said in a soft voice. He extended a hand which Forry shook, although he wished he could ignore it, let it hang out in the air. But, after all, he did not know for sure that Heepish was guilty.

Then he stiffened, and he dropped Heepish's hand.

Over Heepish's shoulder he saw the painting. It was hung at approximately the same place it had hung in his house. There was Dracula sinking those long canines into the neck of a blonde girl!

He became so angry that the room swirled for a moment.

Heepish took his arm and walked him towards the sofa, saying, "You look ill, Forry. Surely I don't have *that* effect on you?"

There were five others in the room, and they gathered about the sofa where he sat. They looked handsome and beautiful and were dressed in expensive up-to-the-latest-minute clothes.

"My painting!" Forry gasped. "The Stoker!"

Heepish looked up at it and put the tips of his fingers together to make a church steeple. He smiled under the walrus moustache.

"You like it! I'm so glad! A fabulous collector's item!" Forry choked and tried to stand up. One of the guests, a woman who looked as if she were Mexican, pushed him back down.

"You need rest! You look pale. What are you doing out on a night like this? You're soaked! Stay there. I'll get you a cup of coffee."

"I don't want coffee," Forry said. He tried to stand up but felt too dizzy. "I just want my painting back."

The woman returned with a cup of hot coffee, a package of sugar, and a pitcher of cream on a tray. She offered it to him, saying, "I am Mrs Panchita Pocyotl."

"Of course, how graceless of me!" Heepish said. "I apologize for not introducing you, my dear Forry. My only excuse

Philip José Farmer

is that I was worried about your health."

The other woman was a tall slender blonde with large breasts, a Diana Rumbow. The three men were Fred Pao, a Chinese, Rex Bilgreen, a mulatto, and George Bunyan, an Englishman.

Forry, looking at them clearly for the first time, thought they had something sinister about them. He could not, however, define it. Maybe it was something about the eyes. Or maybe it was because he was so outraged about the painting he thought that anybody who had anything to do with Heepish was sinister.

Mrs Pocyotl bent over to give him the coffee and exposed large light-chocolate-coloured breasts with big red nipples. She wore no brassiere under the thin formal gown with the deep cleavage.

Under other circumstances, he would have been delighted.

Then Diana Rumbow, the blonde, dropped a book she was holding and bent over to pick it up. Despite his upset condition, he responded with a slight popping of the eyes and a stirring around his groin. Her breasts were just as unbrassiered as Panchita's. They were pale white, and the nipples were as large as his thumb tips and so red they must have been rouged. When she stood up, he could see how darkly they stood out under the filmy gown she wore.

He was also beginning to see that the bendings over were not accidents. They were trying to take his mind off his quest.

Pocyotl sat down by him and placed her thigh against his. Diana Rumbow sat down on the other side and leaned her superb breast against the side of his arm. If he looked to either side, he saw swelling mounds and deep cleavages.

"My painting!" he croaked.

Heepish ignored the words. He drew up a chair and sat down facing Forry and said, "Well! This is a great honour you have done me, Mr Ackerman. Or may I call you Forry?"

"My painting, my Stoker!" Forry croaked again.

"Now that you've finally decided to let bygones be bygones, and, I presume, decided that your hostility towards me was unwarranted, we must talk and talk! We must talk the night out. After all, what with the rain and all, what else is there to do but talk? We have so much in common, so much, as so many people, kind and unkind, have pointed out. I think that we will learn to know each other quite well. Who knows, we might even decide someday that the Count Dracula Society and the Lord Ruthven League can band together, become the Greater Vampire Coven, or something like that, even if witches and not vampires have covens? Heh?"

"My painting," Forry said.

Heepish continued to talk to him, while the others chattered among themselves. Occasionally, one of the women leaned over against him. He became aware of their perfume, exotic odours that he did not remember ever having smelled before. They stimulated him even in his anger. And those breasts! And Pocyotl's flashing dark eyes and Rumbow's brilliant blue eyes!

He shook his head. What kind of witchcraft were they practising on him? He had entered with the determination of finding the painting, taking it down from the wall or wherever it was, and marching out the front door with it. Now that he considered that, he would have to find something to protect it from the rain until he could get it into his car, which was across the street. His coat would do it. Never mind that he would get soaked. The painting was the important thing.

But he could not get off the sofa. And Heepish would not pay the slightest attention to his remarks about the painting. Neither would the guests.

He felt as if he were in a parallel universe which was in contact with that in Heepish's house but somewhat out of phase with it. He could communicate to a certain degree and then his words faded out. And, now that he looked around, this place seemed a trifle fuzzy.

Suddenly, he wondered if his coffee had been drugged.

It seemed so ridiculous that he tried to dismiss the thought. But if Heepish could steal his painting and hang it up where so many people would see it, knowing that word would quickly get to the man from whom he had stolen it, and if he could blandly, even friendlily, sit with the man from whom he had taken his property and act as if nothing were wrong, then such a man would have no compunction about drugging him.

But why would he want to drug him?

Thoughts of cellars with dirt floors and a six foot long, six foot deep trench in the dirt moved like a funeral train across his mind. A furnace in the basement burned flesh and bones. An acid

Philip José Farmer

pit ate away his body. He was roasted in an oven and this crew had him for dinner. He was immured, standing up, while Heepish and his guests toasted him with Amontillado. He was put in a cage in the basement and rats, scores of them, big hungry rats, were released into the cage. Afterwards, his clean-picked skeleton was wired together and stood up in this room as an extra macabre item. His friends and acquaintances, members of the Count Dracula Society and the Lord Ruthven League, would visit here because Heepish would become king after the great Forry Ackerman disappeared so mysteriously. They would see the skeleton and wonder whose it was – since so many people play Hamlet to the unknown Yoricks – and might even pat his bony head. They might even speak of Forry Ackerman in the presence of the skeleton.

Forry shook himself as a dog shakes himself emerging from water. He was getting a little psycho about this. All he had to do was to assert his rights. If Heepish objected, he would call the police. But he did not think that even Heepish would have the guts to stand in his way.

He stood up so suddenly he became even dizzier. He said, "I'm taking my painting, Heepish! Don't get in my way!"

He turned around and stood up on the cushion and lifted the painting off its hook. There was a silence behind him, and when he turned, he saw that all were standing up, facing him. They formed a semi-circle through which he would have to go to get to the door. They looked grave, and their eyes seemed to have become larger and almost luminous. Almost, because it was his imagination that put a werewolfish gleam in them. Of course.

Mrs Pocyotl curled her lips back, and he saw that her canines were very long. How had he missed that feature when he first saw her? She had smiled, and it seemed to him that her teeth were very white and very even.

He stepped down off the sofa and said, "I want my coat, Heepish."

Heepish grinned. His teeth seemed to have become longer too. His grey eyes were as cold and hard as a winter sky in New York City.

"You may have your *coat*, Forry, since you don't want to be friendly."

Forry understood the emphasis. Coat but not painting.

He said, "I'll call the police."

"You wouldn't want to do that," Diana Rumbow said.

"Why not?" Forry said.

He wished his heart could beat faster. It should be, but it wasn't, even under this strain. Instead, his muscles were jerking, and his eyes were blinking twice as fast as usual, as if they were trying to substitute for the lack of heartbeats.

"Because," the blonde said, "I would accuse you of rape."

"What?"

The painting almost slipped from his hands.

Diana Rumbow slipped out of her gown, revealing that she was wearing only a garter belt and nylon stockings. Her pubic hairs were long and very thick and a bright yellow. Her breasts, though large, did not sag.

Mrs Pocyotl said, "Maybe you'd like two for the price of one, Forry."

She slipped out of her gown, revealing that she wore only stockings and a belt. Her pubic hairs were black as a crow's feathers, and her breasts were conical.

Forry stepped back until the backs of his knees were in contact with the sofa. He said, "What is this?"

"Well, *if* the police should be called, they would find this house deserted except for you and the two women. One woman would be unconscious and the other would be screaming. Both women would have sperm in their cunts, you can bet on that. And bruises. And you would be naked and dazed, as if you had, shall we say, gone mad with lust?"

Forry looked at them. All were grinning now, and they looked very evil. They also looked as if they meant to do whatever Heepish ordered.

He was in a nightmare. What kind of evil beings were these? All this for a painting?

He said, loudly, "Get out of the way! I'm coming through! This painting is mine! And you're not going to intimidate me! I don't care what you do, you're not getting to keep this! I might have given it to you, Heepish, if you'd become a good friend and wanted it badly enough! But not now! So out of the way!"

Holding the painting as if it were a shield or a battering ram, he walked towards Heepish and the naked Rumbow.

Philip José Farmer

Chapter 7

Herald Childe drove slowly through the rain and the high waters. His windshield wipers were not able to cope at this moment, so dense was the downpour. His headlights strove to pierce the sheets with little effect. Other cars, driven by more foolhardy Angelenos, passed him with great splashings.

It took him more than two hours to get to his house in Topanga Canyon. He drove up the steep sidestreet at ten miles an hour while water, several inches deep, poured down past him. As he turned to go into his driveway, he noticed the car beneath the oak tree by the road. Another car that had been abandoned here, he supposed. There had been seven automobiles left here within the past several weeks. All were of the same model and year. All had been by the oak tree when he awoke in the morning. Some had been left for a week before the cops finally came and towed them away. Some had been there a few days and then had disappeared during the early morning hours.

He did not know why somebody was abandoning cars in front of his house or, if not outright abandoning them, was parking them for such a long time. His neighbours for two blocks on either side of the house and both sides of the street knew nothing about the cars.

The cops said that the cars they'd towed away were stolen.

So here was the seventh. Possibly the seventh. He must not jump to conclusions. It could belong to somebody visiting his neighbours. He would find out soon enough.

Meanwhile, he needed to get to bed. To sleep. He had had more than enough of that other bedtime activity.

The house was his property. He owed nothing on it except the yearly taxes. It was a five room bungalow, Spanish style, with a big backyard and a number of trees. His aunt had willed it to him, and when she had died last year, he had moved in. He had not seen his aunt since 1942, when he had been a child, nor had he exchanged more than three letters with her in the past ten years. But she had left all her property to him. There was enough money so that he had the house left after using the money to pay off the inheritance tax.

Childe had been a private detective, but, after his experiences with Baron Igeseu and the disappearance of his wife, he had quit. He wasn't a very good detective, he decided, and besides, he was sick of the business. He would go back to college, major in history, in which he had always been interested, get a master's and, possibly, a PhD in time. He would teach in a junior college at first and, later, in a university.

It would have been more convenient for him to take an apartment in Westwood where he would be close to the UCLA campus. But his money was limited, and he liked the house and the comparative quiet, so he drove every day to school. To save gas and also to find a parking place easier on the crowded campus, he rode a motorcycle during the week.

Just now the school was closed because of vacation.

It was a lonely life. He was busy studying because he was carrying a full load, and he had to keep up the house and the yard, but he still needed someone to talk to and to take to bed. There were women who came up to his house from time to time: teachers his own age or a little older, some older students, and, occasionally, a younger chick who dug his looks. He resembled a rough-hewn Lord Byron. *With a clubfoot mind*, he always added mentally when someone commented on this. It was no secret to him that he was neurotic. But then who wasn't? If that was any consolation.

He turned on the lights and checked the windows to make sure again that none were leaking. It was a compulsive action he went through before leaving and after coming back – at least three times each time. Then he looked out of the back window. The yard was narrow but deep, and this was good. Behind it towered a cliff of dirt, which had, so far, not become a mud flow. Water poured off it and drowned his backyard, and the water was up over the bottom steps of the back porch stairs. He understood, from what his neighbours said, that the cliff had been closer to his house at one time. About ten years ago it had slid down and covered the backyard almost to the house. The aunt had spent much money having the dirt hauled away and a concrete and steel wire embankment built at the foot of the cliff. Then, two years ago, in the extraordinarily heavy rains, the cliff had collapsed again. It had, however, only buried the embankment and come about six feet into the yard. The aunt had done nothing about it, and, a year later, had

Philip José Farmer

died.

The entire Los Angeles, Ventura, and Orange County area was being inundated. The governor was thinking about having Southern California declared a disaster area. Houses had floated away, mud slides had buried other houses, a car had disappeared in a hole in Ventura Boulevard, a woman waiting for a bus in downtown Los Angeles had been buried in a mud slide, houses were slipping in the Pacific Palisades and in the canyons everywhere.

There was only one consolation about the deluge. No smog.

Childe went into the kitchen and opened the pantry and took out a bottle of Jack Daniels. He seldom drank, preferring marijuana, but when he was downcast and upset, marijuana only made him more gloomy. He needed something to dull his mind and nerves, and Tennessee mash on the rocks would do it.

He sipped the stuff, shaking and making a face as he did so. After a while, he could swallow it without repugnance. A little later, he could sip on it with pleasure. He began to feel numb and even a trifle happy. The memory of Vivienne was still with him, but it did not shake him so much now.

The three men had entered and one had delicately placed the tip of his sword against Vivienne's neck. She had said something about his breaking the truce.

What truce? He had never found out. But the man with the sword cane had accused her and her people – he called them Ogs – of first breaking the truce. The Ogs had captured Childe and abused him. This was definitely against the rules. He was not even to be aware of their existence or of that of the Tocs.

Moreover, they had endangered Childe's life. He might have been killed because of their irresponsible behaviour. In fact, the Tocs were not sure that the Ogs had not had it in mind to kill Childe.

"You know as well as you know anything that we agreed on The Face of Barrikh and the Testicle of Drammukh that we would let The Child develop until he was ready!" the swordsman said.

"The Child?" thought Herald. "Or did he mean The Childe?"
Later, he thought, "Possibly the two are the same."

Vivienne, still crouching on the bed, had said, "It was an accident that he came to our house – to Igescu's, I mean. He insisted on breaking in and spying on us, and the temptation to partake of his power was too much for us. In that, we were guilty. Then things got out of hand. We did not handle him correctly, I'll admit. We forgot that he would have to be watched very closely; he looks so human it's easy to do, you know. And he acts so stupidly at times, he made us a little contemptuous of him."

"Of The Child?" the swordsman said. "I think you are the stupid ones. He is not an adult yet, you know, so you can't expect him to act like one. Anyway, I doubt the adulthood of any of you Ogs."

Vivienne, looking then at Childe, said, "We've been talking in English!"

She burst into a spew of a language which he had heard before even if it was unintelligible to him. It was the same language that his captors had used when he was a prisoner in Igescu's.

Though he did not understand what followed, he was able to determine the name of the swordsman. It was Hindarf.

Hindarf seemed inclined to run Vivienne through, but she talked him out of it. Finally, Hindarf pricked him with a needle, and presently he was able to function almost normally. He got dressed and allowed himself to be escorted out of the house. He was still too shaky to drive, so Hindarf drove while the other two men followed in their car. Hindarf refused to answer Childe's questions. His only comment was that Childe should stay away from the Ogs. Apparently, he had believed Vivienne's story that Childe was the intruder in this case.

A few blocks before they came to the turn-off to Topanga Canyon, Hindarf stopped the car. "I think you can drive from here on."

He got out and held the door open for a moment while the rain fell into the car and wet the driver's seat and the steering wheel.

He stuck his face into the car and said, "Please don't go near that bunch again. They're deadly. You should know that. If it weren't..."

He was silent for several seconds and then said, "Never mind. We'll be seeing you."

He slammed the door shut. Childe scooted over into the driver's seat and watched Hindarf and the others drive away. Their car swung around and went down Topanga Canyon.

As he sat in the front room and tried to watch TV while he swigged Jack Daniels, he thought of that evening. Almost nothing made sense. But he did believe that Igescu and Krautschner and Bending Grass and Pao and the others had not been vampires, werewolves, werebears, or what have you. They were very strange, bordering on the unnatural or whatever humans thought of as unnatural. The theory advanced by Igescu, and presumably stated by the early-19th-century Belgian, "explained" the existence of these creatures. But Childe was beginning to think that Igescu had led him astray. He did not know why he would lie to him, but there seemed to be many things he did not know about this business.

If he had any sense, he would follow Hindarf's advice.

That was the trouble. He had never shown too much common sense.

Fools rush in, and so forth.

After four shots of mash whiskey on an empty stomach, one also unaccustomed to liquor, he went to bed. He slept uneasily and had a number of dreams and nightmares that he forgot as soon as he awoke.

The persistent ringing of the telephone woke him. He came up out of a sleep that seemed drugged, and was, if alcohol was a drug. He knocked the phone off while groping for it. When he picked it up, an unfamiliar male voice said, "Is this McGivern's?"

"What number did you want?" Childe said.

The phone clicked. He looked at the luminous hands of his wristwatch. Three o'clock in the morning.

He tried to go back to sleep but couldn't. At ten after three, he got up and went into the bathroom for a drink of water. He did not turn on the light. Going out of the bathroom, he decided to check on the condition of the street before he went back to bed. It was still raining heavily, and the street had been ankle-deep in water when he had driven up before the house.

He pulled the curtain back and looked out. The car that had been parked under the oak tree was pulling away. The lights from the car behind it showed that a man was driving it. The car swung around and started slowly down the street towards Topanga

Canyon. The lights of the other car shone on the pale face of Fred Pao, the Chinese he had seen at Igescu's. His lights threw the profiles of the three men in the other car into silhouette. One of them looked like Bending Grass, the Crow Indian, or Crow werebear, but that could not be. Bending Grass had died under the wheels of his car when Childe had escaped from the burning Igescu mansion.

He turned and ran into the bedroom and slipped into a pair of pants and shoes without socks. He ran into the front room, put on a rainhat and raincoat and picked up his wallet and car keys from the bowl of wax fruit – his aunt's legacy – on the dining room table. He got into the car and took off backwards, splashing water as if he were surf-riding as he backed on to the street. He drove faster than he should have and twice skidded and once the motor sputtered and he thought he had killed it.

He caught up with them about a quarter of a mile up Topanga. The lead car was slowing down even more and looked as if it would swing into a private road that went up the steep hill. He had never been up it, but he knew that it led to a huge three-storied house that had been built when the road was a dirt trail. It stood on top of a hill and overlooked much of the area, including his own house.

Abruptly, the lead car stopped. He had to go on by them; they would become suspicious if he also stopped. At the top of the hill he slowed down, found a driveway, turned in, and backed out. He came down the hill again in time to see the two cars heading back down Topanga Canyon.

He wondered what had made them change their minds? Had they become suspicious of him? Perhaps they had seen his lights as he turned on to Topanga?

Childe followed them into Los Angeles. The cars proceeded cautiously through the heavy rain and flooded streets until they reached San Vicente and La Cienega. When the light changed to green, the two cars suddenly roared into life. Shooting wings of water, their tyres howling even on the wet pavement, they sped away. He accelerated after them. They swung left on reaching Sixth and skidded into the traffic island, bounced off, and continued back up San Vicente on the other side of the boulevard, then skidded right as they turned on Orange.

Philip José Farmer

The green light was with them and with Childe, who was about a block behind. His rear tyres hit the curb of the island and one wheel went over and there was a crash. He supposed his right fender had struck the traffic light, but it did not seem to impair the operation of the car. He shot after the other two cars, though he wondered why he was risking his limb and life. But the fact that they were trying so desperately to get away, that they had deliberately led him astray from that road up to the house on top of the hill, kept him going.

Nevertheless, when the car turned west on to Wilshire Boulevard, he began to think strongly about giving up the chase. They had gone through a red light without stopping and by the time he reached the intersection, he saw their tail lights a block away. They were still casting out great sheafs of water.

He continued after them, increasing his speed. He did not know what he would do if he caught up with them. Four against one? And at least one of them, probably all four, was a being with some very strange and deadly powers. He remembered Hindarf's words.

At Wilshire and San Vicente, the two cars went through a red light two seconds after it had changed. Two cars coming south on San Vicente met them. The lead car slammed broadside into Fred Pao's automobile, and the car behind the lead car smashed into its rear. The car following Pao rammed into his rear. A moment later, Childe's car, turning around and around on the wet pavement, slammed its rear into the car that had been following Pao's. The whole mass, five cars jammed into each other, swung around like a five-pointed star, around and around.

Chapter 8

"Very well, Forry," Heepish said. "If you want it that badly..."

He bowed and made a flourish. Forry felt his cheeks warming up. He said, "Do I *want* it? It's *mine!* I paid for it with my money! You stole it, like a common thief!"

"No common thief would touch it," Heepish said.

Forry, deciding that absolutely nothing was to be gained by standing there, plunged on ahead. The others opened a way for him, and Heepish even ran up and opened the door for him.

"See you, Forry," he said.

"Yeah. In jail, maybe!"

As soon as he was in his own house, Forry placed the painting on the wall and then checked the doors to make sure they were locked. The Dummocks had not come home yet, so he decided to stay and sleep on the couch that night. Then he remembered that he was supposed to get the latest edition of *Vampirella* out. He had completely forgotten about it!

He made himself some coffee and went into a rear room, where his "office" was. He worked away steadily until 2:30, when he heard a slight noise somewhere in the house. He rose and started out of the office when the lights went out. That was all he needed to put him hopelessly behind schedule!

He fumbled around in the desk drawer for matches which he did not think he would have, since he had never smoked. Finding none, he groped through to the kitchen. The pantry shelves were filled with books and magazines. He did not eat at the house but took all his meals out or ate at Wendy's. The icebox, except for some cream for coffee and a few goodies, was filled with microfilm.

As he felt around in the porch room for a flashlight, the lights suddenly came back on. He continued until he found the flashlight. If the power failed again, he would work by its light.

On the way back to the office, he looked into the front room. The Stoker painting was gone!

There was no time to stand around and think. He put on his rainhat and raincoat and rubbers and walked as fast as his heart would let him out to the car. He got into the big green Cadillac and backed out into the lake which Sherbourne Drive had become. He went as fast as he dared and within two minutes was before Woolston Heepish's. Fred Pao, the painting in his arms, was just turning away from the car.

Forry blasted his horn at him and flicked his brights on. The Chinese was startled and almost dropped the painting. Forry cried out in anguish and then lowered the window to shout at Pao.

"I'll call the police!"

Pao opened the rear door of the car and shoved the painting into it. He ran around to the other side, got in, and the motor roared. His Mercury took off with a screeching of tyres and sped towards Olympic. Forry stared at him for several seconds and then, biting his lip, took off with a similar screeching of tyres. At the same time, he honked furiously at the Chinese. The man was taking his beloved Dracula where he could hide it until the search was up. And then Woolston Heepish would receive it!

But not if Forry J Ackerman, the Gray Lensman of Los Angeles, had anything to do with it! Just as Buck Rogers trailed Killer Kane to his lair, so FJA would track down the thief!

Pao's car swung west on Olympic. Forry started to go through the stop sign, too, but had to slam on his brakes as a car going west on Olympic, sheets of water flying from its sides, honked at him. His car skidded and slid sidewise out on to the main boulevard. The oncoming car swerved and skidded also, turned around once, and ended up still going westward. Forry straightened out the Cadillac and ran it as if it were a speedboat. Waves curling out on both sides, he passed the car he had almost hit and then continued building up speed until he saw Pao's tail lights going right on Robertson. He went through a red light, causing two cars to apply their brakes and honk their horns. He chased Pao up Robertson and down Charleville Boulevard. Despite its multiplicity of stop signs, neither stopped once. Then Pao turned up to Wilshire, went westward back to Robertson, up Robertson, through all intersections with stop signs and signal lights red or green, and skidded right on Burton Way. He ran a red light going to San Vicente and so did Forry. In the distance a police siren whooped, and Forry almost slowed down. But he decided that he could justify his speeding and, even if he couldn't, a fine would be worth it if the cops caught Pao with the stolen goods. He hoped the cops would show up in time. If they didn't, they might find one dead Chinese.

Pao continued down San Vicente, ran another red light at Sixth, with Forry two car-lengths behind him. Despite their recklessness, neither was going over forty. The water was too solid; at higher speeds it struck the bottom of the car like a club.

At Wilshire and San Vicente the light was green for them, but two cars raced through the red, and Pao hit the lead car broadside. Forry applied his brakes and slowed down the car somewhat, but it crashed into the rear of the Chinese's car. His head hit something, and he blacked out.

Chapter 9

Childe was half-dazed. After the screaming of rubber, the crashing and ripping and rending of metal, and the shatter and tinkle of glass, there was a moment of silence except for the rain and a siren in the distance. Some of the cars still had operating headlights, and these cast a pale rain-streaked halo over the wreckage. Then a huge black fox leaped on to the top of his hood, paused to grin through the windshield at him, leaped down on to the street, and trotted off into the darkness behind Stats Restaurant.

The police car, its siren dying, pulled up by the cars, and two officers got out. At the same time, a big dog no, a wolf – passed by him, also on the way to the rear of the restaurant.

An officer, looking into the cars, swore and called to his partner. "Hey, Jeff, look at this! Two piles of clothes in this one and another pile in this one and nobody around that could have worn them! What the hell is this?"

The policeman had a genuine mess in more ways than one. No one seemed to be dead or even seriously hurt. Childe's car was bashed in in the front and side but was still operable. The car of a Mr Ackerman had a smashed radiator and would have to be towed away. Pao's car was destroyed. The others were leaking badly from the radiators and could not be driven far.

One policeman set out flares. The other still could not get over the abandoned clothing. He kept muttering, "I've seen some freak things, but this tops them all."

Another patrol car arrived after fifteen minutes. The officers determined that no one needed to be hospitalized. They took down the necessary information, gave out some tickets, and then dismissed the participants. The case was far from over, but there had been so many accidents because of the rain and so many other duties to perform that the police had to streamline normal procedures. One did say that the two Mr Paos and Mr Batlang would be sought for leaving the scene of an accident. And if the clothes meant anything, they might be arrested for public nudity, indecent exposure and, probably, would be subjected to a psychiatric examination.

One of the passengers in the car said that they must have

been dazed. He knew them well, they were responsible citizens, and they would never leave the scene of an accident unless they had been rendered half-conscious in a state of shock.

"Maybe so," the policeman said. "But you have to admit it's rather peculiar that all three should take off their clothes – slide out of them the way it looks to me – and run away. We were right behind you, and we didn't even see them leave."

"It was raining very heavily," the passenger said.

"Not that heavily."

"What a night," the other policeman said.

Childe tried to talk to the others in the accident, but only Forrest J (no period) Ackerman would reply. He seemed very concerned about a painting in the rear of Pao's car. He had removed it shortly after the police had arrived and put it in the back seat of his Cadillac. If the police observed this, they did not say anything. Now he wanted to get it back to his house.

"I'll take you as soon as they let us go," Childe said. "Your house isn't far from here; it won't be any bother."

He did not know what Ackerman's part in this was. He seemed to be an innocent victim, but then there was the transfer of the painting from Pao's car. How had Pao gotten hold of it? Also, there seemed to be two Paos. Were they twins?

Forry Ackerman told him something of what had happened on the way to his house. Childe became very excited, because he had met Woolston Heepish when he was investigating the disappearance of his partner, Colben. Another friend had taken him to Heepish's because Heepish had a large file on "vampire" cases, and the film sent to the LAPD showed a Dracula-type vampire assisting in the mutilation of Colben.

Childe decided that he would appear to go along with Ackerman's story. The man seemed to be sincere and genuinely upset and puzzled by what had happened. But it was possible that he was one of the Ogs, as Hindarf called them. It was also possible that he was one of the Tocs.

When he drove up before Ackerman's house, he looked at it through the dark and the rain, and he said, "If I didn't know better, I would think Heepish lived here."

"That man deliberately fixed his house to look like mine," Forry said. "That's why he's called the poor man's Forry Ackerman, though I don't think he's so poor."

They went inside and, while Ackerman hung the painting, Childe looked around. The layout of the house was the same, but the paintings and the other items were different. And this place was brighter and more inclined to science-fiction subjects than Heepish's.

When Forry stepped down off the sofa with a satisfied smile, Childe said, "There's something wrong about this accident, other than the disappearance of Pao. I mean, I was chasing Pao in one car and the three men with him in the other. Yet you say you were chasing Pao, too."

"That's right," Forry said. "It is puzzling. The whole evening has been puzzling and extremely upsetting. I have to get the latest issue of my comic book out to my publisher in New York, and I'm far behind. I'll have to work twice as fast to catch up."

Childe interpreted this as meaning that he should leave at once. The man must really be dedicated to his work. How many could go back to their desk and work on a piece of fiction about vampires when they might have been associating with genuine vampires, not to mention genuine werefoxes and werewolves?

"When you get your work done, and you're ready to talk," Childe said, "we'll get together. I have many questions, and I also have some information you might find interesting, though I don't know that you'll believe it."

"I'm too tired to believe in anything but a good night's sleep, which I'm not going to get," Forry said. "I hate to be inhospitable, but..."

Childe hesitated. Should he take up more of this man's time by warning him? He decided that it would be better not to. If he knew what danger he was really in, he would not be able to concentrate on his work. And knowing the danger would not stop him in the least unless he believed in it and fled from this area. That did not seem likely. Childe would not have believed such a story if he had not experienced it.

He gave Forry his phone number and address and said, "Call me when you're ready to talk this over. I have a lot to tell you. Maybe, together, we can get a more complete picture."

Forry said he would do so. He conducted Childe to the door but before he let him through, he said, "I think I'll take that painting into my office with me. I wouldn't put it past Heepish to try again."

Childe did not ask why he did not call the police. Obviously, if he did, he would be held up even more in getting out *Vampirella*.

Chapter 10

Herald Childe did not get home until seven in the morning. The rain had stopped by four thirty, but the canyons were roaring streams. He was stopped by the police, but when he explained that he lived off the main road, he was permitted to go on. Only residents could use this section of Topanga Canyon, and they were warned that it would be better if they stayed away. Childe pushed on – literally – and eventually got to his driveway. He saw three houses that had slipped their moorings and moved downhill anywhere from six to twenty feet. Two of the houses must have been deserted, but outside the third a family was moving some furniture and clothes into the back of a pick-up truck. Childe thought momentarily about helping them and then decided that they could handle their own affairs. The pick-up truck was certainly more equipped to move through the high water than his lowslung car, and if they wanted to break their backs moving their sofa, that was their foolish decision.

Another car of the same year and model as the others was parked under the branches of the oak tree. The water flowing down the street was up past the hubs of the wheels. So strong was the force of the current, it sometimes lifted Childe's car a fraction of an inch. But at no time was it more than one wheel off the ground.

He parked the car in the driveway. The garage floor was flooded and, besides, he wanted the car available for a quick take-off. He was not sure that the water pouring off the cliff and drowning his backyard would not lift the garage eventually. Or, if the cliff did collapse, it might move far enough to smash the garage, which was closer to the cliff than the house.

He unlocked the door and locked it behind him. He started to cross the room when, in the pale daylight, a shapeless form rose from the sofa. He thought his heart would stop.

The shapelessness fell off the figure. It was a blanket which had disguised it.

For a moment, he could not grasp who was standing before him. Then he cried, "Sybil!"

It was his ex-wife.

She ran to him and threw her arms around him, put her face against his chest, and sobbed. He held her and whispered, over and over, "Sybil! Sybil! I thought you were dead! My God, where have you been?"

After a while she quit crying and raised her face to kiss him. She was thirty-four now, her birthday had been six days ago, but she looked as if she had aged five years. There were large dark circles under her eyes and the lines from nose to mouth had gotten deeper. She also seemed thinner.

He led her to the sofa and sat her down and then said, "Are you all right?"

She started to cry again, but after a minute she looked up at him and said, "I am and I'm not."

"Is there anything I can do for you?" he asked.

"Yes, you can give me a cup of coffee. And a joint, if you have one."

He waved his hand as if to indicate a complete change of character. "I don't have any pot. I've gone back to drinking."

She looked alarmed, and he said, hastily, "Only a shot very infrequently. I'm going to school again. UCLA. History major."

Then, "How did you find this house? How did you get here? Is that your car out in front?"

"I was brought up here by somebody – somebodies – and let into the house. I took off the blindfold and looked around. I found my photograph on your bedside table, so I knew where I was. I decided to wait for you, and I fell asleep."

"Just a minute," he said. "This is going to be a long story, I can see that. I'll make some coffee and some sandwiches, too, in case we get hungry."

He did not like to put off hearing what had happened, but he knew that he would not want to be interrupted after she got started. He did everything that had to be done very swiftly and brought in a tray with a big pot of coffee, food, and some rather dried-out cigarettes he found in the pantry. He no longer smoked, but he had gotten cigarettes for women he had brought into the house.

Sybil said, "Oh, good!" and reached for the cigarettes. Then she withdrew her hand and said, wearily, "I haven't smoked for six months, and my lungs feel much better. I won't start up again."

She had said this before and sounded as if she meant it. But this time her voice had a thread of steel in it. Something had

Philip José Farmer

happened to change her.

"All right," he said. "You left for your mother's funeral in San Francisco. I called your sister, and she said you'd phoned her and told her you couldn't get a plane out and your car wouldn't start. You told her you were coming up with a friend, but you hung up without saying who the friend was. And that was the last I heard of you. Now, over a year later, you show up in my house."

She took a deep breath and said, "I don't expect you to believe this, Herald."

"I'll believe anything. With good reason."

"I couldn't get hold of you, and, anyway, after that horrible quarrel, I didn't think you'd want to ever see me again. I had to get to San Francisco, but I didn't know how. Then I thought of a friend of mine, and I walked over to his apartment. He only lived a block from me."

"He?"

"Bob Guilder. You don't know him."

"A lover?" he said, feeling a pinprick of jealousy. Thank God that emotion was dying out, in regard to her, anyway.

"Yes," she said. "Earlier. We parted but not because we couldn't stand one another. We just didn't strike fire off each other, sexually. But we remained fairly good friends. Anyway, I got there just as he was packing to leave for Carmel. He couldn't stand the smog anymore, and even though the governor didn't want people leaving, he said he was going anyway. He was glad to drive me all the way into San Francisco, since he had some things to do there."

They had driven out Ventura Boulevard because the San Diego Freeway was jammed, according to the radio. At a standstill. Ventura Boulevard was not much better, but ten miles an hour was an improvement over no miles.

Just off the Tarzana ramp, the car over-heated. Guilder managed to get it into Tarzana, but there was only one service station operating. The proprietors of the others were either staying home or were also attempting to get out of the deadly smog.

"You won't believe this," she said, "but I stole a motorcycle. It was sitting by the curb, its key in the ignition. There was no one in sight, although the owner may have been only thirty feet away, the smog was that thick. I've ridden Hondas before, did you know that? Another friend of mine used to take me out on one for fun, and he taught me how to ride it."

And other things, thought Childe without pain. The thought was automatic, but he was glad that it did not mean much now.

There had been no use in her trying to reach 'Frisco on the Honda. The traffic was so thick and slow-moving that she did not see any chance of getting to her destination until the funeral was over, if then. She decided to return to her apartment. Eyes burning, sinuses on fire, lungs hurting, she rode the Honda home. That took two hours. The cars were filling both sides of the street, all going in the same direction, but there was enough room, if she took the sidewalk now and then, to travel.

She got to her apartment, and five minutes afterwards, someone knocked on the door. She thought it must be another tenant. Without a key, it was difficult to get into the building.

But she did not recognize the two men, and before she could shut the door, they were on her. She felt a needle enter her arm, and she became unconscious. When she awoke, she was in a suite of three rooms, not including the bathroom. All were large and luxuriously furnished, and throughout her captivity she was given the best of food and liquor, cigarettes and marijuana, and anything she desired for her body.

Except clothes. She had one beautiful robe and two flimsy negligees which were cleaned each week.

When she awoke, she was alone. She prowled around and found that there were no windows and the two doors were locked. There was a big colour TV set and a radio, both of which worked. The telephone was not connected to the outside line. When she lifted it, she heard a man's voice answer, and she put the receiver down without saying anything. A few minutes later, a door swung open, and two men and a woman came in.

She described them in detail when Childe asked how they looked. One of them could be one of the Paos; the woman had to be Vivienne Mabcrough. The second man did not sound like anyone he knew.

Sybil became hysterical, and they injected her once more. When she woke up again, she controlled herself. She was told that she would not be harmed and that, eventually, she would be released. When she asked them what they wanted her for, she got no answers. Over the year's time, she concluded that her captors

Philip José Farmer

were planning on using her, somehow, as a weapon or lever against Childe.

Childe, thinking of the sexual abuse he had suffered during his short imprisonment in the Igescu house, could not conceive that she was not molested in any way. He asked her if she had been raped.

"Oh, many times!" she said, almost matter-of-factly.

"Did they hurt you?" She did not seem to be affected by his question or any painful memories.

"A little bit, at first," she said.

"How do you feel now? I mean, were the experiences psychologically traumatic?"

He was beginning to feel like a psychiatrist or, perhaps, a prosecuting attorney.

"Come here, sit down by me," she said. She held out a slim and pale hand. He came to her and put his arm around her and kissed her. He expected her to burst into tears again, but she only sighed. After a while, she said, "I've always been very frank with you, right?"

"Yes. But I don't know that a compulsion to honesty was the main factor," he said. "That may have been your rationalization, but I thought that your frankness was more to hurt me than anything else."

"You might be right," she said. She sipped on some coffee and then said, "I'll tell you what happened to me, but it won't be to hurt you. I don't think so, anyway."

Chapter 11

Sybil exercised, smoked more than was good for her, watched TV and listened to radio, read the magazines and books supplied whenever she asked for them, and generally tried to keep from going crazy. The uncertainty of her position was the largest element pushing her towards insanity. However, it was not as bad as being in solitary. The man who answered the phone would talk to her, and she got visitors at least five times a day. The woman who brought her meals would sit with her and talk when asked to do so, and a man called Plugger and a woman called Panchita came quite often. Occasionally, the fantastically beautiful Vivienne Mabcrough would drop in.

"They talked to me about many things, but they also asked many questions about you," Sybil said. "Mostly what I knew about your childhood, although they also wanted to know about your personal habits, what you read, your dreams – imagine that, your dreams! – and other things I might just happen to know because I was your wife."

Sybil had seen nothing damaging to Herald in this. Besides, her drive to honesty almost forced her to give them complete answers. Or that was her rationalization.

After a while, she began to suffer from sexual deprivation. Her nipples swelled whenever they touched cloth. Her cunt itched. She found herself sitting with her foot under her and rocking back and forth on the heel or rubbing up against the bed post or the back of a chair. She even kept a banana from her meal and masturbated with it.

"If it's any consolation to you," she said, "I fantasized that you were my lover. Mostly, that is."

He did not ask her who the others were. Actually, he did not care anymore. And that was strange, because he was feeling a genuine warmth and affection for her, perhaps even a love. He was happy to see her again and to be with her.

Sybil may have changed but she had not changed completely. She still had to tell him everything.

"You needn't be jealous of the other man," she said. "He doesn't exist. He's a fiction. Can you guess who?"

Philip José Farmer

"This isn't exactly the time for guessing games," he said. "But no, I don't know who you imagined at the other end of the banana."

"Tarzan!" she said.

"Tarzan? Oh, for cripe's sake! Well, why not? Bananas, big dongs, and all that. It only stands to reason that the superman of the jungle would be hung heavy."

He was sarcastic, but he was also surprised. There were still things about her he did not know. Tarzan!

There might have been a closed-circuit TV monitoring her, she said. Otherwise, why would Plugger enter that evening, and tell her she did not need to suffer anymore?

Plugger was a tall, rangy man with a deep tan, black hair which came down in a widow's peak, somewhat pointed ears, and a very handsome face. He stood before her and stripped while she asked him what he thought he was doing, though she knew well enough.

"He had a beautiful body with the smoothest skin, almost like glass. But his cock was big. Not enormous, just big and thick and it had the biggest knob at the end of it I've ever seen. I don't mean the glans. That was big enough, but he had a growth, I guess you could call it a wart, on the side of the head. I told him that really turned me off."

You sound as if you were pretty cool about the whole thing," he said.

"Well, I was suffering. The banana was a long way off from being perfectly satisfactory. Or perfectly satisfying. And he was a hell of a good-looking man, and he talked with me enough so that I rather liked him, even if he was my warder. So I just told myself, you know, the cliché, if you have to be raped, lean back and enjoy it."

"Really?" he said.

"Well, not really. I was scared. But then he said he wouldn't force me. That helped relax me a lot."

Plugger sat down by her and kissed her. She tried to turn her head away, but he turned it gently back. She protested that he was forcing her, and he replied that he only asked for one kiss. If she did not like it, he would not kiss her again.

That seemed fair to her, really more than she had expected.

After all, if he wanted to rape her, he could.

She lifted her face to him at the same time that he put her hand on his cock and his tongue into her mouth.

The shock that went down her throat and up her arm was almost as if she had touched an electric eel.

"I mean, it was something like an electrical shock but much weaker. I had an orgasm in my throat and up my arm."

Childe jumped up and said, "What?"

"Yes, I know. It sounds crazy. But it was true. I came. I mean, you know, when I come, I come with my whole body. But the ecstasy was denser, I mean, more intense, in my mouth and throat and in my hand and arm."

He did not say anything more. His experiences with Igescu's crew had opened doors to an exotic enough world. Plugger was one that he had not experienced, and he supposed that there were many other outré beings in that group.

Sybil had not resisted when he took her robe and negligee off. She had allowed him to move her on to the bed, where he got between her legs and thrust his tongue into her cunt. It was like a spark in a cylinder full of vaporized gas. Orgasm after orgasm exploded in her, and then they began building up more slowly, building until she could endure the exquisiteness no more and felt that she would faint.

While she lay panting and moaning with the aftermath, he climbed on to her and pressed her breasts around his dong. The same shock passed through them; the ecstasy was so intense she could see – but of course it was imagination – blue sparks sputtering from the tips of her nipples.

"The funny thing was, his prick was soft," she said. "Even when he stuck it into my mouth, and transmitted that electrical come, it stayed soft."

"He didn't come in your mouth?" he said. "I mean, spermatic fluid?"

"There wasn't any jism, no. I mean, that shock, you might say, was a sort of electrical come."

She had gone into a series of orgasms, one after the other, so fast that she could not count them.

After this, he kissed her all over, and every inch of her skin felt a minor orgasm until he stuck his tongue up her anus. That

Philip José Farmer

almost lifted her off the bed, and she did faint after that orgasm.

She was silent then, as if dwelling with great pleasure on the memory.

Childe finally spoke. "Well, did he ever stick his prick in your cunt?"

He had not meant to sound so harsh but, for the first time, he was jealous.

"No. I tried to get it in even after he said it was no use. It kept doubling back and falling out. But I got orgasms through my hand while I was trying to do it. I said I was sorry I couldn't do something for him. He said it did not matter; he was more than satisfied. I guess that I wasn't far wrong when I said his come was electrical. He had a high-voltage jism, you might say."

She had questioned him about this phenomenon, which became frightening when she recovered enough to think about it. He replied that he was built differently, and he got up, picked up his clothes, and walked out.

He came every four days after that. She asked him why he did not visit her more often, and he said it took time for him to build up a charge. She took him literally, but she was beginning to get frightened again. What kind of weirdos were these? However, when he touched her, her fright went away.

After about five visits from Plugger, two women, Panchita and Diana, came to her room. They talked for a while and left. Every few days, they would drop in. Then, one afternoon, Panchita asked her if she would like some pot. Sybil was very eager to get some, because it would help to pass away the dull moments of her existence. All three lit up.

"But it wasn't real pot," she said. "It smelled something like pot, but it must have been something else. It really turned me on, but it also made me very suggestible. I think it had some hypnotic element in it."

"Really?" Childe said. He anticipated what she was going to relate.

"Yes. I got pretty high, and all three of us were laughing hysterically. I had completely forgotten that I was their prisoner and at their mercy. They seemed like very old friends and very lovable. In fact, uh, desirable."

"One of them made love to you?"

"Oh, yes. Panchita sat down by me and quite casually put her arm around my shoulder. The next I knew, she was cupping my breast with her other hand and then stroking my nipple. I felt a great deal of love – and lust – for Panchita. It seemed the most natural thing in the world. You know I don't swing that way, Herald. I have never had a homosexual experience in my life, not until then. In fact, the idea used to make me sick."

Childe said nothing.

She continued: "Diana, the tall blonde with perfectly enormous breasts, sat down on my other side. She started to kiss me while Panchita pulled up my negligee and began to suck on my nipple. I felt as if I was on fire. I tongued Diana's mouth while she tongued mine. And then I felt Panchita's mouth going down my belly. She kissed me all over there but stopped when she came to my cunt.

"Diana lifted me up then and walked me over to the bed, where she took off my negligee. I got on to the bed and on my back and Diana and Panchita took their clothes off. They stood on each side of the bed and each took one of my hands and placed it against her cunt. They were dripping with lubricating fluid, sopping. I stuck a finger in each slit, and they moved their hips back and forth and jacked themselves off."

"Is it necessary to go into such detail?" Childe said.

"It's good therapy for me," she said. Her eyes were closed, and her head was leaning against the back of the sofa.

The two women had climbed in beside her. Diana kissed and fondled her breasts while Sybil caressed Diana's left breast. Panchita again travelled down her belly with the tip of her tongue. After tracing a triangle around the pubic hairs with her tongue, Panchita got down between Sybil's legs. She spread them apart and then slid a pillow under her buttocks. The next Sybil knew, Panchita was running her tongue over her clitoris and sticking it up her cunt as far as she could.

She kept at it until Sybil had an orgasm.

"Then Panchita traded places with Diana, and Diana tongue-fucked me," she said. "Diana stimulated me better, I came about five times. Then Panchita got on top of me, and I licked her cunt and put my tongue up her slit and vibrated its tip against her clitoris. She came a number of times, after which Diana got on top

Philip José Farmer

of me. Diana came almost at once.

"Then Panchita got down again and turned me on my side and licked my asshole while Diana licked my cunt again. When I had come a number of times, we made a triangle, mouth to pussy, you might say, fingers up twats, and, and, it was wonderful!"

"You say that even in retrospect?"

"I didn't that night after they left. I cried, and I felt so disgusted and dirty. The drug had worn off by then, you understand. But Panchita and Diana kept visiting me, and after a while, I quit having guilty feelings. I got to liking it. Why not? What's so bad about making love to women? Does it hurt anyone?"

"No," he said. "Did their lovemaking lessen the effect of Plugger's?"

"Not at all. Actually, if you were to rate orgasms on a scale, I'd have to rate him as Super A-Plus and theirs as B-Minus."

"Next you'll be telling me that Plugger and the two women got into bed with you at the same time," he said.

She opened her eyes and turned her head to look at him.

"How'd you know that?" she said. "Pour me another cup of coffee, will you, honey?"

He passed her the full cup and said, "Did Plugger touch off the two women, too?"

"Oh, yes. Once Panchita and Diana and I got down in a daisy chain, and he rammed his tongue up Panchita's ass. He said she had the sweetest asshole, which made me a little jealous. Would you believe it, all three of us felt the shock in our cunts and our mouths? That electricity or whatever it was passed through all of us."

"I can understand your making love to the women the first time," he said. "You were under the influence of that drug you smoked. But you knew how it affected you, so why didn't you refuse to smoke it the next time they offered it to you?"

"Like I said, I enjoyed it. Anyway, I didn't think about refusing it the second time. I don't know why."

"Your mind shut down," he said. "You wanted to go to bed with them, so you just forgot how the stuff would affect you."

"I'm not a compulsive lesbian!" she cried. "I don't have any neurotic drive for women! I can take them or leave them!"

"You just got out of prison, so how would you know?" he

said. "However, that doesn't matter. Not now, anyway. How did they explain giving you a hypnotic drug when they said they wouldn't force you?"

"They explained that they did not force me to smoke the pot, or what they called pot. And, later, they said I didn't have to smoke it now that I knew the effects."

"You aren't hooked on the stuff?"

"Absolutely not!"

"Well, you may be right. Time will tell. I just don't understand their non-sadistic treatment. If you hadn't described certain people that I know so well, I would say that another group besides Igescu's had you."

"What are you talking about? Another group?"

"I'll tell you later about my adventures, if you can call them that."

She continued with her story.

He wondered if it was just that: a story. There was no doubt that she knew Panchita Pocyotl and Diana Rumbow and others and to do so she must have been held prisoner. But this sexual narrative? Had it really happened the way she said, or was she unconsciously concealing something more terrible? Had she suffered such traumatic handling that she was repressing it and substituting a fantasy?

It did not seem likely, because she did not act psychotic, but then a psychotic often acted normally.

If the Ogs, as Hindarf called them, had treated her relatively considerately, then they had some sinister end in mind.

There was one confirmation of her story, he thought. That was that Vivienne Mabcrough had left her alone.

"And then, one afternoon, this fabulously beautiful woman, Vivienne, came to my room," she said.

"Oh?"

Vivienne and Sybil smoked the marijuana-like substance, with Sybil knowing well what was coming. The two made love, but the snake-thing remained within Vivienne's womb. Sybil was not aware of its existence, and Childe did not mention it.

Vivienne came to Sybil many times after that, sometimes alone and sometimes with Panchita or Diana or Plugger or with all three. Then Fred Pao, or his twin, showed up. Both only wanted to be sucked off, but when Sybil refused unless she was given something in return, they brought Plugger in with them. While Sybil stood in the middle of the room, bent over, sucking on Pao's long slim dick, Plugger pressed his electric cock against her anus or held its tip against her cunt. Sometimes, he got down on his knees and spread the cheeks of her ass and rammed his tongue up it.

"Every prisoner should have it so good," Childe said. He was thinking of what had happened to Colben and the others and what might have happened to him. But, now that he considered it, Igescu's group may not have been planning mutilation and death for him. They seemed to have been aware that he was something special, if he could believe what Hindarf and Vivienne had said in their short conversation in English.

However, they had been trying to kill him after he had escaped and killed some of them. This could have been from self-defense only, not from a desire to murder for the pleasure of murder.

Mysteriouser and mysteriouser, he thought, paraphrasing Alice.

And Sybil had been a sort of Alice in Sexland. Certainly her adventures were as strange as Alice's.

"You never found anything peculiar about Vivienne?" he said.

"No. Should I have?"

This seemed to confirm her story about her gentle treatment. If Vivienne had revealed the snake-thing, and the two had made love to Sybil, then she was being very considerate to Sybil.

Despite all this enjoyment and the use of drugs, Sybil had many periods of depression, frustration, and a desire to get away. There were times when she felt as if she were a cow being fattened up for slaughter. And even after she became quite at ease with her captors and talked fluently, she could not get them to answer one question about the reason for her imprisonment.

And then, two days ago, all her visitors, except for a woman who brought her meals now and then, quit coming. The woman would not even say Good Morning to her, let alone answer questions.

Sybil had watched TV and smoked pot and wondered what

was going on. Her fears came to the surface, and she fantasized many dreadful things happening to her.

Then, this very night, she was awakened by a hand shaking her. She sat up in bed, her heart throbbing painfully, to find three masked men by her bedside. One told her to get dressed. She did so, while they packed for her. They had brought her clothes in from someplace, presumably from a closet in the house. Then they blindfolded her and took her out of the house and drove her here. The drive, she estimated, had lasted two hours.

Childe did not say anything, but it seemed to him that she could have been located much closer than two hours' drive to his house. If she were prisoner in that house near his, her rescuers might have driven around to make it seem that she had been a long ways from him.

On the other hand, she might have been held in, say, Vivienne's house in Beverly Hills.

"Do you feel all right?" he said.

"What? Oh, yes, I feel fine, except for being tired. And I am happy that I'm out of that, although it wasn't an altogether unpleasurable experience. But very puzzling. What do you think made Plugger the way he was? I mean, how about that electricity of his? Do you think he had a surgically implanted battery of some sort? It sounds sort of science-fiction, doesn't it?"

He kissed her and said, "What about some nice normal sex?"

"All right," she murmured. "It's late and I'm tired, but I would like to have a man who's really in love with me. You are in love with me, aren't you? Despite all our troubles?"

"I must be," he said. "There have been times this past year when I was almost out of my mind wondering what could have happened to you."

He stood up and said, "I'll get into my pyjamas after I shower and shave."

"I'm clean," she said. "I'll wait right here for you. You can carry me to bed. It'll be so nice."

Ten minutes later, having sped through his preparations, he returned to the front room.

She was sitting slumped on the sofa, fast asleep. He grinned wryly and kissed her on the forehead, moved her so that she was stretched out on the sofa, put the blanket over her, kissed her forehead again, and went into his bedroom. The rain had started again.

Chapter 12

Forrest J Ackerman awoke with his head on the desk and the finally edited package of the latest issue of *Vampirella* beside him. He got up and shook his head. When he had finished his work this morning, he had intended to rush down to the post office on Robertson and mail it out. But he had somehow fallen asleep.

The first thought was: The painting! Had he been drugged so that it could be stolen again?

But it was leaning against the wall by the desk. He sighed with relief, part of which could be repressed anger at Woolston Heepish. Something really should be done about that fellow. He was not only a thief, he was dangerous. Anybody who would get two women to strip in order to seduce him out of the painting – and before witnesses – was not only dangerous, he was mad.

Forry stumbled into the kitchen, washed his face in the sink, and then picked up the bulky envelope containing *Vampirella*. He was outside before he remembered that he did not have a car. One more count against Woolston Heepish!

At that moment, like the Gray Lensman or Batman arriving to save the situation, the Dummocks drove up. Lorenzo crawled out of the car and, on all fours, progressed slowly towards the house. He was a youth of thirty-five, of medium height, black haired, ruddy faced, black moustached, paunched, and skinny legged. Hulia, his wife, could walk, just barely. She was a short woman with a magnificent bust, a hawk face, dark hair, and thick spectacles. She was thirty.

Forry said, "I'd like to borrow your car. I have to run to the post office."

"All yours," said Lorenzo, not looking up at him.

"The keys," Forry said. "The keys."

"You want Hulia, you can have her. The cunt's all yours. Just keep me in cigarettes, food, booze, and typing paper, and she's all yours, Forry, old buddy. Ask her, she doesn't mind."

"I want the keys to your car, not your wife!" Forry said loudly.

Lorenzo continued to crawl towards the door. He turned his head and said, "Hulia! Hurry up, help me up! Got the keys?"

Hulia stood swaying and blinking, looking like a giant drunken owl. "What keys? To the car or the house?"

"Fuck it! Forry, can you open the door for me?"

Forry looked into the car. As he had suspected the keys were still in the ignition. He did not see how Lorenzo could have driven in his condition without smashing up, but the luck of drunkards and egoists had held out.

He walked back and opened the door for the two. After Lorenzo had crawled in and Hulia had fallen on her face crossing the threshold, he started to close the door. But he said, "Don't you dare puke on any of my stuff! You do, and out you go! Pronto!"

"Why, Forry!" Hulia said. "Have we ever puked on anything of yours?"

"Just my creature from the Black Lagoon bust," Forry said. "I forgave you, since it could be cleaned. But if you vomit on any of my books or paintings, or anything at all anymore, out you go!"

"You must really be mad at us, Forry darling!" Hulia said. "I've never seen you angry before. I thought you were a saint!"

"If I puke, you can have Hulia," Lorenzo said, looking up from his supine position in the middle of the floor. "Just so you don't toss our ass out of here. I'm writing the Great Cosmic Novel now, Forry. Not the Great American Novel. The Cosmic Novel. It makes Tolstoy, Dostoyevesky, and Norman Mailer look sick. I'm really the greatest creator of them all, Forry, my Maecenas, patron of the arts, protector of the gifted and genius. Your name will go down in history as Forrest J (no period) Ackerman, the man who gave Lorenzo Dummock a roof over his head, a bed to sleep in, a desk to write on, food, booze, cigarettes, and typing paper. And got my typewriter out of hock for me, me, Lorenzo the Magnificent."

The pity of it was that Lorenzo believed that he was the greatest. He had believed it since he was eighteen. The world owed him a living because the world was going to benefit. The world, as typified by Forry Ackerman, owed it to him.

Lorenzo Dummock had said he would do anything, even suck cock if he had to, so he could pursue the call of Apollo. He would do anything except work. Work degraded him, tired him, took precious time from his writing. It was all right for Hulia to work, she should support him while he wrote. Too bad Hulia's asthma and occasional fits of hysteria kept her from holding a steady job. But it couldn't be helped, and if she would suck a few cocks now and then to keep a roof over their head and booze and cigarettes and typing paper at his elbow, what was the harm in that? Forry had turned down an offer by Hulia to blow him. He said that he preferred that she keep the house clean and act as hostess now and then when he had a big party. Hulia had said she would, but it was easier, and more fun, sucking cock. She kept her cunt reserved for Lorenzo, who got killingly jealous at the thought of another man sticking his prick into it. So far, she had done a miserable job as a housekeeper.

Forry turned away from them, swearing that he would kick them out at the first chance, and knowing that he wouldn't. He got into the car, a beat-up 1960 Ford with bald tyres, and verified what he had suspected. The fuel indicator was on zero.

Despite this the motor started up and got him one block down Olympic before sputtering out. He walked to the nearest gas station and returned with a canful. Somehow, he never knew how it worked out, he always borrowed their car when it was out of gas.

When he got back to the house, he found Alys Merrie sitting on the sofa in the front room. There was an odour of vomit in the house. Lorenzo had come through again.

"Hello, Alys!" he said, his heart dropping like an elevator with snapped cables. "What brings you here? And how did you get in?"

"You gave me a key long ago, remember?" she said.

"And I asked for it back, and you gave it to me," he said.

"So I had a couple of duplicates made in the interim. Aren't you glad to see me, Forry? There was a time..."

"Excuse me, I got to attend to something."

He walked to the foot of the steps and looked up. Halfway to the landing was the nauseating pool. And Hulia had not even bothered to clean it up!

He had returned because he had some vital correspondence to clear up before he went to Wendy's to sleep. But Lorenzo's spoor and Alys Merrie were too much to put up with at this time. He would take off like Seaton after Duquesne.

Alys Merrie thought differently. She was a blonde of medium height and good shape, about forty years old. She had been married, but, on meeting him at a world convention, had, as

　　　　　　　　　　　　　　　Philip José Farmer

she put it, "Gone ape over that divine Forry". Forry had been amused and flattered for a long time, but she had become a nuisance. He wasn't in love with her, and while her adulation was pleasing, it got sticky after a while. Especially since her husband had threatened to sue him as co-respondent.

"The Dummocks are too busy to worry about that puke," she said. "I went upstairs to see what was going on, there was so much noise. Would you believe it? That fat-headed Lorenzo was sitting in the chair and Hulia was blowing him! No big deal about that except he was watching her do it and at the same time was taking notes! Taking notes! I wonder if he uses his pen for his prick!"

"Why don't you go back up and watch?" Forry said. "I have to go, now, Alys. I've been up all night, my car is wrecked, I'm exhausted, I'm worried, and... in short, I've had it."

"Yes, I know all about that."

He looked at her with amazement. "You know all about it? Who could have told you?"

"I've been in it from the beginning," she said. She took a cigarette from her purse, lit it, and looked coolly at him. She knew he allowed no smoking in the house – except in the bedroom upstairs – but she was doing this for a purpose. He decided to ignore the gesture.

"You've been in *what* from the beginning?" he said. Despite his tiredness, he was becoming interested.

"The whole business. Starting so many years ago that you would not believe it. Or, if you did, you'd be frightened. Which you're going to be, anyway, because you'll believe before I'm done."

He sat down in the chair across the room and said, "How many years?"

"About ten thousand or so Earth years," she said.

He was silent for a while. Alys Merrie was a great little kidder when she wasn't mad at him or making love. She knew well how deeply immersed in science-fiction he was – sometimes he thought of himself as the leviathan in the great sea of sci-fi or as a sort of Flying Dutchman of the outer spaceways – and she sometimes poked fun at him about it. This did not seem a likely time for it, however.

On the other hand, she just could *not* be serious.

"Look around you," she said, waving her cigarette. "Look at all those wild paintings and photographs. Strange planets, alien forms of life, big-chested, elephant-trunked Martians; winged men; sentient machines; giant insects; synthetic humans; what have you. You've been reading books about weird beings and worlds, and you've collected a monument to science-fiction and fantasy and, incidentally, to yourself. A lifetime of love and labour is represented here.

"You must believe in this exotic otherworld of yours. Otherwise, you would never have gone to such unique lengths to gather the artifacts of the otherworld about you."

Something was different about Alys Merrie. She had never talked like this before. She had seemed incapable of talking seriously or so fluently.

"Ten thousand years," she said. "Would you believe that I'm ten thousand years old? No! What about twelve thousand?"

"Twelve thousand?" he said. "Come on, Alys. I could believe in ten thousand, but twelve? Don't be ridiculous!"

"I look a hard forty years old, don't I?" she said. "How about this, Forry?"

It was like watching *She* or *Lost Horizon*, only it was in reverse. Instead of the beautiful young woman wrinkling into ghastly old age, it was a case of a woman unwrinkling, becoming a beautiful young girl. Helen Gahagan and Jane Wyatt should have had it so good.

He wished his heart could beat faster. Then he wouldn't shake so much. So it was true. Everything he had read and dreamed about was true! Well, maybe not everything. But at least some of it was true.

"Who, and what, are you?" he said. The room was beginning to seem a little fuzzy, and the illustrations by Paul, Finlay, St John, Bok, and the rest of the wild crew had taken on three dimensions. He must be in a state of slight shock.

"Do you like it?" Alys said.

"Of course," Forry said. "But you didn't answer my question."

"I am a, uh, let's say, a Toc," she said. "We are the enemies of the Ogs. You met some of them last night. Fred Pao, Diana

Philip José Farmer

Rumbow, Panchita Pocyotl.
    "And Woolston Heepish."

Chapter 13

"Heepish!" he almost screamed. "You mean Heepish isn't human?"

"We're not only *not* human," she said. "We're extra-terrestrial. Extra-solar system. More. Extra-Galactic. The home of the Tocs is on the fourth planet circling a star in the Andromeda galaxy."

He thought, I've always been a lucky man. I wanted only to work in science-fiction, and I was able to make my living out of it. I wanted to be the greatest collector of science-fiction and fantasy in the world, and I did that as naturally and as easily as a snail grows a shell. I need a job and a publisher wants to put out a series of horror-movie magazines for children, and who else is more capable or more willing to edit those? I have known the greats of this field, I have been their good friend, I have seen the first men land on the Moon, and I hope to see the first men land on Mars before I die. I have been lucky.

But now, this! I would have rejected this as a dream that only a lunatic could believe to be true, even if I have fantasized it many many times. The beings from outer space make contact with Earthlings through me!

That was not exactly true, of course. If what she said was correct, the extees had been in contact with Earthlings for ten thousand years. But had they revealed themselves to any Earthmen before? That was the important thing.

"You're getting too excited, Forry," she said. "I know you have a thousand questions bubbling in your mind. But you'll get things straighter and quicker if you'll just listen quietly to my story. Okay? Good! Lean back and be a good boy and listen."

There was a planet the size and shape of Earth rotating around a Sol-type sun on the edge of the Andromeda galaxy, which was 800,000 light years distant from Earth. The sky was a blaze of luminous gas and giant stars shining through the gas. The planet of the Tocs had no moon, hence was tideless.

The fifth planet out had two small moons but no seas in which tides could occur. This was the dying world of the Ogs, an evil race.

"Geeze!" Forry thought, and the extent of his excitement

could be gauged by his use of the mild expletive. He abhorred the use, even in his mind, of the most dilute of expletives.

"Geeze! This is just like Gernsback! Or Early Campbell!"

The Tocs and the Ogs were not human beings. They were amphibious creatures who passed back and forth from a state of pure energy to that of matter. They formed configurations of bound energy in one condition and configurations of matter in the other. Their shape depended on that which they wished to imitate – or to create. But they did have limitations of size and shape. The smallest body that could be formed was about the size of a large fox or, if they took to the air, a large bat. When they existed as the smaller animals, they carried the energy excess in an invisible form as a sort of exhaust trail. Or perhaps the analogy could be energy packed into an intangible and transparent suitcase.

"What is your true shape?" Forry said.

"You were not to talk," Alys said, flashing white teeth. She looked so beautiful and so young that he felt a pang of desire. Or was it an ache for his own lost youth?

"We have no true shape, unless you would call the shape we use the most our true one. I suppose you could, since long utility of a particular shape results in a certain 'hardening' of that shape. It becomes more difficult to change it as time goes on. And it requires more energy to keep it in a non-human form. So, since most of us have been in the human shape for so long, you might say that that is our true shape."

The Ogs and the Tocs had come into contact when space travel was invented. Neither used rockets or anti-gravitational machines. They travelled from one place in space to another by means of a very peculiar device. That is, it was peculiar from the human viewpoint.

The device was made of a synthetic metal formed into the shape of a large goblet or chalice. That particular form was required because only that form could gather, or focus, the mental energies of a Mover. Perhaps a closer translation of the Toc word would be Captain. The Captain was the only person who could activate the device so that the Tocs could be teleported from one point in space to another.

"Why would the Captain be the only one able to activate the device – this chalice?" Forry said.

"That is the limitation of this device, let us call it the Grail," Alys said. "It has a certain superficial resemblance to the grail of your medieval myths, although the inner surface has a geometry that would be alien, even terrifying, to human eyes.

"The Grail is matter, but it is activated only by a certain rare type of energy radiation. Of brainwave radiation, I suppose you would call it, but there is more to it than that. Anyway, the Grail, to act as a spaceship, or a teleport, must be controlled by a Mover, or Captain. And there were only about a hundred Captains born for every million of us born."

"Born?" Forry said, his eyebrows raising. "How can an energy configuration be born?"

She waved her hand impatiently and said, "I am speaking by analogy only. If I have to explain every detail of an exceedingly complex culture, we'll be here for twenty years. Let me talk."

The Ogs had discovered their Grails and found their Captains the same time as the Tocs. There was travel between the two planets almost at once and war a little later. The Ogs were evil and wanted to enslave the Tocs.

Forry had some mental reservations about this. He would wait until he had heard the Ogs' side before he judged.

The Tocs repulsed the Ogs with heavy losses on both sides. Finally, there was peace. The Tocs and the Ogs then turned their attentions to other worlds. Since distance meant nothing to the Grail, since a hundred thousand light years could be traversed as swiftly as a mile, that is, instantaneously, the universe was open to both races.

But with the billions of habitable planets in the universe, and the limited number of Captains, only a few could be explored. Earth was one of them, and about a thousand Tocs had come here. Almost immediately, the Ogs had sent an expedition here also. The peace did not extend to planets outside their system, so the Ogs had no compunction about attacking the Tocs.

The Ogs and Tocs had waged a mutually disastrous war. They had destroyed each other's Grail and killed each other's Captains. And so they were marooned on Earth.

"We lived *among* the humans but not *of* them," Alys said. "Our ability to take different forms gave rise to a number of superstitions about the supernatural origins of vampires,

Philip José Farmer

werewolves, fairies, and what have you. We Tocs were the basis of the good fairies, although we changed into animal shape, or other shapes, quite often. But we weren't hostile to human beings, that is, if they followed the proper ethics we weren't."

Over the ten thousand years, the War, the occasional killing of human beings, and suicide cut the original number of about two thousand Tocs and Ogs down to about a hundred each. However, every Toc or Og whose material form was slain was not dead. He became an energy configuration again and could regain material form. But this process took a long time on Earth because the magnetic conditions here were not the same as in the mother system.

"That accounts for ghosts?" Forry said.

"Yes. Human beings don't have ghosts. When they die, they are forever dead. But a Toc or Og who has died in material form needs to attach himself to a locale where he has both the optimum magnetic conditions and human beings. He has to, shall we say, 'feed' off the energy of human beings. And when he has gained enough form, in a phase which you humans call ectoplasm, he needs blood or sex to get a completely material body. The Tocs need sex and the Ogs need blood."

She paused and then said, "One of us recently regained corporeal form by contact with Herald Childe. She literally fucked herself into flesh. Of course, she was able to do it far more swiftly with Childe than she would have with one who was completely a human being."

Chapter 14

"What the hell does that mean?" said Forry, who almost never swore.

"I mean that Childe is the only Captain in existence. But he doesn't know it as yet."

"Why not?"

"Because he was born half-human and raised by human parents. Because a Captain has a delicate psychic constitution and must be handled delicately until he has fully matured. Childe is a fully mature man in the physical sense, but he is a baby in regard to his psychic powers."

"Just one minute," Forry said. "I don't want to digress, but if you beings can come back to material life after being killed, why haven't these Captains that were killed come back to life?"

"Some did and were killed by one side or other because their existence could not be kept secret. Others never made it because conditions weren't right. You see, if we had a Captain and a Grail, we could not only return to our home world. We could also bring all our departed comrades back into corporeality. The Toc or Og in his pure energy-complex phase is a rather mindless being. He has some intelligence, but the main reason he gets back to matter is that he has a drive to do so, an instinct. He wanders around until he happens to come across a locale with the proper set-up for reconverting him. And reconversion takes a long long time generally."

"Pardon the interruption," Forry said.

If he had not seen that transformation from middle age to youth, he would have thought he was experiencing the world's biggest hoax. But he was convinced. He was actually talking, face to face, with an extraterrestrial. One that would have made the strangest creature of science fiction, or even those in *Weird Tales* magazine, rather mundane.

He thought, *In a sense, she's telling me the story of the Martians and Venusians waging an underground war for control of Earth. Hugo, you should be here! Oh, boy, if I could just flip a switch and let the sci-fi fans and the Count Dracula Society in on this!*

Philip José Farmer

And then he sobered. If this was true, and he believed it was, this was no mere fiction story or child's delight. It was a deadly war.

"Childe?" he said.

"Let's go back to 1788," she said. "To the birth of the male who would become George Gordon, Lord Byron, the famous, if not great, English poet. At the time he was born, of course, no one, including us, knew that he would become world-famous. Nor did we have any way of predicting whether he would become a Captain or just another human being. Or just another Toc."

"I'm bursting with questions," he said, smiling. "But I refrain."

"He was our first birth," she said. "On Toc, where conditions are optimum, births are very rare. That is, births from a copulation between, or among, our energy configuration phases do not happen often. But then that is counterbalanced by our lack of a death rate.

"Here on Earth, we had never succeeded in producing an infant in the energy configuration. Then a Captain was reconverted into material form. One of us had the idea of preserving his genetic abilities in case he should get killed, which he was later on. The Captain happened to be living near the Byrons at that time, and he became the lover of Lady Byron with the purpose of impregnating her. There were a hundred of us, almost our full complement, gathered together nearby the night she conceived George.

I suppose it is the only case, except one, where a hundred people copulated to produce one baby. We poured our mental energies into Lady Byron, and we succeeded. Coexisting with the fusion of sperm and ovum was the creation of an energy embryo. This embryo was attached, no, was fused with the body of the infant Byron. You might say that he was the only human being up to then who actually had a soul."

"Pardon me, but how did that energy embryo develop? Did it become a separate entity or...?"

"It fuses with the nervous system and becomes one with the corporeal entity. Not identical but similar. It survives after the death of the body.

"However, this creation of an energy baby requires much outpouring of energy on our part. At the same time that we were concentrating our mental energies, we were fucking like mad corporeally. It was probably the biggest gang-bang in history, if you will pardon such language, Forry dear. I know you don't like to use *dirty* words or especially to hear them.

"Unfortunately, though the baby grew up to have some remarkable talents, it did not develop the psychic abilities of a Captain. Not that that would have done much good, anyway, because we did not have the Grail. But we hoped to make the metal for one; we had been creating the metal, bit by bit, over thousands of years. On Toc we could have done it in a year, but here, where the minerals are scarce and the materials for building the *potentializers* are even more rare, we took an agonizingly long time getting what we needed. Then the Ogs made a raid and stole what metal we had.

"They knew that Byron was to be our Captain. They moved in, became acquainted with him, and we could do little about it. Then they abandoned him when they found out that he lacked the Captaincy.

"We were in despair for a while. But Byron still had the genetic potentiality for a Captain, and we decided to take advantage of that. If he couldn't be a Captain, perhaps his child could be."

"Childe?" Forry said, ever alert for the chance to pun.

She nodded and said, "Exactly. We got specimens of his sperm by a method I won't go into and froze it. Not with ice or liquid hydrogen but with an energy configuration. And we waited.

"We waited while our enemies, the Ogs, obtained more metal, enough to make a Grail. Then we chose a woman with suitable genetic qualities, humanly speaking, because those have to be considered, too. You wouldn't want the Captain to be an inferior physical or mental specimen. And we deliberately settled on Mrs Childe because of the name. And its association with Byron, too. After all, we use human languages and so we think something like humans. Only like, not exactly as."

"Thus, Herald Childe from the Childe Harold?"

"If you said H-E-R-A-L-D, yes. Herald. The Child that Heralds the rebirth of our Toc energy ghosts, their materialization. And our return to the Promised Land of our native planet. The dead shall rise and we shall cross the river Zion into the Land of Beulah, if I can mix up a few quotations. You get the idea."

"And what about Childe and the Grail?" Forry said.

Alys Merrie opened her mouth to reply, but she shut it when someone beat at the door and shouted.

Chapter 15

At noon, the ringing of the doorbell awakened Childe. He staggered out into the front room, past Sybil, who was still sleeping, and threw open the front door. A gust of rain wet him and covered the three men standing on his porch. He realized immediately that he should have been more cautious, but by then it was too late. The first man stepped inside, holding a spray can. Childe held his breath and ran towards his bedroom, where he kept a gun. He stopped when the man called, "Childe! Your wife!"

The second man was by Sybil with a knife at her throat. The third, Fred Pao or his twin, held an air gun.

The first man sprayed a gas over Sybil just as she opened her eyes and said, "Wha...?"

She fell back asleep, and Pao said, "It won't hurt her. Now your turn, Mr Childe."

He could still run for the bedroom, he thought. But these men would cut Sybil's throat if they thought they had anything, or nothing, to gain by it. Of course, he might be able to kill all three of them with his gun, but what good would that do Sybil? On the other hand, if he surrendered, wouldn't he and Sybil be as good as dead?

He did not know. That was the paralysing factor. He did not know. And from what had passed between Vivienne and Hindarf he surmised that he was regarded as something special.

"All right," he said. "I surrender."

The man with the spray can approached him and shot the vapour in his face. He wanted to hold his breath, but it was foolish putting off the inevitable. After glancing at his wristwatch, he breathed in.

It was thirty minutes later when he awoke. He was lying on a comfortable bed and looking up at a canopy. He turned his head and saw Sybil beside him. She was still unconscious. He got out of bed with some effort, noting that he had a slight headache and a brassy tongue and gums. His teeth felt enlarged.

Their prison was a single bedroom and a bathroom. There was one door for entrance.

Sybil woke up. She lay there for a while and then got out

of bed. She went to him, and he put his arm around her and said, "I'm sorry about this. If I had made you leave, you wouldn't be in this mess."

"That can't be helped," she said. "Do you think that we'll ever get out of this? I wish I knew what these people wanted."

"We should find out sooner or later," he said. He released her and prowled around the room. There was a large mirror fixed in the wall above the dresser and another wall-high mirror on the opposite side of the room. He supposed that these were one-way.

An hour passed. Sybil had quit trying to talk and had started to read, of all things, a mystery novel she found in a bookcase. He investigated again with the idea of using something to help them get out. He observed that the door was heavy steel and was set tightly against the wall. It swung outward.

An hour and a half after awakening, the door was opened. Pao and two men entered. Sybil spoke to one: "Plugger!"

Plugger was a tall, well-built, dark-skinned man. His hands were long and narrow with long tapering fingers. These were covered with small protuberances, a feature Sybil had not described.

"Our enemies – and yours – were moving in fast," Pao said. "That is why we had to take you two away. I am sorry; we're all sorry. But it had to be done. Otherwise, you would have fallen into the hands of the Tocs."

"Tocs?" Childe said.

"Everything will be explained," Pao said. "Very quickly. Meanwhile, we require your presence elsewhere."

"And Sybil?"

"She will have to stay here. But she won't be harmed."

Childe kissed Sybil and said, "I'll be back. I don't think they intend us any evil. Not now, anyway."

He watched Plugger shut the door. There was a button in its middle; when this was pressed, an unlocking mechanism was activated. Childe reached out and pressed the button, and the door swung out swiftly.

Pao said, "What are you doing?" and pressed the button to shut the door.

"I just wanted to see how it worked," Childe said.

They started down the hall, which was wide and luxuriously carpeted and furnished. He stopped after a few steps.

He had been right. The mirror was a one-way device. He could see Sybil still standing in the middle of the room, her hands clenched by her sides.

He decided to see how valuable he was to them.

"I'd like that mirror turned off," he said. "I don't like being spied on."

Pao hesitated and then said, "Very well."

He pressed a button on the side of the mirror and it darkened.

"I'd like the other mirror turned off, too," Childe said.

"I'll see it's done," Pao said, "Come along now." Childe followed him with the other two men behind him. At the end of the hall, they turned left into another hall and halfway down that turned right into a very large room. This looked like the salon of a millionaire's house as constructed for a movie set. There was a magnificent concert piano at the far end and very expensive furniture, perhaps genuine Louis XV pieces, around the room. A peculiar feature, however, was the glass or transparent metal cube set in the middle of the room. Inside this was a slender-legged dark-red wooden table on top of which was a silvery goblet. Or half a goblet. One side seemed to be complete, but the other was missing. It was as if a shears had cut through the cup part of the goblet at a forty-five-degree angle.

Pao led Childe to the transparent cube and motioned to a man to bring a chair. Childe looked around. There were six exits, some of them broad enough for three men to go through abreast. There were also about fifty men and women in the room, a large number of them between him and the exits. All were dressed in tails and gowns. Pao and his two men were the only ones in business clothes. He recognized Panchita Pocyotl and Vivienne Mabcrough. Vivienne was dressed in a scarlet floor-length formal gown with a deep V almost to her navel. Her pale skin and auburn hair contrasted savagely with the flaming gown. She was holding a big ostrich fan. Seeing his eyes on her, she smiled.

The crowd had been talking when he entered but the conversation softened as he was brought before the cube. Now Pao held up his hand, and the voices died away. A man brought a chair with three legs, a heavy wooden thing with a symbol carved into the back. The symbol was a delta with one end stuck into the open mouth of a rampant fish.

"Please sit down," Pao said.

Childe sat down in the chair and leaned against its back. He could feel the alto-relief of the carved symbol pressing into his back. At the same time, the dull silver of the goblet inside the cube became bright and shimmery. The brightness increased until it glowed as if it were about to melt.

A murmur of what sounded to him like awe ran through the people.

Pao smiled and said, "We would appreciate it if you would concentrate on the goblet, Herald Childe."

"Concentrate how?" Childe said.

"Just look at it. Examine it thoroughly. Let it fill your mind. You will know what I mean."

Childe shrugged. Why not? The procedure and the goblet had aroused his curiosity, and their intentions did not seem sinister. Certainly, he was being treated far better than when he had been a prisoner in Igescu's.

He sat in the chair and stared at the shining goblet. It had a broad base with small raised figures, the outlines of which were fuzzy. After a while, as he studied them, they became clear. They were men and women, naked, and animals engaged in a sexual orgy. Set here and there among them were goblets like that at which he looked, except that these were complete. There was a curious scene in which a tiny woman was halfway into a large goblet while a creature that looked like the Werewolf of London, as played by Henry Hull, rammed a long dick into her asshole. At one side of the base, almost out of view, was a man emerging from a goblet. His legs were still within the cup, but his stiff dong was out and was being squeezed by the tentacle of a creature that seemed to be a six-legged octopus with human hermaphroditic organs. While it was jacking off the man in the goblet, it was also fucking itself.

Childe did not know what the scene represented, but it seemed to him that it had something to do with fecundity. Not with fecundity in the sense of begetting children but of...

He almost grasped the sense of the figures and their play, but it danced away.

The goblet stem was slender. A snake-like thing of silver

coiled around it, its head flattening out to become the underpart of the cup. Its two eyes, distorted, were the only dark spots on the bright silver of the goblet.

The outside of the cup, except for the serpent's head, was bare. But the inside bore some raised geometrical figures that shifted as he looked at them. Sometimes he could pin them down for a half a second and the figures began to make sense, even if they were totally unfamiliar.

The goblet shone even more brilliantly. The room became quieter, and then, suddenly, he could hear the breathing of everyone in the room, except for himself, and, far away, the impact of rain on the roof and the walls of the house and, even more distantly, the roar of waters down the street outside.

There was a hissing he could not at first identify. It was so weak, so remote. And then he knew. He did not have to turn his head to look, and it would have done no good if he had. The thing was hidden under Vivienne's dress. It had slid out and was dangling between her legs. Its little bearded mouth was open, the tongue flickering out, and it was hissing with rage or lust. Or, perhaps, some other emotion. Awe?

The light from the goblet became more intense. Surprisingly, he could look at it without pain. Its whiteness seemed to drill into his eyes and flood his brain. The interior of his skull was white; his brain was a glowing jewel.

There was a collective intake of breath, and the light went out. The darkness that followed was painful. He felt as if something very much beloved had died. His life was empty; he had no reason to live.

He wept.

Philip José Farmer

Chapter 16

When he was finished sobbing – and he still did not know why he had felt so bereaved – he looked up. The people were not talking, but they were making some noise as they shifted around. Also, several were passing through the crowd and serving a liquid in small goblets. The people drank it with one swallow and then put their goblets back on to the large silver trays.

Pao appeared from behind him with a tray on which stood a goblet filled with a dark liquid, and several sandwiches. The bread was coarse and black.

"Drink and then eat," Pao said.

"And if I don't?"

Pao looked stricken, but he shrugged his shoulders and said, "This is one thing that we can't compel you to do. But I swear by my mother planet that the food and drink will not harm you."

Childe looked at the goblet again. It was not quite as dull as it had been a moment ago. It flickered when he looked at it. When he looked away, but could still see it out of the corner of his eye, it became dull once more.

"When will I find out what all this means?" Childe said.

"Perhaps during the ceremony. It is better that you... remember."

"Remember?"

Pao did not offer to explain. Childe smelled the liquid. Its odour was winey, but there was an unfamiliar underodour (was there such a word?) to it. The underodour evoked a flashing image of an infinite black space with stars here and there and then another image of a night sky with sheets of white fire and giant red, blue, yellow, garnet, emerald, and purple stars filling the sky. And there was a fleeting landscape of red rock with mushroom-shaped buildings of white and red stone, trees that looked inverted, with their branches on the ground and their roots feeding on the air, and a thin band with scarlet, pale green, and white threads, something like a Saturn's ring, arcing across the sky near the horizon.

He drained the tiny goblet with one gulp and, feeling hungry immediately afterward, ate the sandwiches. The meat tasted like beef with blue cheese.

When the goblets had been passed around, and everybody was standing as if waiting for something to happen which they were, Childe supposed – Pao raised his hands. He spoke in a loud voice: "The Childe must have power!" That was a funny way to refer to him, Childe thought. *The* Childe?

The crowd answered in a loud chorus, "The Childe must have power!"

Pao said, "There is but one way in which The Childe may gain this power!"

The people echoed, "There is but one way in which The Childe may gain this power!"

"And grow!"

"And grow!"

"And become a man!"

"And become a man!"

"And become our Captain!"

"And become our Captain!"

"And lead us to our long lost home!"

"And lead us to our long lost home!"

"And permit us to triumph over our enemies, the Tocs!"

"And permit us to triumph over our enemies, the Tocs!"

"Through the nothingness and the utter cold he will lead us!"

There was more, none of which made any sense to Childe except for the reference to their enemies, the Tocs. These must be the people of whom he had so far met only three. The three who had rescued him from Vivienne and reproached her for breaking the truce.

The liquor was making him feel very heady by then. And the food had infused him with strength. He looked at the goblet, which glowed as if his gaze beamed radium at it.

Pao finally finished his chanting. Immediately, the crowd became noisy. They started talking and laughing. And they were also stripping off their clothes. Panchita Pocyotl shed her gown, revealing that she wore nothing under it except long stockings held up by huge scarlet garters. Vivienne was not far behind her; she wore a garter belt and stockings. The snake-thing had withdrawn; her auburn bush looked very attractive.

Pao, naked, his skinny dick dangling halfway down

between his thighs, said, "Would you please undress, Captain?"

Childe, feeling dizzy, rose. He said, "Captain?"

"You will know what I mean – I hope," Pao said.

Childe remembered with a pang of dread his treatment at the hands of the enormously fat Mrs Grasatchow when he was a prisoner in Igescu's house.

He said, "Am I to be abused?"

"No one would think of that now," Pao said. "Vivienne made a very bad mistake, and if we did not need her so much, we might have killed her. But she was overcome by your power, and that is a reasonable excuse for her actions. Nevertheless, she will not be permitted to touch you tonight."

Childe, looking at the naked and superbly shaped woman, felt his penis rising. The liquid seemed to have gone down warmly to the place behind his navel and there caught fire. The blaze spread out, up, and down, but mainly down. The base of his cock was rammed with a boiling and heavy liquid metal; it expanded upwards, filling out his cock, lifting it up, and making it throb.

He said, "All right," and he undressed.

Pao took his clothes and left the room. Childe, standing there, felt foolish, and so he sat down. The others seemed to know what was expected of them; they began embracing and caressing each other, standing up, or lying down on the floor, or on the sofas. They were not putting their whole hearts into their love-making, however; they were waiting for someone or something.

Pao returned. He walked up to Childe, took his hand, and said, "Your blessing, Captain."

He placed his long slim peter on Childe's upturned palm, and the dead worm came to life. It became red and swollen and rose up off the hand as if launched. Pao backed away and bowed and kissed Childe's hand where his peter had lain.

"I thank you, Captain," he said.

There was a scramble among the couples after that. They arranged themselves in a double line in an order of precedence which they seemed to know well. There was no quarrelling or struggling to get ahead of one another.

The first two in line were Panchita Pocyotl and a big blond man with Scandinavian features. They stood before Childe, between him and the goblet in the cube.

The man said, "Your pardon, Captain," and took Childe's hand and closed the fingers around his half-erect dong. At the touch, the big-knobbed dong filled up like a blimp being engorged with gas. It lay hard and throbbing in Childe's hand, and a small drop of fluid oozed out of the slit in the glans. The man stepped back and Panchita got down on her knees and took Childe's penis in one hand and kissed it on the head and the shaft. Then she arose, looked once into his eyes with her large luminous dark-brown eyes, and withdrew with the man.

Childe watched them. They walked to a sofa and lay down on it. Panchita spread her legs out and over his shoulders, and he inserted himself into the thick black glossy bush and began pumping. His red Swedish ass went faster and faster and then, suddenly, both groaned and writhed. After they had come, they lay quiescent and then, a few minutes later, he was fucking her dog fashion.

This excited Childe, who wanted the next woman kissing his cock to continue. But she backed away, murmuring, "Thank you, Captain," and went away with her squat Indian partner and his thick stubby penis.

The couples came quickly, the men laying their dongs in his hands and the women kissing or licking his cock. There were exceptions, however. Some of the men also got down and kissed or even sucked briefly on him, and some of the women took his hand and placed it on their cunts.

Childe had been slightly repulsed by some of this at the beginning. But as more couples approached him, as more couples began fucking or sucking, he accepted it as something natural to him. He began thinking of it as his due, and then as something old and familiar. The flashes of the exotic and extraterrestrial landscapes occurred more frequently, each time coincident with the placing of a dong in his hand or the slide of lips over the head and shaft of his cock.

The goblet had increased its illumination during this ceremony. As each couple passed, it shone a trifle more brightly. And the white glow in his skull was exceeded only by the hot whiteness in his penis. It was so strong a sensation, he was disappointed when he looked down and did not see glans and shaft radiating with a white light.

Philip José Farmer

Pao, he noticed, had no steady partner. He wandered around, and when he found a vacant cunt or empty mouth, he filled it. He did not seem to care whether or not the other was male or female. He came each time he rammed his partner with a few strokes, and then he would withdraw his dripping but still rigid dick and go on to the next person.

The only one missing, he suddenly noticed, was Plugger. He had shown up early in the line and given Childe a slight shock when he closed Childe's hand around his warty cock. Childe had felt an increase in the ecstasy building up in him but that was all. He had the feeling that Plugger was withholding, that he had, somehow, turned down his bioelectricity to a minimum. And then Plugger, after briefly fucking his partner but leaving her passed out, had disappeared.

Childe considered this for a second. He had an image of Plugger walking down the hall towards Sybil's room. Was the bastard going to her? And then he forgot about him when the next woman ran her tongue over the head of his penis.

Although the line had been sedate enough, considering the actions of the couples, the people became wild once they had left him. They talked loudly, swore, smacked loudly when kissing or sucking each other off, and filled the room with the slap-slap of wet cocks driving against wet cunts or into wet assholes. They groaned and moaned or screamed with the ecstasy of orgasm oncoming or occurring. And the air was heavy and musky with the odours of sweating bodies, lubricating fluid, and sperm.

The fantastically beautiful Vivienne, although denied touching him, was taking advantage of her liberty with her fellows. She was standing bent over, sucking on a big black's cock while Pao thrust his dick into her anus and the snake-thing looped under Pao's balls and slid back and forth into his anus. They all seemed to come at once, judging from their writhings and shakings. The black's cock dwindled to a half-erection and came out of the mouth of Vivienne, who swallowed the jism. Pao's dick withdrew and was at half-mast, dripping. The snake-thing left Pao's ass reluctantly with its mouth still vomiting spermatic fluid and coiling and uncoiling in the final spasms of orgasm.

At that moment, the last woman in line quit tickling his glans with her tongue. Pao, his cock beginning to rise again but still expelling the grey fluid, walked across the room to him. Childe looked at him with a mute appeal. He was close to coming, and his peter was throbbing in the air. In one corner of his mind, he noted the goblet had begun to pulse. The whiteness flared and dimmed, flared and dimmed.

Just before Pao reached him, he made the connection with full awareness. The goblet was emitting pulses of light in phase with the throbbing of his dong.

Pao took Childe's hand and lifted it. His dick rose so high it almost touched his navel. Childe's own organ seemed to lurch, and its head touched his belly. The throbbings increased, the warm grey tide in his testicles and ducts rose more swiftly, and the glory in him threatened to shoot out.

"Come on!" he said fiercely to Pao.

Pao waved his hand, and Childe understood that he was to take his pick.

Childe looked quickly around. He had a superb choice, because there were very few women in the room who were not extraordinarily beautiful.

Childe said, "Vivienne!"

Pao was startled and opened his mouth, apparently intending to protest. But he closed it, and crooked a finger at Vivienne.

Vivienne was startled, too. She pointed a finger at herself and mouthed, "Me?"

Pao nodded and gestured for her to come a-running. She did so with the snake-thing flopping between her legs, banging into her knees and protesting against the treatment. When Vivienne got to Childe, she dropped on her knees and said, "Forgive me, my Captain."

Then she started to suck the end of his cock. The ecstasy came in slow waves, and from the inside of his navel to his knees he became ice.

He managed to gasp at Pao, "Jerk that thing out!"

"What?" Pao said.

"Pull that thing out of her cunt! Quick!"

Pao got down behind Childe and reached through his legs and grabbed the snake-thing, which was trying to wrap itself around Childe's thigh. Apparently it intended to climb up and into Childe's

Philip José Farmer

asshole, although it was doubtful that it was long enough to reach its goal. But Pao grabbed it behind its head and gave a savage yank.

Vivienne fell apart.

Childe stood with her head between his hands and his penis in her mouth. The eyes stared up at him with a violet fire, and the lips and tongue kept on sucking and thrusting. The other parts of her body, having gotten on to their legs, began to scuttle around the room. The big black who had been sucked off by Vivienne picked up the many-legged cunt and stuck it on the end of his cock and began sliding it back and forth. The cunt's legs kicked as if it were having an orgasm.

The goblet's pulses came faster and faster. Childe held the head by the ears and rammed his prick faster and faster between the lips. Its head drove down her throat, backed out until it almost left those beautiful lips, and then rammed in until the hairs around his cock were crushed against her lips.

Faster and faster. Brighter and brighter. Pulse and ecstasy.

The ice turned to fire. He spurted with a scream and a writhing that was so violent he almost dropped the head. His pubis was against her nose and his dong was far down her throat. He came and came, and the goblet glowed as if it were in the heart of the sun.

Pao got down underneath the head and swallowed the jism that fell down her throat and out the open neck.

The others scrambled to catch the drops that Pao had missed. They rolled him away, and stuck their heads under Vivienne's, and then they were pushed away. Those who could not get any directly ran their fingers over the lips or down the mouths of those who had been lucky and got the stuff second-hand. Some tasted it and then rubbed the residue over their cunts or pricks.

Childe quit shaking and spurting. The goblet's light waned swiftly, and soon it had only a faint glow.

He pulled Vivienne's head off his peter and threw it to Pao, saying, "Now you can put her together again. I had my revenge."

He sat down and stared dully at the goblet. He felt very tired.

The people crowded around and spoke in awed tones. At first, he did not understand what they were talking about. When he heard a woman say, "It did grow, just a little, but it grew!" he saw

---

what they were marvelling at.

The incomplete side of the cup of the goblet was now half-filled in. It had grown more of the metal.

"You are indeed the Captain and The Childe," Pao said, holding Childe's limp cock in his hand. "But you are no longer a child."

Childe understood what he was saying, although he did not know the details. During that last explosion of orgasm, he had seen many things on the screen of his mind. Somehow, this experience had tapped a racial memory. No, not racial. That was not the correct term. A genetic memory was closer to an exact definition.

Chapter 17

Forry Ackerman jumped when the poundings came on his door. He opened the door without checking on the identity of the visitor, a lack of precaution indicating his upset condition.

A tall good-looking man with yellow hair and dark blue eyes stood there. Two other men were with him.

He said, "I'm Hindarf. This is Bellow and this is Grunder. We're friends, old friends, of Alys Merrie. We'd like to come in."

"No smoking," Forry said and then remembered that Alys was puffing on one cigarette after another.

He let them in and closed the door. Two sat down without asking his permission; Hindarf stood in the middle of the room as if he intended to dominate it. And he did.

"I'm here to carry out the rest of our plan," he said.

"What plan?" Forry said.

"He looked around the room. It had always seemed the centre of the universe, this room. It contained illustrations from all over the cosmos by men who had never left the planet Earth in the flesh. Memos from Mars. To others, it appeared weird, but to him it was home.

Now it was shifting from reality, slipping its moorings. The very intrusion of genuine alienness rendered this place alien. The aliens were the real people, and the products of imagination were fake. Contrary to what he had always maintained, reality was more real than fantasy.

"You must be wondering why you've been chosen," Hindarf said. "Why should we bring in an Earthling in our battle against the Ogs? Why do we need you in our effort to recapture the Captain?"

Forry bent his head and looked at them from under raised eyebrows. He drawled, "Yes. I had been wondering about that. Many are called but Fu are Cho-sen, as the Korean said."

Hindarf did not smile, but he did not look puzzled either. He said, "There are some Earthlings who have what we call *resonance*. Through the chance of genetics, they are born with a psychic affinity, or a psychophysical complex, which generates what, for want of a better term, we call *white noise*. This vibration is quite in phase with those radiated by the Tocs. It makes the

Earthling immediately sympathetic and empathic with the Tocs, and, conversely, it generates disturbance and confusion in the minds of the Ogs. But it exists, and its effect is to blank out the vibrations radiated by the Tocs. In other words, we Tocs and Ogs know when we're near each other. We sense it just as a lion downwind from an antelope smells it. But when one of the resonant white-noise generator Earthlings is around, the Ogs can't sense us."

Forry put his fingertips together to form a church steeple. He said, "I've never been one to make everything black or white. There is much more grey in this universe than black and white."

"Did you ever have a good word to say for the Nazis?" Hindarf said.

"Well, they did get rockets launched and that led to the first men on the Moon."

Alys Merrie guffawed and said, "Well, kiss my ass and call me Hitler!"

"Woolston Heepish is a member of the Ogs," Hindarf said. "He has not only set himself up as a rival of yours, he has become a caricature of you, and he has stolen from you. Do you think he's more grey than black?"

"Black as the devil's hindbrain," Forry said. "Why, just last night...!"

Hindarf waved his hand impatiently and said, "I know. The question is, will you help us? It will be dangerous. But it will be less dangerous for us if you accompany us. We intend to rescue Childe. He is a prisoner of the Ogs. And the emanations from the house today indicate that he's participating in a grail-growing ceremony. He probably doesn't know what he's doing, but that makes no difference. He is doing what they want him to do."

"Aren't there any other Earthlings you know who could go with you?" Forry said. He remembered some of his youthful fantasies in which he had been the focus of attention from the secret band of Martians and Venusians operating in an underground struggle for control of Earth. Generally, in his fantasies, he had been on the side of the Martians. There was something sinister, damp, toadstooly, and creepycrawly about the Venusians. All that rain... Now that he thought about it, the deluge of the past seven days had turned Los Angeles into a Venus such as the sci-fi writers had projected back in the good old days of *Science Wonder Stories* and

Astounding.

"No," Hindarf said. "There are none available in this area, and none anywhere who can generate white noise to compare with yours."

"This may seem irrelevant to you at this moment," Forry said, "but why does Heepish steal from me?"

"Because he wants your stuff for the collection he intends to take to the planet of the Ogs. He's a greedy and short-sighted person, and that is why he's stolen a few things from you instead of waiting to take the whole collection just before he leaves."

"What?" Forry said shrilly. "The whole collection?"

"Oh, yes," Alys Merrie said, blowing smoke at him. "He has planned on emptying your house and your garage. He can do it in a few minutes, you know, if he can get a Captain to do it for him. The collection would be moved to a huge room in a barn behind the present headquarters of the Ogs. Then, when the Captain moves all the Ogs to their home planet, he will also take the collection. Which, by the way, will consist of many of Earth's art treasures in addition to artifacts and books and so forth, for the Og museums."

"You can visit our planet, if you wish," Hindarf said. "And you might as well have Heepish's collection too. It won't do him any good after he's dead."

"Dead?"

Hindarf nodded and said, "Of course. We plan to kill every Og."

Forry did not like the idea of killing, even if Heepish did deserve it. But the thought of going to an alien planet, one so far away that it was not even in this galaxy! He alone, of all men, would voyage to another world! He had wanted to be the first man on the Moon and the first man on Mars when he was a child and then that dream had glimmered away. He wouldn't even be able to go to those places as a tourist. And now, he was offered a free ticket to a planet far more alien and weird than the Moon or Mars could ever be. Under a strange sun on an unimaginably exotic world!

"I can come back any time I wish?" he said. "I wouldn't want to leave Los Angeles forever, you know. I have my collection and all my wonderful friends."

"No trouble," Hindarf said.

"I must warn you, if it involves anything strenuous, I'll be handicapped," Forry said. "My heart..."

"Alys has told us all about that," Hindarf said.

Forry's eyes widened. "Everything?"

"Just the medical aspects," Hindarf said.

"All right then," Forry said. "I'll help you. But just as a white-noise generator. You can't ask me to take part in any killing."

The three men and Alys smiled.

Forry smiled, too, but he was not sure that he was not making a pact with the devil. It seemed that the Ogs really were evil, but then the Tocs might not be so good, either. It could be a case of one band of devils fighting another.

Chapter 18

Childe awoke with a feeling of emptiness and of shame.

He looked at Sybil, who was sleeping by his side, and then he stared upward for a long time. Something had happened to him last night, or he presumed it was last night, since he did not know what time it was. His wristwatch was gone.

As if a key had been turned in, unlocking a memory or releasing a programmed tape, he had gone through that ceremony without a false step or being told, really, what to do next.

When he had evoked that pulsing light, he had felt an ecstasy that was superior, in some undefinable way, to that of sexual orgasm. It was difficult to untangle the sexual from the photonic, but a part of the glory had been from that goblet.

That final incident, the one with Vivienne's unattached head, had seemed at the moment to be fully justified and exquisitely delightful. But this morning it looked ugly and perverted. He could not understand what had possessed him.

The hell of it was, he thought, that the next time he was seated before that goblet, he was likely to do the same thing or something equally uninhibited. He did not fool himself about that.

The worst thing about this was that he was cooperating with people – beings, rather – who were evil.

But when he had been placed before that goblet, he had been unable to refuse to act. In a sense, the goblet had activated him more than he had activated it.

What was supposed to be the final result of this ceremony and of others that would undoubtedly follow it?

He decided that he would refuse to do anything more unless everything was fully explained.

He thought of Sybil. Would she be tortured if he refused to carry out the Ogs' desires? Knowing what he did of them, he could not doubt that they would do whatever they thought was required. And so Sybil would be... He shuddered.

Somebody knocked on the door. It was faint because the door was of such thick metal, but he was aware of it. His sense of hearing seemed to be sharper after last night's experiences. He rose, noting that he was naked and not caring, and went to the door. He

---

rapped on it, and the door swung outward. Vivienne was standing there with Pao behind her.

"You people are so technologically advanced, you could find some easier way to get my attention," he said.

"You indicated you wanted privacy in your room," Vivienne said. "So we polarized the one-way windows and turned off the TV monitor and the intercom."

"That's nice of you," he said, thinking that they were really trying to sell him on how extremely nice they were. "Show me where this intercom is, and I'll contact you when I want you. And be sure to keep the other devices off."

"What the Captain wishes..." Pao murmured.

"What I wish now, after a good breakfast, are answers to my questions."

Pao said, "Of course," as if he was amazed that Childe could have any reason to think otherwise.

"I'll see you in ten minutes," he said. "You'd better tell me where the breakfast room is. And leave the door unlocked."

Pao looked embarrassed. He said, "I'm sorry indeed, my Captain, but you'll have to stay in here. It's for your own safety. There are evil people who want to hurt you. You cannot leave this room. Except for the Grailing, of course."

"The Grailing?"

"Growing that goblet. The Grail."

"There is to be more of that?"

"There is."

"Very well then," Childe said. "I'm a prisoner."

Pao bowed slightly and said, "A ward, Captain. For your own protection."

Childe closed the door in their faces and woke up Sybil. She did not want to get out of bed, but he told her he wanted her to hear everything that would be said. He started towards the bathroom but stopped when he saw a hairy pointed head sticking out from under the bed. It looked vaguely like a sleeping black dog about the size of a Great Dane. He rapped it on its wet doggy nose, and it opened its eyes wide.

"What the hell are you and what the hell are you doing under my bed?" he said.

The eyes were dark brown and looked familiar. But the

Philip José Farmer

animal that crawled out from under the bed was unfamiliar. Its front part resembled a giant water spaniel, and the back part was monkeylike. It stood up on its semi-human feet and staggered over to a chair and sat down. It leaned its shaggy floppy-eared head on its two paws. The monkey part was hairy but not so hairy it entirely concealed a pair of human testicles and a warty penis.

"I was hungry," Childe said aloud. "But seeing you, whatever you are..."

He felt repulsed but not scared. The thing did not look dangerous, not, at least, at the moment. Its weariness and its big wet gentle eyes added up to harmlessness.

One thing its presence did for him. It reaffirmed the sense of alienness, of unhumanity, about these people.

Sybil did not seemed frightened; he would have expected her to be screaming with hysteria.

He said, "Was this your bed partner last night, Sybil?"

"Part of the time," she said.

"There was more than one?"

The only one missing from the ceremony, as far as he knew, was Plugger.

"I don't think so," she said. "He seemed to have changed into this about a half hour before we quit."

He did not have to ask her what they had quit doing.

"He said he was almost emptied," Sybil said. "He had been to the three Toc prisoners before he came to me. I suppose he buggered them, I mean, he applied his limp prick to their anuses and shocked them with the only pleasant shock that I know of. Then he came to me."

Childe did not feel that he was in a position to rebuke her. What good would it do, anyway? She took sex where she found it and enjoyed it. And all the time professing that he was her only true love. The truth was, sex was her only true love. Impersonal sex.

The unbelievable element in this was not so much the metamorphosis of Plugger into this dog-monkey thing as it was her calm acceptance of the metamorphosis. She should have been in a deep state of psychic shock.

"Why did Plugger feel it necessary to stimulate the prisoners?" he said.

"He told me that everybody in the house had to be hooked

into the Grailing and that only if the prisoners and I had sex with an Og could this be done."

A voice spoke from a jade statuette on a table against the wall near the bed: "Captain, is there anything you want?"

"Yes!" he said, facing the statuette. "Get this thing out of here! Plugger is making me sick!"

A moment later, the door swung out, and the blond man who had been first in the line entered. Behind him came two women holding trays. The man took one of Plugger's paws and led him out while the women served the food. The coffee was excellent, and the bacon and eggs and toast and cantaloupe were delicious.

While he ate, he looked steadily at Sybil. She chattered on as if unaware of his scrutiny. She had certainly acquired a set of stainless steel nerves during her imprisonment.

After breakfast, she went into the bathroom to fix herself up for the day, as she put it. Pao and Vivienne entered. The first thing she did was to get on to her knees before him, murmuring, "Your permission, Captain!" She kissed the head of his penis.

He did not object. When in Rome, and so on. The custom certainly beat that of kissing the hand of royalty.

Pao touched his penis with one finger, also murmuring, "Your permission, Captain."

That was where the power and the glory were stored, Childe thought. No wonder that Igescu and Grasatchow and Dolores del Osorojo and Magda Holyani had been unable to resist using him sexually. The Ogs were supposed to have left him alone to develop into something, according to what he had garnered from the brief conversation between Vivienne and the leader of the three who had rescued him from her.

He wondered if the two werewolves had intended to kill him, as he had thought when they attacked. Maybe they had only meant to herd him back to his prison. And when he had been jumped by that wereleopard while he was killing Igeseu in his oak-log coffin, he may have just been the object of her efforts to drive him away.

It was obvious now that he was supposed to develop into a Captain. But there were a number of questions to which he required answers. For one thing, what about those abandoned cars in front of his house?

Vivienne said, "Several years ago, we had about half of a grail in our possession. It was the result of several thousands of years collecting the materials needed to make the metal. Then the Tocs stole it. We pursued them and cornered the one with the grail after killing his two companions. He had run into a railroad yard to get away from us, and when he saw he could not escape, he threw the grail into a gondola full of junk. At that time, we did not know that. Later, we got the information from him."

"I can imagine," said Childe, closing his eyes and shuddering.

"By then, the grail and the junk had gone into a steel mill furnace. We had to do some very intense detective work, very expensive, too, and we found that that particular load had ended up as metal in a certain number of cars of a certain make and model. So..."

"But you did not know which cars exactly?" Childe said. He was beginning to understand.

"Luckily, they were cars which were transported to this area. We had narrowed the number to about three hundred. And so we started to steal them and leave them in front of your house. We were lucky, very lucky. Three of the cars contained traces of the metal in the grail. They activated when you went near them, but you couldn't see that because the paint hid the glow, which was extremely feeble, anyway.

"We junked the cars and had them melted in a yard by a man whom we paid well. We *strained out* the grail metal, as it were, and used the tiny bits as a detector for those other cars that contained the metal. When one bit of grail is brought close to another, both glow. We no longer had to leave cars in front of your house, because we knew exactly what group of cars contained the metal. We had to do some more bribing of authorities to get the owners' names, and it was impossible to steal all the cars.

"But we got enough to act as a seed for the growth of more metal. It is a procedure that is terribly tiring for the Captain. And it exhausts those who take part in the ceremony. But it has to be done."

Childe did not completely understand. He asked that Pao explain everything to him. This took an hour and a half with several questions still to be asked.

Nor did he accept Pao's word that the Tocs were the evil ones and the Ogs the good. The Tocs could be evil, but if they were, they were certainly matched by the Ogs.

However, what the Ogs wanted of him was not something that he had to refuse for the good of Earth. Far from it. If he took the Ogs to their home world, he would be doing his world a vast service. He would never be rewarded by humans for his heroism. In fact, if he were to bring his deeds to their attention, he would be put into an insane asylum.

There were several disturbing things about being a Captain. One was that he could return to Earth and there arrange to transport the Tocs to their home planet, too. If the Ogs could scrap cars and make a grail, the Tocs could do the same. There were plenty of cars left for that purpose.

The Ogs must have thought of this possibility. What did they intend doing about it? He hated to ask them, because he was afraid of both the truth and of falsehood. If they meant to kill him or hold him prisoner on their world, they would not, of course, tell him so. And if he asked them about it, they would know that he would have to be killed or imprisoned. Either way, he would lose.

"It will be glorious," Vivienne was saying. "When the Grail is complete, then you, my Captain, can materialize all the Ogs who are wandering the face of this planet as energy complexes."

Childe was startled, and he had thought he was beyond being surprised anymore.

"You mean that I am expected to give all your, uh, dead, new bodies?" he said.

"You will enable them to give themselves their material bodies," she said.

"It will be a resurrection day for us," Pao said. His slanting vulpine eyes glowed. The light from the lamp was reflected redly in them.

"And just where will this resurrection or rematerializing, or whatever you call it, take place?" Childe said.

"They will materialize in the barn behind this house," Vivienne said. "There is more than enough room, even with all the goods stacked there."

"Approximately nine hundred of them," Pao said. "They

Philip José Farmer

won't be brought into matter all at once. You can control that, Captain. Ten or twenty or so at a time, and these will be conducted out of the place into this house or into rooms in the barn."

Theologistics of resurrection day, he thought. And am I really a sort of god?

"Will Lord Byron, my real father, be among them?" he said. Pao said, "Oh, no. You forget that..."

He did not want to continue. No wonder. Byron would be among the Tocs, who would not be materialized. And Pao must be trying to guess what Childe was contemplating. How could he avoid the conclusion that the Tocs might be the good ones, if his own father was a Toc?

"Byron was a very talented man, but a very evil man," Pao said slowly. "History does not reveal how evil, though there are hints. The world never knew the story behind the story, of course. If it had, it would have executed him. I am sorry to say that about your father, but it has to be said. Fortunately for you, we saved you from the Tocs."

The implication was that they had also saved him from following the evil ways of his father.

"I have a lot of thinking to do," Childe said, "so I'd like to be alone. What are your plans for me today, if any?"

Pao spoke in an apologetic tone. "The Tocs will be gathering for an attack on this house. Time is more essential than ever because of this. We were hoping that you would be quite rested by evening and ready for another Grailing."

"See me after dinner," he said.

Pao bowed and Vivienne started to suck his cock again, but he stopped her. "I'll save my power," he said.

Pao looked pleased at this, but the woman frowned and bit her lip. She turned to go, but Childe said, "One moment, Vivienne. Last night. You know what happened? I mean, are you conscious when you, uh, come apart?"

She said, "I must be dimly conscious. When I came to, all put together, I remembered vaguely what went on. It was like a poorly remembered dream."

"Can you have an orgasm when you're disconnected?"

"Not that I remember. If you were getting revenge, you got a pale shade of it, just as I probably got a pale shade of orgasm."

Childe said, "I can understand even the weirdness of the others, since they are known in folklore and superstition. But I have never heard of your type. Was your kind ever known among humans?"

Vivienne said, "If you're referring to my structure, to the thing in me, to my discreteness, as I call it, no. I am unique. And I am recent. I was rematerialized in 1562. I had died in 1431 A.D., by present reckoning. The thing in my womb died in 1440 A.D. He was my very good friend then in our public human life and in our private Og life."

"That thing was human?"

"Yes. You see, when we succeeded in rematerializing in 1562, we constructed ourself in our present arrangement. We can do that within certain limits, you know. We have to conform to biological laws, but if you have great knowledge you can do things with matter that you humans would think impossible.

"We had talked about such a symbiosis as this, where we could double the intensity of our sexual activities. So we materialized with this structure. Only we made a mistake. I did, rather. I had an idea that if I could be separated into various parts, and these parts could also have a sexual life, orgasm, that is, and the parts could communicate each other's orgasms... well, it didn't work out that way."

Childe wondered if he was being told the truth. It seemed too fantastic. Would anybody deliberately build herself like this? Wasn't it more likely that her enemies, the Tocs, had caught her as she and the thing were rematerializing and shaped her like this? He did not know why they would do it, but it was more probable that someone would do this to another for a sadistic joke than that anyone would purposefully do it to herself.

"Both of us had very traumatic experiences in our 15th century lives," she was saying. "He was hung and burned at the same time, and I was burned at the stake."

"You were a witch?" Childe said. "Then all the witches burned were not innocent?"

"Oh, no! I wasn't innocent, but I was not a witch in the sense that my executioners thought. It was the English that burned me, you know."

"No, I didn't know," he said. "Who were you? Anybody I

Philip José Farmer

might know?"

"I think so," she said. "I was Joan of Arc. And the being in my womb was Gilles de Rais."

Chapter 19

After the two Ogs had left, Childe lay down on the bed. Sybil had heard only the last five minutes, so he went over the entire conversation with her. She said, "I always thought Joan of Arc was unjustly burned by the English, that she had been proved innocent of the charge of witchcraft?"

"She was condemned by the Church, but it was the Church that later removed the charge and then canonized her. I think that that happened because she was too big a hero to the French."

"I don't understand," Sybil said. "What was Vivienne, or Joan, or whatever she was, doing? Why would an Og try to save France from the English?"

"Maybe for herself. Who knows what she intended to do after she had saved the nation for the French ruler? It's possible that she meant to take over from him or perhaps to control France through him. She may even have intended to drive the English out and then invade England and bring both nations under one ruler again. I didn't ask her what she and de Rais meant to do. But I'll have a chance later on. Just now, I'm too stunned."

"Who was Gilles de Rais?"

"He was a Grand Marshal of France, one of the best warriors and generals the French had. He was also savagely sadistic, a psychotic homosexual who abducted, tortured, mutilated, and sacrificed hundreds of little boys. Little girls, too, I think. A member of the royalty or the nobility could get away with a lot in those days, but he went too far. He was charged with witchcraft, ritual murder, and a number of other things, including sodomy, I think. He was executed and quite properly, too. Few people have ever been so bestial. He made Jack the Ripper look like a gentle old fuddyduddy."

Sybil shuddered but did not say anything. He got off the bed and undressed while she looked wide-eyed at him.

"Take your clothes off," he said.

"Why?"

"Because I want to make love to you. Is that surprising?"

"Yes, it is, after last night," she said.

She started to unbutton her blouse and then stopped.

"Aren't you supposed to save yourself for tonight?"

"Here, I'll help you undress," he said.

He began to unbutton her.

"Yes, I am. But what they want and what I want do not necessarily coincide. Besides, if I'm dry, what can they do about it?"

"Oh, no! You shouldn't do that!"

"Whose side are you on?"

"Well, yours, of course! But I don't want them to get mad at you, Herald. Or at me."

"You can always tell them I made you," he said, grinning. "In more senses than one."

"I really shouldn't," she said, staring at his slightly swelled cock.

"Go ahead. Touch it."

"I'm not an Og," Sybil replied. "But if you say so." He stripped her blouse and unhooked her bra and took it off. She had full well-shaped breasts that had not yet begun to sag. He kissed the nipples and saw them swell and then he sucked on both, one after the other. She stood against him, her back slightly arched, and moaned. She reached down and tenderly fondled the shaft of his cock, which was expanding with his kissing and her caressing. He kissed her breasts all over and then backed her towards the bed, where he eased her down. He removed her skirt and her panties, and moved in between her legs. The thick black fleece of her cunt was beginning to run; she had always over-lubricated. He licked along the slit, putting the tip of his tongue in between the lips and running it up and down. Then he pressed the tip against the clitoris, ran it back and forth, and inserted two fingers into her slit and moved them slowly back and forth and then more swiftly. She came finally with a fierce deep groan and pulled the hairs off his head.

After this, he came up from between her legs and slid on up by her. He pushed her head down towards his penis, which was sticking up straight and hard and swollen. The head was purple, glistening, and the skin was stretched so tight it seemed about ready to burst. The blue veins stood out like unmined mineral under the reddish skin.

Sybil sucked on his testicles a while, one after the other, while she ran a finger partway up his anus. He moaned with the delight of the mouth and tongue and the finger. Then she ran her tongue lightly along the shaft of his peter, wet his pubic hairs with her tongue, and took the big head into her lips. Her tongue trembled on the slit of the glans, and her lips moved noisily with their sucking. The edges of her teeth brushed against the tight tender skin.

He blew into her mouth with a writhing of belly muscles and hips and a feeling of flying apart.

Sybil continued to suck, having swallowed the fluid. She worked at him, occasionally stopping to murmur endearing words. His dong began to rise again and when it was fully rigid, he told her to lie down. He got down on top of her and eased his prick into the slit until the pubic hairs were crushing each other. He lay there for some time, luxuriating in the warmth and the moisture and the tenderness. Her sphincter muscle squeezed on his cock, gently working it.

"I'm no superman, you know, Sybil," he said. "Once or twice a night, and I'm done for, usually. But when I was at Igescu's that hog of a woman, Grasatchow, put a suppository up my rectum that acted as an aphrodisiac and an energy source. And last night they gave me a drink that had the same effect. Maybe some of that effect is still with me, which is why I could get a hard-on so quickly after coming. Or maybe it's just because I've been so long without you, and you're my aphrodisiac. Anyway, I love you, and I intend to fuck all day."

"I love you, too," Sybil panted. "Do you want to move now, Herald?"

He began to thrust, slowly at first and then more swiftly as he felt the tide in him increasing its forward swings. He came with a moan at the same time that she screamed with ecstasy. Tears rolled down her face on to the pillow.

His speculation that the drug he had taken was still affecting him was probably true. He lost some rigidity after the shooting out of his sperm, but he kept his peter in her, and within a minute or two it was rigid and apparently ready to tap on new reserves.

However, this time, the grey liquid in him would not rise so soon. He hammered her for what seemed like fifteen minutes and though the ecstasy built up, he could not come. Sybil was having one orgasm after another. Her eyes were open and her

Philip José Farmer

hands were flung out and she was rolling her head back and forth and groaning and weeping.

Suddenly, she gave a scream, and seemed to fall unconscious. He was not worried, since she had behaved like this frequently. When she had an especially exquisite orgasm, she would faint.

But the white body beneath him became reddish. The smooth but wet-slippery skin was covered with hairs as red as an Irish setter's and as wet as if it had just climbed out of the water. The face became elongated and snouted, the long head hairs shrank to a bristle, the eyes shifted towards the sides of the head, the small and delicate ears became large hairy pointed organs.

The long-fingered well-manicured hands became paws with blunt hooked nails. The legs on his shoulders became hairy, and a big hard penis was against his body. It was spurting jism over his belly and down on to his own cock, which was buried to the hairs in the hairy anus of the creature.

It was too late for him to stop. He had been on the verge of ejaculating as the metamorphosis took place. Moreover, he had suspected that this thing was not Sybil. She had been too blasé about the change of shape of Plugger, too calm about what was happening, and too eager to fuck him. Sybil might have wanted to fuck him, but she would have been too afraid of emptying him and so making their captors angry. This thing should have been afraid of that, too, and probably had been, but it could not resist the temptation to get the power and the glory of the Captain's cock all to itself.

That had been the thing's undoing. It had become overwhelmed and had lost control. Apparently, it still was not aware of this.

He exploded inside the red-haired ass of the creature. The intensity of the orgasm was such that, afterwards, he felt almost forgiving. Almost but not quite.

Panting, he lay for a while on top of the wet and hairy body.

Then he got off the bed and seized its neck between his hands. It was as tall and almost as heavy as he, but it was terrified. Its brown eyes bulged out as its air was squeezed off, and its paws flailed.

Childe turned, swinging it off its feet, and then dragged it by its ears to the door. He shouted until the door was opened and then he shoved the thing out with a kick just under its long bushy tail. The three who received it looked shocked.

"That'll be the last trick you play on me!" he shouted. "Where is my wife? You had better produce Sybil, and quick, or you'll get nothing out of me anymore! No matter what you do!"

The thing got off the floor, rubbing its spine with a paw, and whined. It said something, but the shape of the mouth was not appropriate for human speech.

"Kill it!" Childe shouted. "Kill it and prove to me that you did! And then bring me Sybil, my wife, alive and well!"

The door swung inwards and locked. He raged around the room for a while. Finally, he burst into tears and wept for a long time. Then he got up and took a shower and dressed again. Pao and the big Swedish blond, O'Brien, entered.

Chapter 20

At nine that evening, Forry Ackerman and four Tocs, including Alys Merrie, set out for their rendezvous. Forry had had to exercise his imagination to the rupture point to explain to Wendy why he wasn't going to the monthly soirée with her and to the host and hostess why he couldn't make it. He didn't think he satisfied anybody with his excuses, but certainly they were far more satisfactory than the truth.

The rain had stopped for several hours after five o'clock, and some of the clouds overhead thinned out. Then darkness and lightning had moved back in and thunder had come. A half hour later, it began raining savagely.

Every channel was filled with news of the damage done by the floods and the lives lost. The radio seemed to talk of little else, between bursts of rock music. Over two thousand homes had had to be abandoned. At least that number were in danger of sliding down a hill or being floated away. Most of the canyons were closed even to those who lived in them. The rivulets and brooks roaring down from the hills had become small rivers and frightening tidewaters. The Basin and the San Fernando Valley were sometimes knee-deep in water. Business was at a standstill; most of the bus lines had quit running. The governor had finally declared the three counties a disaster area. Citizens were screaming about flood control, and an insurance man was gunned down by an enraged citizen who had lost his home under an avalanche of mud.

The grocery stores were beginning to run short of supplies. There was water contamination and a backing up of the sewers. Despite the almost continuous rains, fires were numerous, and one fire truck, answering the twentieth call that day, dropped into a tremendous hole created by the torrents slamming down from the hills. No one was drowned, but the truck was lost.

Just before he left, Forry received a call from Wendy. The party had been called off, even though most of the guests lived within a few miles of the house where the monthly party of science-fiction people and normals was being held. It should have been cancelled days before, but the hostess was unusually stubborn.

He sighed with relief. Telling the lies had burdened him

down, and at the same time he resented the burden. Why should he worry about breaking an engagement for a party when the fate of the world depended on what he and the Tocs did tonight? Nevertheless, he did worry.

Hindarf drove a pick-up truck which was several times in water higher than the wheels. At Sunset and Beverly Drive, he pulled to the curb. A semi with a big van came along five minutes later and stopped with a hissing of air brakes. They got down out of the pick-up and waded through water up to their ankles to the van. They had to hold on to each other to keep from being swept off their feet by the current. A piece of timber, which looked as if it had been a post for a billboard, swept by them. If it had struck a leg, it would have cracked the bone.

There were twenty others in the van. The back doors were closed, and the truck pulled away. With its high body and its power, it should get through water which would drown out an automobile.

On the way, Hindarf gave them instructions. Apparently, everybody except Forry had heard these before, but he was making sure that they understood them. The instructions took about fifteen minutes, and the putting on of the diving suits, flippers, tanks and goggles about ten. Forry objected that he had never been scuba diving but was told that he would be underwater for only a minute. The main reason they were wearing the suits was to keep from getting cold while they went through the water.

The truck stopped on a steep slope. The doors were opened and a small ladder let down for Forry while the others leaped out on to the road. They were parked on Topanga Canyon just outside the entrance to the road that ran up to the house of the Ogs. The brown flood running off it joined the ankle-deep current coming down Topanga. Forry was glad that he wore flippers and a suit and that the tank gave him more weight to resist the current. But he did not think that he could carry it up the hill.

"Sure you can," Hindarf said. "Put on the goggles and start breathing through the mouthpiece."

"Now?" Forry said.

"Now."

Forry did so, and at the first breath he felt more energetic than at any time in his life since he had been a child. The air filled his whole body with a strength and a *joie de vivre* that made him want to sing. This was impossible, of course, with the piece in his mouth.

Hindarf said, "We may have a hard fight ahead. The vaporized drug in the breathing system will charge our bodies. The effect is intense but short-lived."

They walked up the road, their flippers slop-slopping. They looked like Venusians, Forry thought, what with the frog feet, the slick black skins of the suits, the humped air tanks, the goggles, and the big mouthpieces. Some even carried tridents or fishing spears. The rain fell heavily on them, and everything was dark and wet, as if they were under the clouds on the nightside of the second planet from the sun.

Before they came to the turn of the road that would have placed them in view of those in the house, they started to climb the hillside. This was steep and muddy, and they could only get up by grabbing bushes and pulling themselves up. He appreciated the suit now, since it kept him from getting wet and muddy. The weight of the tank seemed negligible, so strong did he feel. His heart was chugging along at its accustomed pace, which meant that the extra demand for energy was being taken care of by the drug in the air system.

After slipping and sliding and hanging on to the bushes, they crawled out on to the top of the hill. Another hill to their right hid them from view of those in the house, although Forry did not understand how they could be seen in the dark.

Hindarf led them around the larger hill and up to a high brick wall. This was topped by a barbed wire fence about three feet high. Several Tocs unfolded a ladder, a stile, really, and put it over the wall and the wire fence. Hindarf cautioned everybody not to touch the wires, which were charged with high voltage. One by one, they crawled up the stile and over the wall and down to the other side.

They were in an orchard which seemed to run several hundred yards north and south from where they stood and an indeterminate distance west. The stile was taken down, telescoped, and placed under some bushes. Hindarf led them through the trees until they came to another slope. This rose steeply to a low brick wall. There was a flight of steps made of some stone which glowed red and black in the light that Hindarf and others flashed on it.

Forry had been upset by their careless use of this light, but Hindarf assured him that it was a form of black light. Forry could see it simply because his goggles had a specially prepared glass. Hindarf doubted that the Ogs had anything which could detect this form of illumination.

When they got to the top of the steps, they could see the black bulk of the house about fifty yards away. It was dark except for a slit of light. They went on and then were at the end of a long swimming pool. This was brimming over, flooding the cement walks, the patio, the yard, and running down the steps up which they had just climbed.

Hindarf gave Forry his instructions again and then went down into the pool via the steel ladder. The man assigned to watch Forry led him into the pool. For a moment, everything was black, and he had no idea which was up or down, north or south. Then a light flooded the area around him, and he could see his guide just ahead of him, holding the lamp. Hindarf's flippers were visible just ahead of the globe of illumination.

They swam the sixty-yard-long pool underwater as near the floor as they could get. Forry caught a glimpse of strange figures painted on the cement floor. Griffins, werewolves metamorphosing from men to beasts, a legless dragon, a penis-beaked flipper-winged rooster, a devilfish with a shaven cunt for a mouth, a malignant-faced crab being ridden by a nude woman with fish heads for breasts, and something huge and shadowy and all the more sinister for being so amorphous.

Then they were at the deep end of the pool, and Hindarf and his guide were removing a plate from the wall. It looked like any other section of the wall, but it was thin and wide and its removal exposed a large dark hole. Hindarf swam into it, the guide followed, and Forry, after a moment's hesitation, and knowing that the honour of Earthlings depended upon him, swam through the hole. The tunnel had been dug out of the earth, of course, but it was walled up with many small plates screwed together. He wondered how long the Tocs had been working on this. It must have taken them years, because their time would be limited to the early hours of the morning before the sun came up.

It was possible, however, that this tunnel had been built by

Philip José Farmer

the Ogs as an escape route. The Tocs, having discovered it, were taking advantage of it.

He did not know how long they swam through the tunnel. It seemed like a long time. It led downward, or at least he got that impression. Then they were popping up in a chamber illuminated by a bright arc light hanging from a chain set into the cement ceiling. A ladder gave access to a platform at the end of which hung row on row of suits. Shelves held many goggles and air tanks.

His second speculation was correct. This had been made by the Ogs for escape. But then, wouldn't they have set up guards or alarms?

Hindarf explained that they could go no farther in that direction. The door in the end of the chamber was locked and triggered to alarms. So, they would go through another tunnel, which they had dug and walled themselves.

They dived again, and Forry plunged to the bottom of the tunnel. He saw Hindarf go through a hole which was so narrow that the air tank on his back scraped against the plates. The tunnel curved rapidly and took them on a course that he estimated would bring them about even with the ending of the Og tunnel but about forty feet westward.

He came up in another chamber, much smaller than the first. There was a raft made of wood and inflatable pontoons. It was near the wall, which held a ladder that ran to the ceiling, twelve feet up.

Hindarf pulled Forry on to the raft. A man handed Hindarf a paper in a sealed package. He opened it and took out the paper and spread it out. Under the lights they had brought, with the only sound the slight splashing of the men and heavy breathing, they studied the plates which constituted the ceiling of this chamber. The plates were being removed by two men standing on the ladder. There was a great boom from above them.

The shock was sudden and savage. The platform rose into the air above the water and the men on it went with it. Dirt fell in on all sides, striking the men and sending up gouts of water and clunking into the raft, which was tilting to one side and then to the other.

But the walls did not fall in, though the plates were bellied out or buckled and broken here and there. The booming noise had come and gone, like an overhead explosion. All was quiet except for the loud slap-slap of the see-sawing water against the sides of the pit and the groaning of the platform moving up and down.

Hindarf was the first to break the silence. He said, "That was either an earthquake or the house is starting to slide. In either case, we go ahead as planned. We'll be out of this place and into the house in a few seconds."

The two men on the ladder had clung to it as it had threatened to topple over. Now they went to work and removed the plates to make a wide opening above them.

Forry wondered why they worked so slowly. He felt like clawing the plates out and anything else that stood between him and the open air. But he managed to subdue the panic. After all, as he had already told himself, he was upholding the honour of Earthlings.

Hindarf climbed the ladder and began to chip away at the dirt with a small pick. Forry moved to one side to avoid the falling matter, which came down in big chunks. His guide, pointing at the diagram, said, "We are directly below the floor of the room where Childe should be held."

"How did you get hold of the diagram?" Forry said.

"From the city archives. The Ogs thought that they had removed all of the plans of the house, which was built long ago. But there was one plan which had been misfiled. We paid for a very expensive research, but it was worth it."

"Why do you think Childe is in the room above?"

The Ogs have held important prisoners there before, both Toc and Earthling. We could be wrong, but even so we'll be inside the house."

Hindarf quit scraping away the dirt and was listening through a device, one end of which was placed against the stone. Then he put the device in a pocket and pouch of his suit and began to work on the stone with a drill. Forry listened carefully but could hear no sound from it. His guide told him that it used supersonic waves.

The removal of several blocks of stone took some time. Hindarf and another man stood side by side on the narrow ladder and eased each block down between them, and this was passed slowly between the men standing together on the ladder.

Philip José Farmer

Then Hindarf listened again. He looked puzzled as he put the device away.

"There's a strange swishing and splashing noise," he whispered.

He took the large square of metal which a man handed him and screwed it to the underside of the floor. A wire led from one side of the metal square to a small black metal box held by a man on the raft.

Everybody except Hindarf got off the ladder and stood to one side. Hindarf nodded to the man holding the box, who pressed a button on its top.

The metal square and the section of floor within it fell down past Hindarf.

A solid column of water roared through the opening. It knocked Hindarf off the ladder, struck the small platform, sprayed out over the raft, and swept those standing on the platform into the well or on to the raft.

Forry Ackerman was one of those swept off.

Chapter 21

Pao said, "Your wife died three months ago."

"You killed her!" Childe raged. "You killed her! Did you torture her before you killed her?"

"No," Pao said. "We did not want to hurt her, because we meant to bring her to you when you were ready for us. But she died."

"How?"

"It was an accident. Vivienne and Plugger and your wife were forming a triangle. Plugger was stimulating Vivienne with his tongue in her mouth, your wife was being stimulated with Plugger's cock in her mouth, and Vivienne and your wife had their cunts almost touching each other, face to face as it were. Gilles was up your wife's cunt or alternating between her cunt and her asshole, I believe."

"I can believe that Sybil might engage in some daisy chains," Childe said. "But I can't believe that she'd let Vivienne even get near her. That snake-thing would horrify her."

"When Plugger is charging you, you get excited enough to do a lot of things you wouldn't otherwise do," Pao said. "I have no reason to lie to you. The truth is that Gilles was driven out of his mind – he doesn't have much, anyway, just a piece of brain tissue in that little skull, he doesn't even know his own name and his talking is automatic and unintelligible even to him... Anyway, he went out of his head, too stimulated by Plugger, I suppose, and bit your wife's rectum. He tore out some blood vessels, and she bled to death. She kept moving and responding to Plugger's electric discharges even after she died, which was why neither Plugger nor Vivienne knew what was going on."

Childe felt sick. He sat down on the edge of the bed, his head bent. Pao stood silently.

After a few minutes, Childe looked up at Pao. The man's face was smooth and expressionless. His yellow skin, thin-lipped down-drooping mouth, thin curved nose, high cheekbones, slanting black eyes, and black hair with its widow's peak made him look like a smooth-shaven Fu Manchu. Yet the man – the Og, rather – must be very anxious behind that glossy sinister face. He could not use the usual methods to force cooperation from Childe. Even the worst of tortures could not extract the power for Grailing or star voyaging from a Captain. Under pain, the Captain was incapable of performing his duties.

Childe thought of Vivienne, Plugger, Gilles de Rais, and the creature that had metamorphosed itself to look like Sybil. What was its name? Breughel?

O'Brien had left. Had he gone out to obey Childe and to kill Breughel?

Pao swallowed and said, "What can I do to make this up to you?"

What he meant was, "What kind of revenge do you wish?" And he was thinking, must be thinking, that Childe would hold him responsible for Sybil's death.

Childe said, "I only require that the snake-thing be killed."

Pao looked relieved, but he said, "Vivienne will die, too!"

Childe bit his lip. The revenge he was planning did not involve killing anybody except the snake-thing, and that thing could not be called an entity. Not a sentient entity, anyway. He wanted that thing killed, but he wanted Vivienne alive to appreciate what had happened to her and the other Ogs.

"Bring Vivienne in," he said.

Pao left and a few minutes later returned with Vivienne behind him. O'Brien and several others also entered.

"I need a butcher's cleaver and bandages and ointment and morphine," Childe said.

Vivienne turned pale. She alone seemed to grasp what he intended to do.

"Oh, yes, and bring a wooden stool and a pair of long pliers," he said.

Trembling, Vivienne sat down in a chair.

"Stand up and take your clothes off," Childe said.

She rose and slowly removed her clothing.

"Now you can sit down there," he said.

O'Brien returned with the tools ordered.

Childe said, "I saw the film where you bit off Colben's cock with your false iron teeth. So don't plead with me."

"I am not pleading," she said. "However, it was not I who

bit his cock off."

"I won't argue. You are capable of doing it; you probably have done that, and far worse, to others."

He wished that she would weep and beg. But she was very dignified and very brave. What else could you expect from the woman who had once been Joan of Arc?

"Hold on to her," he said to the others. "Spread her legs out."

Pao and O'Brien pulled her legs apart. They were beautiful, absolutely perfect legs, with flawless white skin. The brush on the mound of Venus was thick and auburn. She probably had the most attractive pussy that he had ever seen. There was no hint of the horror that lived coiled inside it.

Childe felt like ordering one of the men to take the next step, but if he had the guts to order this, then he felt obliged to have the guts to do it himself.

Carefully, he inserted the pliers. Vivienne started and began quivering, but she did not cry out.

He pushed the pliers in and felt around. His original intention to close the jaws of the pliers around the head now seemed foolish. He could not get them open enough, and that thing was too active. But he could drive it out, and he did.

Its wet, black-haired and black-bearded head shot out past the pliers handles. Its tiny mouth was open, exposing the sharp teeth. Its forked tongue flickered at him.

With his left hand, he caught it behind the head. He pulled it out slowly as it writhed and then placed the head and a part of the body on the stool.

Pao sucked in his breath. Apparently, up to that moment, he had expected Childe to yank the thing out by its uterine roots and so disconnect the parts of Vivienne again.

Childe said, "Hand me that cleaver."

Vivienne watched him take the chopper. She did not blink.

"Inject the proper amount of morphine in her," Childe said to O'Brien. "You do know how to do it, don't you?"

"I do," O'Brien said. "You have recognized me as a doctor, obviously. But this morphine will do no good. She is resistant to it."

"I don't want to inflict physical pain on her," Childe said. "As little as possible, anyway. What kind of anaesthetic do you

Philip José Farmer

have? I do want her to see this. She is not to be unconscious."

"Never mind that!" Vivienne said. "Get it over with! I want to feel the parting in its fullest!"

He did not ask her what she meant by that. He looked down at the snake-thing, which twisted and hissed. Then he raised the cleaver and brought it down hard across the flexible spine.

Blood spurted out across the room. The head rolled off the stool and fell on the floor. Pao picked it up and put it beside the still bleeding trunk. The head moved its mouth several times, and its eyes glared up at Childe as if wishing him evil even after its death. Then the eyes glazed, and the lips ceased to work.

Vivienne had turned grey. Her eyelids were open, but her eyes had rolled up to expose only the whites.

O'Brien smeared an ointment over the amputation. The blood quit flowing entirely. Probably, that ointment was not known to Earth doctors nor used by O'Brien in his Beverly Hills practice.

O'Brien bandaged up the body, and Vivienne was carried out on the chair. The snake body dangled down and scraped against the floor until one of the men coiled it up in her lap.

Two women came in and began to clean up the mess. Pao said, "What shall we do with the head?"

"Put it down the garbage disposal."

Pao said, "Very well. Will you be ready for the ceremony tonight?"

"I'll try," Childe said. "Of course, Breughel emptied me."

"Breughel maintains that you asked him to go to bed with you," Pao said.

"I would think that his duty would have been to find some excuse for putting me off. He knew that I should be full again for tonight."

"That is true, but the temptation is very great. And you did ask for what you got. However, if you require it, Breughel will be killed."

"Let him live," Childe said. "Now, if you don't mind, I would like privacy. Complete privacy. Turn off everything, except the intercom, of course. Don't bring me anything to eat until I ask for it. I want to meditate and possibly to sleep later on."

"As you wish," Pao said.

Childe sat on a chair for a while. He had considered doing

what the Ogs wished up to the point of taking them to their home planet. Then he had intended to land them on some other planet. Maroon them. They would find themselves on a world which could support life but would offer them little except hardship. And he would go on.

Pao had explained some of the results of the Grailing, and he knew that during the voyaging ceremony he would be able to scan through a part of the cosmos. He did not know how he could do this, but he had been assured by Pao that it was open to him. The implication was that he could go to any world he was able to see during the ceremony because the power would make him courageous.

But now, he had changed his mind. He wanted to escape. He had to get out and away. The chopping off of the snake-thing's head had sickened him. He was becoming an Og by association with them. If he continued with them, he might end up as cold and cruel as they. He had to get out.

An hour passed. Then, knowing that he did not have too much time to carry out the plan he had conceived, he arose. He went into the bathroom and turned on all the faucets. He used a nailfile to unscrew the grate over the shower drain, and he stuffed the drain with sheets. He put the plugs in the bathtub and washbasin drains. Then he looked around for weapons and tools. The Ogs had taken the pliers and the cleaver.

The nearest thing to a weapon was the jade statuette, which he could use for a club. He could also use it to listen in on anything on the intercommunication system, since it operated without wires.

He prowled around, looking for other useful items, and could find none. Then he sat down on the bed and waited. It would take a long time for the water to fill the room as high as the canopy on top of the bed. He would be on top of it when it occurred, since he had determined that the canopy would support him.

The hours passed. The water flowed out of the bathroom and spread over the bedroom floor. It rose agonizingly slowly. But the time came when he had to climb up on the canopy and wait there.

The statuette in his hand spoke. "Captain, it is dinner time. Do you wish anything to eat?"

"Not now!" he said. He gauged when the water would rise

Philip José Farmer

to the level of the canopy. "In about an hour. I'll take the same food as last night! Oh, by the way, when does the ceremony start?"

There was a pause and then a voice said, "About nine, Captain. Or later if you prefer."

"I think I'll sleep a little now," he said. "Be sure to wake me about ten minutes before you bring dinner in."

When the water lapped at the canopy, and wet his rear through the cloth, he swam out into the room. The door to the bathroom was almost under by then. He dived through the door and came up to the airpocket between the bathroom ceiling and the surface. Then he dived down again. The ceiling light was still on, so he could see somewhat in the clear water. He turned off all the faucets in one dive and then returned to the top. Another dive through the door, and he swam back to the canopy.

As he pulled himself on to it, he felt a shock. The water slipped to one side of the room, as if the house had been tilted, and then it rushed back.

For a moment the motion confused him. He was panicked. What the hell had happened?

The voice said, "Captain! If you felt that lurch, do not be alarmed! It's not an earthquake! We think that the front of the hill gave way! We're inspecting the damage now! But do not be alarmed! The house is at least forty feet from the edge of the hill!"

Everybody in this house was so engrossed in the Grailing that they had forgotten about the deluge and its possible effects. Other houses were slipping and sliding, tumbling down hills which caved out from under them. But these people had felt themselves insulated from the disaster. They had far more important matters to attend to.

Now was his best chance. If a large number of them were out of the house, looking at the slide, he had a clearer road out than he had hoped for.

He spoke into the statuette: "I'll take my dinner right now."

"Sir," said a voice. "It isn't ready yet."

"Well, send a man in. The slide broke a water pipe in here. It's flooding my room."

"Yes, sir."

He waited. He had slipped the statuette between his belt and his stomach. He poised now, hoping that the pressure of the water would spring the door outwards even more swiftly than it normally travelled.

The caving in of the hill front had undoubtedly been the main factor in making the house lurch. But the enormous weight of all the water in this room had helped. Now, if only things worked right.

Suddenly, the door swung out. There was a yell, cut off by the roar of the water pouring out through the door. The water churned and frothed as it fought to get through the narrow exit.

Childe hesitated several seconds and then he dived. He was caught by the current and hurled through the doorway, brushing it as he went by and hurting his ribs and hips. He smashed into the wall on the side of the corridor opposite the door and then was shot, turning over and over, helplessly down the hall. The house must have been tilted slightly forward, towards the road, when it had shifted in response to the cave-in. Most of the flood seemed to be charging in that direction.

Philip José Farmer

Chapter 22

The water fell through the hole in the floor as if it were a waterspout. It pounded the narrow platform, making it shudder and threaten to break up. It swirled the raft around so that several men in the water, clinging to the side of the raft, were crushed between the raft and the wall.

Forry, hanging on to another man on the raft, thought that this time the house had slipped forward after another cave-in. This time, it was not going to stop. It would go down the hill, and everybody in it would be buried under tons of mud. Especially those in this underground hole!

The worst part of it was that they had removed their air tanks and so could not swim back through the tunnel.

Or could they? It was difficult to think coherently while the water was roaring through that hole and the raft was spinning and he could not see much because of the splashing and spraying around him. But it had seemed to him that the swim through the tunnel was a very short one and that he would not have to swim under the surface of the swimming pool to its end. He could emerge at once.

But the thought of going through the curving tube when its side might collapse at any second unnerved him. Bad as it was being shut in this hole here, he would stay.

By then all the lights had been extinguished, and he was in total darkness.

Suddenly, though the raft was still turning, the turbulence was much reduced. A light came on, and he could see another light. This was shining down through the hole in the floor. Water was still coming through but it was a trickle compared to the first discharge.

Hindarf was shouting at them to be quiet. Miraculously, he was unhurt.

Under his directions they erected the ladder again, and he climbed on up through it. His men followed him. Presently, a man pushed Forry and urged him to get going. Forry scrambled up the ladder swiftly but reluctantly. He poked his head through the floor and saw a bedroom that had been submerged only a few minutes before. The only exit was blocked with chairs, tables, and a bed, which had been swept against the door by the current.

The Tocs worked furiously to clear the furniture away. Hindarf and another looked for Childe, but he was not in the room.

"What happened?" Forry said to Hindarf.

"I don't know. But I would guess that Childe or whoever was a prisoner in here flooded this place. When the door was opened, he went out, riding the waters. He may have escaped."

"Good!" said Forry. "Maybe we can leave then?"

Hindarf looked down the hall at the wreckage. Several tables and vases and a crumpled carpet were piled at the corner where the hall turned. Part of the wall, where the water had first struck, was broken in. A man with a broken neck lay against the wall. He was identified as Glinch, an Og who had once terrorized medieval Germany as a werewolf. For the past twenty years, he had been working in the Internal Revenue Service, Los Angeles.

Hindarf gave direct orders. Part of the Tocs were to go down the hall, looking for whatever they could find in the way of Childe, the Toc prisoners, and the Grail. He, Ackerman, and the rest of the party would go in the other direction.

As they split up, they were hurled off their feet by another shock. Somewhere in the house, a great splintering and crashing sounded.

"We may not have much time left!" Hindarf said. "Quickly!"

They broke in a door which was jammed because of the twisted walls. They found the three Tocs, naked, hungry, and scared, in that room. The next room contained Vivienne, whom everybody except Forry recognized. She was lying in bed, moaning with pain, a sheet over her. Hindarf pulled off the sheet, and Forry's eyes bulged. A three and a half foot long penis with an amputated head was lying between her legs, its other end stuck into her cunt.

"So somebody killed Gilles de Rais at last?" Hindarf said.

"Childe did it," Vivienne moaned.

"Where is he?"

She groaned and shook her head. Hindarf reached out and gave a savage yank on the thing between her legs. What happened next was something that Forry would never be able to forget.

Hindarf picked up the many-legged cunt and smashed it against the wall. "Here's something for your collection," he said, handing the head with its kicking legs to Forry by the hair. Forry

Philip José Farmer

backed away and then ran out of the room.

There were shouts and then shots and screams somewhere in the house. Hindarf pushed past him and ran down the hall. Forry followed the others and eventually entered an enormous room where about twelve Tocs were struggling with ten Ogs. In the middle of the battle was a glass cube with a dully glowing grey goblet on a pedestal.

A Toc shoved the cube with his foot, and the enclosure fell with a crash, taking the pedestal and the goblet with it. There was a desperate scramble, during which the floor suddenly tilted with a deafening crash of rending timbers from nearby. The cube slid down to one end of the room while the combatants, knocked off their feet, chuted after it.

Forry was knocked down and sent sliding on his face for perhaps ten feet. He suffered friction burns on his hands and knees, but he did not notice them at that moment. The goblet had tumbled out of the cube and come to rest a foot before his face.

"Get it and run!" Hindarf yelled, and then an Og woman, whom he recognized as Panchita Pocyotl, leaped upon Hindarf from behind and bore him to the floor.

Forry would not have touched the goblet if he had thought about the effects of his act. But, excited and impelled by the Toc's order, he scrambled to his feet, scooping the goblet up. Even in his frenzied state, he noticed that it felt extraordinarily warm and that it seemed to pulse faintly. He also felt a resurgence of energy and an onslaught of courage.

He ran, even though he was not supposed to run. He went out of the room and down the hall and then there was a terrible grinding noise, a groaning, a shrieking, and a rumble as of thunder. The floor dropped; he fell, though still holding the goblet.

The room seemed to turn upside down. He struck the ceiling, which cracked open before he hit it. The lights had gone out then, but a flashlight from somewhere, maybe held by an Og who had just entered the house, threw a beam on the goblet and the surrounding area.

Half-stunned, Forry saw the goblet slide away from him. A dark figure hurtled into the area of light and sprawled after the goblet. It was not clad in a diving suit and it was not Childe, so he presumed it was an Og.

He kicked the Og as he rose with a triumphant cry, holding the goblet to his chest. The bare foot – he had long since shed his flippers – caught the Og under the cheek of his right buttock. At the same time, the house lurched again, and the Og, screaming, went flying forward. The goblet fell from his grip and rolled out through the door which was collapsing.

Cold wet mud lifted Forry and carried him as if he were on a rubber raft through the doorway just before it closed in on itself. He shot out through another room as if he were a cake of soap slipping out of the wet hands of a bather. The goblet appeared before him, riding upside down on a wave of mud. Forry reached out and grabbed it and held it to his chest even through his terror and his screaming.

Then he was turned upside down. Mud covered him and filled his nostrils and mouth. He choked and fought against the wet heavy stuff killing him.

Something struck the side of his head, and he fell into a darkness and silence blacker and quieter than the mud.

Philip José Farmer

Chapter 23

Partly stunned when he hit the wall at the first turning of the corridor, Childe was hurled down the next hall, spun off lightly at the second turning, turned aside by a great curling wave, and shot down another hall. At its end it opened on to the front door and, on the side, to a large room. The waters split here, one torrent shooting through the doorway after having broken down the door, and the other torrent spilling into the room.

The parting of the flood greatly diminished its force and its level. Childe scraped his knees and hands on the lintel as he went through the front door and was deposited at the foot of the steps at the bottom of the porch. Staggering because of the water that was falling on his back, he crawled away and then got to his feet. He took two steps and screamed as he fell outwards and down. The mud of a very steep bank took him, and he slid face down for some distance before plunging up to his shoulders into the sticky stuff. He fought his way out and then lay on his back, staring upwards.

Light was streaming out through the open door and several other windows. He was lying on top of the cave-in. And if he did not get out of the way soon, he would be crushed by the entire weight of the mansion. It was groaning and swaying, and the slides of mud around him heralded a greater slide.

Though he would have liked to stay there and rest, he turned over and slipped and slid to his feet and sludged away from the building looming above him as fast as he could go. Once he tripped over a solid object, which he would have thought was a small boulder if it had not moaned. He got down on his knees and felt the roundness, which was the head of a woman buried up to her neck.

"Who is it?" he said.

"It's me," the woman said.

"Who?"

"Diana Rumbow, who're you?" And then, "Help me!"

Mud abruptly covered his legs to the ankles. He looked up but could not see much except that the house seemed to be tilting a little more. Suddenly, the lights went out, and a great grinding noise came from the house.

He went on as swiftly as he could. It would take him a long time to dig her out, and the house was surely coming down on them at any minute. Besides, he owed an Og nothing except death.

When he had gotten to one side, far enough out of danger from the house, though not from the slippage of the hill beneath him, he turned. Just as he did, the great structure screamed and toppled down the steep slope. Though it was so dark, he could still see that it had turned over on its side, so swiftly had the earth beneath it fallen in.

He wanted to make for the ruins as fast as he could, but he was too emptied and shaken. He sat down in the mud and wished that he could cry. After a while, he got up and sludged through the mud, sinking to his knees with every step. He went even more slowly than the effort accounted for, because he was never sure that he would not keep on sinking.

The first body he found was Forry Ackerman's. It was lying on top of the mud, though sinking very slowly. He was on his back, his face covered with mud but his spectacles still on. A glow of headlights coming up the road below showed him palely to Childe.

"Forry?" he said.

The mud-covered lips parted to show mud-covered teeth. "Yeees?"

"You're alive!" Childe said. And then, "How in hell did you get here? What's been going on?"

"Help me up," Forry said.

Childe hauled him up, but Forry got down on his knees and started groping around. The headlights of the car came up over the top of the road below them, and Childe could see much better. But he could see nothing that Forry might be groping for.

"I had it! I had it!" Forry groaned.

"What?"

"The Grail! The Grail!"

"You had it? How? Forry, tell me, what's going on?"

Forry, feeling into the mud and cursing curses which were completely out of character for him, told him.

Childe pulled him to his feet. "Listen, you'll never find it in this mess. We better go into the house, if we can get into that mess, and look for our friends. If they are our friends."

Forry raised his head sharply. "What do you mean, if they

Philip José Farmer

are our friends?"

"How much do you and I really know about the Tocs?" Childe said. "They've been nice to us, but then they have a reason to be so. Even the Ogs became better after they had a reason to get my cooperation. So..."

"I have to find that Grail," Forry said. "I want to go to the planet of the Tocs. It'll be the only chance I'll ever have!"

"All right, Forry," Childe said. "We'll get it somehow. I'd like to have it, too, so I could settle this thing once and for all! But we'd better see who we can save. After all, Toc or Og, human or not, they feel pain, and they're going to need help."

The car had approached as closely as its driver dared. Four people got out and walked through the mud to them. It took a few minutes of questioning by both parties before it was established that the newcomers were Tocs. They had been summoned from the other side of the world and had just managed to get here.

"I wouldn't worry about finding it, Captain," the leader, Tish, said. "You can concentrate on it, and it will glow. The glow will come up even through tons of mud."

Chapter 24

The Tocs and the Ogs had hired a hall.

Over two-thirds of the big dance floor of the American Legion post had been marked off in squares. The remaining third was given over to the hundred or so surviving members of both groups. And to Childe, the Captain, the Grail and its pedestal. And to Forry Ackerman, who sat on one side to observe. He would participate in the ceremony but only as one caught in the sidewash of radiation. When the time came for the voyaging, he would move into the direct influence of the power and, if all went well, travel with the others to the stars.

Childe sat in a chair before the Grail. Beyond him the Tocs and Ogs stood in ranks of twelve abreast. They were naked. Everybody in the hall was naked.

They were here because Childe had ordered it. He had told them that if both groups did not declare, and keep, a truce, he would destroy the Grail and would refuse to act as their Captain. If they agreed to keep the peace and to participate together, he would transport both groups to their home planets.

They did not take long in reaching an agreement.

Childe was still dubious about his ability to move them across intergalactic spaces and pinpoint the exact world for each. But he hoped that it would work. It meant ridding the Earth of a number of monsters and potential monsters. He wished that he could do this with others than the Tocs and the Ogs.

Hindarf and Pao had died under some heavy timbers and several tons of mud. Tish had been elected master of ceremonies. It was he who had arranged that the authorities did not investigate the ruins. With the spending of much money, he had kept the police and others out of the area, and the Tocs and Ogs who survived had secretly buried the dead.

Now Tish called up the couples, one by one, to begin the ceremony. These were male and female with each couple composed of a Toc and an Og. There were about four females left over, and these were also to couple in the beginning.

Male and female, they approached Childe and knelt before him. They touched his genitals and kissed his penis and then rose.

Philip José Farmer

He stared at the Grail while his cock became bigger with each kiss until it had reached its utmost rigidity. The Grail began to glow and to pulse. Its glow waxed and waned as the throbbings of his dong built up.

One by one they knelt and kissed or sucked his cock. Then they returned to their stations to wait, hand in hand, or hand on cock or cunt, for the last couple to return.

The light from the Grail grew brighter and brighter until it could not be looked at directly by anybody but Childe. The light filled his eyes and his skull, but he could still see the Grail and the people beyond.

Finally, Tish approached Childe and knelt and stroked his balls and cock and then kissed the glistening glans. Childe's body from behind his navel to his knees had turned to ice, and the peter was giving little jerks while the fluid moved more swiftly towards its exit. He beckoned to an exquisite Thai woman, a Toc, and she ran to him and bent over to take his cock into her mouth. Immediately, the man who had been her partner came up behind her, got down between her legs, and buried his face in her cunt. Another woman got down on all fours and began sucking his dong; a man went down on her; a woman crawled between his legs and sucked on his peter; a man thrust his tongue up her slit; a woman got under him and started to work on the head of his penis with her mouth; and so forth. The result was a daisy chain with the woman on the end lying on her back blowing a man and nobody on her cunt.

Tish walked down the line of the grunting, moaning, smacking, writhing men and women. He straddled the last woman and let himself down, not too easily, into her split.

But even while he was pumping away, Tish called out in a strange language. He chanted, and Childe understood the words, though he was not able later to translate them.

Childe sat still and let the woman mouth his glans and run her tongue over his prick while the ecstasy mounted and mounted and mounted. Suddenly, he gave a little scream and spurted. The Grail seemed to burn; it shot out a pulsing light that drove away every shadow in the hall. Tish continued to chant. Apparently, he had not come yet. And then, as Childe's peter gave its final jerk and spurt, Tish cried out.

The air over the squares darkened. Little clouds formed.

The air became very cold, chilling the hot sweating bodies. There was a wind, as if the air was moving towards the clot of duskiness over each square. At first, the air moved gently, but within a minute it was whistling from every corner of the hall and rattling the windows. Dust from the floor rose up and whirled in small cyclones.

The Grail continued to pulse dazzlingly, though Childe had ceased to ejaculate. It did not obliterate the shadows above the squares; it seemed to make them darker.

The first one that Childe recognized was Igescu, the Toc whom he had killed in his oak-log coffin by thrusting a sword through his heart. Afterwards, the body had been burned to ashes in the fire of the great house.

Childe had never expected to see that long lean face with the high forehead, thick eyebrows, high cheekbones, and large eyes, nor the very long and skinny dick.

And there was Magda Holyani, the beautiful blonde weresnake.

And there was Hindarf and beside him was Pao.

They were all naked and all in their human form.

And where was Dolores del Osorojo, the beautiful California-Spanish "ghost" who had literally fucked herself back into a materialization of flesh and blood and bone, only to be killed and skinned by the Ogs?

He saw her in a square in the middle of the crowd. She was as beautiful in her nude body as she had been in her early nineteenth century gown. She was smiling at him, and her hips were rotating as if she were relishing the memory of their times together.

The air warmed up, and the wind ceased.

The hall was filled with many voices. The living and the recently dead were chattering, yelling, laughing.

Tish waited for five minutes and then shouted for silence.

It came slowly and reluctantly, because the Tocs and the Ogs were human in that they had to express their emotions.

"Now for the voyaging!" Tish shouted.

They all faced him expectantly. Childe noted, out of the corner of his eye, Forry sitting on his chair. His eyes were bulging out, and he was covered with sweat. Childe did not know whether

Philip José Farmer

this reaction was caused by the ceremony he had just seen or the thought of the trip.

It was up to him whether or not he went along. If he decided to go, he just had to move from the side of the hall to the middle of the floor, and he would be taken along automatically.

Tish had not liked the idea that Forry was not participating in the ceremony, but he admitted that his non-involvement would reduce the effect of the Grail by only a negligible amount.

Tish indicated that a woman should bring up a bowl with a dark liquid in it. She took a position by Childe after kissing his penis and the second ceremony began immediately. She sprinkled his genitals with a few drops of the dark liquid before each person kissed his peter. Tish stood on the other side and every third person dipped his finger into the bowl and passed it over Childe's lips. The stuff tasted like honey with a trace of rancid cottage cheese. When the bowl was empty, Tish signalled for it to be refilled, and the ceremony went on.

The Grail kept on pulsing brightly. Its white light was beginning to affect Childe. He did not become blind or any less able to see what was going on around him. But he was receiving flashes of strange scenes. Usually these were seen as if he was standing on the surface of a planet, but several times he whizzed by a star burning redly, greenly, or amberly. He seemed to be no more than a hundred thousand miles from the great luminaries. Despite the brightness and nearness, he felt no heat, only a bone-crystallizing cold.

Tish began to chant in the foreign language. Childe beckoned to Dolores, who ran gladly towards him, her big shapely breasts bouncing with the impact of her feet. She got down on her knees and buried her face in his crotch and wept. Then she took the end of his half-limp organ and began to suck on it. It rose as if she were blowing air into it, became hard and throbbing, and gave him that first warming under his belly button.

The Grail pulsed faster, and the flickers of alien topographies and brilliantly coloured stars increased in number and variety.

Dolores sucked harder and moved her head back and forth. Igescu came up behind her then and lifted her up so that she was standing up but with her knees bent. He rammed his dick into her asshole and began pumping. Plugger got down on his knees behind Igescu's buttocks, spread them, and thrust his tongue up Igescu's asshole.

His body rocked back and forth as he rode the vampire's ass with his face.

Even through the woman and the man, Childe could feel the shock of Plugger's tongue. He hoped that the others would form the daisy chain quickly, because if they didn't they were going to get caught short. He was going to come soon. This would require starting the voyage ceremony over again, because the chain had to be complete, or nearly complete, when he came.

The room started to rotate. The naked bodies of the men and women seemed to be skating on the edge of a spinning disc. They slid here and there, catching each other, going down, tonguing cocks and cunts, ramming cunts, mouths, and assholes.

And there was Vivienne. And there was a tall man with a black beard and burning eyes. His face had much more distinct features, of course, but the resemblance was close enough for Childe to identify him as Gilles de Rais. He had materialized in his original body, and he was sticking his dong into the spread buttocks of a slim blond man who was sucking off Vivienne.

Then Vivienne and de Rais and everybody receded on the edge of the whirling plate that had been the big ballroom. Lightning was flashing from the Grail, white strokes, scarlet flashes, emerald zigzags, yellow streaks, purple swords with jagged edges. The flashes spurted upwards from the Grail, bounced off the ceiling, spiralled down, caromed off the naked writhing bodies of the men and women, fell to the floor like coloured and shattered stalactites.

Childe felt the grey fluid thrusting upward. But when he looked down, he saw only the red lips of Dolores, like an unattached cunt, squeezing around his cock. He could see into his own body, and the grey fluid was red as mercury in a thermometer and rising as if the thermometer had been thrust into a furnace. The red thread sped upward and then leaped out between the disconnected red lips and spurted like a scarlet gunpowder exploding.

The Grail blew up soundlessly with a crimson-and-yellow cloud expanding outwards and pieces of whitely glowing metal flying through the cloud.

Philip José Farmer

Chapter 25

Until the last moment, Forry could not make up his mind.

He had been repulsed at first by the orgy. Seeing such things in stag films was one thing, but seeing them in the flesh was very uncomfortable and even sickening. After a while, the aura of reeking sexuality, of uninhibited orgasms, of penises and vaginas and anuses and mouths, began to excite him. He even got jealous when he saw Alys Merrie sucking on the red-skinned cock of a big Amerindian, and he felt an impulse to get off the chair and dive into the welter, that raging sea, of hair and flesh.

But he was, in the end (I always pun, even here, he thought), too inhibited.

Nevertheless, the vibrations were getting to him, and he hoped the ceremony would not last too long. Otherwise, he might abandon his restraints and join in the fun.

A few seconds later, he got his first view of what was taking place in the mind of Childe. He did not know that it was Childe's mind that was broadcasting, but he surmised that it was. There was no doubt that Childe and the Grail, hooked together in some psychosexoneural manner, formed the focus and the distributor of the strange power emanating throughout the hall.

The glimpses of the alien worlds were like seeing the paintings of Bonestell, Paul, Sime, Finlay, St John, Bok, Emshwiller, and other greats of science-fiction become three dimensional and then become alive. Painting turned into reality.

The worlds were only slices; it was as if Childe was cutting the cosmic pie into slim pieces and hurling them at him.

He jumped up from the chair and unsteadily made his way towards the complicated shifting structure of flesh. It was only a few feet from him but it seemed to have sped towards the horizon. Between him and the bodies writhing in the glory of the power from the Grail was a vast distance.

He had to hurry. The Childe – Child? – was coming. If he did not get within that blaze, he would be left behind. He would be standing alone, naked and erect and weeping in the big American Legion hall. This was the only chance he would ever get. He, Forry Ackerman, the only human to get a ticket to intergalactic space, to alien and weirdly wonderful worlds in a foreign galaxy. His childhood dreams come true in a universe where he had no right to expect that any dream would ever be reality. Where he had built a house to embody dreams with only half-reasonable facsimiles. Where the pseudoworlds had seemed to be real in the shadow world of his home but real for split-seconds only. Where stars like giant jewels, and crimson landscapes, and trees with tentacles, and balloon-chested Martians with elephant trunks and six fingers, and huge-eyed feathered nymphs, and long-toothed red-lipped vampires dwelt in startling fixity forever.

Now he could go voyaging.

He ran towards the dwindling figures while the Grail sent up a mushroom cloud of red, green, yellow, purple, and white shoots. He ran towards them, and they shot away as if on skates.

"Wait for me!" he cried. "I'm going, too!"

The horizon, so distant, suddenly reversed its direction and charged him and was on him before he could stop running. Like a locomotive appearing out of a tunnel, it ran over him with flashing emerald, topaz, and ruby lights screaming at him instead of a train whistle, and swiftly rotating puffs of brilliant white and deep-space black cutting through him instead of iron wheels.

Whatever the objective length of time, to him it seemed instantaneous. He was in the hall and then he was in a huge room with grey walls, floor, and ceiling. It had no furniture and no doors or windows. The only light was that escaping in waves from the Grail.

Childe and the others were with him. They were all looking at each other dazedly. Some of them had not yet uncoupled.

The Grail and its pedestal stood before Childe.

Hindarf strode to the wall and spoke one word. A large section of the wall became transparent, and they were looking out over the bleakest landscape that he had ever seen. There was only naked twisted rock. There was no vegetation or water. Yet the sky was as blue as Earth's, indicating that there was an atmosphere outside.

Childe said, "Come here, Forry. Take my hand."

"Why?" Forry said, but he obeyed.

Hindarf activated another window on the opposite wall. This showed more windswept rock, but far away, near the horizon, was a spot of green and what looked like the tops of tall trees.

"This isn't our world or the Ogs' either!" Hindarf shouted. He pointed into the sky and Forry could barely see the pale moon there. It looked as large as Earth's, but it was darkly mottled in the centre and resembled the markings on the wings of a death's-head moth.

Childe beckoned to Dolores del Osorojo, who smiled and came to him and stood on his left, holding his hand. Childe said something in Spanish to her, and she smiled and nodded.

"That about uses up my knowledge of Spanish," Childe said. "But she prefers to stay with me. And I want her to be with me."

"That is the moon of Guthrath!" Hindarf shouted.

He wheeled upon Childe, "Captain! You have brought us to the desert world of Guthrath!"

Childe said, "It's a desert, but it can support you and the Ogs quite comfortably, if you get out and dig, right?"

Hindarf turned pale. Weakly, he said, "Yes, but surely you are not thinking of...?"

"My ancestral memory or genetic memory or whatever you call it has been opened," Childe said. "I know that there is very little chance that either you Tocs or Ogs would let me go once I made the first landing on either planet. You have Captains greater than I who could neutralize my powers long enough for your people to physically capture me. You'd have to, because I am partly an Earthman, and you could never trust me. And whichever planet I got us to first, the home of the Toc or the Og, the people there would catch me. And they would take captive the enemy people, too."

"That isn't true!" Hindarf and Igescu yelled.

"I know," Childe said. "You two were taking a chance in a cosmic lottery, as it were. You did not know which planet I would pick out to land on first, and you couldn't even ask me, because I would not know which one until I was presented with a choice. Also, if you tried too hard to sway me, I might get suspicious. So you took a chance. And both of you lost."

"You can't do this!"

The Tocs and Ogs rushed towards Childe.

Forry almost let loose of Childe, because it looked as if the three of them were going to be torn to bits.

Childe gripped Forry's hand so hard that the bones cracked. He shouted, "Fuck you!" and they were off.

There was a thin triangle of nothing wheeling by Forry, a gush of soundless purple flame around his feet, and the familiar walls of the American Legion hall were all around him and the familiar floor was under his feet.

Forry did not say anything for a moment. Then, slowly, he spoke. "Where's the Grail?"

"I left it behind. I can do that, you know, although it means that the Grail is now forever out of my reach. Unless another Captain brings one here."

"That's all?" Forry said. "You mean the trip's *over?*"

"You didn't get *killed,*" Childe said.

"I made a better trip when I saw the movie *Barbarella,*" Forry said.

Childe laughed and said, "You'd gripe if you were hung with a new rope."

They got dressed and prepared to leave the hall. Childe said, "I wouldn't tell anybody about this, if I were you. And I think we'd better not see each other again."

Forry looked at Dolores. She was dressed in a white peek-a-boo blouse and tight orange slacks that one of the Toc women had left behind.

"What about her?"

Childe squeezed the dark-haired woman and said, "I'll take care of her. She may have been one of *them,* but she was one of the good ones."

"I hope so," Forry said. He stuck out his hand. "Well, good luck. *Adiau,* as we Esperantists say."

"Don't take any wooden grails," Childe said.

Forry watched him walk away with his arm around the slender waist of Dolores, his hand resting on the curve of her ass. How could the fellow so easily give up that power, that chance to go star-voyaging?

But he felt good again when he came out into the familiar world of Los Angeles. The rains had stopped, the night sky was clear and full of stars, car horns were blaring, water was splashing on to the pedestrians as reckless drivers roared through pools, a

Philip José Farmer

radio was screeching rock, an ambulance siren was wailing somewhere.

A half hour later, he entered his house. He stopped and gasped. The Stoker painting was missing again!

Lorenzo Dummock came down the steps then, scratching his hairy chest and swollen paunch. He said, "Hi, Forry. Say, could you loan me a coupla bucks for ciggies and a beer? I'm really down in the dumps, I..."

"That painting!" Forry said, pointing his finger at the blank space on the wall.

Lorenzo stopped and gaped. Then he said, "Oh, yeah, I was going to tell you. That guy, what's his name, Woolston Heepish? He showed up about an hour ago and said you had told him he could have the Stoker. So I let him. Wasn't it all right?"

Forry charged into his office and dialled Heepish's number. His heart chunked when he heard the smooth voice again.

"Why didn't you go with the others?" Forry said.

"Why, Forry! You're back! I thought sure you'd be gone forever! That's why I stayed behind. I like this life, and I couldn't pass up the chance to add your collection to mine!"

Forry was silent for a moment and then he said, "Hold on! I thought you were buried in that landslide?"

Heepish chuckled. "Not me! I was slid out as nice as pie and took off. I had enough of Childe and the Tocs and the Ogs, even if the Ogs are my people."

"I want my painting back!"

"Would you consider trading it for a rare Bok?"

Forry wondered if the fellow had slipped some LSD into his coffee. Perhaps everything that had happened was only a lysergic acid fantasy?

Heepish's voice, fluttering like the wings of a bat in the night, said, "Maybe we could get together soon? Have a nice talk?"

"You can keep the painting if you'll promise never to cross my path again!" Forry said.

Heepish chuckled. "Could Dr Jekyll get rid of Mr Hyde?"

www.creationbooks.com